Th

ALSO BY R.W. MARCUS

The Fate of Tomorrow: Tales of the Annigan Cycle
Book One

Shadow of the Twilight Lands: Tales of the Annigan Cycle
Book Two

Whispers from Nocturn: Tales of the Annigan Cycle
Book Three

Agents of the Void: Tales of the Annigan Cycle
Book Four

R.W. Marcus

The BANE *of* EMPIRES

A Tale of the Annigan Cycle
in Three Acts

BOOK FIVE

R.W. MARCUS

LAUGHING BIRD PUBLISHING
SAINT PETERSBURG, FL USA

The Bane of Empires

Copyright © 2022 by Jeff Morris

Published by Laughing Bird Publishing
St. Petersburg, Florida

Visit us on the web!
https://AnniganCycle.com

Cover art by SelfPubBookCovers.com/ FrozenStar
Cover layout and design by Laughing Bird Publishing

Laughing Bird Publishing® is a registered trademark of Mark W. Phillips

Manufactured in the United States of America
10 9 8 7 6 5 4 3 2

First Printing, 2022
Revised Second Printing, 2023
ISBN 979-8-9877180-0-1

R.W. Marcus

*Dedicated to the memory of
Edgar Rice Burroughs...
with a wink and a nod to
Philip José Farmer &
Quentin Tarantino*

CONTENTS

ACKNOWLEDGEMENTS

On the cover of every book rests the author's name. To most, this is the sole creator associated with the work before them. However, behind every author stands a crew of dedicated believers responsible for bringing the final creation into the world. It is to those people I am eternally grateful.

First and foremost, my thanks go to my partner in crime Cheryl Pepper, who, after all this time, truly appreciates the eccentricities of the writer's life and yet still decides to stay with me.

A special thank you to my trusted and indispensable creative muse of thirty years, Mark Phillips. This insanely talented individual had his hand in almost every one of my projects.

I can't say enough about my steadfast, elite group of beta readers; Dave (Captain Proton) Holman, Lynn Marie Firehammer, Max Yrik Valentonis, Chris Breton, and Tom Lancraft. Their various eyes on the work and insight caught many a discrepancy.

Special technical kudos to Keenan Pepper, because what writer doesn't want a brilliant physicist on call; and to Jessica Pepper RN, whose advice on what occurs when horrible things happen to the body made more than a few readers cringe in disgust.

Finally, a grateful tip of the hat to the good folks at Laughing Bird Publishing and Self Pub Book Covers for taking the production burdens off my shoulders, freeing me to create more disturbing content to shock and amuse.

WELCOME TO THE ANNIGAN

This mostly aquatic planet travels in a geosynchronous orbit around a small yellow sun. It's set far enough back in the solar system's Goldilocks Zone it maintains an atmosphere conducive to a wide variety of life.

Sentient creatures, terrestrial, marine or amphibious, share a hyper-fertility devoid of genetic boundaries. Any sentient creature may mate with any other and produce offspring.

Lumina basks in perpetual sunlight on one side of the Annigan. Humans dwell alongside many other sentient races thriving across its various continents and island chains. The fertility enriching rays of the sun, and the warmth of the Shallow Sea, support a vibrant and rich ecosystem.

Although life is abundant there, Lumina is hardly a serene place as you will see. Millennia of feuds, ruthless ambition and individual hatreds forged a fragile peace, barely sustained under the rule of the Great Houses.

Because of the incredible diversity of sentient creatures, all races, genders and hybrids in Lumina enjoy social equality, judging each as an individual based upon their own merits. Beneath the veneer of peace, however, dwells a hotbed of totalitarian torture, raider uprisings and a constant escalating cold war between the Great Houses.

Nocturn, languishes in constant darkness on the other side of the Annigan. Only moonlight, starlight and bioluminescence illuminate the land of endless night. Without the warming rays of the sun, Nocturn's oceans froze over, but constant geothermal activity heats the land masses, creating a temperate and misty terrain teeming with exotic and predatory sentient races.

Imperialistic cat people rule aboveground and hive nations of humanoid mantises swarm beneath the surface. In the Ocean Deep, a race of sentient octopoids dwell in vast underwater cities worshiping the ancient ones of the abyss. You are predator or prey in Nocturn's despotic societies.

The Twilight Lands reside at the fringes of the Annigan and remain in a constant gloaming. Here, warm and cold air currents clash, generating a perpetually stormy climate.

Ruled by the amphibian Bailian race, the Twilight Lands serve as a neutral zone for cultures from every corner of the Annigan. Many encountering the other races for the first time, and like the weather, their clashes can prove tempestuous.

Only the sun of Lumina keeps back the nocturnal predators of the dark side. Legends tell of a prophesied great eclipse stripping away all boundaries and igniting an apocalyptic war. Until then...

...these are the tales from the Annigan Cycle.

The Annigan struggles
With the balance.
Chaos and order,
Evil and good.
The rumbles of conflict
Echoes from the east.
With many warnings given,
But few understood.

ACT ONE

The Chaos Within

Alto peered down the line of extended sword tips and furrowed his brow.

"Forty-five degrees, people," he said sternly.

He placed his hand on the top of the nearest practice sword and adjusted it to the proper height.

"Any other position when you recover from a crouch leaves you vulnerable to attack."

The row of students all craned their necks for a better view, and then awkwardly adjusted their weapons.

"Now, advance continuously in the guard position and execute an overhead strike," he ordered. "Remember... forty-five degrees."

The young novices started moving across the floor when Alto saw the young mermaid enter the training hall and stand quietly in a corner, silently observing.

Alto quickly recognized her, even in her human form. Her simple green dress hung loosely on her petite barefoot frame and long brown hair flowed down to the small of her back. The swordmaster smiled and nodded at her before continuing with his instruction.

He vividly remembered finding her naked and helpless, three Kans ago, on the Makatooa docks. A tall, thin, lipless gang leader threatened her, wanting to skin her and wear her scales. When Alto intervened, the assailant mocked the very code which demanded the swordmaster protect the young mermaid. Even when Alto killed most of his henchmen, the gang leader showed no fear.

She escaped without a word as her attackers fled. Alto remembered feeling relieved at avoiding any maudlin displays of gratitude. Now, he wasn't sure how he felt about her seeking him out. A twinge of guilt, perhaps?

The trainees all lined up in a kneeling position, with their swords laying reverently in front of them, facing their teacher as the class ended. All bowed and touched their foreheads to the floor with the bark of a single command.

With the class now officially over, Alto's demeanor changed from studious taskmaster into congenial mentor while milling about the dispersing class. When the last student exited into the crowded street, the smiling woman slowly approached.

"Your appearance has greatly changed from the other Kan," the swordmaster said, studying her youthful face.

"I imagine so," she admitted, modestly looking down. "I just wanted to thank you for saving my life."

"May I ask how you located me?"

"From what I saw on the dock," she said, shyly grinning, "I thought you to be a master swordsman. There are very few in this city."

Alto nodded at the explanation. "You are undoubtably a Mer of some sort. I assumed your kind kept to themselves in the deep ocean."

"I am called Jullinar," she said, sweeping back a strand of hair. "My people gave up our deep diving ability long ago when we acquired the gift of walking on land. We are few and lead a solitary existence in the Shallow Sea."

"Well, Jullinar, I'm glad I happened to be passing by."

"Believe me, I am too."

"Why were you being accosted?" Alto asked. "It was obviously not a robbery."

Jullinar's face turned sad. "His name is Serobini, and he's been pursuing me for several fog cycles."

The swordmaster was about to press the question further when she reached out and hugged his neck.

"I must go," she said. "It's not safe for me on land. Thank you again, Master Alto."

Breaking from the embrace, she hurried out the front door, past Mal leaning against the door jamb with arms folded. The Spice Rat eyed Alto up and down.

"I thought we agreed you were going to keep the whores to a minimum?" she teased, her face softening with amusement.

"I certainly hope this isn't going to become a habit," Wikk the First, Lord of Tannimore and Keeper of the Faith, frustratingly muttered.

Wikk stood of average height, clean shaven, with short brown hair. His narrow eyes constantly shifted over slightly sunken cheeks. A set of full lips cast in a permanent dour frown completed his slightly ominous deportment.

He impatiently drummed his fingers on the table and glared at the empty seat across from him. The other council members, Da-Olman the Minister of Etheria, Soldi the Regent of Currency, and Onarim the Minister of Works, shifted restlessly in the council chambers of the floating city built from the converted ships of pirate fleets.

"Should we start the meeting without her, Lord Wikk?" asked Onarim.

"I have a schedule to keep," Da-Olman grumbled, his Gila eyes rotating independently, seeking support.

"As do we all," Wikk answered, sighing in annoyance. "This is the first high council meeting since the ascension of the Proffitt. All members should be in attendance."

They heard a commotion in the hallway just before the door flew open and Mistress Ve-Qua, tenth level Kinjuto dominator, swept into the room with hips swaying sensuously. The naked Bailian stood just a little over five feet, but radiated intensity. Tightly kinked, shoulder length ebony hair bounced across her pale blue skin. The light from the bay windows exposed the sunken black circles around her eyes, giving her baby face a sinister quality.

This was the first encounter with the torture mage for most of the stunned council. They openly winced at the one-quarter-inch diameter rod impaling the center of her ample breasts and bolting them together into a morbidly evocative cleavage. Large twin bolts locked the rod in place. Delicate chains hung from each bolt, extending the length of her exposed body, tautly hooked to her vaginal lips, spreading them obscenely open.

She held two leashes in her right hand, leading a pair of naked men in pet collars. They shuffled behind her on their hands and knees, frantically attempting to keep pace.

"Hello dearies," she greeted, with elitist disdain. "Well, if *this* isn't the biggest bunch of pathetic losers."

"How good of the Minister of Justice to finally decide to grace us with her presence." Wikk sarcastically announced.

Mistress Ve-Qua ignored the slight and started for the remaining open seat.

"I'm afraid your pets must remain outside," Wikk said, stopping her. "Council meetings are private."

The mistress of pain dramatically sighed and led her two slaves back into the hall. She waved her hand and called them to their feet. A fluttering of her fingers and they rose to their tiptoes. She raised their leashes and secured them to an overhead beam so any attempt to escape the stressful position would cause strangulation. She briefly admired her work before returning to the meeting.

Mistress Ve-Qua sensuously slinked into the remaining open chair, seated between Onarim and Soldi. Her proximity visibly unnerved both former gangsters-turned-bureaucrats.

Soldi, a slight man with bobbed hair and a scraggly beard, meekly stole side glances, surreptitiously eyeing her grotesque piercings. Ve-Qua mischievously grinned and spun, facing the uncomfortable treasurer.

"Is there something you want to ask me, Regent?"

"Um, uh…" Soldi stammered, averting her penetrating gaze.

"Don't be shy," she coaxed.

Soldi summoned his courage, quickly surveyed the front of her body, and then looked her directly in the eyes.

"Isn't that painful?" he asked timidly.

She playfully rested her head on his shoulder and rolled her eyes rapturously.

"Exquisitely painful," she cooed.

Wikk noisily cleared his throat. "If we can get down to business."

The rattled Soldi quickly focused his attention back on Wikk, thankful for the interruption.

"I believe the first order of business is an audience with the Proffitt's Na-Kab companions."

They escorted two fire mantids in human form into the room. The temperature noticeably rose when the humanoids with glowing red eyes stepped up to the council's table, causing several members to break into a sweat.

"Fleshy ones," Valvur gruffly began. "Our bargain is complete. You will arrange passage to our new hive and queen."

Wikk bristled at the creature's curtness but remained calm and congenial.

"Of course, my fiery friends," he agreed. "I have already arranged transportation. Go with our gratitude and the knowledge that you brought the word of the lord to our city."

"We care nothing for your so-called god," the Na-Kab brusquely said. "The bargain is concluded. Send us home."

A flash of anger stormed across the Keeper of the Faith as a thin, cruel smile pulled at his lips.

"A vidette boat awaits you on the docks."

The glamoured fire bugs hesitated, briefly assessing the sincerity of the offer.

"Very well," Valvur snapped dismissively.

The two abruptly departed without another word. Once the door closed, the taut smile on Wikk's face transformed into a scowl. Everyone except Ve-Qua shifted nervously in their seats while waves of righteous rage emanated from the young man. A long, tense moment passed before Wikk abruptly stood and went over to the doors leading out to a wide landing overlooking the docks. He paused before opening the door and looked back at the seated Kinjuto.

"Ve-Qua," Wikk summoned, voice trembling with anger.

He stepped out onto the rail-less balcony. All eyes around the table turned to the naked Bailian.

She quickly rose to her feet with a sadistic grin, retrieved one of her slaves from the hall and led him out onto the veranda. She ordered him back on his tiptoes and then tied his leash to an exposed beam beside the doors.

Ve-Qua joined Wikk, and the pair watched the two Na-Kab clumsily climb aboard the small boat. The single human pilot cast-off and lowered the Ukko rudder into the water. The craft slowly made its way through the city's outgoing maritime traffic before picking up speed once it acquired a westerly course.

"Now," Wikk calmly ordered once the craft reached fifty yards out.

Ve-Qua gave a depraved giggle, then without warning, pushed her slave over the edge of the balcony. The startled submissive didn't have time to cry out before the collar snapped tightly around his throat. He gurgled and sputtered, his legs flailing wildly while grasping at the taunt leash suspending him.

With the first jolt of her submissive's choking and pain, Ve-Qua swayed in ecstasy, feeling the psychic power build within her. She extended one arm towards the departing craft, her eyes wide with excitement and her face lit up in enraptured concentration. Slowly closing her outstretched hand into a fist, she held it in front of her face before quickly opening it in a flourish of widespread fingers.

When she heard the driver of the boat scream, she shyly peeked past her hand with a satisfied smile. The fast-moving vidette now spun in tight circles in the calm water while the terrified driver attempted to escape some unseen horror just in front of him. The pilot's hysteria soon reached a fevered pitch and his flailing sent the boat into a series of choppy, erratic turns until it capsized, sending all three of its occupants into the water.

The Ukko wood Nolton Boat automatically righted itself and the frenzied squeals of the Na-Kab replaced the cries of the pilot. In their initial panic, the fire mantis shed their human facade and returned to their original form. They clawed frantically at the side of the boat, but their bulk and lack of buoyancy pulled them under. Thrashing about violently, they fought to keep their heads above the surface.

The driver climbed back over the other side of the empty craft just as the Na-Kab's exoskeletons cracked. Cold seawater rushed into their fiery innards, sending massive plumes of steam jetting into the air. The fire bugs floundered about wildly, and their screams reached a screeching crescendo when the surrounding water began boiling.

Panicked bolts of flame erupted from their mouths and shot harmlessly into the sky. They finally descended below the surface of the scalding water, boiling alive into the inky blackness of the ocean's depths.

Ve-Qua uncontrollably tittered while the pilot pulled back up to the landing. He looked around, relieved that the horrific phantom was gone.

"I guess it's true," Wikk said, staring at the bubbling water still belching steam. "Bugs really can't swim."

At first glance, the morning bustle in the streets of central Makatooa appears to be complete chaos. Wagons clatter noisily on the cobblestone streets coming to and from the nearby docks. The various shops and walkways lining the major thoroughfare bustled with activity. The crowds were mostly human, with a sprinkle of Piceans and the occasional EEtah. A pervasive odor, the unique combination of fish and human waste, with notes of cooked food from the many street vendors, drifted throughout this large, busy seaport.

No one noticed the six men loitering about the alley entrance. Their brutish presence and disheveled clothing gave them the appearance of laborers waiting for a ride. One of their numbers, a short stocky man with a considerable paunch, spit on the ground and sneered.

"I don't much like taking orders from crazies," he grumbled. "Loonies will get you killed quick as fuck."

A young man with thickly muscled arms and long blond hair gave him an annoyed look.

"Can you do anything without bitching, Telek?" he asked, pulling himself up on a crate.

The older man pulled a large knife from his boot and waved it menacingly.

"I don't imagine I'd complain too much carving you up like a ham!" Telek threatened.

"Knock it off, Telek," ordered a man leaning against the alley wall with short brown hair. "Ciro didn't mean nothing by it. Besides, he's new."

This didn't faze the insulted thug, and he circled the blade toward the young man's face.

"Yeah, well," he said, "new or not, you open your yapper at me one more time and I'll slice up that pretty boy face so bad that whores will run away screaming."

Spittle now sprayed from Telek's mouth and drool flowed from the corners of his puffy lips down his stubbly chin.

"It's bad enough we gotta work for a lipless freak, but I don't have to put up with…"

Telek abruptly halted his threatening monologue when he saw the faces of his companions go pale. He lowered his knife and slowly turned to see Serobini a mere five feet away. He stood there smiling in a floor length, formal, black funeral dress, which starkly contrasted his long thinning white hair. All stood frozen, staring at their boss while a curtain of fear and chaos descended on the area.

"I see you've noticed my lips, or rather lack of them," he said in a casual, almost friendly tone. "Did I ever tell you what happened?"

The six men, now paralyzed with dread, shook their heads. Serobini quickly ran a tongue across his teeth before targeting the explanation directly at Telek.

"You see," he began, "my mother was a pious woman, very devout. Well, as you can imagine with all that religion around the house, there were rules, lots and lots of rules."

Serobini reached out and gently placed a long, bone white hand on Telek's shoulder, continuing his explanation.

"My mother was also an extremely strict woman who could get very creative with the punishments. So, one day, when I was eight years old, she saw me kissing little Bekka from down the street. Well, she was having none of that. Did I mention she was a pious woman?"

All meekly nodded.

"Well," he continued, "she had a *very* strict interpretation of the part of scripture that says, 'if a body part offends you, remove it.' Anyway, she prayed the entire time she worked on my face with my father's straight razor."

Serobini shrugged and snapped his fingers, releasing a fine blue talc in Telek's face.

"And poof," Serobini continued. "The offending appendage was gone!"

Telek sputtered and sneezed. Wiping away the powder from his face, his features shriveled in pain before he began coughing and convulsing.

"I'm very sensitive about it," Serobini said in a hurt tone.

Telek clutched at his throat and dropped to the alley floor. His face grew sickly pale and eyes bulged.

"So, I'd appreciate it if you didn't mention it again." Serobini said, leaning over the dying man. "Okay?"

Telek vomited a small amount of greenish fluid on the ground beside him and stared lifelessly forward.

"Okay then, no hard feelings!"

Serobini continued staring down expectantly at the dead man for a response. When he didn't see one, he gave a resigned shrug and glanced over at the remaining five henchmen, silently staring in shock.

"Ah, all's well that ends well," he proclaimed.

Serobini withdrew a black shawl and veil from a hidden pocket in his wide, hooped dress.

"Come on boys, let's go do some banking."

The interior of an Imperial Bank contained the same layout, no matter their location. The newest branch in Makatooa proved no exception. They all had a high-ceiling, large main room with an uncomfortable sofa against one wall. A closed conference room door adorned the opposite end of the room and a large vault filled up the adjoining facade.

They arranged four desks, so the corners touched and faced each other in the center of the spacious room. Three men and one woman sat at their respective workstations. Each studiously manipulated an elaborate abacus before them, intricately sliding and placing the beads. They then carefully examined the resulting design and noted it in a ledger.

No one heard the thump of the EEtah guard toppling to the ground outside the front door. They continued working obliviously when Serobini and two henchmen entered. He peered up at a chandelier in the form of a giant ship's wheel adorned with glowing gems.

"Would ya look at that!" came his astonished voice from under the veil.

By the time the bankers finally glanced up from their work, the hoodlums were halfway across the room.

"Remember," Serobini whispered. "Ciro does the talking. Are the other two in place?"

"Yeah boss, one on the roof the other in the wagon."

"May I help you?" one banker asked, his voice dripping with superiority.

Serobini walked within three feet of the desk and then made an abrupt turn to the right. Ciro stepped into his place with head meekly bowed.

"I certainly hope so," Ciro said, flashing a big smile. "We work with our aunt here. She owns a small fishing fleet."

Everyone curiously watched the person in the black dress take three paces and then turn again.

"Fishing fleet, huh?" the banker said, obviously unconvinced. "So *that's* what that smell is."

Ciro leaned on the desk and his long blond hair tumbled forward, framing a smile and turning to a contentious sneer.

"I know her ways may seem odd," Ciro said gravely, "but I think you'll find her gold as good as anyone's."

"I suppose so," the banker reluctantly said.

Serobini took four more paces and then turned right again, placing him directly in front of the human female banker. She looked up quizzically from her desk and could only make out a pair of bloodshot eyes and wisps of grey hair behind the veil and shawl.

"She just lost her husband, and she's a little out of it," Ciro offered, stepping next to her desk.

"I'm so sorry for your loss," the woman said, clearing her desk and pulling out a blank ledger page. "I'm Colette, the bank manager. Perhaps I can help?"

"I like your necklace," Serobini said, pointing to the large ornate key dangling around her neck.

The young woman blushed slightly at the compliment and brushed back her shoulder-length brown hair.

"Hardly a fashion accessory," she said. "I *have* to wear it. It's the key to the vault."

She then picked up a pen and slid the ledger page in front of her.

"Now…" she said, attempting to direct the conversation down to business.

"You know," Serobini began, "I like to play a little game in my head whenever I enter a room. I try to imagine how many people in that room I could kill all at once."

The woman's expression of bored impatience suddenly transformed into shocked disbelief. "I beg your pardon?"

Serobini cackled loudly, pulling the headdress and veil off. The woman's face went ashen with terror and she started screaming. Her hands involuntarily held the sides of her head as if to keep her mind from blowing. Her blaring outcries sent Serobini into peals of hysterical laughter.

Between the two of them, no one heard the ceiling cracking above them. When dust began falling on her desk, the bank manager looked up in time to see the ship's wheel above them break loose and fall.

Through her renewed round of shrieks, Serobini lashed out and snatched the key from her neck. Her screams ended abruptly when the massive lighting device crashed to the ground, crushing the desks and their occupants.

Serobini stood unharmed in his carefully calculated position between the spokes. He looked over at his men, then peered around the dust filled room.

"Four at once," the gaunt bank robber gleefully noted, discarding the dress. "It's not a record, but it'll do!"

He satisfactorily surveyed the destruction and spun the key chain on his forefinger while he did a little happy dance before heading for the vault. He stopped at the crushed body of the bank manager.

"Looks like a change of plans," he said to her mangled corpse. "We're making a withdrawal, not a deposit."

"Asad, you're fucking killing me here," Mal groaned.

The fat mobster, seated at the desk in front of her, reached again into the bag of mushrooms laid out on the desktop. He gingerly held one fungus aloft in his pudgy fingers and carefully examined it before placing it back with a frown.

"Sorry Mal," he said, "but these were picked too early. The spores didn't have time to fully develop."

"Yeah, well, time was a bit of a factor when I got those."

He sat back in his chair. "I'll bet. They're not worthless, just not top quality. My offer still stands, twenty Secors."

The Spice Rat gave a resigned sigh. Asad had always been fair to her in the past.

"Just give me the fucking money."

Asad smiled sympathetically and reached into a side drawer, retrieving two ten-secor Spice Notes.

"A pleasure doing business with you," he said, placing them on the desktop.

"Yeah, yeah," Mal replied, picking up the rectangular Ukko wood wafers and putting them in her pocket.

Out in the streets, the shrill report of a city guard's whistle cut short any further conversation. Several more whistles rapidly joined in and the uproar drew closer.

"Are they coming for you, Asad?" Mal half joked.

The mob boss quickly placed the bag of mushrooms in a desk drawer and stood up.

"If the city guards wanted to talk to me," he explained. "They wouldn't announce their arrival. They would just kick in the door. Besides, I keep the locals pretty well paid."

Mal curiously followed Asad onto the walkway just outside his office. Off to their right, a loud commotion headed their way with the alarm whistles not far behind.

When it got close enough, both saw an open-top wagon moving rapidly through the congested streets. Mal could make out three passengers and a driver.

One occupant, tall and pale with a black top hat, stood near the rear of the wagon. He reached into a bag and tossed handfuls of its contents onto the road behind the fleeing wagon. Townspeople swarmed into the street in the carriage's wake, greedily grabbing up the items. The behavior of the chaotic throng proved quite effective in hindering any potential pursuers.

When the wagon drew closer, the Spice Rat could hear the peals of deranged laughter over the rattling of the wheels on the cobblestones and the roar of the crowd.

"That's gold!" Asad said in disbelief. "He's throwing gold in the streets!"

Mal shook her head in bewilderment. "What the fuck!"

Mal and Asad finally got a good look at the crowd's generous benefactor while the wagon rumbled by. Serobini's ghoulish appearance visibly shocked them. Sensing their revulsion, he removed his hat with an elaborate flourish and did a grandiose formal bow.

"That is one ugly son of a bitch," Mal commented while the frenzied procession passed.

"And more than a little crazy," Asad added. "He must be the one I've been hearing about."

"Oh?" Mal asked, observing several fist fights break out.

Asad's eyes narrowed while watching the chaotic parade move off, replaced by a troupe of city guards slogging their way through the riotous throng.

"Yeah, one thing for sure," he said, "a loose spoke like that is always bad for business. Speaking of business, I've a quick, simple job for you, which pays pretty good."

Mal chuckled. "I didn't think there was anything like a quick, simple job in my business. Talk to me."

The buggy plodded cautiously through the streets of Zor and Demetrius could see the ornate gables of the Demon's Gate Inn through the early Kan fog.

"Are you going to tell me what's going on?" he guardedly asked Okawa, nestled closely beside him.

"I wanted to surprise you with a special dinner out," she softly admitted, wrapping her arms around his waist, "and I reserved one of their private dining rooms."

"I wondered what you were up to when you said to get dressed up," Demetrius said, smiling his approval. "What's the occasion?"

"I just wanted a little privacy while someone waits on us," Okawa replied, before kissing him on the cheek.

"Well, this was definitely a surprise," he said.

When the carriage stopped before the Inn's wide front porch, Demetrius offered her his hand while she exited onto the street. He stepped back and took in the statuesque brunette. The form fitting blue dress came down to mid-thigh and accentuated her ample curves.

He whistled softly. "You're a stunner."

"And you look very handsome," she said, adjusting his collar.

"Gee, thanks," he replied. "I hardly ever get to wear my good threads. I hope I don't spill anything on them."

"You'll be fine," she assured, making their way up the stairs.

They led them through a half full main dining room and back to a small, private room.

"Pretty fancy," Demetrius beamed, pulling back the curtain. "I mean, I didn't expect..."

Demetrius froze in stunned silence.

A well-dressed, elderly man and woman sat side by side at a solitary table in the center of the room. Both had close cut, grey hair, and the man wore a tightly trimmed, white beard. They were clearly just as shocked as the young pilot.

"Surprise!" Okawa announced sheepishly.

"Mother? Father?" he finally stammered. "What are you..."

Santo de Vana rose to his feet, glaring at his son.

"Demetrius, what is the meaning of this?!"

Okawa immediately stepped forward.

16

"Please, don't be angry with him," she pleaded. "This was my idea. He knew nothing about it."

Santo relaxed slightly and focused his scowl at Okawa.

"Very well then," he said tersely. "I'll ask you, whoever *you* are, what is going on?!"

"My name is Okawa de Dryden," she said modestly. " I'm Demetrius's girlfriend. I just thought if I could get you all together, you might resolve your differences."

Alyanna de Vana slowly stood facing Okawa. "Then Santo is not being honored by the Quartermaster's Guild?"

"No, I'm sorry," the Valdurian said, lowering her head apologetically. "I needed an excuse to get you here."

"I see," the older woman said, face souring. "Well, I must say that the letter was quite convincing."

Santo gave a frustrated sigh. "Well, young lady, I'm afraid you have wasted all of our time. My son and I have nothing to discuss!"

"You *do* realize I'm standing right here?!" Demetrius asked defensively.

Santo's eyes shifted angrily to his son.

"I realize where you are standing because I have eyes," Santo retorted. "I, however, was not addressing you!"

Demetrius's demeanor shifted from stunned and meek to hard and resolved.

"Then, I would appreciate you not referring to me as if I were absent!" he growled.

"I will refer to you any way I wish!" Santo blustered. "*I* was the one dragged here under false pretenses."

"Please," Okawa said, stepping between them. "I can see now that this was a mistake."

"I should say so," Alyanna coldly agreed. "If our son wants to waste his life as a common smuggler, we want nothing to do with him or his corrupt lifestyle."

"He doesn't do that anymore," Okawa corrected calmly. "He works with me in the Valdurian Air Service."

Santo's expression remained dour. "House Valdur, I see. So, you're no longer transporting illegal goods, but you have turned your back on House Aramos."

Demetrius turned away. "That's it. I've had enough of this nonsense! I'm going home."

"Thank you for an enchanting evening, my dear," he snapped sarcastically at Okawa before disappearing back through the curtains.

For a city of its considerable size, Makatooa surprisingly has no air station. A small clearing, hewed from the jungle just to the North of the main inlet, provided only the most basic accommodation to all air ships. Landing on the tropical location offered its own set of challenges. The thick, triple canopy jungle limited access to this rare open expanse, forcing entrance at the inlet, along with the nautical traffic.

Two pairs of eyes cautiously peered from the foliage, while the Kan fog enveloped the rainforest, and surveyed the crude airfield.

"Where's the guard?" a young thief with badly pockmarked skin and long greasy hair asked in a whisper.

"Probably on the other side of the clearing," an older, skinny, bald man softly replied. "The fog's so thick I can hardly see shit."

The landing field held only two airships, a medium sized transport berthed beside a solitary one-room guard post, and the *Haraka* parked next to the dense jungle.

"We'll go for the smaller one," the older thief said, squinting into the fog. "That transport's too close to the maintenance shed for my liking."

The young thief nodded in agreement and started forward. A hand on his shoulder halted him, just as a Valdurian marine came into view, walking the perimeter. Dressed in the traditional green jumpsuit, he carried a medium crossbow lowered, but loaded and at the ready.

Hefting a crowbar, the older thief picked up a rock and handed it to the younger one. When the marine passed them, the young man tossed the rock into the clearing. It bounced loudly off the wall of the shack.

The guard spun toward the sound, raising his weapon. He didn't have time to take a step when the curved end of the crowbar streaked out from the bush and violently hooked his neck. The young marine gagged in surprise when it brutally yanked him backward into the thick bushes. He landed on his back, dropping the crossbow to the ground, desperately grabbing at his throat. The old thief brought the iron bar down hard, crushing the marine's forehead with a sickening crack.

"Grab the crossbow," the older thief ordered.

They started out into the clearing, moving quickly and carefully around the jungle's edge approaching the *Haraka*.

"The cargo hold is in the rear," the older man said. "Now, let's see what goodies we've got in here."

He wedged the crowbar between the cargo hatch and the hull, tugging with both hands, but the hatch refused to budge.

"We gotta tough one here."

The old man wiped away the sweat from his brow and closely examined the seal. "Come give me a hand."

The young thief joined him, and both pulled when they heard a loud clunk from inside. The rear hatch slowly descended and they both stepped out of the way. Filtered sunlight crept in through the ship's windshield, washing the open design of the interior in deep shadows.

"You smell that?" the young man asked, his nostrils flaring at a thick, musky aroma.

"Yeah, smells kinda like sex," the elder answered.

"Not much of a haul," he scoffed, noticing only a few crates and barrels.

"Eh, never can tell what's in those containers," the older burglar replied, lifting the blood-stained crowbar. "What say we pop a few open and see what we've got?"

"Let's go."

They'd only taken a few steps up the ramp when the young thief's foot became entangled.

"There's something sticky over here," he said, wrestling his boot free.

"Over here too," the older thief answered next to him.

He pressed his hand against tacky, thin strands of silk across the hull just inside the craft.

They quickly forgot their curiosity over the gummy material when sudden movement drew their attention. Shadows partially obscured the details, but from the shoulder length hair and buoyant breasts, a naked woman ducked behind one crate.

The burglars grinned salaciously at each other and stepped fully inside the air ship.

"Come on out, luv," the older one coaxed. "We're not gonna hurt ya."

"Yeah, we're just lookin' for a little affection," the younger one added, setting the crossbow down.

They slowly advanced around both sides of the crate to prevent her escape.

"We promise to be gentle."

"Yeah, we promise."

Kumo leapt straight up toward the ceiling. She gripped her webbing across the cargo bay and hung upside down, staring curiously. Both burglars screamed upon seeing her arachnid lower body and multiple eyes.

The older man raised the crowbar. A stream of sticky webbing shot from the tip of her thorax, circled his assaulting arm and pinned it to the inner hull.

The younger one staggered backward in a panic, screaming and flailing his arms into the webbing lining the walls. Now trapped, he whimpered and sobbed, struggling in vain against his constraints.

Both men realized the powerful, musky odor emanated from her. The spider-woman lowered herself within a few feet of the ensnared older man. She hung there, tilting her head from side to side, studying the curious mixture of fear and arousal on his face.

Slowly and seductively, she reached out and unlaced the older man's tunic. He batted away her first two attempts with his free hand before realizing he had developed a rampant erection.

When she pulled away the tunic from his free arm, she sensuously stroked his chest. His terrified gaze followed her delicate fingers playing with his nipple. When she gave it a pinch, he grunted in ecstasy and ejaculated in his pants.

The spent man slumped over as far as his restraint would allow and tried to regain his breath. Kumo pressed her voluptuous black lips against his ear.

"Hungry," she whispered suggestively.

The young burglar trembled so badly he heard his teeth chattering. He watched in terrified confusion while the spider-woman stroked his companion's chest, and his stomach twisted with dread, but his loins ached watching the old man buckle in orgasm. When two large, curved fangs rapidly extended from her mouth, he screamed hysterically.

She bit down on the older thief just above the collarbone and the victim went into shock instantaneously. Powerful injected neurotoxins paralyzed and liquified his muscles and organs. A look of ravenous hunger descended over her face and she retracted her fangs quickly, burying her mouth into the growing area of goo on his upper chest.

When the young man's throat grew horse, and no screams could escape, it forced him to listen to the voracious slurping and sucking sounds of her devouring his companion.

Mal and Alto walked the solitary road to the airfield with their arms around each other. Mal rested her head blissfully on his shoulder and contentedly sighed over their wonderful evening of food and drink at the Storm Watch Pub. She felt especially nostalgic when Alto stopped her for a kiss on the very spot they first embraced.

"Just let me get my bag, then we can head back to your place," she offered.

"You'll be more comfortable there." Alto assured.

"Yeah," she agreed, "just don't let me oversleep or try to distract me tomorrow. We've got a quick but profitable run to make once the Kan lifts."

"I would never seek to delay you." Alto said, feigning indignation.

Mal stopped and put both arms around him. "You know just the right way to delay me."

She kissed him but couldn't help noticing something distracting the swordmaster. Breaking the embrace, she gave a questioning glance.

"What?"

"Is the ship's cargo hold supposed to be open?" Alto asked, looking over her shoulder.

"No!" Mal said in alarm.

The Spice Rat spun to see the *Haraka*'s aft entrance unlocked and aggressively drew her sword. She sprinted to her airship with Alto in tow. Mal stepped over the dead guard and peered through the wide open hatch.

The female Makari was just finishing wrapping the young thief in a white cocoon of spider silk. He frantically mouthed the words "no" and "please."

Off to her left, the partially eaten older thief sat propped up against a crate. His bald head dangled unnaturally forward into his missing chest cavity.

"Kumo, what in the name of the goddess are you doing?!" Mal asked indignantly, putting her blade away. "We talked about this!"

Kumo briefly halted to watch the two enter the hold. A look of hope passed over the young man's face when he saw Mal and Alto.

"Please help me!" he croaked in a horse whisper.

"Hungry," she said guiltily. "They break into ship."

"Oh," Mal replied.

She shot the thief a merciless look, before walking past the encased victim to the cockpit and retrieving her backpack from the back of the captain's chair. She gave the burglar another disdainful glance before addressing her pilot.

"Chow down," Mal said in an aloof voice, "but have this place cleaned up by morning, and please don't forget to do something about that dead guard outside. We sail at the lifting of the Kan."

Even though it was a short walk from the Zorian Forum to the headquarters of the Imperial Bank, by the time Bartol Aramos made it to the main promenade, the corpulent patriarch was sweating profusely.

Six strapping men, armed with pole arms and short swords, surrounded the new king and pushed their way through the crowds leading to the upscale bustling merchant's row. They wore the purple sashes of the Szoldos mercenaries and weren't gentle parting the affluent crowd.

Forsvara Guards traditionally protected Aramos royalty, however, in this instance, Bartol took no chances on a coup. He remembered how insanely jealous his uncle Dolan, commander of the Forsvara, became when passed over for the position of Aramos' sovereign.

Bartol stopped briefly in front of the large ornate doors of the Imperial bank and a lone EEtah standing guard saluted smartly. Bartol glanced down at the small piece of paper he clutched in his pudgy hand and sadly sighed before nodding grimly. Two of his mercenaries opened the doors.

The procession then made its way through the busy lobby of the financial engine for the mercantile and royal class alike. Bankers occupied large ostentatious desks scattered about the huge open room, softly conversing with merchants and envoys tending to their accounts or soliciting loans. A small army of clerical staffers glided about, passing around stacks of official documents.

The industrious activity paused and everyone stared when the royal party passed through the lobby and disappeared into the offices of the Zorian Monetary Council.

Bartol approached the office of Senior Fellow, Cedar Aramos. He again stared down at the paper in his hand with a mournful frown. He knocked with a resolved sigh and, without waiting for a reply, entered. A wiry older man with salt and pepper hair sat at a lone desk. He stood when the patriarch entered and smiled broadly.

"Nephew!" he exclaimed, opening his arms. "Excuse me… I mean, your majesty."

Bartol gave a subdued smile and nervously played with his eyebrow. "Uncle Cedar, we've just received word from Makatooa."

"Yes," Cedar answered, "I heard from my little muffin the other day. The new bank is off to a distinguished…"

The pained look crossing Bartol's face when he mentioned his daughter caused the senior economist to cut short his thought.

"What?"

"There was a robbery at the bank, Uncle," Bartol gently answered. "Colette and her staff were all killed."

Cedar's face went ashen with the news. He dropped back into his chair staring vacantly forward. Bartol watched the tears well up in his uncle's eyes.

"I'm so sorry, uncle."

"What... how?" was all Cedar could manage.

"Apparently, someone dropped the lobby's chandelier on them before robbing the vault."

"She... she was my sunshine," Cedar sputtered as he wiped away a stream of tears. "Who could have done that sort of thing to such a gentle soul?"

"We've got a good description," Bartol answered. "They didn't even attempt to disguise themselves. I'm dispatching a detachment of Forsvara along with a few Black Talons. We'll get them."

Now openly weeping, the older Aramos could only nod his head.

"I'll arrange for her body to be sent back to Aris," Bartol continued. "Aunt Ferro will probably want to arrange the funeral service."

Cedar now sat, staring into the distance, tears streaming down his face. Bartol reached down and reassuringly touched his uncle's arm.

"Once again uncle," he offered, "I'm so sorry. I hadn't seen my cousin in a while, but I'll always remember her sweet nature."

Cedar broke from his tearful trance when Bartol opened the door to leave.

"When they are caught," he said, his voice cracking. "I would very much appreciate it if I could dispense justice to the guilty party."

A sad, cruel smile crossed the family patriarch's face.
"In whatever manner suits you, uncle."

"Asad's running late," Mal said, when she heard the
Turine in Makatooa's harbor ring thirteen bells. "And we
sure can't go anywhere until he delivers the cargo."

"What's the cargo, captain?" Zaad asked, standing and
stretching. "I mean, we've been waiting for nearly a deci."

"Not what, *who*," Mal answered. "We're supposed to take
whoever it is over to Shun-Dra."

"Nocturn, huh?" Zau said with a mercenary gleam. "Well,
that explains the generous fee,"

"Yep," Mal answered. "'Quick and simple' is how Asad
described it."

"Don't forget profitable," the Singa added, greedily
eyeing the bag containing a sizeable stack of commodity
notes on the floor by the captain's chair.

"Here they come," Wostera said, looking out the lowered
back hatch,

A large lizard drawn coach and two riders on horseback
entered the crude airfield. The entourage came to an abrupt
halt by the open side hatch. One rider dismounted and
opened the coach's double doors. Asad, along with two
bodyguards and a small, hooded figure stepped out onto the
grassy field.

"What's with all the muscle?" Zau asked, furrowing her
brow.

"Maybe they know something we don't," Zaad offered.

"I'm sure they do," Mal said, getting up. "Zau, Kumo, be
ready to get us the fuck outta here if need be."

She shuffled out onto the ramp and gave a short wave at the crime boss.

"Bout damn time you got here, Asad."

"Sorry," he apologized, "we were unavoidably detained."

"We got company!" Zau cried out.

Four Singa females broke from the tree line and bound on all fours in their direction. Thin blindfolds covered their eyes and they wore leather bandoliers lined with sickle-shaped throwing daggers.

Mal lashed out, grabbing the arm of the hooded figure beside Asad and yanked it into the craft. When she felt fur in her hand, it surprised her. A collision with Kumo at the wheel knocked back the hood, revealing a fawn-colored, female mongrel.

Well, Mal thought, *at least the destination now made more sense.*

She drew her sword and bounded out of the *Haraka*. By the time Mal made it down the ramp, Wostera and Zaad were rushing out the rear of the airship with their weapons brandished.

"Get those hatches closed!" Mal ordered.

One of the Singas vaulted on top of the transport airship parked next to them. In a fluid motion, she launched herself at the remaining mounted gangster. They collided while he attempted drawing his sword, pushing both off the horse and the mawl simultaneously raked her claws across his chest as they fell to the ground. The unfortunate mobster struggled briefly against the much larger and heavier mawl on top of him until it leaned in and bit out his throat. It licked its bloody jaws and peered around for its next target.

Two others charged Mal, and she braced herself to deal with both attackers, but to her surprise, only one leapt at her. The impact drove the Spice Rat on her back and sent her sword flying. Mal could feel its claws dig into her shoulder, pinning her to the ground, and quickly snapped her head to one side, narrowly avoiding the ferocious gnashing jaws aimed at her neck. Anticipating a second strike, she quickly wrenched her head in the other direction, avoiding another killing bite.

It sunk its claws in deeper, attempting to hold her still, and searing pain wracked Mal's right shoulder. The beast lunged at her again and she smelled its rancid breath just before pain erupted from the side of her head. Its sharp teeth missed another fatal blow, but bit off part of her earlobe.

The Spice Rat felt herself growing weak and unsure of her ability to dodge the next attack. Out of the corner of her eye, she noticed the other Singa leaping for the closing side hatch. The door caught its tail just past the entrance, but it wiggled free and the hatch closed behind it.

Zaad charged around the craft bellowing and waving Bowbreaker. One of the Singa attackers unsheathed two sickle daggers and threw them at the berserking EEtah. The small blades lodged harmlessly in the thick skin of the man-shark's chest. Zaad screamed in rage and brought Bowbreaker down with full force.

The agile lioness saw the blade descending and lurched to the right. The dodging attempt proved partially successful in avoiding a body severing blow, but the Singa screamed in agony when the great sword completely cleaved both of its back legs off. It rolled around clawing at the grass and crying out, while blood pumped onto the ground from its amputated stumps.

The Singa mounting Mal reared back to strike when the *Haraka* suddenly shot nose first into the sky. The Spice Rat felt a powerful jolt then a warm shower of blood spraying her. Something propelled the assaulting creature ten feet away, and it lay lifeless on the ground, most of its chest missing. Wostera rushed over to her, arm extended. Her arrow returned to her hand in a cascade of blue sparks just as she reached her fallen captain.

"Valorous, you're injured," she exclaimed.

Mal groaned in pain, watching her airship hover a hundred feet up when the cargo hatch opened. The Singa which made it inside toppled out of the opening and plummeted to the ground. It landed with a resounding thud and the crack of its shattered spine.

The *Haraka* leveled off and gently descended to its former berth. The side hatch dropped and Zau sat in the navigator's chair clutching the trembling mongrel. A single, thick strand of spider silk crossed their torsos and secured them to their seat.

In a flash, Kumo scurried down the ramp and over to her captain laying in Wostera's lap. Surveying the situation, the humanoid spider ripped open the torn bloody shoulder of Mal's shirt.

"Must stop bleeding," she said softly, moving the tip of her thorax just above the wound.

Several short silky bands flowed from the quivering orifice, covering the bleeding incisions with a thick white coating. A single, large drop covered the missing lobe of her left ear.

Zau used a single claw to sever her makeshift seatbelt. She motioned for the mongrel passenger to stay in the ship and then bounded to Mal's side. The airship captain kept her eyes closed and her mouth contorted into an agonized scowl.

Rotating one seashell on her belt, Zau knelt over Mal. She rubbed the solitary rune which adorned the shells' underside with one hand and placed her palm over the spider silk bandages. They sparkled with a light blue glow as she touched them. When the light faded a sudden look of relief appeared on the Spice Rat's face.

"This should help with the pain," Zau explained. "It will also keep rot from setting in. My people's mouths are notoriously filthy."

With a flutter, Mal's eyes opened and she looked around.

"What the fuck was that all about?" she asked sitting up.

"I'm pretty sure they were after your passenger," Asad answered, picking up one blindfold. "They were all wearing these... whatever they are."

Zau reached out and took the long strip from Asad's hands and examined it.

"The skin of the Dalla eel," she said authoritatively. "This is eye protection. The sun is much too bright here for the beings of Nocturn."

She tapped the dark spectacles on her face.

"They act much the same way as my glasses," she continued, "but did you notice that our new passenger apparently doesn't need them?"

Mal glanced through the hatch at the mongrel staring back at them, and then to Asad. "So, who gave you the money to hire us?"

The gangster paused apprehensively.

"I'm not fucking around here Asad!" Mal scowled. "We almost got killed!"

"The mayor," the mob boss admitted, resignation crossing his pudgy face, "Blyth Calden."

Mal sighed resolutely and rubbed her wounded shoulder.

"Okay, Zaad stash these bodies in the woods somewhere, then watch over our passenger."

She reached into the *Haraka* and retrieved the bag containing their payment.

"I need some more answers before we agree to this shit," she declared, looking over at Zau and Asad. "We're gonna go have a 'stand before the gods meeting' with the mayor."

Mal proceeded over to Asad's carriage and noticed Kumo webbing up the body of the broken, but uncut, Singa which fell to its death.

"Kumo, what are you doing?" Mal asked.

The Makara smiled shyly and easily hoisted the entombed body up onto her shoulder.

"Feast," she said innocently, before carrying it up the rear ramp, disappearing into the cargo hold.

Chu-Chu loved it when humans pissed themselves. The Cul-Ta leader reveled in the fear and power the rat-men could impose on the unwary who ventured out too late in the Kan. All too often, his kind were the target of violence and scorn at the hands of humans.

The old couple trembled in front of his slowly circling blade and he could smell the distinct odor of urine. The Cul-Ta leader started giggling.

"Please," the old man begged. "You've taken everything! What more could you want?"

"Shut up stupid human!" Chu-Chu scolded.

He knew the man was right though. Glancing over at the small pile of their belongings laying nearby he smiled conceiving a final humiliation.

"Clothes!" he demanded, motioning towards the pile.

The couple froze in shock. The old woman silently shook her head in a panicked no.

"Please, you don't need to do this." The man's voice trembled, trying to reason.

"NOW!" Chu-Chu squealed, threateningly swinging his sword in front of them.

The elderly couple quickly disrobed while the surrounding rat-men launched into peals of laughter. The humans cringed in fear and embarrassment, vainly attempting to cover their wrinkled, naked bodies. Their distress caused even more taunting laughter. The four-foot-tall creatures mockingly pointed at the frightened humans.

"Okay, you go now."

The two shuffled away, vainly attempting to cover their nakedness, but Chu-Chu became frustrated with their pace.

"GO!" he screamed, the admonishment reverberating off the high walls.

The couple shed all modesty and hurried, as quickly as possible, out the exit from The Old City below the seaport. They ran until they disappeared into the fog shrouded streets of Makatooa.

With the victims now gone, the small mob of Cul-Ta descended on their pile of loot with gleeful abandon. Several inspected the various jewels and gold coins. Two played tug-of-war with the man's scarf. They chattered wildly, fighting for possession of the garment. Still another walked around completely encased in the comically oversized dress of the woman, blindly bumping into his companions.

"Not a huge haul for all that work," Serobini interrupted, stepping from the shadows.

The Cul-Ta froze and then panicked. Squealing loudly, they jumped about, desperately scanning around the room for an escape route. They, however, had chosen their robbery location too well, because the only exit lay past the thin man in the tall hat. With no escape, the man-rats drew their weapons and began hissing.

"Whoa, what's with all the hostility?!" the lip-less human said, unfazed by their threats.

He calmly sat down cross-legged on the floor, licked his teeth and looked around smiling. "So, here we are!"

The rat creatures stared at each other, unsure what to do with this odd looking human.

"What you want?" Chu-Chu asked apprehensively.

"Ya see," Serobini began, animatedly waving his arms. "That's what's wrong with society nowadays. Everybody assumes you want something! When you start thinking everyone has ulterior motives, it's a slippery slope descending into a completely nihilistic way of life..."

Serobini paused and smacked his gums, looking around at the simple creature's blank faces. He sighed, sensing his audience didn't appreciate his philosophical rant.

"I have a gift," he said, his pleasant tone returning.

Serobini reached behind him and retrieved a small bag from the shadows. He placed the sack between his legs. The contents clattered noisily when they landed on the floor. Without waiting he opened the drawstring and began pulling out oblong wooden wafers, stacking them in six orderly piles.

The Cul-Ta leader recognized the commodity notes immediately. His eyes fixated on the number etched into the front of the wafer, *one-hundred-secor*. A greedy smirk tugged at the corners of his mouth while he quickly calculated their value at one thousand struck gold pieces each.

Serobini smiled broadly at the Cul-Ta, who stared intently at the notes. He extended his arms towards the stacks with a flourish.

"Your gift!"

The rat-men eyed each other suspiciously.

"Why?" Chu-Chu asked cautiously.

Serobini enthusiastically bound to his feet and the Cul-Ta nervously jumped backwards.

"I have a soft spot for the downtrodden, the overlooked, the oppressed. All who have to live by someone else's rules or measure up to another's standards."

Confused stares met him once again. Sighing, he gave a satisfied grin.

"Enjoy yourselves!" he said, before bounding through the doorway and disappearing back into the shadows.

Asad watched an unusually quiet Mal stare pensively out the carriage window at the congested streets of Makatooa. Zau sat beside her admiring the coach's opulent interior.

"Nice ride," Zau said. "You would think someone in your line of work would choose something a little more low-key."

An amused, superior smile crossed the mobster's face. "And exactly what kind of work would that be?"

"Umm..." the Singa shifted nervously in her seat and tugged at her tunic. "Uh..."

"Exactly what *kind* of carriage would you expect from a successful import/export broker?"

Zau's eyes darted back and forth and the whiskers on her short snout twitched furiously. "Well... I... I mean..."

Mal smiled at her navigator's awkward situation.

"Nice job, Zau," she said. "Why don't you just ask him how many kneecaps he's broken today?"

Zau's head snapped around at her captain, her face masked in shocked disbelief at the question. Now, Asad, and the burley bodyguard seated next to him, also grinned.

"Oh, I don't break kneecaps anymore," Asad said obviously amused. "I have people to do that for me."

The mountain of a man seated next to Asad smiled broadly in silent surety.

"I meant nothing by it!" Zau said, her voice raising a register.

"It's all right," Asad said with a chuckle. "In my line of work, my associates and I are seldom at odds with the local governments. We act as a sort of silent partner."

Asad turned his attention back to Mal, who resumed staring out the window. He noticed her clothing and face were still blood stained and tattered.

"Speaking of governments," he suggested, "don't you want to get cleaned up before meeting the mayor?"

"Fuck that," Mal said defiantly. "I want him to get a firsthand look at what we're dealing with."

"Very well," Asad said. "Have you *met* the mayor?"

"Nope," she answered. "I've had some dealings with his brother Pierce. He's the Calden ambassador to Zor."

"He's a personable-enough lad," Asad said, nodding. "Former naval officer, Brightstar, well-liked by his men. His father pulled him out of naval service right after he earned the Brightstar pin, married him off to the daughter of a wealthy shipping magnate and assigned him here as mayor. He doesn't like it much. He'd rather be at sea, but they expected him to serve the family politically, like his older siblings... and here we are."

Asad's bodyguard opened the door and Mal looked out at the four nondescript buildings surrounded by a wrought-iron fence comprising the governmental compound. A Sunal EEtah stood guard just outside the gate, holding his Yudon harpoon before him ceremoniously.

"You'll forgive me if I don't accompany you," Asad said stepping out. "It's best if they don't see the mayor and I together. It's the silent part of our silent partnership."

"I get it," Mal said.

She and Zau stepped out onto the street and the coach quickly sped off. The EEtah guard suspiciously eyed Mal's gruesome appearance.

"I'm pretty sure I'm going to need your help to get in," Mal whispered to Zau.

The Singa turned over the fifteenth of sixteen shells comprising her belt and rubbed the rune etched on the reverse side.

"We're here to see the mayor," Mal announced, craning her head up to address the twelve-foot-tall man-shark.

She could tell he stood poised to challenge them and then Zau's spell took effect. He quivered in frustration, and then reluctantly nodded.

"Weapons in the bin," he ordered.

They deposited their weapons in a long oblong box against the fence.

"It's that building," he said, pointing out the two-story structure on the end.

They approached the building and discovered a young pageboy, in a blue tunic, squatting by the front door.

"We're here to see the mayor," Mal proclaimed.

The page stood. His face registered a brief look of shock at Mal's appearance before silently leading them inside and up to a set of double doors on the second floor. There, another young pageboy met them, also squatting by the entrance, and dressed identically. The young boy escorting them knocked three times before scurrying back off down the stairs.

"Come in," a masculine voice answered from within.

When they entered, a young man stood from behind a large ornate desk strewn with papers. He appeared in his early to mid-twenties, with a medium build, pleasant facial features sporting tightly trimmed dark brown hair and a closely trimmed beard. He wore the formal blue waist coat of a Calden naval officer. The rank of lieutenant commander adorned the epaulettes on each shoulder and his chest displayed various ribbons and the striking Brightstar pin.

He couldn't contain a wide-eyed look of surprise at Mal's bloody, disheveled appearance and her humanoid lioness companion wearing round dark glasses.

"C... Can I help you?" he stammered.

"I believe you can Si. Mayor," Mal replied, placing the bag of commodity notes on his desk. "I'm Captain Maluria of the airship *Haraka*. That's my navigator, Zau."

"And I'm Blyth Calden Mayor of Makatooa," he said, unable to take his eyes off Zau. "Please forgive me for staring, but I've only *heard* of your kind before. I've never met one. You're a Singa, are you not?"

"You get the prize, Your Honor," Zau replied. "We inhabitants of Nocturn don't get over here much."

"Yeah, that shit's about to change." Mal declared, motioning to the bag on his desk. "You recently had a visitor from Nocturn. That's the money you gave Asad to hire us. I've got a few questions before we take the job, questions Asad couldn't answer."

The mayor's face went from quizzical to guarded.

"I'm afraid I'm…"

"Save it, Your Honor," Mal interrupted. "I don't work for House Calden, so the whole *need to know* shit doesn't work with me. This was supposed to be a 'simple, quick job,' but three dead Singa assassins back at the airfield say otherwise. I'm not putting my crew in danger when I damn sure don't know why! If you can't or *won't* tell me, you can have your money back and use it to hire someone else… *and good luck with that*, because the only other air-jockey that's flown to Nocturn works for House Valdur."

Mal knew he assessed a precarious situation from the way the mayor's gaze bounced back and forth from her to Zau.

"There are those more qualified than I to fill you in." Blyth said, sighing in resignation.

The Mayor of Makatooa reached for a small bell in a corner of his desk. The young pageboy squatting outside the door appeared the moment he rang it.

"Fetch Kem and Velitel," he ordered.

The page silently nodded and disappeared down the hall.

"The hiring and payment were supposed to be anonymous," Blyth lamented, sitting down.

"Don't worry your Honor," Mal said reassuringly. "Your secret's safe with me. Besides, I've worked with your family before."

"Oh, really?"

"You got your Ukko wood back, didn't you?"

The young mayor's face lit up. "That was you?!"

"Damn right," Mal replied. "We worked with your brother, Pierce."

There was a knock on the door ending the reminiscing banter.

"Come," Blyth called out.

Two people stepped into the room, a large dark skinned, balding man with a close-cropped white beard and a much shorter demure female with attractive features and short brown hair. They abruptly halted and stared at the mayor's unusual guests.

"You sent for us, sir?" the man asked, sounding slightly confused as his gaze locked on Mal.

Blyth nodded at his two officers. "This is Kem, the local Intelligencer and…"

"Hello Velitel," Mal greeted with a smirk.

"Captain Maluria," the commander of the city guards answered, breaking into a wide grin. "I never thought you would make an appearance in my little drama under these circumstances."

He then surveyed her shabby appearance.

"You've looked better though," he added. "Your costuming seems amiss."

"Still a theatre buff I see," Mal noted pleasantly.

"You two know each other?" Blyth asked, watching the reunion.

"Yeah, from back in my smuggling days," Mal answered.

"I could never catch her," Velitel admitted.

"I wouldn't feel bad about that," she replied. "You're in good company."

"We hired captain Maluria to return our visitor back to Nocturn," Blyth said, tapping his finger nervously on the desk. "In the light of recent events, she feels the need for more information about the job before she commits to it."

Velitel rapidly searched everyone's faces. "Events, what events?!"

"We were just attacked by a Singa hunter/ killer pack over at the airfield," Zau chimed in. "They were after the mongrel."

Velitel examined Mal's bloody features. "This explains the bad stage makeup."

"You call it a mongrel?" Kem finally spoke up.

"Mongrels are the result when any of the predominant pure races in the Land of Mists crossbreed," Zau explained.

"I brought you two in to catch her up on the more unusual goings on around here." Blyth said formally.

Kem and Velitel traded apprehensive glances.

"Speak freely," the mayor said.

Kem's mouth went taunt in disapproval, clearly uncomfortable sharing information with strangers.

"Four cycles ago," she reluctantly began, "a Caldani patrol ship came across a small vessel they had never seen before. It was open top with six... mongrel... as you call them... four oarsmen, a humanoid tiger captain and their only passenger, the mongrel now in your custody."

"Orange or white?" Zau quickly asked.

"I beg your pardon?"

"The tiger, was it orange or white?"

"Orange," Kem replied, baffled.

Zau scowled and gave a low sigh. "Rank and file Tiikeri."

"Tiikeri?" the spymaster asked.

"Those are one of the pure-bred races I mentioned," Zau answered. "They pretty much run the show over in the Land of Mists."

"Go on please," Mal said, staring intently at Kem.

"According to standard practice, the Caldani stopped the ship and attempted to board her to inspect for contraband. The crew put up a fight, and they killed them. The ship sank, and they pulled your little guest out of the water. We were the closest port with an intelligencer, so they brought her to me."

"Did she talk?" Mal asked.

"She was quite forthcoming," Kem answered, "told us her name was Pamje and that she had no love for the tigers. It surprised me we understood each other, but she claimed this was because of a piece of crystal she carried."

"What the fuck were they doing all the way over here in the Spice Islands?"

"She said she was special," the spymaster continued. "Something about the way they bred her. She also said she was always uncomfortable, like people were in her head looking through her eyes."

"Worrg!" Zau gasped.

"The breeding center they held you captive in!" Mal added.

"The Kharry Institute!" Zau clarified.

"Excuse me," Blyth said, interrupting their private revelation. "Anything you would care to share with the rest of us?"

"Sorry, Your Honor," Mal said, slightly embarrassed. "One more thing, were the sentients on that boat wearing eye coverings?"

"Everyone except Pamje. She said she didn't need it."

Mal and Zau sat silent for a moment, staring concerned at each other. Blyth clearing his throat brought them out of their collective trance. The mayor extended his hands with a serious and inquisitive expression.

Mal gave a frustrated sigh and nodded at Zau.

"Tell them."

All eyes fixed on the Singa.

"The peoples of Nocturn have trouble seeing in the bright, constant sunlight of Lumina. We need eye protection." The Singa lightly tapped on the side of her glasses. "It's a great disadvantage. It looks like the Tiikeri have discovered how to breed mongrels that this light doesn't bother, but it gets worse, they've combined this enhanced sight with Worrg psychic abilities."

"Worrg?" Kem asked, betraying the first signs of alarm.

"Remote viewers, the perfect spies," Zau said in a matter-of-fact tone. "When she complained of people looking through her eyes, she wasn't kidding. There are Worrgs back in the Land of Mists psychically connected to her and under direct Tiikeri control. They see what she sees. That's how those Singas found us."

A moment of somber silence descended on the room.

"So, what do we do now?" Velitel's deep voice broke the stillness.

"I want any mongrels spotted anywhere, detained and questioned," Blyth ordered.

"Yes sir," the commander responded with an enthusiastic nod.

"You should share this information with the forum over in Zor," Mal said directly to Kem. "House Valdur has had dealings with all things Nocturn. Working with Joc' Valdur's people, as well as the Zorian spymaster, Rafel, will be of mutual benefit."

Mal then reached over and picked up the money sack from Blyth's desk.

"As for me and my crew," she added, "we've got a delivery to make to the Unaligned City of Shun-Dra. Pamje is right, it's the only safe place for her."

"Uhh boss," Zau asked apprehensively, "you *are* gonna tidy up first, right?"

The knock was so soft, Demetrius almost didn't hear it. He opened the door to discover Okawa, dressed in her green jumpsuit, staring down embarrassingly. A silent, awkward moment passed while she fidgeted slightly. Summoning her courage, she looked up at her pilot and lover.

"May I come in?"

Demetrius stepped aside without answering, extending his arm in a stiff welcoming gesture.

She immediately spun to face him when he closed the door.

"Demetrius, I'm, I'm..." she paused and lowered her gaze.

He let the moment hang before stepping over to her.

"You're sorry?"

She nervously nodded, all the while keeping her eyes lowered. "I mean, I..."

She fell silent again and peered up sorrowfully. He put his hands gently on her shoulders.

"You were just trying to get me and my folks back together because of what happened to yours, weren't you?"

Keeping the forlorn expression, she nodded once again.

"Back to your old talkative self, eh?" he asked through a thin smile.

"Demetrius!" she scolded. "This isn't easy for me."

"So I can see."

"You're not mad?"

"I was, but mostly at my parents. They do a pretty good job of holding a grudge."

Before she could speak, he softly slid his hands down to her forearms and gazed into her eyes.

"Captain Okawa," Demetrius continued, "I know you are a top fixer for House Valdur, but there are some things in this world, one just can't fix."

"It's just..."

Demetrius smiled and shook his head, cutting her off.

"Apology accepted."

He then leaned in and gently kissed her. It lingered and they fell into each other's arms.

"I've got an idea," he mischievously whispered. "What say we adjourn to the bedroom where you can give me a proper apology."

Okawa returned a lecherous grin. "Oh, I think I can conjure up the appropriate gesture of penance."

"Well then," Demetrius said taking her hand and guiding her towards the bedroom door. "Let the contrition begin."

Okawa chuckled and slipped her arm around his waist while they made their way across the living room.

"Just as long as we're prepared to fly with the lifting of the Kan," she added.

Demetrius paused. "This is the first I'm hearing of it."

"I just got the orders, we're to report to Landagar. They want to finish the upgrades they started."

Nodding, he resumed guiding them on their amorous trek.

"I just love new toys."

Wikk the First, Lord of Tannimore and Keeper of the Faith led the small procession through the crowded walkways making up the streets of the floating city. Behind him, two armed guards flanked an older bearded man in saffron robes.

The guards tightly gripped each arm and muscled the robed prisoner along, even though he didn't resist. His calm demeanor cracked a bit when they led him onto the Kinjuto barge and he heard the cries of anguish drifting up from within. The priest of Santi trembled while they descended into the darkened interior, staring wide-eyed at a dozen nude victims, both men and women, secured to heavy wooden crosses.

Strips of leather bound their hands and feet to the X shaped beams. They'd applied thin brown cords wet and, now dried and shrinking, they dug deeply into the flesh. Long slender wires pierced various tender parts of their naked bodies suspending weights of various sizes from their ends. The wounds, while extremely painful, weren't life threatening, but designed to inflict constant pain. At prescribed intervals, one of Ve-Qua's Kinjuto pupils adjusted or moved a weight for maximum effect.

His knees buckled when they entered the Mistress of Pain's chambers and found Ve-Qua still busy with a client, a naked older woman bound spread-eagle on a low table. They'd scrawled sordid, derogatory words across her pale frame. Another of Ve-Qua's pupils knelt between her legs, violently ramming a dual, phallic-tipped, pitchfork-shaped implement into both exposed orifices. Ve-Qua straddled her face, viciously grinding her open vaginal lips on the squirming woman's mouth and nose, all the while keeping up a torrent of demeaning verbal abuse.

The Santi cleric began softly praying when Ve-Qua suddenly rocked in the throes of orgasm. Her pelvis pounded mercilessly on the woman's head while torrents of clear female ejaculate squirted all over the squirming client's head, soaking her hair and face. Ve-Qua took a moment to compose herself, keeping the head between her thighs in a vice-like grip. Her impaled breasts heaved in unison while catching her breath. The mistress' spent fluid seeped off the table in a slow drip and pooled on the floor.

The Kinjuto master climbed down from the table and eyed her assistant still impaling the woman's nether regions with wild abandon.

"Keep this up until you're certain she will have trouble walking," she said, disdainfully watching the human female struggle and writhe against her bonds. "Then you can take her if you wish. When she leaves, do not allow her to dress or clean up."

"Yes mistress," the naked young man eagerly replied, not missing a stroke.

"Giving the customers their money's worth I see," Wikk said when Ve-Qua approached.

"Lord Wikk," she said, scanning the group, "welcome to my little chamber of horrors. What brings you by today?"

"They caught this one begging and proselytizing on the docks," Wikk announced, indicating the robed prisoner.

Ve-Qua stepped in close and the Santi priest stopped his prayer under his breath and swallowed hard.

"Tisk, tisk, naughty boy," the mistress said, stroking his cheek. "Don't you know other religions are forbidden?"

The bearded cleric recoiled at her touch.

"The word of Santi is for all to hear," he blurted before resuming his mumbling prayer.

Wikk lashed out and slapped him hard. The blow rocked the priest's head and a thin ribbon of blood appeared in the corner of his mouth. Ve-Qua shuttered with pleasure from the pain the blow caused.

"Blasphemous pig," Wikk sneered. "Your ways are repugnant to Pa-Waga and everything we are attempting to accomplish!"

Ve-Qua stared down, amused at the two zealots.

"I really don't care about your holy wars," she said in a bored tone before addressing Wikk. "Am I to assume you brought him here for my special form of discipline? Why are you involved in such a trifling matter?"

"Blasphemy against the lord is hardly a trifling matter. I bring him as an offering for the oracle."

Ve-Qua's eyes grew wide in excitement and a sadistic smile erupted from her lips.

"The Oracle of Agony," she said breathlessly, toying with the captured cleric's beard. "This is your lucky day."

Barely able to conceal her enthusiasm, she headed for the door. "Right this way, dearies."

She led them down to the third level skipping with glee. The Santi priest kept his eyes closed, praying in a low rapid voice. Eventually they entered a large, virtually empty room with obsidian walls. One of which had a large rectangular hatch to the outside.

A slender, three-foot-tall stone pyramid rested on a wooden stand before the hatch, surrounded by a network of restraints and pulleys hanging from the ceiling. The floor around the structure contained a shallow channel draining out to the sea. An ominous shade of reddish brown stained both the channel and the pyramid.

Two naked, collared assistants—a young man and woman—relieved the guards and led the prisoner to the macabre obelisk. The woman stripped him of his robe while the young man placed his wrists and ankles in the restraints.

The Santi priest, now naked, didn't resist and continued praying with eyes closed. They opened with a start when the young woman fondled his small, shriveled member. He reeled in fear and she stared back at him, her face contorted in diabolic glee.

"When the mistress is done with you," she whispered, "I'll add this to my collection."

The Santi priest snapped his eyes shut. His benediction took on a panicked cadence when Wikk stepped in close.

"Your worthless god of peace, love and... poverty," he said, spitting the last word, "has forsaken you. Perhaps now, you can prove useful to my lord."

Wikk nodded and the young man winched him up over the pyramid. The young female assistant gripped his naked buttocks and positioned them just over the capstone's tip, while Ve-Qua settled back onto a nearby couch.

"You have a question for the oracle?" the mistress asked, lewdly spreading her legs and closing her eyes.

"A new institution has opened in the western Goyan Islands with great potential to serve my lord and the prosperity he seeks to bestow upon the world," Wikk explained. "I have received news of a troubling, yet unspecific nature and seek clarity."

Without opening her eyes, Ve-Qua nodded and motioned to her assistants. They slowly lowered their victim and the young woman methodically inserted the tip into his anus. When the cold stone penetrated him, the old man gasped at the painful disruption of his prayers.

The young man released the rope once he felt sure she securely inserted the tip and the Santi priest screamed when his weight impaled him on the obelisk. Ve-Qua wantonly writhed about on the couch and she slipped into a trance. Thin trails of blue lightning danced across the black crystal walls while the Kinjuto mistress converted the priest's excruciating pain into psychic energy.

Both assistants stood transfixed in masochistic rapture before the impaled man. The woman's breath grew ragged with excitement and the male assistant's erection bobbed carnally in front of him.

"Chaos," Ve-Qua said breathlessly. "A powerful spirit of chaos has arisen and seeks to challenge the laws your lord would impose. It has already struck the first blow."

"What is it?" Wikk asked over the tortured moans filling the room.

Ve-Qua opened her eyes. They danced back and forth wildly, before they locked on Wikk standing over her.

"It was once human," she continued animatedly. "It is clever, but impetuous. Your lord's mission cannot take root while its presence is in the city."

"What can be done?"

"Already, there is one who opposes it," she answered. "More will arrive soon. You must act quickly if you wish to secure your lord's presence there."

Ve-Qua slowly came out of her hypnotic state. The young male assistant lifted the priest off the pyramid and the lightning on the walls subsided with his agony.

"You have served Pa-Waga well," Wikk said, watching the Kinjuto collect herself.

"There is only one god," she said with a mocking laugh, "and that is suffering. All creatures know her, and I abide in her turbulent bosom."

Wikk smiled approvingly at the mistress of pain. The Proffitt had been wise to enlist her aid. She certainly would prove useful in the future. Right now, though, he needed a course of action against an unpredictable enemy. Time was rapidly running out, if they were to believe the oracle.

Commander Truden de Tonck spit over the side railing of the Aramosi combat frigate, *Doyus*, and watched the tall, thickly forested peaks of the Makatooa inlet pass by. They joined a half dozen ships of various sizes entering one of the busiest seaports in the entire Spice Islands. Cargo ships rode low in the water off the starboard side, making their way back out to sea.

The leader of the Forsvara guard detachment didn't especially like hitching a ride on a privateer vessel, but in this case, they had no choice. His men had just finished quelling a native insurrection on nearby Anumi Island when a gull dropped surprise orders in his lap.

"First time in Makatooa, Skipper?" Lieutenant Doosara asked, leaning on the rail beside him.

Truden nodded to his second-in-command and kept studying the rapidly approaching docks and city. The freckle-faced young officer scowled at his superior's silence. He knew from experience it didn't bode well if the normally boisterous commander grew quiet.

"The men will be relieved we're pulling a city assignment," Doosara added, trying to fill the silence. "They'll be glad to get out of the jungle for a change."

"This ain't gonna be no cushy assignment, Doo," Truden scoffed, running a hand through close-cropped brown hair. "We're sailing, uninvited, straight into the heart of Calden territory. By the time we're through, if we don't start a war, the men will realize just how good they had it only protecting spice plantations."

"I thought we were babysitting those four civilians in the cabin back there," Doosara said, brow furrowed.

"Twenty of us?" Truden challenged. "Then there's the Black Talons," he said, indicating the four men in grey tunics playing cards on the stern.

"I thought we were guarding whatever is in those three chests in the storage hold."

"We are," Truden said, pulling out a single leaf of paper from a pouch on his sword belt and handing it to him. "You may as well see it before I brief everyone."

The lieutenant read the order and gave out a whistle drowned out by the rattle of the rigging from the crew preparing to dock.

"Robbery, huh?"

Truden nodded. "They killed the original staff and cleaned out the vault a couple of cycles ago. The civilians are the replacement staff."

"And the Talons?"

"My guess is their job is to find the ones that did it."

"Skipper, sounds like our job just shifted from protecting fat ass plantation owners to protecting fat ass bankers?"

"We are, after all, the guardians of House Aramos, its citizens and property." Truden declared, watching the gangplank lowered. "All right, we're here. Gather everyone around."

"You bet, Skipper."

The Aramos commander looked past his lieutenant rallying the men, to the four Black Talons slipping down the gangplank and disappearing into the bustling city.

As his soldiers assembled, Truden climbed halfway up the stairs to the quarterdeck and studied the youthful faces of the battle-hardened jungle fighters.

"All right lads," he shouted, drawing their attention. "Quite simply, our mission is to escort the civilians on board and the three chests in the hold, to the Imperial Bank and then secure the position."

"For how long, sir?" a soldier asked.

"Until we're relieved," Truden said, with a touch of reservation.

A wave of perplexed chatter rustled through the crowd.

"We drew the short straw on this assignment because we were the closest unit," Truden added. "I can't imagine command wasting our talents in the city, getting our hair and nails done. We're much better suited to slaughtering filthy savages in the bush."

The unit erupted in laughter and cheers.

"Seriously though," the commander continued, cape fluttering out behind him. "We're not in friendly territory anymore. House Calden calls the shots here. Stay sharp and don't provoke a fight. This ship sails the moment we disembark and we'll be on our own, but it won't be the first time, eh lads?"

More cheers and Truden nodded confidently.

"The city may belong to House Calden," he roused, "but the bank belongs to Aramos and it's our job to protect Aramos property. So, let's get to it! We'll travel in columns of two with the civilians and chests in the middle."

They trotted in double time, flanking the wagon through the narrow streets. Their boots clacked rhythmically on the cobblestones drawing the stares of curious onlookers. Truden drove a single large work-lizard pulling the open-top wagon containing the three locked chests and four well-dressed young men.

Flustered citizens and merchants hastily got out of the way of the passing martial parade all along the route. They had made it off the wharf and into central Makatooa before a commotion coming from side streets around them drew their attention.

City guards, wearing the traditional blue tunics of the Calden Maritime Legion, filled the boulevard in front and behind them. They held medium crossbows lowered but at the ready.

Truden stopped the wagon and signaled his men to a halt. His troops automatically assumed a classic defense position. Pivoting in place, the back half of both lines faced the threat behind them.

"Easy lads," Truden cautioned. "We're not here to fight."

Both sides eyed each other suspiciously until two figures, a man and a woman, stepped forward from the platoon of twenty guards. Despite their similar uniforms, both could not have appeared more different.

The petite woman stood just over five feet tall. She had pleasant, delicate features and wore her short hair up in a pompadour style. She spoke softly with the large man standing well over six feet tall with dark brown skin. His short, neatly trimmed white beard framed a jovial face. Truden could make out a colonel rank insignia on the shoulder of his garment. The woman wore no identifying marks, but the Aramos officer knew a spymaster when he saw one. They walked to the front of the caravan and the man flashed a wide toothy grin.

"It appears new players have arrived on our stage!" he announced in a booming friendly voice. "Welcome to Makatooa, Commander Truden. If we had known you were coming, we would have prepared a more fitting welcome."

Any doubt about dealing with a Calden Intelligencer evaporated in an alarmed moment when Truden realized they identified him. Recovering quickly, he returned a contrived smile at the silent woman.

"Well," Truden answered, "I'm afraid you've got me over a bit of a barrel. You obviously know me, but I got no idea who you are."

"Oh, your reputation precedes you, Commander," the man replied, not relinquishing his jovial demeanor. "Tales of a jungle fighter with abilities bordering on the supernatural are told over many a tankard of ale."

"Allow me to introduce myself," the large man continued. "I am Colonel Velitel, Commander of the City Guards in this tropical paradise."

"Colonel," Truden greeted with a nod then smiled at the description. Sniffing the manure laced air he sarcastically gazed about at the rustic, somewhat ramshackle architecture.

"So, commander, to what do we owe the pleasure of this unexpected visit?" Velitel asked, his gaze sweeping across Truden's wagon and men. "Perhaps you offer your considerable skills in helping us rid ourselves of the various bandit gangs which call the jungle home?"

"Nothing would make me happier, Colonel," Truden answered, chuckling, "but we're here to provide security for the new bank and its staff."

The smile vanished from Velitel's face. "I believe that falls under my people's job."

"Well, Colonel," the Aramos commander countered, "I have my orders and, it seems to me, I wouldn't need to be here if your people *were doing* their job."

A blanket of tension descended and the two commanders locked gazes while their men peered nervously about. The dull thud of a crossbow bolt embedding into wood broke the uneasy silence, followed by the clattering of swords drawn and men shouting. The four unarmed bankers dove to the floor of the wagon.

"STAND DOWN!" Truden screamed.

"CEASE FIRE!" Velitel yelled.

The leaders needed to repeat themselves several times before they restored order. Once the fighting stopped, they only heard their soldiers' ragged breaths while the two sides stared menacingly at each other. The two commander's eyes swept over their charges and settled back on each other.

The once congenial Velitel scowled angrily, marched to the rear of the wagon and examined the bolt protruding from the wagon's side, mere inches from the head of a cowering banker. He yanked out the projectile and stomped over to the

Calden guard holding an empty crossbow. The young man sheepishly bowed his head, profoundly intimidated by the glowering giant before him.

"I believe this is yours," he said sternly, handing him the spent bolt.

The guard meekly accepted it. Without warning, Velitel backhanded the unsuspecting soldier, sending him hurtling backwards onto the cobblestone streets with a resounding thump.

"Latrine duty until further notice," Velitel ordered in a low growl, before returning his attention to the Aramos commander.

Truden's demeanor turned conciliatory. "Look colonel, I don't want to be here anymore than you want us here. You say the word and I'll turn my men around and head right back to the docks. However, *you're* the one who has to explain to your mayor why the bank isn't open."

Velitel hesitated, weighing Truden's words.

"Very well," he conceded.

With a jerk of his head the city guards parted and he stepped aside, eyeing Truden suspiciously.

"I trust you'll keep your men in check?" he asked. "No going off script?"

Truden nodded. "And I would ask the same of you."

The colonel returned the nod and the Aramos caravan resumed its passage. Lieutenant Doosara heaved a sigh and looked up at his commander on the buckboard.

"That was a close one, Skipper."

"You ain't kidding," Truden concurred. "That was exactly what I didn't want to happen. Luckily, the colonel didn't want a fight any more than we did."

"You can bet they'll be keeping a close eye on us," Doosara said.

Truden chuckled knowingly. "You can bet Colonel Velitel will know how many times a day we take a shit."

The moon shone down bright and full, amplifying the weak rays of the sun in the West. Wikk Roncel peered down from his balcony onto the wide aquatic passage framed by the main docks of the free city of Tannimore.

To his left, on the second level of the floating city, the sound of construction clattered away. The burnt down theatre was now being rebuilt on an even grander scale, as the new banking complex and temple to Pa-Waga.

The former gangster turned dark priest smiled, watching a dozen rowdy revelers disembark a large, docked yacht. His plans to transform this city was proceeding nicely since they abolished the crime families. Word of mouth amongst the other societies already rebranded the remote local into a place of pilgrimage for all things forbidden. Now, all prospered under the guiding principles of the lord and it quickly filled the city's coffers.

The doors to the balcony opened with a slight creak and Ve-Qua stepped up beside him at the railing, just as an agonized cry rose from beneath them. The mistress of pain shuttered in ecstasy at the sound.

Da-Olman led several acolytes forcing a bound, naked man across the first level. They dragged him before an orange crystal log, a foot in diameter, laying on its side. The man screamed and struggled against his bonds to no avail.

"Another Santi follower," Wikk said, his voice ringing with contempt. "Looks like we've got a lively one this time. Normally they meekly accept their fate praying quietly whilst they die."

Wikk noticed Ve-Qua's breath grow heavy with excitement when they laid the man so the back of his head rested on the hard surface of the crystal pole. Da-Olman loomed over the terrified man's head and stared down at him crying and pleading.

"It's the pleading that gets my pussy wet," Ve-Qua remarked, unable to take her eyes off the grim spectacle.

"No? Please? Are you sure you want those to be your last words?" the Gila asked, placing the tip of a long thin diamond Etheria rod against his forehead.

The condemned Santi follower continued babbling and whimpering. Da-Olman looked up questioningly at Wikk and Ve-Qua.

"Slowly, for the benefit of the mistress," Wikk ordered.

Nodding, the powerful humanoid lizard exerted pressure downward. Wikk and Ve-Qua heard the crack of the rod piercing the front of his skull, followed by a prolonged series of screams while Da-Olman leisurely pushed the rod through the victim's head.

Ve-Qua had to steady herself on the balcony's rail when the screams led to a piercing orgasmic climax.

The shrieking abruptly ceased when the tip of the rod exited the back of the skull and contacted the Etheria log. Bolts of blue lightning erupted from the back of the dead man's head, cascading around and through the pole, charging it with his psychic essence.

Wikk gave a satisfied smirk.

Once the lightning dissipated into the crystal, Da-Olman removed the rod and nonchalantly tossed the corpse over the side. The ocean became a thrashing tempest where the body landed, with sharks rending and devouring the fresh sacrifice. The Gila Etheriat then ordered the acolytes to move the bloody pole into position, before addressing the pair staring down from the balcony.

"Lord Wikk, that's the last of the Trinilic and we're running low on Rhodosite and Lolite."

Wikk nodded. "Make sure you secure more. Meanwhile the mistress and I are going to take a brief trip."

He then pointed to the purple Azurite pillar prominently on display. "Is that Etheria charged and ready to go?"

"Yes, Lord Wikk."

"Excellent, you will be temporarily in charge here in my absence."

"Thank you for your confidence in me," Da-Olman said, obviously surprised.

"May the lord guide your hand," blessed the dark priest.

"Thanks for the little pick me up back there dearie, but *where* are we going?" Ve-Qua asked, regaining her composure.

"Makatooa," Wikk declared. "We've got to deal with that chaos your oracle saw. I also need to consecrate the bank as a temple before it's claimed by other parties. Then, we'll need to appoint a competent cleric to watch over the sanctuary. There's a good chance I'll need your powers."

"Sounds like we're going to be busy," Ve-Qua said.

"Yes, yes, with plenty of anguish for you to spread around," Wikk replied, staring at the purple pillar which would transport them through the Middle Realms.

"You sweet talker," she purred, putting a hand on his shoulder. "You always know the right thing to say."

"Just one thing."

Her sensuous demeanor turned suspicious. "Oh?"

Taking his eyes off the pillar he surveyed her pierced naked body.

"You're going to have to wear clothes."

Kisa loved to kill even more than sex. To be so close you can feel their last breath, and see the light go out in their eyes, thrilled him beyond compare. He knew that was the reason they chose him from the ranks of the Aramos Forsvara Guards to join the elite Black Talons. Not all missions involved death, but he savored the ones which did.

Now, as he and his three team members moved through the Makatooa Kan, he could feel the anticipation building. This was one of *those* coveted assignments; find the ones responsible for the bank robbery and kill them. Make it messy and public to send a message.

This would prove easy if the thieves remained in town. The fools did not try to conceal their identities and the leader wore a ridiculous looking top hat.

Kisa checked back on his companion, Vrases, who followed ten feet behind, watching the rear. He enjoyed working with the lanky youth. You could always depend on Vrases and he liked killing almost as much as Kisa did. Across the street, he could barely make out the other two members of the team moving surreptitiously through the fog in the same manner.

Thankfully, with the streets mostly empty, only the occasional passing wagon and loitering drunks interfered with their search. When they reached one of the major intersections off the docks, Kisa peered down the cross street and glimpsed the telltale shape of a top hat moving slowly away from them through the fog.

Kisa signaled Vrases and the two quickly slipped down a parallel alley, allowing Quattiel and Mordare a more direct pursuit, while they attempted to cut their quarry off in a pincer maneuver. Kisa felt his heart beating faster in anticipation. The Black Talon sprinted, fearing his quarry would escape, and drew his dagger.

Kisa and Vrases waited at the next intersection, confident they had gotten ahead of the ambling suspect. They peered around the corner and could see the figure wearing the top hat just off the road near the intersection. He appeared to be talking with three other men.

They flattened themselves against the nearest wall and silently advanced. They got within twenty feet of the suspect, when across the alley, Mordare accidentally kicked a bottle and drew the attention of the man in the hat.

"Woo Hoo, boys, we got company!" he cheerfully barked. "I love a party!"

Kisa cursed to himself over the blown element of surprise. They rushed the gang while they focused on Quattiel and Mordare, but their footsteps off the pavers betrayed them.

"More uninvited guests!" Serobini's voice rang out and the group scattered.

"Follow the hat!!" Mordare screamed.

Kisa felt a flash of anger. Mordare always fancied himself in command, but in this case, he was right. All four Black Talons took off after Serobini, who now ran down the alley, occasionally doing an exuberant hop.

Kisa grunted in irritation when the gangly Vrases sped past him following the equally thin Serobini around a corner. They had no sooner turned the bend when all four came to an abrupt halt.

The alley was a dead end. Locked doors, along with various crates and barrels, lined either side. Serobini stood calmly at the alley's end, leaning against a barrel. His wide lipless smile and casual demeanor raised the Black Talons' suspicions. They cautiously advanced with daggers drawn.

"Ya know the only thing worse than a bunch of dumb-ass soldiers?" Serobini riddled, holding his unnerving grin and licking his teeth.

The pursuers continued silently forward.

"Greasy ones!" he answered jovially.

With a jerk of his arm, he sent the barrel toppling over, spilling its contents of rancid cooking grease across the alley. He then quickly reached up and pushed on a single brick. The sound of grinding stone preceded a section of the wall sliding away. Giving a mocking laugh he disappeared through the opening.

Vrases took off in pursuit first and the enthusiastic youth slipped the moment his feet stepped in the viscous pool. He grunted, landing in the rancid smelling oil and organic debris.

"Idiot!" Mordare admonished, cautiously stepping around him.

The four now stood peering at stone stairs descending into the darkness, listening to Serobini's contemptuous laughter echoing up from the depths.

"He's getting away!" Quattiel cried out.

"What can we do?" Vrases asked. "We can't see anything down there."

Kisa glanced around the alley and started rummaging through a pile of rubbish. He wrapped a torn apron around the end of a broken broom handle and swabbed the makeshift torch through the pool of oil.

"Flint," he requested.

Mordare produced flint and steel from a tunic pocket and soon the grease-soaked rag was blazing.

"Be careful, our boots are still oily," Mordare warned, slowly descending.

The staircase ended in an immense room with ornately carved walls. Holding the torch aloft, Kisa could see several wide passageways across the room.

"What is this place?" Quattiel asked, in awe.

"I don't know," Kisa answered, peering at the tunnels, "but the laughter is coming from that direction."

"Quiet," Mordare snapped. "Let's go."

They plodded through the waist high Kan fog. Kisa shivered in the dampness, all the while marveling at the walls apparently carved from a single colossal piece of wood.

They seemed to be gaining on the laughter. It sounded just ahead when it abruptly stopped. The group paused and shared questioning glances. Mordare put a single finger to his lips and motioned them onward.

Up ahead, they found a smaller opening with a partially open thick wooden door. The hinges creaked when Mordare pushed it the rest of the way open.

He hefted his torch and dagger before him, leading the rest through. The flickering light lit up a room extending about a hundred feet square with high ceilings and no other apparent doors or passages.

"A dead end," Quattiel said, clearly disappointed. "We lost him."

"Let's double back," Mordare quickly offered. "We can still…"

The sound of the door slamming closed and the bar on the other side locking into place cut off the proposal.

"The door!" Kisa yelled, rushing over and running his torch close to the slatted wood blocking their exit.

Quattiel ran up beside the torch bearer and rammed his shoulder against the heavy wooden surface with no effect. The stout commando then lashed out with a powerful kick which echoed off the walls, but otherwise did little good.

"We're trapped!" Vrases cried out in a panic, looking wildly around. "What are we going to do?!"

"We better think of something," Kisa said, looking at the torches burning tip. "This isn't going to last much longer and then we'll be in the dark."

"Burn the door," Mordare ordered authoritatively.

Kisa spun with a look of disbelief. "Are you fucking kidding me?! This whole place is made of wood!"

Mordare snatched the torch from his hand. "You got a better damn idea?!"

Mordare knelt in the fog and placed the flame directly on the bottom of the barrier. The mist muted the light, limiting visibility in the room.

"It won't burn!" Mordare reported after a few moments.

"Ukko," Kisa noted in a defeated tone.

"There's gotta be some way out of here," Mordare said, standing up and handing the torch back to Kisa.

When the flame rose above the fog, it illuminated the room once again. The Black Talon cried out in surprise. A smiling female ghoul stood beside him, her emaciated, hairless body a pallid shade of white. Her eyes sunk into her sockets and two shriveled, pendulous breasts drooped over her chest with her long nipples stirring the fog.

More figures rose from the mist all around them, both male and female. All with the same emaciated appearance.

The female stared hungrily at Mordare and licked her lips. He panicked and plunged his dagger deep into her chest. The weapon didn't seem to affect her and jutted from between her breasts. Mordare pulled violently on the handle, desperately trying to dislodge the blade from her ribs, when she leaned over and bit his neck. He screamed while the female ghoul thrashed her head from side to side until she came away with a large bloody chunk between her teeth. Geysers of blood erupted from the wound instantly and drenched her pale body in a morosely contrasting shade of crimson.

The three other Black Talons cried out in panic, wildly flailing their knives. Something suddenly and violently yanked Quattiel below the surface of the mist. They heard the thud of his body hitting the floor followed by his screams over rending and tearing flesh.

Kisa spun with the torch and caught sight of two ghouls grabbing Vrases' gangly body. He had no time to cry out when an ice-cold hand wrapped around his forearm holding the torch. He watched in shocked disbelief, when, with an inhumanly powerful tug, it rended his entire arm from his body and casually tossed it away.

The light in the room dimmed to the glow of the torch resting ten feet away beneath the fog. Kisa slowly lost consciousness. His last sensations were of cold hands against his head holding him erect, while multiple mouths ripped away chunks of flesh from his legs. He lost consciousness when his abdomen opened and steaming bowels poured into eager mouths.

The aroma of roasting meat attracted Ve-Qua to the smoky food cart on the side of the road. She mentioned to Wikk how the act of being shot across the middle Realms from Tannimore to Makatooa made her ravenous.

Wikk agreed, because the food vendor was located just across the street from the entrance to the Imperial Bank and he felt a bit peckish himself. Two coppers later, each picked away at a paper sleeve full of steaming fare.

"So, explain something to me," Ve-Qua said, popping a finger full of meat into her mouth. "You know I don't give two flying shits about your religion. Why is Stryder, and now you, interested in me?"

Wikk glanced away from the two Forsvara Guards standing outside the bank's wide double doors. "My lord favors you even though you deny him, because it's not just about money."

"You could have fooled me," Ve-Qua countered, searching her sleeve for another morsel, "with all your talk of prosperity."

"Physical wealth is just one of the easiest ways to measure prosperity. In your case you covet certain things in life and then go about manifesting them. This is good in the eyes of the lord."

Ve-Qua giggled. "Even though most days I just lie around playing with my pussy whilst listening to people being tortured?"

Wikk finished his meal and discarded the paper.

"Doesn't your stable of the punished grow by the day?" he asked. "The carpenters can barely keep up building your various implements of pain. In your case, this is *prosperity*. Whereas the followers and Priests of Santi are truly repugnant in the eyes of my lord, with their incessant talk of peace and poverty."

Wikk watched the guards stop and question a wealthy merchant before allowing him to enter.

"I must sanctify this as a temple," Wikk said, "but I fear the guards won't allow me access."

Ve-Qua finished eating and licked her fingers. "Don't you worry about those guards, dearie. I'll take care of them. After that, you're on your own."

Wikk gave her a skeptical look, but she returned a reassuring nod.

Ve-Qua stepped into the street and walked up behind the busy food cart cook. She waited until he was turning a hunk of meat and, with a slight bump of her shoulder, she sent his fist plunging into the grease fueled fire. The vendor cried out in pain, quickly recoiling his hand.

"Ya stupid fucking quim!" he screamed, nursing his burnt fingers. "Watch what the fuck you're doing!"

The Kinjuto mistress tuned out the man's tirade and watched Wikk cross the street. Her eyes rolled back in her head, harnessing the pain of the cook into psychic energy and directing it at the bank.

It pleasantly surprised Wikk when the guards remained at attention when he ascended the wide stairs and stepped onto the portico. They continued to ignore him as he raised his hands in prayer.

"Lord Pa-Waga, hear my plea," he said, in a booming voice which stopped people passing in the street. "Bless this institution and its holy mission."

More people gathered and stared curiously.

"I consecrate this as holy ground," Wikk continued, tracing an "X" and an "I" in the air, "and dedicate this as a temple to your service."

A gasp rippled through the small crowd when the double doors slowly opened by themselves and Wikk strode inside.

Kassade de Orta sat back at his workstation reveling in his accomplishments and supervising his three assistants busy at their desks.

From numbers' runner in the slums of Zor, to bank president by twenty-six, not bad, he silently mused.

The sound of a commotion just outside the front doors, followed by someone shouting, broke his daydream trance. Kassade stood in surprise when the doors opened of their own volition and a young man, wearing a bulky, long black robe, cinched closed by a red sash around his waist, walked into the lobby like he owned the place. He raised his hands and face to the ceiling when the doors closed behind him.

"Oh, great Pa-Waga," Wikk prayed, "we thank you for accepting this temple. Bless it and those who serve. May the spirit of prosperity rain down upon all who enter and a curse upon those who have stolen from it."

Kassade lowered his head and sighed upon hearing the name Pa-Waga. He knew of this strange, fanatical religion from Nocturn. It already attracted a small group of rich and ruthless followers in the financial community. He'd considered it a fad which hopefully would quickly pass.

The two guards on the inside of the door turned to him for guidance on how to deal with the boisterous young zealot.

Kassade held up his hand for them to hold and approached him, extending a hand.

"Hello," he greeted with a placating smile. "I'm Kassade the bank president. What can the Imperial Bank do for you?"

Wikk ignored the outstretched hand and looked around at the architecture. "It is what *I* can do for you. I have brought this fine temple the blessing of the Lord."

Kassade's wide nose turned up disdainfully and his thick lips contorted into a sneer. "I'm afraid I don't know what you're referring to. This is a bank, a *financial* institution, not a place of worship."

"All banks are hallowed ground, whether or not they acknowledge the Lord." The dark cleric's gaze settled on Kassade. "I just consecrated this as a temple to Pa-Waga."

"Really?"

"You doubt," Wikk offered, "I understand. Perhaps a demonstration as to the prosperity which can be yours."

Kassade was on the verge of having the nut job tossed out onto the street when curiosity befell him. "Show me."

"First, I will need some seed money," Wikk declared.

"Here now!" Kassade protested.

"Nothing in nature grows without a seed," Wikk said, on the verge of indignation. "Trees and flowers cannot grow without first planting a seed. Such as it is with the lord. The size of the seed determines the size of the harvest. Rest assured the lord rewards all offerings tenfold."

One of Kassade's assistants, a young woman with long hair pulled back into a bun, had sat listening to the conversation, enraptured by Wikk. Suddenly, she stood up, took a single one-hundred-secor commodity note from a stack on her desk, and handed the Ukko wafer to Wikk with her head bowed.

Kassade's mouth fell open in shock. "Zdacca, what is the meaning of this?!"

The young clerk kept her head down while Wikk accepted the offering.

"A woman of vision," Wikk said, gently placing a hand on the top of her head.

He then spun with a flourish back to Kassade. "Behold!"

Wikk produced a three-inch-long orange crystal needle from his sleeve. Everyone in the room watched in beguiled fascination, unable to turn away. The dark cleric then lanced his fingertip and wrote a line of binary of "X's" and "I's" on the Ukko surface in his own blood. He then scraped the Trinilic needle across the markings and the note burst into flames.

A profound hush descended on the room until the crackling of the fire became the only noise. When almost consumed, Wikk let the charred wood drop to the floor. The moment it hit the ground, thin fingers of blue lightning erupted and began coursing across the door of the bank's vault. With a loud click, the thick steel door swung open.

All in the room gasped in disbelief at a thousand gleaming Imperial Gold Ingots neatly stacked atop a desk just inside the vault.

Wikk pointed to the currency. "Tenfold."

The room erupted in excited chatter immediately quelled by Kassade's outraged voice. "I don't know what kind of parlor trick you just pulled, but I'll have none of it! This is a respectable institution. I won't have it besmirched with smoke and mirrors. And... you're bleeding on my floor."

Wikk looked down at the small pool of blood and smiled. He then pointed the oozing digit at Kassade.

"You are not worthy to lead this temple!" He gestured to Zdacca. "If she will receive the Lord's mark, I shall make her priestess of this holy place!"

Kassade had heard enough.

"You are fired!" he sneeringly proclaimed to Zdacca. "Guards, remove them!"

The soldiers began approaching. Wikk stared calmly at them while he reached out and drew a bloody "X" on the open door of the vault.

"You do not deserve the lord's bounty."

The words barely escaped Wikk's mouth when a crackle of energy reverberated through the lobby. Bolts of blue lightning danced and filled the vault's interior. When they finally subsided, the gold secors on the desktop were gone.

"The lord gives freely and takes on a whim," Wikk condescendingly spat at Kassade before they gruffly escorted him out the front door.

Out on the porch, the two guards flanking the entrance remained frozen at attention, staring blankly forward.

Wikk faced Zdacca and smiled sympathetically. "Are you prepared to receive his mark?"

She silently nodded and the dark cleric guided her down to her knees. He stepped behind her and produced the once more Trinilic needle.

"In the name of the most high god..."

He traced an "X" on the back of the right side of her neck. The sharp tip sizzled as it cauterized, giving off the smell of burning flesh. Zdacca remained motionless, neither wincing from the pain, nor crying out.

"And the blood of the Proffitt," he continued, etching an "I" on the other side. "I pronounce you a true devotee of Pa-Waga and priestess of this temple. Arise."

Wikk reached into his robes, pulled out a one-thousand-secor commodity note and handed it to her when she rose to her feet.

"The lord has taken from the unworthy and bestowed it on the worthy."

"Thank you," she said meekly, staring at the enormous sum of money in her fist.

"Thank Pa-Waga, from whom all blessings flow," Wikk replied. "Continue down this path and prosperity will surely follow you. I must go. You are now his priestess here. I charge you with reclaiming this temple. Drive the blasphemers out. Follow the laws of prosperity and resist the chaos within and without."

She nodded in understanding. Wikk made his way down the stairs and navigated across the busy street where he met Ve-Qua standing on the corner.

"All finished?" she inquired.

"Not quite," Wikk replied, "but we're well on our way. Let's go home. By the way, you did an excellent job on those guards back there."

The Kinjuto mistress looked back before she walked away. The sentries still had not moved.

"Yeah, I might have gone a little too far. I think I scrambled their brains."

Her name was Kopit and Alto loved watching her work. She was easily twice his age, short, squat with wide flaring hips and enormous breasts. Her plump face occasionally could be soft and matronly, however most of the time it bore an impatient scowl. Quick to berate an indecisive customer, Mz. Kopit did not suffer the fool. The only reason she kept such a brisk business, with steady repeat patrons, was because she ran the best produce stand in Makatooa's central open-air market.

Alto shifted the wrapped mutton chop under his arm and examined the selection of squash, while watching the mercurial vendor's gaze latch onto a middle-aged well-dressed man caressing a melon.

"Are you going to buy it or fuck it?!" Kopit snapped, waddling over to the stunned customer. "I tell you what, buy it first, then take it home and fuck it. Two coppers, cheaper than a whore."

The wide-eyed man quickly pulled two coins from a pouch on his belt, clutched the melon and scurried away into the thinning crowds.

When she began verbally accosting the next person, Alto grinned at her theatrics and chose a small onion and a squash.

"Ah, Mora," she said, in a much-softened tone, stepping over to him and taking the squash out of his hands. "This one's no good for you." She promptly replaced it with another. "This one is better."

Alto accepted the substitute with a broad smile. "Thank you, Mz. Kopit for always looking out for me."

"You remind me of my eldest son," she said, patting his cheek. "By the way, Widow Tomlin came by earlier today."

Alto nodded, happy that the widow who owned the boarding house where he lived since his arrival several grands ago was still getting around.

"She's going to cook that for you tonight," Mz. Kopit added. "Why you no let her shop for you?"

"And miss seeing you?"

"Ah, Mora Alto, you sweet, just like my eldest."

Alto was about to take his leave when alarm whistles sounded from down the street. Their shrill drew steadily closer, causing all in the market to stare. Alto watched suspiciously when he glimpsed a black top hat rushing through the crowd directly for them.

The swordmaster's hand automatically rested on Defari's hilt when he spied the pale, lanky Serobini barreling through the crowd hooting and laughing. Alto felt torn. He recognized the potential threat Serobini posed and the chaos he brought with him, but he *was* unarmed.

The fleeing fugitive spied the pickle barrel while passing the produce stand and came to an abrupt halt. Smiling at Kopit and Alto, he popped open the lid and pulled out a large dill pickle. Shuttering in ecstasy, the briny cylinder gave a resounding crunch when he took a big bite.

"Hey, no sampling the merchandise," Kopit admonished fearlessly. "That'll be one copper!"

Serobini ignored the outraged merchant and calmly chewed his treat.

"We meet again," Alto said, stepping forward. "And, as before, you seem to have a propensity for harassing women."

"Actually, when the mood strikes," he said, waving the partially eaten pickle in front of him, "I harass just about everyone. I can't help myself. I also just can't resist a good pickle; and, madam, may I say, this is *superb*."

"I believe you owe the lady a copper piece," "Alto said, slowly advancing.

"Sorry, I'm a little short right now but…"

Two city guards entered the market, interrupting Serobini's excuse. They spotted him immediately and sounded the alarm again before charging towards him.

"I gotta go," he said, taking another quick bite. "Put this on my tab."

"No tabs!" Kopit shrieked. "Cash only!"

With a slight bow Serobini reached down and flipped over the table full of produce. A cascade of fruits and vegetables spilled out onto the street.

Kopit placed her hands on either side of her head and screamed in shock. Serobini took full advantage of the distraction and obstruction. He bolted towards a nearby alley with the city guards in tow.

Alto leaped over the table in front of him and fell in behind the pursuing guards. At the far end of the long and gently downward-sloping alley stood a wide, door-less opening with a thick, ornately carved frame. The guards slowed to a stop just before the entrance and Alto came up quickly behind them.

"Why are you stopping?" he asked, indicating the partially eaten pickle on the ground. "He obviously went this way. This delay will allow him to escape."

The two guards shared an apprehensive glance.

"Uhh, that leads down to the Old City," one said, clearly unnerved. "We've lost a bunch of guys down there over the grands. Besides it's a maze down there, he's probably long gone by now."

"And the Kan's about to start," the other added. "You don't want to be *down there* when the fog rolls in."

"Our quarry has left us a trail." Alto said, unsheathing Defari.

He aimed the sword downward, pierced the tip into the pickle, picked it up, and examined it on the end of his blade. The canine inside the Etheria weapon took in its scent. Satisfied Defari cataloged the odor, he flicked the blade, discarding the pickle back onto the alley floor. Alto sheathed the sword but kept his hand firmly on the hilt as he sniffed the air.

"This way gentlemen."

The wide wooden staircase led down to a large, tall-ceilinged plaza. Intricately carved Ukko wood lined the walls, with no apparent seams between the massive panels. An omnipresent orange glow dimly illuminated everything, revealing the plaza branched out into three wide boulevards.

Alto channeled Defari and sniffed again, catching the distinct odor of dill trailing down the thoroughfare to the right.

"Let's go," he said, indicating the direction.

"Look!" a guard called out, nearly panicked.

He pointed up the staircase where the Kan mists flowed downwards around them.

"It's not worth being caught down here during the Kan for some stolen fruit."

"You were obviously chasing him for some previous infraction." Alto replied, starting down the passage. "I'm sure your superiors will be interested in your diligence."

"If we live," one guard complained, before reluctantly following the swordmaster.

After traveling several hundred yards, the fog grew waist high. They entered another large courtyard forming an intersection into four more hallways.

"Didn't I tell ya it was a maze down here?" the other guard lamented. "We'll get lost and never find our way out!"

Alto ignored their complaining and pressed onward. The guards searched each other's faces and reluctantly followed. With every step the guards grew more jittery. Strange sounds and whispers seemed to echo from around every corner.

The trio paused at the next intersection.

"Look, over there," one said, pointing. "Something just moved in the fog!"

"I would advise quiet," Alto whispered, before deciding on the hallway to their right.

"What was that?!" the other cried out, spinning toward a scraping sound on the floor.

Both gasped when a dozen hairless, gaunt figures with bone white skin rose from the mist surrounding them.

The three drew their weapons and formed a small circle facing outward. Defari uttered a low growl in Alto's hands. The creatures slowly advanced and the swordmaster's eyes shifted back and forth strategically. The two guards trembled nervously and held their swords out before them.

When the ghouls drew within ten feet, they halted and began circling. With each rotation, one would step forward and sniff in their direction before continuing around. On the third revolution, one of the older appearing ghouls stepped in front of Alto and sniffed furiously. It took another short step and Defari mysteriously quit growling.

Slowly bringing his face close to Alto's, its long tongue snaked out of its mouth and flicked Alto's cheek. The swordmaster shuttered when the ice-cold, wet appendage brushed against him.

"I do not know your name," it said in a resonating baritone echoing off the walls, "but you are a friend of Soshanna."

With the utterance of her name Alto relaxed and slightly lowered his sword.

"I am," he confirmed. "Soshi and I were friends and traveling companions."

"Then, as promised, you are a friend to the Zoande Clan. We offer you safe travels through our realm."

Alto sheathed Defari and gave a curt bow.

"Alto de Gom, at your service. Thank you for passage. We seek a man in a tall hat."

The ghoul nodded his head. "Serobini is who you seek. He is an unwelcome traveler through our city. He no longer dwells here."

"Put your weapons away," Alto ordered the still terrified guards.

He returned his gaze to the ghoul leader. "Is there nothing you can do about this trespasser?"

"No, he travels with a powerful spirit of chaos and actually draws chaos to him. We dare not approach lest it pull us in and destroy us. Because of that, he can use the streets of the Old City to move about unseen and strike at the inhabitants living above at will."

The swordmaster silently processed this revelation.

"You, and your travelling companions, may go in peace," the ghoul declared. "If you truly wish to be of service to the Zoande, rid us of this spirit of turmoil plaguing our city as well as yours above."

Kassade de Orta still reeled from the calamitous events of the previous cycle. He lost three people. Something rendered the two Forsvara guards stationed at the door mysteriously catatonic. Unfortunately, the mental affliction seemed permanent. The biggest loss came from the very valuable assistant he had to fire, who was now apparently some sort of religious fanatic. Commander Truden's understandable unhappiness about losing two men made things even worse for the new bank president.

In a change of strategy, he divided his remaining eighteen Forsvara Guards into two shifts. He would take personal command of the day watch, while his second led the Kan shift. He just needed to replace an accountant arriving within the next few cycles from the Imperial Bank of Zor.

Hopefully then life could get back to normal, he wishfully thought, sliding three beads across the abacus.

The commotion at the Bank's main entrance immediately squashed *that* wish. High pitch chattering, accompanied by gruff male voices, drifted through the ornate wooden doors.

Kassade's shoulders slumped with a defeated sigh. He clearly heard the argument on the porch when the doors cracked and a patrol sergeant's face peered through.

"Uh, sir?" the guard started, hesitantly. "We've got two sentients out here demanding entrance. They claim to have business with the bank."

"Are they armed?"

"No, sir."

"Did they say what sort of business?"

"No sir, but one has a commodities bank note."

Kassade closed his eyes and rubbed his temples, he could feel a tension headache coming on. When he opened them, the guard still stared at him with a questioning look.

"Oh, very well, show them in. Let's get this over with!"

The banker instantly regretted his order when the door fully opened and two Cul-Ta strode into the lobby. Both humanoid rats stood about four feet tall and wore filthy brown tunics. Their mangy, matted black fur reeked like they had just crawled out of a sewer. One Cul-Ta, slightly taller than the other, kept his eyes straight ahead and walked with a purposeful stride. Kassade could see the wafer-thin oblong commodity note in his hand. The smaller one trailed behind, staring about in wonder.

Kassade rose from behind his desk and stared disdainfully at their approach.

"Can I help you with something?" he asked, nostrils flaring from the stench.

The rat-men stopped in front of his desk, their heads peaking just above the surface.

"I am Chu-Chu," the larger one said, placing the note on the desk. "Wooden money no good, trade for gold coins."

"I see," Kassade said, picking up the note.

The thin rectangular token *seemed* like a genuine one-hundred-secor note worth a thousand struck gold coins. Made of Ukko wood, it measured the standard two-inches-wide by four-inches-long. Burnt onto the front was the number one hundred and the rear contained the standard of the Imperial Bank of Zor, along with their motto written in Yassett, *"Full Faith and Credit."*

"Where did you get this?" Kassade asked, eyeing the money suspiciously.

"Not your business!" Chu-Chu said, with a defiant squeak. "Trade for gold coins."

This left Kassade genuinely torn. Cul-Ta possessing this kind of money proved highly irregular. However, according to the Zorian Monetary Compact of 3850 P.A., he was duty bound to honor the note.

"You realize that's a lot of money?" he asked, in a last attempt to dissuade the humanoid rodent.

"Trade for gold coins!" Chu-Chu said, remaining firm.

The bank president gave a resigned sigh. *Full faith and credit,* he silently assured himself. He called over one of his remaining two clerks, a freckle-faced junior accountant, with a wave of his hand.

"Peega, see that one thousand gold coins are bagged and given to these two sentients."

"Yes sir," he said, heading for the vault.

"Good," Chu-Chu said triumphantly. "Back tomorrow for more."

Back tomorrow for more! Kassade thought in astonishment.

While the Cul-Ta took possession of the gold, Kassade turned the note over in his hand, staring at it. He couldn't shake the question of how some of the lowest denizens of the city got ahold of such sophisticated monetary counters. He watched them comically drag bags of coins, nearly as large as them, across the lobby and out the door.

They had only been gone for a few moments when Kassade abruptly stood and walked over to Peega's desk.

"Something's not right," he said, holding the note up between two fingers and shaking it. "I'm going to report this to the authorities. I'll be back."

At age forty-two, Sergeant Taw de Sury was also one of the oldest and most senior of all noncommissioned officers in the entire Aramos Forsvara Guard, which made him a ruthless and experienced jungle fighter. His haggard, hardened features and gruff demeanor only perpetuated his deadly reputation, despite his average height and build. His pernicious experience afforded him an almost sixth sense with spotting potentially dangerous situations. Right now, all his alarms were going off.

He, and five of his men, were one round of drinks in and ready for their second at the Stormwatch Pub on Makatooa's Wharf. The service had been slow since they arrived. The soldiers had just ended their shift of babysitting the bank and the tedium had made them thirsty.

Taw watched the newest member of the team, a baby-faced young man named Ozel, navigate through the crowd back to their table, carrying four full tankards.

"Hey that didn't take too long," remarked a corporal seated to Taw's left.

"Better than that damn serving wench," a private, seated across the table, said in disgust.

"What ya expect," Taw snarled. "We're in a Calden bar wearing Aramos uniforms."

A grumble of agreement rounded the table. Taw went silent when he heard a group of Calden dock workers make kissing sounds when Ozel passed. Taw couldn't help but think they wouldn't be doing that if they'd seen him ten-cycles ago, his face bloodied from killing three insurgents.

"Hey, he's got whore lips," one dockworker called out as Ozel set the tankards on the table. "Send him over here when you're done with him."

"Yeah," another spoke up. "He can even keep that cute beanie on while we're doing him."

They roared with laughter and a scowl descended over Ozel's smooth pleasant features.

"Let it pass kid," Taw advised, sliding one drink in front of him.

"They can say and think what they want about me," Ozel said with a sneer, "but I earned this beret the hard way."

"Maybe so," Taw said, scanning the crowd. "But I don't like our odds."

The young private reached for a few of the empty containers. "Let me get these back up to the bar."

"Sit down and drink," the corporal said. "That's the serving wench's job."

"By the time that bitch gets around to us the table will be full of empties." Ozel said, before heading back to the bar.

Taw knew this was a potentially volatile situation. He kept his eye on the studious young man and tensed when the same laborer taunted him again. Taw gave a proud sigh of relief when Ozel passed them by, ignoring the lewd instigation, but this proved short lived. The aggressive dock worker, thinking he could take advantage of Ozel's hands being full, reached out and patted the comely private on the ass as he passed.

Without winding up or taking another step, Ozel spun and smashed an empty tankard against the side of the man's head, dropping him where he stood. When one of his companions lunged forward, swearing, Ozel doubled him over with a front kick to the groin.

"Aw shit!" Taw lamented, springing to his feet.

By the time the Aramos soldiers made it to the bar, they found Ozel actively trading punches with the other two laborers. Several other patrons joined the altercation when a deafening bellow resonated above the clamor of the brawl.

Taw looked up in time to see the meaty hands of an outer clan EEtah grab both Ozel and his opponent. The eight-foot-tall man-shark separated the two combatants with ease. He lifted them and smashed them together, before dropping their stunned bodies to the floor.

"Knock it off!" he roared.

All activity in the pub stopped and a woman with long thick white hair calmly approached the EEtah. She wore a floor length green gown cinched tight at the waist, pushing her golden breasts up until they looked like they might explode from the top of her low-cut dress at any moment. Taw guessed her to be in her fifties with a beautiful face pursed into a serious expression.

Nice, he thought. *She must have been a real looker when she was younger.*

She smiled serenely at the combatants and cleared her throat. "I'm afraid I'm going to have to ask you rowdy boys to leave."

"Even us?" the patron who instigated the incident asked, nursing the side of his head.

"Even you, Stig."

"Come on Malika," Stig protested. "You'd think you'd kick out the Aramos swine in here stinking the place up."

"Aramos money spends just as well as yours," she countered casually.

"We shouldn't have to leave," Taw said indignantly. "They started it!"

"I don't care who started it," Malika said, turning her attention to the outraged sergeant. "Do you know why my place is so popular? I don't water down my booze, my whores are clean—some of them are even good looking— and I don't put up with *this kind of activity*. So, you can go somewhere else and cool off. Come back when you can behave yourselves, *but not tonight!* Or you can continue this little skirmish outside. I can assure you though, Velitel's city guards won't be treating you as gently as my bouncer just did. The choice is yours, gentlemen, but either way you can't stay here."

Taw waited for the other party to reluctantly leave before directing his men out into the damp Kan fog.

"You handled yourself pretty good back there, kid," Taw said, slapping Ozel on the back. He blushed slightly as the others enthusiastically agreed.

"I thought you'd be mad at me for, you know, going against your orders."

"You obeyed. Right up to the time he touched you. Can't fault you for that. I'd have probably done the same thing."

"Yeah sarge," the corporal jeered. "But you ain't pretty like Ozel there. Nobody's going to pat your butt."

Everyone laughed and Taw could feel the collective tension receding.

"You boys look like you could use a drink," a feminine voice called out of the fog.

They could make out through the mist an attractive young woman standing beside a nondescript door down the street to their left. The Aramos soldiers traded curious looks.

"Come on," she said, provocatively. "I know what it's like to get kicked out of the Stormwatch. It's a lot friendlier over here and I need a warm lap to sit in."

Taw eyed the young woman suspiciously. The woman met the veteran sergeant's gaze with a vulnerable expression.

"It's been really slow," she beseeched. "We could use the money. Come on, the first round's on me."

She opened the door and light streamed out through the fog and revealed she wore only a sheer white dress with nothing underneath.

"I'm still thirsty," the corporal said.

"Me too," another agreed.

"I didn't even get a chance to have a drink," Ozel rationalized.

The woman stepped inside and the men turned to Taw.

"Why not?" he proclaimed. "We'll just spend our money here instead."

The room stood only about thirty feet square. Two small tables were set up before a ten-foot-long serving bar with a backdoor behind it. The only other patron was a lone man standing at the end of the bar nursing a drink. He didn't even look up when they entered.

A female barkeep and another waitress sitting directly across from her—both wearing similar skimpy white dresses—turned and greeted the soldiers with seductive smiles.

"Well, hello," beamed the barkeep. "Come on in and make yourselves comfortable."

"Have a seat, boys," the waitress from the street said. "What are you drinking?"

"Ale," they replied, sitting down.

"Set them up, Tudy. The first round's on me," she said, dropping into Ozel's lap. "My, my, aren't *you* the cute one?"

"Now, this is what I call service," the corporal announced when the waitress promptly brought the tankards.

"A toast," the woman in Ozel's lap said, raising her mug in the air. "To prompt…"

She paused briefly and brushed Ozel's cheek.

"…and *very* friendly service."

The table erupted in cheers and laughter before all took several large gulps. When they set down the mugs, frothy foam coated most of their mouths.

"To warm companionship on a damp Kan!" Ozel toasted, raising his glass while simultaneously reaching around and cupping the waitress' breast.

All hooted in agreement and drank to the toast.

"I can't place this ale," Taw said, smacking his lips.

"It's from a small local brewery," the barkeep explained. "Careful, it's potent."

"Ah, don't you worry about us," the corporal scoffed. "If there's one thing the Forsvara Guard can do, it's hold down our drink. Now, I've got a vacant lap right here."

Taw watched the woman start for the corporal's chair when the first wave of light-headedness swept over him. He blinked several times and shook his head to clear it, but to no avail. Through a fog, he heard the clatter of tankards dropping as his men slowly slumped over. He saw the woman get out of Ozel's lap as he teetered before falling forward onto the table. The last thing the Aramos sergeant saw before passing out, was a tall gaunt man in a top hat being let into the room by the barkeep through the rear door.

The Kan fog was so thick, the three humans in the cart could barely see the narrow trail ahead of them. Their lone horse snorted in protest when Royd Sorbornef flicked the reins and made a clicking sound out of the side of his mouth. The large, bearded man knew he had to be cautious and not drive the skittish horse too hard in these present conditions.

"Even the horse doesn't want to be out in this," Lagun said, nervously looking around from the back of the small cart. To their right, fields of grain towered, completely obscuring their vision. Just to their left, a winding tributary of the mighty Otoman River gurgled placidly. A mile away in the distance, they could hear the roar of rushing water as the Western fork raced outward from the wide body of water which flowed down from Mount Otoman.

Royd shared an annoyed glance with the grim-faced young man seated next to him on the buckboard. Soku almost never smiled or talked, except to bark orders to the field slaves of the Sorbornef's Staghorn plantation.

"Well, we can't do it in broad daylight," Royd said, betraying his irritation at his friend's constant complaining.

The eldest Sorbornef son guessed he really couldn't blame the gentle, good-natured, Lagun, who served as Staghorn's head animal tender. He obviously enjoyed spending his time with the estate's various livestock instead of humans. Lagun also apprenticed under Albaitari, the local traveling Samar mage. Even though the young man's powers over the animals paled compared to his teacher, they would come in handy this Kan.

Just as all the other times, Royd felt a touch of trepidation when he slowed the wagon by a bend in the river that flowed around a large tree. Poaching the protected Caskel fish was very dangerous, but because of its popularity, just a few of the coveted fish were worth quite a bit of gold. Tonight's yield could quickly net them a small fortune tomorrow on the streets of Locian.

By treaty, only Dreeat could harvest the delicious, medium-sized Caskel fish. Royd, along with most humans in lower Otomoria, hated the humanoid crocodiles inhabiting the end of the Otoman River's Western fork. The smart, aggressive Dreeat took a dim view of anyone stealing their main source of food, hence the real peril. Royd however was eager for a quick infusion of gold, and to prove his ability to broker lucrative deals. This Kan, greed motivated him more powerfully than fear.

"All right," Royd said, bringing the wagon to a stop just before the tree's canopy. "Let's get this done."

Shoku silently leapt to the ground, holding two lines of Darian Silk with multi-barbed hooks.

"I'm not so sure about this," Lagun said, climbing out of the wagon's bed. "Once I start, it's going to be like sounding an alarm to any creature in the water. We'll have to work fast."

"Quit worrying," Royd said, accepting one line from Shoku. "With that little trick of yours we'll load up and be gone before any of the fucking crocs know we're here."

Lagun reluctantly nodded his acceptance and knelt on the riverbank under the tree while Royd and Shoku positioned themselves by the cart with their lines ready.

Placing both hands into the gently flowing water, Lagun closed his eyes in concentration and began wiggling his fingers. Royd and Shoku saw blue sparkles emanating from Lagun's fingertips under the surface. After a few moments of the magical summoning, the water before them came alive with hundreds of spawning fish answering the call.

Royd cast his line with a satisfied smile, followed by Shoku. The hooks immediately grabbed hold and they yanked their catches from the teeming waters into the back of the cart.

With robotic-like precision, the two friends repeated the action again and again, each attempt never failing to retrieve an aquatic bounty. When the cart reached half full, Royd noticed Shoku tiring a bit and slowing down.

"Just a little while longer," Royd encouraged.

The ever-quiet Shoku merely nodded and threw out his line, but this time, when he tried to pull it back, it wouldn't budge. He tugged harder, but it didn't give.

"Ah, Royd?" Shoku asked, growing frustrated.

"What?" Royd asked, annoyed at the delay.

"I'm caught on something."

Shoku wrapped the line around his arm, gave it another hard yank and it suddenly gave way. He lost his balance, falling backwards on the ground, and the water exploded in spray. Two seven-foot-tall male Dreeats erupted from the river, roaring furiously.

Shoku's hook had lodged in one of the humanoid crocodile's shoulders. The Dreeat lashed out, grabbed the line and violently heaved the frightened Shoku towards him. Once close enough, its powerful jaws clamped down severing the forearm at the elbow and it swallowed it in one destructive bite.

Shoku screamed in shock and agony. He looked on in horror as jets of blood pumped from his severed limb just before he slumped back to the ground.

The other Dreeat bounded onto the bank in front of Royd. It bellowed again and swung its powerful tail, knocking the Sorbornef youth to the riverbank before smashing into the back of the cart. The impact crushed the rear axle and ripped open the back of the wagon.

"Thieves!" it hissed.

Royd rose to his feet, holding his side. Dead fish poured out the back of the damaged wagon and onto the ground. He caught a glimpse of Lagun bolting into the grain fields, disappearing into the Kan fog.

The other male stepped over Shoku—lying unconscious and bleeding out. Coming up rapidly on the panicked horse winning and rearing, the Dreeat bit out a large section of the beast's elongated throat. It gave out a final bray of pain and dropped with a resounding thump.

Royd realized the tail broke most of the ribs on his right side and he was having difficulty breathing. Hunched over in anguish, he found it all but impossible to move and the Dreeat closed in on him.

"I am the son of Lord Don Sorbornef," he wheezed out in a vain attempt to intimidate.

The man-croc lashed out and grabbed him by the throat. He lifted Royd off his feet and sneered contemptuously at the wounded human.

"If you are who you say you are," it cackled menacingly. "Then you should have known better."

The Kan fog lifted and a nude Demetrius watched the sunlight glisten off the peaks of the Atarian Mountains from his bedroom's large picture window. For the last two and a half cycles, he and Okawa had been guests of the Valdurian government in the balloon city of Landagar while the *Drakin* underwent a series of upgrades.

With little to do until they readied his ship, he and his new girlfriend had taken some much-needed time off for rest and relaxation. The amenities this remote location offered pleased the airship pilot, the primary feature being security. He discovered he could truly relax on a station only accessible by air.

Behind him, Okawa stirred in bed.

"I still can't get over this view," he said, with reverential awe.

"Mmm," she purred. "Come back to bed."

"I'm too excited to sleep. I can't wait to see what they did to my ship."

"Who said anything about sleep?"

The amorous suggestion caused Demetrius to abandon his lofty vigil. Okawa had the sheets pulled back invitingly, revealing her voluptuous nude body.

"Speaking of a magnificent view," Demetrius said, in a low husky voice, sauntering over to the bed. "Good morning."

He leaned in for a long slow kiss and inadvertently found his hand cupping one of her ample breasts. Reaching up, Okawa wrapped her arms around Demetrius's frame and rolled, sending him tumbling into bed with her on top.

"It could be a great morning," she cooed.

Demetrius felt the beginnings of an erection and gave a frustrated sigh. "As tempting as that sounds, we've got a meeting with The Dwarf in less than a Deci, which doesn't leave much time to get breakfast."

"Forget breakfast. I've got what I want to eat right here," she said lecherously, beginning a slow series of kisses down his stomach.

The lone sentry saluted Okawa when they entered the secure hangar. Demetrius saw considerable activity around several airships sporting unique designs, but the *Drakin* was nowhere to be seen.

Tresna de Warton, the head of the Landagar group, codenamed 'The Dwarf,' supervised a crew working on one ship. He waved them over to a small table. His code name fit him well. Tresna was a little under five-foot-tall and squat, with an almost square-shaped head. His eyes appeared bulbous through the thick glasses he wore which looked like goggles.

"You're late," he admonished.

"Yes," Okawa admitted with an awkward grin, "we had a very important meeting take a little longer than expected."

"I see," the research chief answered skeptically, watching Demetrius blush. "Nevertheless, I've got some items I'm sure the both of you will find interesting."

On the table lay two pistol crossbows accompanied by four-inch-long curved magazines. The Dwarf held up one crossbow for display. Even with Demetrius's limited knowledge of weaponry, he immediately noticed these were sleeker than Okawa's current pistol crossbow.

"These are the new M-3s," Tresna said with pride. "You'll both be carrying these from now on. You'll notice we've added a barrel and, just like the M-2 you now carry, the bow is vertical, so it rides comfortably next to your body. The new bolts we've developed make the M-3s so compact."

He set the weapon down, picked up one magazine and deftly popped out a bolt with his thumb.

"As you can see, it's *considerably* smaller at just under three inches," he said directing their attention to the base of the petite arrow. "The fletching is more streamlined. They don't need to be as large, because we've etched the inside of the barrel with spiral grooves which spin the projectile when fired, giving it greater range and accuracy. The bronze end you see here is an Ukkonite cap. It matches the Ukkonite striker on the bowstring. The natural repellant properties of the Etheria crystals give this an incredible velocity." He ran his fingers lovingly over the metal tip. "This makes it especially deadly, courtesy of our new fire bug friends under Mount Goya. We fashioned this tip from Na-Kab Carbon. It's lightweight and incredibly strong."

"Nice!" Okawa said, obviously impressed.

"Would you care to try it out?" he asked, indicating a large three-inch-thick wooden target propped up beneath the open hangar door.

"What a question!" the Valdurian agent enthusiastically exclaimed, picking up the weapon and magazine.

Okawa deftly examined and loaded the magazine in the slot on top of the barrel with a confident pat. Demetrius was still clumsily examining his pistol by the time Okawa pulled back the slide, cocked the bow and dropped a round in the chamber.

"The cocking lever's smoother," she noted. "And there's no gear noise."

"An extra feature," Tresna smugly said.

Stepping away from the table, Okawa aimed at the target and pulled the trigger. The M-3 made a slight click as the two Ukkonite surfaces collided and a soft whoosh when the bolt left the barrel.

Just before reaching the target, a loud crack reverberated through the hangar when the miniature arrow broke the sound barrier. The thick wooden target exploded with a roar when the projectile struck. It blew a massive six-inch diameter hole completely through the hardwood, just before the adjoining portions of the door cracked into dozens of jagged pieces and scattered about the floor.

Demetrius's mouth dropped open. "Wow! Not too stealthy, but it packs a real punch."

"We don't know why it's explosive," The Dwarf admitted. "It may have something to do with the projectile's velocity."

Okawa nodded appreciatively. "If this doesn't take down what you're shooting at, you're in trouble."

"And we have a little something for you too," Tresna said, staring up at Demetrius. "Can't forget the air-jockeys."

Demetrius glanced around. "Yeah, I've been meaning to ask, where's my ship?"

"I'm so glad you asked." the Dwarf said, raising his hand and snapping his fingers. "Normally I save the best for last, but in this instance, we'll lead with it."

The air shimmered twenty feet away from them and the *Drakin* appeared out of nowhere, gently floating a few inches above the hangar floor. It rendered Demetrius speechless and even Okawa's face betrayed surprise.

"What... I mean how?!" he finally sputtered, his gaze shifting from the *Drakin* to The Dwarf.

"I told you this was the good part," Tresna said.

He led them over to the now visible airship and the side hatch popped open and an assistant in a green jumpsuit climbed out, leaving the door open.

"Thanks, Balin," Tresna said when the young man passed.

"Running down the length of the craft are two Etheria strips," he said pointing to the underside of the airship. "One of Howlite and one of Planchite. The way we combined the two, bends the light around the craft, making it invisible. It won't work on anything that sees heat signatures or like the Ash-Ta sees by bouncing sound off things."

The Dwarf then pointed to two orange cylinders on either side of the *Drakin's* nose. "Those Trinilic rods discharge fire magic."

Demetrius tilted his head back. "You mean?"

"Yeah, they shoot fireballs, or a continuous stream, depending on how much PSI you've got. Obviously, the stream burns through the PSI faster."

He then pointed inside to the back of the ship. "We've set you up with an Obsidian PSI battery in the back. It holds enough of a charge for about twenty fireballs. When you're out, we'll have to have one of our Goy-Ardia's charge it up again. We added both the cloaking and fireball controls to the overhead panel we installed last time."

Demetrius and Okawa could only stand in stunned silence.

"Well, there you go," The Dwarf said with a satisfied look on his face.

"You said you liked toys," Okawa whispered to Demetrius.

"I did, didn't I?"

The Dwarf chuckled. "With all this heavy hardware I'm not sure what they've got in store for you, but Joc' Valdur is waiting to talk."

"I'm betting we're about to find out." Demetrius said with resignation.

When Nikki Sorbornef saw her father in an animated conversation with their head animal handler Lagun, she bolted out the front door of the Staghorn plantation house. She had a bad feeling in the pit of her stomach ever since her oldest brother Royd wasn't at breakfast that morning.

"Where are they?" Don Sorbornef asked the petrified youth.

"Over by the river," Lagun gasped, his trembling hand pointing North. "I ran the whole Kan."

Her father glanced at Nikki and concern etched his face. "Nikki, find Paz and saddle up three horses from the corral."

"Four," Nikki defiantly said. "I'm coming with you."

"Go!"

Nikki sprinted past her mother to the barn, where she had seen her older and younger brothers sneak off a little while ago. The gangly nineteen-year-old knew what to expect as she approached the closed double barn doors. Her brothers were probably in there fucking—or more accurately, Paz was fucking Dobet, the youngest sibling. For some reason the boys always got horny after breakfast.

Nikki knew it could be months between taking a harvest to town, where Paz could do some serious whoring. He'd already fucked his way through all the female house and field slaves. He even tried fucking her once until she stabbed him. She wasn't interested in any man, especially her brother. Paz's lusty intentions finally settled on his little brother, Dobet. The youngest Sorbornef was quiet and sensitive with a love of poetry and a shapely ass. The arrangement seemed to work. Paz left all the women of Staghorn alone and Dobet really liked taking it in the ass.

She threw the double doors open and flooded the barn with light. Just as she suspected, she found both brothers inside. Dobet bent over a large bale of hay with his legs spread and pants cast onto the floor. Paz's pants hung down around his ankles and he heatedly pumped away at Dobet's firm behind.

Both immediately ceased their passionate moans and looked up, startled at the interruption. Paz quickly jumped back from his brother with a wet plop when his rigid member disconnected and shrank.

"Nikki, I…" Paz stammered in embarrassment.

The tomboy ignored the compromised scene. She ran a hand through her short brown hair and made her way over to a rack of saddles on the wall.

"Something's happened to Royd," she said, pulling two saddles off the rack. "Dobet get your pants on and go to mother. Paz, wipe the shit off your dick and grab a couple of saddles. We have to go now!"

She ignored her brother's panicked questions while they hastily dressed.

"Come on, let's go!" she yelled, lumbering out the doors to the corral, a saddle in each hand.

Nikki, Paz and Lagun rode up on their horses in front of the wide porch when Don came marching out the front door at a determined pace, now armed with a longsword and carrying a full-sized crossbow in his meaty hands. A small group of curious field slaves gathered around the bottom of the porch stairs.

"You and the boy stay in the house," he said, passing his wife Matka. "We'll be back soon." He then faced the slaves. "Get back to work!" he angrily bellowed.

"I really don't approve of Nikki going with you," Matka said, her thin, angular features, which rarely displayed warmth, were now especially drawn and tight. "It could be dangerous."

The family patriarch shook his head. He had long since given up trying to make his second daughter into a lady. She would always be "one of the boys." Matka, however, still hoped to marry her off to one of the other River Lord's sons and cement another alignment.

"I'll be all right mother," Nikki called out from the saddle.

"Stay in the house," her father said.

He kissed her gently on the cheek, tossed the crossbow up to Paz and climbed into the saddle.

"Take us there," he ordered Lagun.

The four promptly rode off in a gallop and the trip took barely enough time to tire the mounts. They could see the damaged cart by the riverbank and two objects dangling from a low branch of the lone tree.

They slowed their mounts cautiously. Nikki's heart sunk when she recognized her brother and their field boss, Shoku, both hung by the neck at opposite ends of a fishing line tautly draped across a thick limb. The weight of their dangling bodies caused the thin spider silk to cut through their necks in a garrote-type fashion.

The cord had sliced completely through their necks and only their spinal cords kept them suspended. Their heads bobbed about gruesomely while their bodies swayed in the wind and blood drenched the fronts of their shirts. The

Dreeat had jammed a Caskel in each of their mouths with its tail jutting unnaturally outward.

Don Sorbornef could only sit and stare in shock at his oldest son—his spitting image—dangling before him. Royd's already wide features were bloating and blood caked his close-cropped hair and bushy beard.

Nikki looked away briefly and sighed before staring back at the corpse of her favorite brother.

"The Dreeats did this," Lagun sorrowfully said.

"I'm going to kill every one of those fucking crocs!" Don spat, unable to take his eyes off the macabre spectacle.

"Father, you can't do that," Nikki softly pleaded.

"Can't I?!" he said, finally taking his eyes away from his dead son, gazing angrily at his daughter.

"Father, you know what those fish mean as well as I do. They caught them poaching. The penalty for poaching is death."

"I thought you *loved* your brother," Don said with a sneer.

Nikki became defiant. "I loved my brother... I *love* my brother, but by treaty the Dreeat were within their rights to kill them."

"And I am within my rights to avenge my oldest son!" he screamed.

"Father..."

"Get them back to Staghorn and prepare a pyre. I ride for House Kenyev and Volga. It's time to finish what our ancestors started!"

The small, pilotless airship shuttle seated only four. Demetrius and Okawa were the lone occupants on the brief

93

trip as the craft zipped between the separate sections of the balloon city of Landagar.

"So, what's with the different sections?" Demetrius asked, eying the cable they were riding.

"Security," Okawa replied. "This station is the most secure location run by House Valdur. Each section performs a unique form of research and development as well as intelligence gathering. If any one section is compromised, we can quarantine it." She pointed to the oblong wooden badge hanging around his neck. "Each of the six sections has a different color. Your badge is black and blue. Those are the only two sections we authorize you to be in. We're leaving the blue airship research section and heading for the black intelligence section."

"You folks really have the security thing down," Demetrius said watching the opening to Section Black swallow the shuttle.

"We have to be," Okawa said, blinking so her eyes adjusted from sunlight to the orange glow of the crystal interior lighting. "The Unification War severely depleted our house in both land and personnel. I mean we're down to one island now. That'll make anybody paranoid. Luckily, we had a jump on everyone in the Etheria department and we mean to keep it that way."

They stepped out onto the landing and the shuttle sped off. The sentry by the double entry doors eyed their badges and saluted Okawa when they passed. The extremely busy corridor bustled with humans, and a few Outer Clan EEtah, all wearing green jumpsuits.

Up ahead on their right, Demetrius saw a large doorless opening guarded by two sentries on either side. A steady stream of people moved in and out, accompanied by a cacophony of squawking.

When they passed by, Demetrius looked inside a large active room with an open window to the outside running its entire length. Dozens of gulls perched on a metal rod a foot above the window's ledge and running the entire length. When one arrived on the perch, a person would remove a rolled piece of paper in a leather sleeve from the bird's leg.

They determined the message's recipient without opening it. Then a delivery runner took off down the hall with the message. Black badged Valdurians urgently rushed in, reattached a new message, and sent the bird on its way.

"We call that the squawk box," Okawa said when they walked past. "Reports from spies and ambassadors from all over the Annigan come in at all times of the cycle. They subsequently send orders out on it as well. The room never closes."

"Impressive," Demetrius said turning down another busy corridor.

She stopped before the third door, adjusted her uniform and knocked. Without waiting for a reply, she swung the door opened and the duo stepped into a small, plain windowless office with a single desk and a large map of both Lumina and Nocturn on the wall.

Joc' Valdur sat directly behind the desk with an elderly man seated next to him that Demetrius didn't recognize.

The man wore a more formal looking jumpsuit than the others he had seen with medals and decorations littering his left breast. Both stood and Okawa snapped to attention.

"Air Lord Osip!" she said in surprise. "I didn't expect to be called into your presence."

When Demetrius saw a slight grin on the Air Lord's face, he surmised she wasn't in trouble.

"Quite all right, Captain," he said, stepping over to the edge of the desk where a small box and rolled piece of paper rested.

Joc' gestured toward the senior officer. "Air Lord Osip is here to do a little housekeeping before I send you off. Air Lord…"

Osip picked up the box and stepped up to Okawa who was still at attention.

"Captain Okawa de Dryden," he formally began. "For meritorious service and multiple displays of gallantry under fire. The Supreme Air Lord has authorized me to promote you to the rank of major," he said, opening the box to display small gold clusters. "Congratulations Major."

Out of the corner of his eye, Demetrius could see Okawa beaming and a profound sense of pride swept over the pilot.

"Thank you, sir. I'm honored," she said, taking the box from him.

"Well-deserved Major," he said, picking up the roll of paper.

Osip then stepped over in front of Demetrius and unrolled the small scroll.

"Demetrius de Vana," he said with equal formality. "For your exemplary skill and dedication to House Valdur, I am bestowing on you the rank of Pilot in the Valdurian Air Scouts."

"Golly thanks," Demetrius said, accepting the paper. "Does this mean I have to salute and everything now?"

Okawa tensed but the Air Lord broke out into a broad grin. "Only if you're wearing a uniform."

"Yes sir!"

"Ambassador," Osip said returning his attention to Joc'. "My work here is done. I'm sure the three of you have things to discuss. Once again, congratulations to both of you."

Okawa saluted as he left and Demetrius clumsily followed suit.

"All right," Joc' said upon the door closing. "We've fed you the molasses, now it's time for the sulfur."

"I had a feeling," Demetrius quipped.

Joc' smiled at the new scout and sat down. "Three cycles ago Calden Intelligencers interrogated a captured mongrel in Makatooa. She was the only passenger on a Tiikeri spy ship skulking around the Zerian Reef Chain. The crew died and they sunk the boat."

"What in the name of the gods were Tiikeri doing over here in Lumina?" Demetrius innocently asked.

"It gets worse," Joc' continued. "The mongrel said they had specially bred her not to need eye protection over here. She also confessed to being a worrg."

Okawa lowered her head and loudly exhaled.

"I need you two to go over to the Land of Mists. Locate the breeding center. The mongrel claims it to be near the Tiikeri capital city of Hai-Darr. Find out what's going on. If the Tiikeri's have improved their Worrg capabilities, we need all the information we can get."

"I imagine you're going to want us there quickly?" Demetrius asked.

Joc' shook his head. "As soon as you take on provisions. However, I want you to take the long way."

Demetrius' quizzical look prompted Joc' to continue. "We've been getting reports that the Tiikeri have built a settlement on the far Western tip of the Twilight Lands at Gar-Yesh Point. I need you to do a fly-by and take a look."

Demetrius gave a gentle shrug. "When you think about it, the Tiikeri are about the only race capable of settling there. The Spine of the World starts no more than ten miles off that point. The Tiikeri and Ash-Ta are friends. Heck, the ruins of at least a half a dozen failed Bailian fishing communities litter the point. The Ash-Ta are just too dangerous for anyone but the Tiikeri to live there."

"No matter," Joc' grimly said. "If the Bailian's are right, the Tiikeri are getting dangerously close to the Etheria forests of the Barrens and the processing operations in the Oasis of the Dark Waste."

"Sounds like we've got our work cut out for us." Demetrius said getting to his feet.

"Oh, I almost forgot," Joc said reaching into a desk drawer and pulling out two one-thousand-secor commodity notes.

"That's okay," Demetrius said sweeping them up and pocketing them. "I figured you were good for it."

Out in the hall Demetrius put an arm around Okawa's shoulders as they walked.

"So, tell me, how do majors feel about pilots?"

Okawa looked over at him and smiled. "The same way captains did."

"That's good to know. Seeing how we're leaving as soon as we stock up, I'm glad you convinced me to skip breakfast this morning."

"Me too. Uh, Demetrius…"

"Yes major?"

"Speaking of stocking up. You're not getting any of that disgusting smoked salted fish, are you?"

"What are you talking about?! They're delicious and really portable!"

"Yeah, but they stink up the cabin something terrible."

"Oh, all right."

Blyth Calden leaned back in the large tub and felt the warm waters swirl gently around his body. Dipping his head briefly below the surface and closing his eyes, he could hear the turine in the Makatooa harbor ring eleven bells.

The Kan would be starting soon.

Closing his eyes, he swirled his hands through the water enjoying the silence. His wife Shantal and their two children were visiting her parents and he reveled in their absence.

There was a time, not to long ago that he actually resented her, them, his family and the entire situation. His father tore him away from a promising naval career, forced him to marry a woman he didn't love or even know for that matter, and then made them bear children.

He was told they would grow to love one another.

Bullshit, he loved the adventure of the sea.

Then there was the assignment, a prestigious one to be sure; Mayor of Makatooa, the largest, busiest seaport in the Spice Islands.

He reluctantly agreed, all for the family name.

He did have to admit, he was growing used to the luxury. The Calden estate near the outskirts of town stood far removed from the smells of the seaport and having servants was reminiscent of his childhood as the son of the family patriarch.

"Sir," a squeaky voice disrupted his musings.

Blyth opened his eyes and his gaze fell upon a male Picean wearing an apron over his nude scaly frame. The thin fish-man placed a small, neatly folded stack of clothing on a nearby bench.

"Sir, here are your evening clothes and your dinner is prepared," he said, gill flaps fluttering over his ears.

"Thank you Riba," he said not bothering to stir.

"And sir, your Spymaster and commander of the city guards are here to see you. They say it's important."

Blyth grudgingly raised his head out of the water and sighed. "Very well, show them in. Then you may retire for the evening."

"Thank you, sir," he said before backing out of the room.

The young mayor returned to his reclining position with his face just above the water. Within moments he heard the clatter of two people entering the private bath but did not acknowledge their existence.

"We're sorry to disturb you sir," Velitel cautiously said after an awkward silence, "but there are several matters that need your attention."

"Very well,' Blyth said sitting up and indicating a vacant bench near one of the large picture windows. "What has transpired that needs my immediate consideration?"

"Once again. Sorry sir, we will try to be brief," Velitel began just before the duo sat down. "The new bank president has informed me that for the past two mornings Cul-Ta have been cashing in one-hundred-secor commodity notes for gold coins. He finds it very suspicious and says at this rate of one thousand per day, the bank will run out of struck gold coins in three cycles. The Cul-Ta say they are coming back tomorrow for more."

"We can't allow that to happen," Blyth said with a scowl.

"Your Honor," Velitel countered. "The bank president says his hands are tied. He is duty bound to honor the exchange under the full faith and Credit clause with the commodities exchange."

"Not only that sir," Kem said sitting forward. "The Cul-Ta have descended on the marketplace and artisan shops, spending like drunken sailors. It's causing absolute pandemonium with the merchants and patrons alike."

Blyth actually smiled at the visual. "I imagine it's bringing old prejudices to the surface."

"Oh yes," she continued, "the Populus are torn. On one hand, the crude garish behavior repulses them. I mean, they're buying anything that catches their eye, no matter how stupid or frivolous..."

"But in the other hand, they've got gold." Blyth finished her thought.

"Yes sir," she said sitting back. "There's even a new nickname for them on the street, Pacuk."

This caused the mayor to chuckle. "It's a Calden-Ya word. It means rat, in the most derogatory of terms."

Blyth gave a knowing stare to his two subordinates. "Tell me, is there any doubt in your minds that these are the notes stolen in the bank robbery?"

"None whatsoever," Velitel vehemently stated.

"Well, there you have it," Blyth said, swirling the water in front of him. "The furry little bastards are in possession of stolen property. This lets the bank president off the hook and us just cause to arrest them."

"The whole troupe sir?" Velitel asked with a touch of uncertainty.

"Let's start with the ones cashing in the notes. We'll go from there. Have your men in position when he shows up tomorrow."

"With pleasure, sir."

Blyth then turned his attention to Kem. "Once in custody that's where you come in. I want to know who they got them from and where they are. It's time we nip this little incident off at the stem."

"I'm willing to bet it's the mysterious guy in the top hat that robbed the bank in the first place." Kem offered.

"We still haven't been able to catch him," Velitel said in a frustrated tone. "Patrols have caught glimpses of him during the Kan, but he always manages to elude them."

Blyth sighed. "I mean how is it, he sticks out like my mother-in-law's ass, and nobody manages to see, much less catch him?"

"We don't know how he's moving around the city unobserved sir."

"Very well, anything else to spoil my dinner?"

"One more thing," Kem replied. "A patrol sergeant and four of the Aramos bank guards have gone missing."

"Disturbing, what do you make of it?"

"I don't know sir, Velitel's people haven't found any bodies. It may be a simple act of desertion."

Blyth nodded wearily. "Alright, keep me informed. Velitel you're dismissed. Kem, you stay, there are a few matters I need to discuss with you."

The mayor and spymaster silently watched the commander of the city guards leave. Both smiled after they were sure he was long gone and Blyth leaned back against the side of the tub.

"Intelligencer Kem," he said seductively. "You appear rather tense."

Kem returned the provocative smile. "I have many duties Your Honor."

"Perhaps joining me in a relaxing bath might ease your burden?"

The spymaster raised a curious eyebrow as she unbuckled her belt and let it drop to the floor. "Relaxing?"

"Of a sort," he replied watching her slide off her tunic and underdress.

Now naked he marveled at her petite frame and taunt breasts that were so different from his wife's.

"Intelligencer Kem would like to propose a motion to the Honorable Mayor," she said slipping into the tub and placing her arms around him.

"What is "Your motion?"

"Your Honor," she purred, straddling him. "This intelligencer seeks permission to fuck your brains out?"

"Motion carried and approved; you may proceed."

Harper had arrived long before the whistle indicating the end of the work cycle sounded over the docks of Aris. He stood on the deck of the Tannimore shuttle ship *Satala* and watched the freemen dockworkers rowdily exit from the paymaster's office and disperse. Harper found his attention automatically focus on a small purse of coins each worker clutched.

A group of twenty made their way over to the gangplank but he found his focus had settled on four coworkers slightly segregated from the others.

Harper decided to eavesdrop on the little group. They would be a good sample of the people which would frequent the city of Tannimore with its variety of forbidden delights. The boat ride out was free as were the tankards of ale served by a naked hostess upon entering the ship.

He had to admit, Wikk's business model seemed sound and perfectly in line with the teachings of the lord. The free boat ride and alcohol were the seeds which would bear prosperous fruit.

The success of Lord Wikk caused a wave of failure to sweep across Harper. He was on the ship to deliver a chest of the Etheria Notes gained from the sale of the stolen Zerian Forest. There was little doubt that his uncle Cedar would descend on Aris any day now with a group of auditors from the Zorian Monetary Council as well as some military muscle. The money simply could not be in his possession when they arrived. Tannimore now seemed the perfect refuge for the funds which would guarantee the lord's place in the financial hierarchy of the Annigan. Watching the reveling dockworkers below, he couldn't help but wonder if transmuting the Imperial Bank branch in the Aramos ancestral city to Pa-Waga was a gross overreach.

No matter, he thought watching the ship pull away from the dock. They should be in Tannimore by the time the Kan fog fell here, and the moon descended in their destination. Now that they were under way, it was the perfect time to listen in on those soon to be separated from their money.

The leader of the group was Gavin, tall, overweight with an enormous pot belly and bald. His boisterous, overbearing, and even bullying nature accentuated his slovenly appearance.

The object of Gavin's taunts appeared to be the youngest and newest of the group, who sported short blond hair and a

103

baby face. He was quietly sipping his ale, shyly ignoring Gavin's goads.

As for the other two, both were quite muscular with a distinctive blue-collar appearance. Orn was bald, with a simple yet almost retarded demeanor who found everything Gavin said to be humorous. Aurek had a head full of brown hair and seemed to have a smart-ass comment for everything.

Harper leaned on the mezzanine's railing. A naked hostess came by and freshened his wine while he listened to Gavin regale stories about Tannimore, including wild Bailian whores with pussies so wet and cold you would shoot your load in no time. Free food and drink so long as you were engaged in the city's many leisure activities. Central to Tannimore's entertainment was the gambling. The most intriguing to the laborer was a particular game, forbidden in all the Goyan Islands, called Ramu.

Harper sipped his wine and smiled. This influential workhand would be the perfect individual to lead the other gullible colleagues straight into the bosom of Lord Pa-Waga.

High above there was a chorus of inhuman cries causing all on the ship to look up.

Coursing across the sky were a herd of large flying lizards. The unruly Kells snapped and hissed at each other with each beat of their wide leathery wings.

Driving the herd were six Avions with long tridents. They poked and prodded the vicious creatures, moving them as a unit through the air.

Gavin stood staring at the winged spectacle, totally enraptured.

"I had Kel meat once," Aurek said returning his attention to the drink in his hand. "It was kinda chewy."

"Avions are just beautiful," Gavin said, continuing to stare. "So pure, one of the first races of sentients."

He continued watching until they flew out of sight then sighed deeply and took a drink.

"You know," Gavin began, attempting to sound intellectual. "It's a little-known fact that Avions don't have pinky fingers."

Aurek's face scrunched in disbelief. "Bullshit! When have you ever been around Avions?"

"I know stuff!" Gavin defensively said.

"Yeah, Gavin's smart," Orn said, coming to his aid.

Aurek shook his head and took another drink, letting the subject drop.

"You just wait," Gavin said, determined to get the last word. "One day I'll be able to prove it to you."

Eventually, moans of pleasure and frantic cries of passion gave way to guttural resonances of release and labored breaths.

After savoring a moment of her warm embrace, Alto rolled off Mal onto his back. The two panted and stared at the ceiling, their naked bodies covered in a fine sheen of sweat.

"Well shit, *that* was some homecoming," Mal said between gulps of air.

"Indeed, you were only gone a short time," Alto noted. "I'm glad you missed me that much."

"What the fuck are you talking about? You attacked me the minute I came through the damn door!"

"Funny, my recollection is altogether different."

Casually reaching over, she playfully swatted his chest with the back of her hand. "Asshole."

They lay in silence for a moment until the Turine in the harbor rang thirteen times, signaling the Kan was well under way.

"It was a long flight," Mal noted. "With that and your hanky-panky I could use a bite to eat and a drink."

"Well, Widow Tomlin has probably shut down the kitchen by now." Alto thoughtfully said. "There is always Hanno's Tavern next door."

"He serves a mean mutton sandwich," Mal conceded. "Let's go."

"So how was the job and flight?" Alto asked watching Mal take a large gulp of ale across the table.

"The flight was a piece of cake," Mal said wiping the froth from her mouth onto her sleeve. "Damn that's good ale! anyway, it was the cargo and circumstances that were a clusterfuck, and not in a good way."

"Oh?"

"The cargo was a very special mawl mongrel we had to deliver to Shun-Dra for protection. A small pride of Singa assassins attacked her, and by default, us, before takeoff."

Alto lowered his eyebrows. "Really? For what reason would the Singas want a mongrel on the other side of the world from their empire dead?"

"Not just any mongrel. This one was special. And the Singas were working for the Tiikeri."

Alto continued to stare contemplatively into space allowing Mal to continue. "I tell ya Alto, from everything I've been seeing and hearing, the Tiikeri Empire is going to be a major fucking problem sooner rather than later."

"What kind of problem?"

Mal shook her head. "I don't exactly know. Besides, I can't worry about that now. I leave in the morning for Rophan. Shommy says he may have a big job for us."

"Please give my regards to his majesty," Alto said, before they placed two plates of food were placed on the table in front of them.

"Sure," Mal said with a chuckle, picking up her overstuffed sandwich. "Are you having any luck tracking that fucking psycho bank robber?"

Alto nodded. "Through a number of new, unexpected friends I think I've learned enough to at least start the hunt. It used to be human and indeed there may be an element of humanity still residing there, but a powerful spirit of chaos completely overshadows it. Its name is Serobini, and it is using the Old City below us to move about Makatooa with impunity, striking at random. Believe me, when I say random, I mean random. It is near impossible to predict where the next strike will be because *he* doesn't even know. His impetuousness borders on self-destructive, so predicting him is all but impossible. Though I believe I've discovered an obsession which will draw him out into the open."

"That must be some obsession."

Alto nodded. "You remember the young lady I was speaking with in my dojo several cycles ago?"

"The whore?"

"Jullinar is no prostitute, in fact she is only partially human. Jullinar is a were-mer. I had rescued her from Serobini several cycles prior and she had tracked me down to thank me. For some reason, he seems obsessed with her. I plan to exploit that preoccupation to my advantage."

"How?"

"Quite simply, I'll use her as bait around the accesses to the Old City he has frequented."

"Do you think you can find her again? If she knows he's after her she's probably hiding somewhere in the Shallow Sea."

"I believe so," Alto said with a confident tilt of his head.

Mal raised her mug and paused, eyes narrowed. "You just be careful. Were-Mer's are notorious seductresses."

Alto smiled mischievously then took another sip. "Why my dear, if I did not know better, I would say that sounded a touch jealous."

Gavin was in awe, as were his three companions. Being dockworkers in Aris they had heard sailor's tales of the mysterious Doldrums and the Free City of Tannimore, but they paled compared to the reality before them.

When the ship crossed into the Doldrums from the rolling ocean swells, the laborers broke from conversations with their naked attendants and stared out the large side windows at the now flat, smooth waters.

"Well, I'll be fucked!" Gavin gasped grabbing his drink off the bar and heading out onto the deck for a better look.

In the West, the moon was setting and a dense blanket of stars emerged in the Eastern sky, reflecting off the calm sea like a twinkling blanket. When the lunar orb finally dipped below the horizon, the retreating globe appeared to flare as it back lit the floating metropolis in the distance, leaving only a glowing promise in its wake. The multi-colored beacon of decadence and avarice grew closer with each passing moment as the luxury craft sped across the tranquil, smooth patch of ocean.

All four stood on the bow in hushed reverential silence when the tops of the city's spires peeked above where the moon dipped. Gavin caught Aurek's appreciative nod, then an excited downing of his drink when the giant purple Etheria tower came into view.

"How about that shit?!" Gavin called out when they neared the eight-story structure set atop a massive bed of ships. Every facet of the nautical anomaly twinkled invitingly and Gavin felt his pulse quicken in anticipation.

The senior dock worker already had his agenda loosely panned out. Free exotic drinks and food definitely factored in as did the wild Bailian whores he had heard so much about. However, gambling drove the principal desires of this balding, potbellied dock worker. Not the regular games of chance—the wheels of fortune, the plethora of dice and card games where one could wager anything—no, he sought the pinnacle of the bettor's challenge, a game banned in every corner of the Goyan Islands.

He sought Ramu.

Ever since he'd heard about the bowling style game which wagered slaves limb's, he had become obsessed with the notion. Having never served in the military, the idea of killing someone—or severing human limbs—was a foreign but beguiling concept. His violent past had always been one of bloody bar fights, lacerations and broken bones, not dismemberment and death. The thought of being able to experience the sensation of maiming and killing without the consequences of retribution was heady and overwhelming.

Passing under the entrance archway between the huge, windowed sterns, everyone peered up at the prostitutes and barkers lining the rails, waving and cheering their welcome.

"Pretty girls!" Orn reveled, unable to take his eyes off the half-naked welcoming committee above.

"I think I'm gonna like this place," Aurek said waving back. "Nice and friendly, just the way I like it."

"Ya know," Gavin said in a somber tone. "As tempting as it may be to go taking off when we dock, I say we stick together, this being our first time here and all."

Aurek nodded in agreement at their ring leader's suggestion. This entire trip was Gavin's idea and he had heard stories of how dangerous this place could be. Despite Gavin's sometimes cruel overbearing nature, he had always looked out for his workmates. "Yeah, maybe you can help thread Orn's dick into his whore in case he has trouble."

"Fuck off Aurek!" Gavin responded as he watched the simple, oblivious Orn giggle excitedly, unable to take his eyes off the amorous welcoming group crowding around the lowering gangplank.

"Keep a tight grip on your coin purses you horny bastards," Gavin warned just before a wave of disembarking revelers swarmed around them. Tabor, who had been shyly watching the unfolding spectacle, nervously reached down and gripped his purse when the crowd surrounded him and carried him ashore.

The quartet was still in sight of one another when they made their way onto the Tannimore docks. Their naked greeters immediately shoved into their hands drinks. Prostitutes draped themselves on each passenger while barkers enthusiastically circled the newcomers, soliciting the city's many adult attractions.

The sudden sensations and choices almost overwhelmed Gavin. Glancing over at his companions he saw Orn pick up a naked Bailian prostitute and carry her on his shoulders while wrapping an arm around another, chuckling deliriously. Aurek was all smiles, groping a human prostitute as he walked along. Even Tabor had seemed to shed his self-conscious demeanor and was joining in the party atmosphere.

"All right crew!" Gavin announced above the celebratory clamor. "We've already got us some drinks and whores. What say we get us a bite to eat before trying our luck at some games?!"

The others hooted in agreement. Even though he mentioned gaming, there was only one he was interested in, and he was sure the others would follow.

Back aboard the *Satala,* Harper Aramos smiled. He watched the latest crowd of eager customers escorted off the dock below and into the city to begin the elaborate process of relieving them of their gold.

Once the crowd had dispersed, he nodded over at the two cloaked members of the Piety Watch. Without a word they lifted the small case containing the Etheria Commodity Notes.

Now for the first time, he was going to meet his counterpart in faith. The only other person appointed as priest of Pa-Waga by Saint Stryder the Proffitt; Wikk the First, Lord of Tannimore was waiting.

"Brothers, I believe we are expected."

The large outer chambers to the Ramu hall struck Gavin and the dock workers as a grimy and chaotic scene. Dozens of people yelled to be heard, bumping against each other and waving bank notes in the air.

Gavin noticed Tabor wincing from the thick smoke in the air and the rancid stench of body odor. Squinting, he tried to make sense of the frenzied activities around them. Off to his right was a table with people crowded around it, excitedly waving money. He guessed it to be the registration area. On the left were the slave pens. Gavin could see contestants choosing their live betting tokens, then moving into the hall just beyond where the Ramu game board was located.

It was then Gavin caught another smell permeating the avalanche of sensations flooding the room.

Fear.

It radiated from the slave pits, and for those who could perceive it, permeated everything. He could see it in their quickly shifting, jerky motions and anxious expressions.

Gavin closed his eyes and took in a deep intoxicating breath. This was going to be life changing, he could feel it.

"I think I got this figured out," he proclaimed to the other three. "This way."

"Welcome to Tannimore brother Harper," Wikk said standing from behind his desk.

"May the prosperity of the lord be upon you brother Wikk," Harper greeted, indicating a spot on the floor for the two Piety Watch to place the chest.

"And you," Wikk replied when the two politely embraced.

"I had gotten word that you were making a sudden visit," Wikk said taking a step back and glancing over at the chest. "What brings you to this haven of Pa-Waga?"

"Brother, the enemies of the lord grow wary of us," Harper said in a dire tone. "Even now they gather to strike at the temple in Aris."

"How so brother?"

"One by the name Shom Eldor has alerted the Zorian Monetary Fund concerning the nature of our Etheria holdings."

Wikk paused. "You mean Shom Eldor, the new Eldorian sovereign?"

"Yes. I'm afraid he's a much more hands-on leader than his late father. His methods are also much more egalitarian than his predecessor's."

"This is little better than begging and hateful in the eyes of the lord," Wikk said, his mood turning anxious. "For the Proffitt says 'Productivity is the only way to prosperity.'"

Harper nodded in solemn agreement.

"How can I help you along the lord's path my brother?" Wikk finally asked.

"I expect the enemies of the lord to descend on the temple in Aris at any time. I have removed the Etheria Commodity Notes and brought them here for safe keeping."

Wikk glanced over at the chest on the floor. "Brother, of course we will keep the lord's treasury safe, but Tannimore has never seen the need for a formal bank."

Harper placed a hand on Wikk's shoulder. "Our lord Pa-Waga now controls the Annigan's supply of Etheria. Perhaps it is time to revisit that strategy."

The atmosphere surrounding the Ramu tournament room was absolutely electric. Gavin stood on one side of the twenty-by-twenty square game board and stared over at his three opponents nervously occupying the other sides.

Across the field of play were eighty-one evenly spaced holes. Each were six inches in diameter and all arranged in nine rows of nine, with a one-foot alley in between.

On each corner of the board, they gagged and secured the purchased game token slave to a heavy wooden cross. Beside each bound slave was a rack containing bladed instruments of every size resting just above glowing coals.

Three of the walls were crowded bleachers filled with noisy, anxious spectators. A murmur swept through the crowd when attendants appeared and placed a rack of three balls by each of the contestants. Each of the hard spheres were the same size as the holes in the board.

The crowd began stomping and cheering in anticipation as a lone referee walked out onto the center of the board and welcomed them.

When the referee began the introductions of the players, Gavin turned to his companions.

"Keep an eye on Tabor," he yelled into Aurek's ear above the crowd. "He's looking a little pale. He may not have the stomach for this."

Aurek nodded and positioned himself a little closer to the peaked looking young man.

When the announcer finally got around to Gavin's name, the dock worker raised both fists in the air, playing to the crowd which went wild with appreciation.

"Here are the rules," the referee called out to everyone in attendance. "The player wagers a body part on their slave. Other players may then either call, raise or pass. The player then attempts to roll their ball across the board, past all the obstacles and holes to win. If the ball falls in a hazard or hole, the player must dismember the body part wagered from their slave. If the ball makes it past the hazard holes the other players must dismember the wagered parts from their slaves. If the player's slave dies, they're out. The winner gets to keep their slave. Is everybody clear?"

All players signified they understood.

Introductions and instructions now complete, the crowd calmed a bit, and the referee signaled to each player, asking if they were ready. All nodded, 'yes.'

With a forceful flourish he pointed at the man to Gavin's left, another unkempt laborer, for their bet.

The man lifted his left pinky high into the air and the crowd roared its approval. The referee then pointed to each of the other three contestants. Each called the bet by raising the same digit. They then pointed to the player, indicating they were betting with him against the house.

Satisfied at the wager, the judge then pointed back at the laborer who picked up a ball from the rack and positioned himself, ready to throw.

Wikk examined the label on the bottle before pouring a glass full of amber liquid and handing it to Harper. "Isn't the head of the Zorian Monetary Fund your uncle?"

Harper nodded and accepted the drink. "Yes, but in matters of money, Uncle Cedar shows no favorites."

"What will he do?" Wikk asked pouring himself a drink.

"I expect him any cycle with a team of auditors. If he doesn't like what he sees he can pull my charter."

"Given the Etheria notes are now here, does that matter?"

"Not as much," Harper said, taking a sip. "But he could still call for my arrest."

"Would he?"

"Perhaps," Wikk responded. "In matters of finance, Cedar Aramos is quite neutral."

"Then there is no reason to return. Let Tannimore be your refuge."

"A most kind offer," Harper said thoughtfully. "I'll send word for my people to join us."

"A consolidation of power," Wikk rationalized. "Now what about that change in strategy?"

Winding up, the man released the ball with a grunt. It rolled down the narrow alley, past the first two rows. Once past the danger zone, the crowd's mood picked up and they cheered the ball onward.

It rolled two more rows before veering into a hole in the sixth row. The people groaned their frustration at the negated shot and the referee scissored his arms in front of him, indicating no score. Lifting his pinky to confirm the bet, the heavy-set woman across from Gavin added her left ring finger, raising the bet and pointing to the judge showing that she was now betting with the house. The audience enthusiastically whooped their approval.

With all contestants agreed, he rolled the second ball. This one rolled straight and made it all the way across the board. The losing woman scowled and cursed. Stomping over to her bound slave, she reached into the blade bin and retrieved a large pair of shears whose tips were glowing red from the coals. Holding it up in front of her terrified slave, she gave a sadistic smile, causing him to struggle futilely against his bonds. She watched his fear-filled eyes follow the scissors to his left hand. Pausing for effect, she allowed the victim's eyes to focus and brain to anticipate the impending pain. Once she calculated the proper amount of anguish had accumulated, she quickly snipped off his ring and little finger. The slave writhed in agony as the fingers dropped to the floor. The roar of the crowd drowned out his screams muffled by the gag.

They retrieved the balls and the judge pointed to Gavin. Gavin paused, momentarily staring at the slave's amputated fingers, not out of revulsion, but revelation.

Something stirred deep within the excited dock worker. Something ancient and profound. He wasn't sure what seeing the fingers—especially the pinky—meant. That singular action triggered something deep within him. Something that meant freedom and change.

Harper's eyes danced with excitement and he quickly downed the rest of his drink. "If we control the Etheria, we can set our own rules. We no longer need the approval of the

Zorian Monetary Council. They will need to bargain with us."

"Already Tannimore has one of the largest physical holdings of Etheria," Wikk said, his interest building. "A bank and temple to Pa-Waga could be the perfect way to secure a place for our lord and his followers in this world."

"A pilgrimage destination!" Harper added.

"Yes! And not just a temple. The entire city shall be called holy!"

Gavin tried unsuccessfully to block out the din of the audience. Sweat poured off him, soaking his shirt and making it difficult to grip the smooth six-inch diameter ball in his hand. He glanced over at the referee who was staring expectantly at him for a bet.

Fuck it, he thought. *It's time to raise the stakes*!

Raising his left fist into the air, he showed his bet was the whole left hand.

The audience thundered its approval then immediately booed the woman across from Gavin who waved her hand, signifying that she was passing. The other two called the bet, but pointed at the judge, demonstrating they were betting with the house.

There was now nothing left to do but play. Stepping forward to roll the ball, Gavin felt his front foot slip in a small pool of sweat. He struggled to catch his balance, but it was too late. The ball slipped from his hand and clattered into the first row of holes on the board, an instant loss.

A nervous murmur crept through the bleachers. The woman who passed gave him a condescending sneer while the two other opponents celebrated their choice of betting against him.

Gavin felt a wave of anger at his own carelessness sweep over him. In a flash of white-hot rage, he marched over to his bound slave who watched his approach in a wide-eyed panic.

Reaching up he slid the restraints off the man's wrist and up around his forearm. The gagged victim looked pleadingly as he frantically shook his head, 'no.'

"You cost me on that one," Gavin said with a merciless sneer.

He then reached over and pulled a wide butcher's chopping knife from the rack. As with the others, its blade glowed red.

Tears now streamed down the slave's face. He continued to shake his head and mouth the word 'no' over and over through the gag.

For the briefest of moments Gavin felt a touch of pity watching the captive's helpless face while the blade drew near.

Gavin paused, allowing the slave's eyes to travel from the blade, now poised by his wrist, and locked with his unrelenting gaze.

"Sorry, rules is rules," he said before sinking the blade into the victim's skin.

The heavy knife was sharp. It rapidly passed through the wrist's muscles, bones and tendons with a sizzling sound and the smell of burning flesh. The moment Gavin completed the cut, two previously unrealized things about his personality manifested themselves. This sadistic activity breathlessly enraptured him to the point of sexual arousal, and he needed to cut slower to savor the moment.

The audience thundered its approval when the cauterized hand dropped. The amputated slave thrashed back and forth in anguish just before passing out.

Returning to his position, Gavin noted Tabor was nowhere to be seen. Aurek was staring at him in stunned shock while Orn looked on, grinning in simple amusement.

"We must secure a strong foothold on the Etheria production if we are to keep our advantage," Harper said taking it upon himself to pour another drink.

"I'm sending one of my top lieutenants to the Dark Waste to procure some Etheria we have run out of," Wikk replied. "I'll make sure he understands his additional duties."

"You're sure he's up to it?"

"He's a native of the Dark Waste and a master Etheriat," Wikk reassured.

"What about Shom Eldor?" Harper asked draining his glass once more.

"What about him? I fail to see how he can cause any more trouble."

"By the gods, he's still the Eldorian king."

Wikk chuckled. "I think that in the world of international finance the king of Eldor is going to find his reach and input quite limited, while ours will continue to grow."

Gavin had been losing badly and now his slave was dead. It had only taken two rolls from the man on his right and the same amount of bad bets to cost his once living token both his arms. He had died of shock with the removal of the second limb and his heart gave out. This was due to the sadistic dock worker drawing out the amputation, allowing for maximum suffering from the slave and extreme pleasure for himself.

One thing he was sure of, he had definitely acquired a taste for it and couldn't wait to do it again, with or without Ramu.

Right now, the only thing left to do for the remainder of this brief hedonistic junket was get drunk.

Kassade watched the two Cul-Ta enter the bank in the same arrogant manner as the last two cycles. This time, a cruel vindictive grin followed his contemptuous sneer. This time, they were ready.

Gripping the one-hundred-secor note tightly, Chu-Chu came to a halt in front of the bank president's wide desk and peered over the top with an unnerving stare. Kassade pretended not to notice the repulsive creatures that plagued every civilized city in Lumina.

With a loud clack, the rat-man slammed the Ukko note on the edge of the desk as far as he could reach.

"Trade for gold coins!" Chu-Chu curtly demanded.

Kassade slowly lifted a bored, scornful glance toward the Cul-Ta leader.

"And a good morning to you," the elitism dripped from his voice. "How may the Imperial Bank help you?"

"Trade for gold coins!" Chu-Chu impatiently repeated.

Taking his time, Kassade arrogantly stared at the Cul-Ta leader before casually reaching over and picking up the note.

"Where did you say you got this?" he asked suspiciously while nonchalantly examining the wooden rectangle.

"Not your business!" Chu-Chu angrily squeaked. "Trade for gold!"

"Oh, but I do believe it is my business," Kassade said with a condescending smile. "You see, I believe these are stolen goods."

"Cul-Ta steal nothing!" Chu-Chu defensively said.

Kassade chuckled. "I seriously doubt that your kind doesn't steal. In this case, however, you may only be in possession of stolen property. A violation of the law none the less."

Chu-Chu was about to protest when the bank president continued. "And I'm afraid that some of my friends agree with my assessment."

Kassade raised his hand and the lobby noisily swarmed with city guards. They surrounded the two man-rats, crossbows aimed. Both Cul-Ta looked around in a panic for an escape route only to find none.

From outside the circle the towering figure of Velitel appeared and stepped up to the captured duo.

With an amused shake of his head the commander of the city guards assessed his prisoners. "Well Chu-Chu, it looks like you've managed to rise from understudies to stars in your own little drama."

The simple creatures blinked uncomprehendingly at Velitel's theatrical reference.

"Money is ours!" Chu-Chu vigorously defended. "Not your business where it came from!"

"Oh, but it is," Velitel calmly countered. "A short while ago, some notes just like these were stolen from this very bank. Now your people, normally of meager means, show up with some of them." Velitel shrugged. "You can see how some would find that suspicious?"

"Cul-Ta steal nothing!" the sentient man-rat was adamant.

Velitel gave a frustrated sigh at the creature's inability to grasp the concept that possessing stolen property was wrong. "Where did you get the stolen money Chu-Chu?"

"Cul-Ta steal nothing!" Chu-Chu repeated pointing a tiny finger up at the much larger dark-skinned man.

A sad look of resignation crossed Velitel's face. "Take him," he ordered, and several guards seized the four-foot-tall man-rat. "Maybe a few cycles in The Hole will loosen up that tongue of yours," he said watching Chu-Chu squirm in the guard's grip. "And if that doesn't, I'm sure a session or two with my spymaster will."

Velitel then turned to the leader's companion. "Do you understand me?"

The smaller Cul-Ta nervously shook his head 'yes.'

"Good," Velitel said, making sure Chu-Chu was still within ear shot. "Go back to your brood and deliver a message. I want those bank notes returned within two cycles or I'm going to turn your leader over to my cousin, Thorn the Wheel, for a rather painful public interrogation and execution. Then I'll put a bounty on your kind just like my colleague Zekoff did in Zor. Do you understand?"

The Cul-Ta nodded once more.

"Excellent, now go!"

The Kan fog was just receding over the lush, rolling agricultural hill country of Southern Otomoria. Dew drops glistened on the gently waving grass making the entire countryside sparkle like a blanket of jewels under the morning sun.

Youra, an eight-foot-tall aging mother Dreeat, gazed lovingly at her daughter, Saba, and gently handed her a speckled egg the size of a small melon. The young female nervously accepted it, holding it gingerly in her hands. Youra smiled, remembering her first time tending the birthing Yerms. Her little girl was growing up. This rite of passage would signify her place in the community as well as her eligibility to mate and lay her own eggs.

"This one is a female," she said, indicating the dozen small, crude enclosures lining the river.

Nodding she understood, Saba set off past the thatched huts containing peaked roofs and headed for the coverings that were dome shaped. Youra was proud of her daughter's cautious gate. The breaking of an egg was a grave offense that would bring great dishonor to her family.

The sound of a horse whinnying broke the mother Dreeat's watchful gaze and proud musings. Youra looked up to see a line of men on horseback spanning the ridge of a nearby hill.

On the hilltop, Don Sorborneff pulled his mount to a stop and peered down the line of fifty men. In the shallow valley below was one of the Northern most tributaries of the Otoman River.

Lining the banks of the narrow waterway, several large female Dreeats moved in and out of the water, tending to the birthing Yerms lining the banks. Their ferocious humanoid crocodile appearances conflicted with the tender way they attended to the delicate structures. Birthing season was upon them now that winter had finally passed. Each of the individual Yerms contained up to a dozen eggs. The shape of the enclosed huts kept them all a precise temperature. Males gestated in the Yerms with peaked roofs, females under the domes.

The elder Sorborneff watched the maternal activity below with a scowl.

"This'll do for a start," he called out to the riders lined up beside him. "No survivors."

The line of grizzled, hardened faces nodded in acknowledgement. Each stood armed with the specialty weapon of their respective houses, identified by the family crests emblazoned on their medium round shields.

House Sorborneff, with their leaping stag crest, carried long pikes designed to distance them from the Dreeat's sizable range. Likewise, the men from house Kenyev, who fought under the wild boar standard, armed themselves with bows and heavy barbed arrows to keep them away from powerful jaws and tails. The men of House Volga with their castle tower sigil, sported long-handled maces and torches.

With a shout from the elder Sorborneff, the horsemen charged, yelling and screaming above their mount's thundering hoofbeats.

The dozen Dreeats stared at the charging humans, pointing and honking out their alarm. Several more of the humanoid crocodiles climbed onto the bank from the water, armed with heavy-bladed machetes.

The archers arrived first, circling twenty feet out, firing with deadly precision. Three Dreeats dropped with the first volley of arrows.

The Sorborneff pikemen came next, running through several more. An arrow pierced one of the enraged females in the shoulder, making her drop her sword. Grabbing the protruding spear, she pulled the rider off his mount. The terrified Sorborneff man cried out before a heavy tail came crashing down on his head, pulping it on the ground, silencing him forever.

A tail clipped a horse's front legs, throwing a Sorborneff pikeman over his mount's head. The horse pitched forward braying in pain and landed on top of his rider, crushing his legs. The trapped rider's agony from his crushed legs ended with machetes frantically hacking his upper torso and head to pieces.

Don Sorborneff finished running a female through, stabbing it several times when he saw the Volga mace wielders smashing open the roofs of the Yerms, tossing lit torches in. Within moments the thatched mud birthing chambers were burning, sending plumes of pungent smoke into the clear Lumina sky.

The entire encounter was over quickly. The humans had only lost three. Fifteen slaughtered Dreeats littered the ground around their burning offspring while some floated lifeless in the river.

The sound of the crackling fires and horses whinnying had replaced the clash of combat. Don wiped the blood from his lance tip and looked around at his men's handiwork. He nodded in satisfaction to Pax who cut off a Dreeat's hand to keep as a souvenir. The Sorborneff patriarch couldn't help but feel disappointment that his tomboy daughter had refused to be a part of the raid.

No matter, she would serve the family in other ways.

Riders from House Targoff were on their way and he had promised her hand in marriage to unify the houses. Tonight, they would light the funeral pyre and he would say goodbye to his eldest son. Tomorrow, a wedding would insure he had enough forces to destroy the Dreeat pyramid city of Hasteen. They would record his name in history as the one who rid the Otoman River's Western fork from the croc scourge once and for all. The accolades would pale compared to avenging his son and bringing honor to the family name.

Cedar Aramos, renowned as a studious, serious man, was considered as uncompromisingly honest as he was mathematically shrewd. These qualities made him a natural as one of the Senior Fellows of the Zorian Monetary Council.

As he watched the Aramos frigate *Candeed* pull up to the docks in the city of Aris, he found himself anxious and more than a bit troubled. If Shom Eldor was to be believed, his nephews had perpetrated one of the most egregious acts of robbery, extortion and market manipulation in history. The worst of it was all they had carried out the unlawful acts under the auspices of the Imperial Bank of Zor. It was now up to him to discover what was going on. He now travelled with two of his brightest auditors, Hartman, his personal assistant and five Forsvara Guards... just in case the allegations proved true.

Disembarking, Cedar realized there was no time to lose. As soon as Hartman procured a wagon, they quickly made their way along the busy streets of the Aramos ancestral capital.

The trip itself was short and Cedar warily surveyed the bank entrance when they came to a halt out front.

The first thing he noted was the lack of activity. There were no guards stationed at the entrance and the place seemed locked up tight. Cedar scowled at the bronze placard above the doors containing a single 'X' and 'I.' He recognized it as the symbol of the new—and as far as he was concerned—dangerous cult of greed known as Pa-Waga. Several rich clients and many influential commodity traders had already embraced this unscrupulous movement from Nocturn. Cedar vehemently opposed the cult being associated with the Imperial Bank.

This was not a good sign.

Sighing deeply, he ran his hands through his head of short snow-white hair, then removed a key from his pocket and handed it to his assistant.

"Open her up Hartman," he firmly said. "Sergeant, secure this establishment."

"Yes sir," the lead guard said, jumping from the wagon and motioning to his men.

Cedar watched the Aramos guards follow Hartman while he slowly climbed down to the street. The young man's ponytail swayed when he turned the key, opened the door, then stepped aside allowing the soldiers to enter.

By the time Cedar joined Hartman on the wide portico, the guards had completed their sweep of the bank's interior.

"Sir, you're going to want to see this," the bearded sergeant ominously said when he appeared in the doorway.

The banker's footsteps echoed against the bare walls. Looking around, Cedar could hardly believe his eyes. The entire bank was completely empty.

"Not even a stick of furniture left," Cedar mumbled, examining the barren rooms.

"Back in the vault is the most interesting part," the sergeant said, perplexed.

The thick vault door was ajar and just as the rest of the building, it was empty.

"Everything's gone except for that," the sergeant reported, pointing to a small oblong object laying in the center of the floor.

Keeping his eye on it, Cedar cautiously walked over and picked up the one-hundred-secor Etheria Note.

"Huh," the sergeant grunted as Cedar held it up and examined the Ukko wood rectangle. "It's weird they would have forgotten this when they did a pretty good job of cleaning the place out."

"They didn't forget it," Cedar grimly said, not taking his eyes off the currency. "They left this on purpose as a taunt."

Gavin's head felt like it was going to explode. He winced in pain, shielding his eyes from the onslaught of light. The combination of a newly risen moon and the ever-present sun on the permanent station in Tannimore's western sky was relentless.

Then there was the person kicking his foot.

"Come on," a belligerent voice rang out from above. "Get to your feet you lazy bastards!"

Squinting through an incapacitating hangover haze, Gavin could see several men in red shirts and black capes surrounding him and his companions. All were being subject to similar harassment.

"Hey, knock it off!" Gavin angrily grumbled.

They had just gotten to sleep a little while ago, when they staggered out of an all-moonless pub just as the Eastern sky was alighting. Plopping themselves in a remote alcove near The Outskirts seemed like the perfect idea.

They were wrong.

With shouts and curses, the black caped men yanked the debilitated dockworkers to their feet.

Gavin stared into the face of a bald, clean-cut man with a youthful face carrying a serious disposition.

"Whatcha' think yer doing?!" Gavin incredulously roared. "We were just tryin' to sleep one off!"

The young man's face went from serious to stern. "So, you freely admit your transgression?"

"What the fuck are you talking about?!" Gavin said, attempting to pull his arms free. "We didn't do nothin' wrong!"

The Piety Watch gripped the protesting dock workers firmly as the young man's tone became commanding. "I'm placing you all under arrest for Public Sloth. And because that is a crime against the lord, we will take you before the High Priest for his judgment."

"Judgement?!" Gavin protested. "What judgement? We weren't hurting anyone!"

The men of the Piety Watch didn't respond. Muscling them roughly along, they led them to a set of double doors on the third level of Tannimore's central city. After giving three resounding raps from a large ring knocker, a guard opened one door. A brief conversation ensued between the Piety Watch leader and the sentry. He then stepped aside and granted them entrance.

Through waves of pain and nausea, Gavin could see that this was obviously a receiving room, mostly empty with a row of six ornate chairs grouped together along the far wall. The floor had highly polished wooden planks while dull, subdued draperies adorned the walls. Two human males, a grotesquely pierced female Bailian, and a blue skinned Gila hybrid occupied four of the chairs in the middle. They halted their conversation when the group approached.

"You are now in the presence of Lord Wikk the First," the leader said as they stopped twenty feet in front of the seated foursome. "Defender of Tannimore and Keeper of the Faith! You will kneel!"

The four captured dock workers shared hesitant glances.

"I'm a loyal subject of House Aramos," Aurek defiantly said. "I kneel before no man save the leaders of that noble House."

A blanket of tense silence descended on the room.

"Your loyalty to House Aramos is most admirable," the seated young human said in a calm, unnerving voice. "Your quandary not to bow before the majesty of Pa-Waga or any other sovereign must be quite a burden. Please, allow me to unburden you. Ve-Qua, assist our troubled guest."

Gavin watched the Bailian giggle and stand. Her pale blue, impaled breasts jiggled when she reached over beside her chair. Cooing sensuously, she lifted a black, bejeweled long handled mace and stroked its shaft.

The captives nervously eyed the Kinjuto mistress sauntering over to them, deftly twirling the petite mace in one hand, while her face betrayed a sadistic grin. She stopped just in front of Aurek and gave him a suggestive pout.

"Hello Dearie," she purred, just before sending the mace crashing into Aurek's kneecap with a loud, horrific crunch.

The dock worker screamed and doubled over. A second solitary blow to the other knee sent the insolent prisoner to the floor, clutching his crushed joints and howling as he rolled around. Ve-Qua immediately dropped the mace. She then straddled the man's agony ridden face, burying it deep within the folds of her open vaginal lips. She bore down muffling his cries of pain. Grinding her hips, waves of her victim's agony transmuted into psychic power and she threw back her head in ecstasy. Small blue currents of energy traveled from the hooks which held her vaginal lips lewdly open, up the attached chains flanking her torso, which connected to the bolts on the outsides of her impaled breasts.

The other three stared on in terror and inadvertently dropped to their knees.

Wikk gave a sardonic smile when Ve-Qua stood and returned to the seat on his left, leaving Aurek moaning and whimpering beside his kneeling companions.

"I hope this has helped you in your dilemma of whom to kneel before," Wikk calmly said.

"Put him in dungeon level three and bind those wounds," Ve-Qua said to the door guards. "We want him to be somewhat productive in the future."

The sentries nodded and dragged the wounded Aurek out the door.

"Now to the business at hand," Wikk said, returning his attention to the three prisoners. "What is their sin?"

"Public sloth," the head of the Piety Watch proclaimed.

Wikk sorrowfully shook his head. "The Proffitt tells us you can only achieve prosperity through productivity. This is a grievous sin before the lord. What punishment do you think would be fitting, brother Harper?"

The human to Wikk's right sat forward and stroked his neatly sculpted beard.

"Brother Wikk, in this instance mercy may be the just course. They are not citizens of Tannimore nor are they among the faithful to our lord. Because of such, they are ignorant of our ways."

The Lord of Tannimore nodded, considering the suggestion. "Perhaps you are right. Arise."

The dock workers got to their feet; their faces bathed in relief.

"It is repugnant in the eyes of the lord not to be productive to the community in public," Wikk admonished, "but we understand you are ignorant to our ways. Remember this the next time you visit us. If you must rest, do so in private. You are now free to purchase tickets for your return trip home."

The dock worker's eyes shifted nervously.

"Uh sir," Gavin apprehensively began. "The boat ride out was free. We just assumed the ride back was too. We blew all our money this moonless, while enjoying the city."

Wikk's face became stern once again. "Travel to our city is complimentary. The passage home is not. You have no money left?"

"We spent it all sir," Orn finally spoke up.

"To have no money is also a grievous sin before the lord," Wikk scolded. "Two sins committed at the same time are much harder to overlook."

The relief on the prisoners faces evaporated while the high priest of Pa-Waga quietly consulted with those seated next to him.

"Are you prepared to work to earn your passage home?" Wikk finally asked.

"We already have jobs," Gavin defended. "And we gotta get back to them."

Wikk nodded solemnly. "You are saying you are unwilling to work for return passage. This is unfortunate."

"Wait," Gavin began, but it was too late.

"I sentence you to four hundred cycles of punishment slavery. To be carried out by any willing to purchase you. Until that time of sale, I commend you to the disciplinary care of Mistress Ve-Qua."

The Kinjuto mistress smiled at the prisoners' looks of panic when the Piety Watch seized them once again.

"Don't worry dearies," she called out, "the auction block needs you in shape to work, so we're just going to have a little short-term fun." She paused thoughtfully watching them led away. "Well, fun for *me*."

As they were being led out the door, the mistress of pain pointed toward Gavin. "That one, take that one to my private dungeon."

Passing the dock workers and heading home, Alto could see the Kan fog rolling in from the Shallow Sea. Soon a thick damp cloud would envelope the entire city and island. Most citizens, such as the wharf personnel, wisely stayed inside. The Kan was notoriously the time when the more nefarious elements of civilization came out to play.

The swordmaster wasn't concerned about the various criminal elements that thrived in the murky vapors of society's respite. This undisciplined rabble posed little threat. It was the more supernatural aspects of the world that the mist concealed that gave him pause.

The vapors were already slipping over the tops of the wharf's decking, causing a thin sheen of dew to accumulate on the thick wooden planks as Alto arrived at the end of Pier Six. In the distance, he could see the pinpoints of light on board vessels moored just offshore.

Kneeling in a meditative stance, he could hear the turine in the harbor ringing six bells, indicating that the Kan was fully upon them.

Facing out to sea, Alto began his breathing regiment and cleared his mind. Slowly, his consciousness and perception extended outward. At first, he became in tune with his immediate surroundings. He could feel the gentle panting of his beloved dog's essence resting within his long sword. From there, his awareness began expanding, encompassing the wharf, then the city, finally embracing the entire area.

The passage of time was inconsequential and Mora Alto did not know how long he had been kneeling there when he felt the presence rising from the water behind him. Sensing a shift in the entity's shape once on land, the soft padding of feet from behind him reverberated through his head.

"Hello Alto," came a softly lyrical feminine voice and an accompanying gentle hand placed on his shoulder. "I felt you reaching out to me."

"Greetings Jullinar," Alto replied, opening his eyes but remaining motionless. "I felt you too. It is as if the events of the other day joined our spirits in some manner."

The mermaid slipped up to Alto's side. Sitting down on the dock's edge she let her legs dangle over the side.

Alto tilted his head to watch the naked young lady join him. She was as tall as he was and slender, with small perfectly formed breasts. A flowing head of long whiteish blonde hair with blue green streaks now crowned her hairless body. The swordmaster felt a twinge of arousal at her close proximity and he fought to control it.

"I'm glad you reached out to me," she said, staring directly at him. "I can't help thinking about you."

"And I, you," Alto confessed. "Though I cannot say why."

Jullinar smiled, gazing back out at the fog shrouded water. "It is my kind's natural ability. Once encountered, the thought of us almost becomes an obsession. There are some of my deep ocean cousins which use it to lure sailors to their watery death."

"Why would they do such a thing?"

"It amuses them. Remember, their ways are not yours."

"And your ways are different?"

The mermaid sighed and caught Alto's attention. "Yes, the major difference is we shed our wild ways at the same time we gave up our deep diving abilities. This coincided with our ability to walk on the land, making us prisoners of the Shallow Sea."

Alto gave a self-conscious smile. "And your sensual allure?"

"An effect which still clings to us," Jullinar admitted, blushing. "Ironically, my special kind are the only one of our greater species that can mate with humans."

There was a long silence between the two, accentuated by a lone foghorn echoing across the bay.

"Alto," she said, her voice little more than a sensuous whisper. "Speaking of mating..." She gently touched his shoulder, hand lingering. "Our souls have already linked. It is my fondest desire to physically join with you. I wish to bear your child."

With that amorous admission, Alto felt a wave of desire flood his senses, overwhelming and overshadowing the shock of that revelation.

He sat without speaking for several moments. Feeling a nervous compulsion to do something with his hands, he rested one on the hilt of Defari. Immediately, the sensations of love and loyalty flooded from his treasured canine within the sword. They swept over him, completely suppressing any inappropriate sexual attraction.

"I am flattered of course," Alto said, in an apologetic tone. "However, I am promised to another. Besides, in your current state of flight, I would think caring for a child quite dangerous."

Jullinar silently stared down at the water.

"Speaking of your pursuer," Alto said, attempting to change the subject. "That is the reason I sought you out. We must do something about him and I was hoping you could help."

"His name is Serobini," she said, continuing to stare off the dock. "And he has been trying to kill me since I witnessed his transformation."

"Transformation?"

The mermaid nodded. "He was once human. I saw his small boat crash into the Zerian Reef, marooning him on one of the small out islands of the chain. I was curious, and I watched him for several cycles before the totem washed ashore."

"A totem? What kind of totem?"

"One of your human storm warding totems," she replied, her tone just shy of accusatory.

Alto scoffed. "Surely you do not mean the superstitious practice of placing statues on the shore to drive off hurricanes?"

"Many believe in it," Jullinar replied. "On top of every totem is the likeness of Huatau, the chaotic god of the sea, but there I felt a very real presence. As I watched Serobini drag the totem from the surf to the beach, I heard him cry out. He must have thought the likeness of Huatau scraped him as he lifted it upright. But I saw the blood around its mouth and knew it was a bite. Huatau had chosen a disciple in this world and possessed him with the spirit of pure chaos. It fills and surrounds him. He draws the chaos to him like insects drawn to the light. He saw me watching and knows I am the only witness to this. As far as he is concerned, I must die."

"But why is he here?" Alto asked, clearly perplexed. "I have some limited experience with supernatural things of this nature and they are rarely isolated incidents. Surely something lured him here."

"The new bank."

"What?!"

"Once the bank established itself, any of a sensitive nature could feel the balance tipping toward lawful malevolence. The invisible force behind that bank is not from here. It is one of inflexible rules and a sadistic order fueled by greed. Serobini is the natural counter. It is an ancient law; evil to counter evil."

"I must stop him," Alto softly said, after a moment's reflection. "He is about to attempt something catastrophic. I can feel it."

"This is an ancient battle between the forces of law and chaos. What can you do against such formidable entities?"

Alto gave a confident smile. "As I said, I have some experience with things of this nature. I have an idea, but I will need your help."

"Anything!" she quickly agreed.

Alto paused and raised an eyebrow. "It will be dangerous."

"It's better than looking over my shoulder for the rest of my life," she resolutely said before adopting a more appreciative tone. "Besides, if you deliver me from him again, I will be doubly indebted to you."

"You are not indebted at all," Alto assured. "Meet me back here tomorrow at the same time. If you draw him out of hiding, I can deal with him."

There was something about Gavin that intrigued Ve-Qua. In some ways he was just another simple laborer like his friends. However, she saw him looking around at the other half dozen bound captives in her private dungeon. His eyes were wide, but not with fear.

She had made sure they secured him nude to one of the X-beam crosses closest to the atrium's opening. There he could watch her special treatment to those closest to her couch and hear the cries of anguish from the dungeon levels below. It was an intimidation technique meant to terrorize. Here, it seemed to have the opposite effect.

"Tell me all your dirty little secrets," she said, in a seductive growl while tracing a sharpened fingernail from his chest down to his groin.

Gavin's breathing quickened, but he remained silent.

"Aww," Ve-Qua said, with a pout. "No need to be so shy. I've got something to help you find your voice."

Stepping over to a small brazier filled with glowing crystals, she pulled out a long needle from the variety of implements nestled within. Holding the glowing tip in front of her, she slowly approached the bound dock worker. To her surprise and delight he showed no fear.

"Now let's see if this does the trick," she said, bringing the needle up to his hand.

When he still showed no response, she slowly pushed the needle through his open palm.

The smell of burning flesh filled the air. Gavin winced and closed his eyes but refused to cry out. Ve-Qua watched him thrash slightly on the cross and gave a subtle chuckle when she saw his cock stiffen.

"What have we here?" she said, with a twinge of excitement. "I think I know what gets you going," she continued, pulling the needle from his flesh. "You were at the Ramu board last moonless."

She quickly examined the small, cauterized wound on his palm before stepping back to the brazier. Returning the needle, she removed a small carving knife. Like the prior instrument, the blade glowed red.

Keeping her eyes on Gavin, she approached the man bound to the cross next to him. The man was thin with long black hair and a scraggly beard. His scarred and bruised body told Gavin he had been here awhile. His eyes widened in dread when she moved the blade closer to his hand and Gavin felt his cock growing.

"Mistress, NO PLEASE!" he begged, straining against his restraints.

A quick check by Ve-Qua revealed Gavin's now rampant erection and labored breathing. The man before her kept begging, shaking his head 'no.'

The mistress gave a breathless giggle. "Between the two of you, you've got my pussy dripping."

Bringing the knife up to his hand, she blew him a kiss. "Now is when you show me how much you love me. How about a small sacrifice for your mistress?"

Without waiting for a reply, she brought the knife down on the last two fingers of his hand. The unfortunate amputee let out a piercing scream while the severed digits toppled to the floor. A trail of smoke from the burnt flesh rose to the ceiling. Closing her eyes, she took a deep breath of the pungent vapors and sighed contentedly.

Opening her eyes, she glanced back at Gavin to find that he had just finished several powerful ejaculations. Ribbons of cum streaked his chest and stomach, but his member remained rigid, with thick milky fluid still seeping from the tip.

Abandoning the severed man, who was now sobbing in agony, she stepped up to Gavin, eyeing him up and down. Her gaze came to rest on the thick streams of cum which dripped down his torso.

"There may be hope for you yet," she purred, while collecting a thick dab of ejaculate on her forefinger. Locking her eyes on his in a lecherous gaze, she raised her coated finger to his mouth. Once again to her delight, instead of turning his head in revulsion, he eagerly took the slimy digit into his mouth, greedily sucking down his own seed.

"Good boy," she praised, stepping back. She began gently stroking his still hard cock with the tips of her fingers. "I think I can really work with you," she said in a seductively appreciative voice. "You will be my masterpiece."

Wikk and two Piety Watch guard's arrival interrupted the sadistically prurient scene.

"Ah, there you are," the lord of Tannimore greeted. "I thought I might find you here playing with your new toy."

"What can I do for you, Lord Wikk?" Ve-Qua replied with a touch of irritation. "I'm very busy."

Wikk eyed the semen doused Gavin, who's erection had still not abated. "So I see. Brother Harper and I have consulted," he began, business-like. "We both agreed on an undertaking better suited for him and his friends. One that I'm sure you will find beneficial. We'll return them to the Goyan Islands and they'll be responsible for procuring slaves for your dungeons. This should keep you fully powered for the foreseeable future. If they agree, I am prepared to commute their sentences."

"I was just getting somewhere with this one," the Kinjuto mistress pouted. "I really feel like he will be much more use to you if I can complete his training."

Wikk paused and assessed her demand. "If you must," he conceded. "You have two cycles."

"Oh, all right," she said, still pouting. "Two cycles."

When Wikk left, she stepped up to Gavin and gave a resolute nod. "Well dearie, we've got a lot of work to do and not a lot of time."

With a sudden, hard open-handed blow, she gave his rigid member a resounding slap, which caused it to finally recede.

She realized that she must quickly formulate a training regimen. She had never created a monster before and the challenge excited her.

Kazza couldn't see them, but he could smell them. The twelve-foot-tall EEtah of Garf Sunal, House Bran sniffed the air furiously and peered as far as he could down the fog laden streets of Makatooa. The Turine had just rung seven times, indicating the Kan was well under way and his shift as gate sentry to the municipal complex would be over. As usual, his vigil had been quiet and uneventful until moments ago when the stench of wet fur and sewage assaulted his nostrils. He wasn't sure what was happening, but he didn't like it.

Slipping the Yudon harpoon off his back, he peered both ways down the street. To his right he could detect movement in the fog. When he heard squeaking to his left, he saw the first wave of Cul-Ta rushing toward him. An even larger second group followed them. Bellowing, he raised his weapon at the advancing rat-men just before realizing they were behind him too.

A swarming mass of tiny claws, jaws and weapons flooded over the man-shark. Kazza stabbed and slashed at the tide of vermin overtaking him. Soon, a growing pile of rat bodies littered the surrounding ground, but they kept coming. They vaulted from the bodies of their fallen comrades onto his massive frame.

He had felt little pain in the attack so far. Individually, their small, sharp weapons were almost ineffectual against his tough skin, but their sheer numbers began doing real damage. Thrashing about dislodged several rat-men from his arms and back but more immediately replaced them.

When three managed to climb up to his head, he knew he was in trouble. He finally felt real pain and roared in agony when they began stabbing at his eyes and gill slits on the side of his neck.

Their foul-smelling bodies covered his face, and Kazza felt them remove the keys from his belt but couldn't stop them in time. Just before they gouged out his eyes, he glimpsed the municipal compound gate opening and Cul-Ta swarming through. They headed for the city jail, which was an old, abandoned well with a locked grate on top.

The EEtah dropped to his knees in shock as everything went black. They completely sliced open his gills and one burrowed into his body, gnawing furiously. The man-shark lost consciousness and pitched forward, completely engulfed by viciously assaulting Cul-Ta.

Too weak to fight, and now completely blind, Kazza listened to them pull Chu-Chu from the jail and escort him out the front gate. The EEtah's final thought was one of gratitude, thankful for the honor of dying in combat, instead of facing the utter humiliation of his failed mission.

Serobini watched his five men slipping on the tunics of the Forsvara Guards he had poisoned several Kans ago.

"Hey boss," one said while examining the baggy apparel. "These don't fit so good."

"That's okay boys, you don't have to fool all the people all the time," Serobini said. "Besides the Kan just started and they won't be able to get a good look at you."

"So why do you want to start something between Calden and Aramos?" another asked, buckling his sword belt.

"I figure these two houses have been sucking each other's dicks long enough." He licked his teeth and grinned. "I say it's time to shake things up!"

It was clear by the blank looks that none of the thugs comprehended.

"That's okay. We've got a bunch of money left from the bank job and a boat waiting to take us out of this backwater cesspool. Just start at the bank in midtown and work your way down to the docks."

The men nodded and continued dressing.

All quickly turned when the door flew open and a young man with long brown hair raced into the room.

"Boss," he said, through labored breaths. "That fish lady is down on the docks talking with that sword guy."

"Woo Hoo, boys, we just got handed a gift, tied up with a fancy bow. And to think, we were headed in that direction, anyway. Oh, and remember, whoever gets to him first, I want that sword of his."

Everyone nodded again and finished with their Aramos disguises.

"All right boys, let's go check a few things off our to do list."

Shom was getting bored. It had been a day of tedious meetings and a long receiving line of merchant's, bureaucrats and everyday citizens who sought to petition the crown on several mundane topics. Right now, all the sovereign of House Eldor wanted to do was call it a day and get a drink.

"How many more?" Shom asked, slumping back on the throne. "This damnable chair hurts my ass."

Attina, who was standing dutifully next to her king and lover, smiled. He had been complaining about his father's throne since day one. "Only one more. It's a late addition to your schedule."

Shom groaned. "Can't it wait until tomorrow?"

"It's a representative of the Dreeat Empire. They say it's urgent."

Shom sat up straight and sighed heavily. "Very well, send them in."

Attina motioned to the door guard and three Dreeats entered.

"Presenting Sobek, representative of Queen Rani and the mighty Dreeat Empire!" The guard completed the announcement and closed the large double doors.

Shom had only seen Dreeat merchants from afar. He was curious what could be so urgent, but they had every right to petition the king. Technically, they were one of the Otoman River Lords and subjects of House Eldor.

A large twelve-foot female led the group. She wore flowing red and purple robes and carried herself with authority. The two smaller males followed. One was carrying a large sack.

The trio stopped at the stairs leading up to the throne and gave a shallow bow.

"Your majesty," Sobek growled, a bit raspy. "I thank you for adding me to your busy schedule. Queen Rani sends her congratulations on your ascension to the throne as well as a gift of our finest confections."

At her direction, the male placed the bag on the bottom step then backed away.

Shom's mouth watered at the thought of Dreeat candy. The small brown balls were a rare treat and beastly expensive. That was because the swampy end of the Otoman river's Western fork was the only place in the Annigan that grew sugarcane. The Etheria laced waters gave the cane and the candy restorative powers treasured across Lumina by healers for their medicinal properties and those with discerning palates.

"Please convey my thanks to your queen for such a gracious gift and well wishes. Surely you didn't travel all the way across the Goyan Islands to exchange pleasantries?"

The Dreeat's face grew solemn. "No, my sovereign. The news I bring is dire."

Shom sat forward. "Dire you say?"

"Yes, your majesty. A short while ago, the Dreeats caught one of the river lord's sons poaching. They executed him in accordance with the treaty, of course."

"Of course," Shom concurred.

"They now seek vengeance and there have been skirmishes. The river lords are massing and we fear they wish to eradicate our race once and for all."

Listening intently, Shom's lips grew taunt. It was a legitimate concern. The Dreeat Empire used to encompass the entire Otoman River before the humans arrived. For a thousand grands the Otoman River Lords had been waging war on the peaceful Dreeats for no other reason than their appearance. The countless battles had pushed them farther and farther down the river until the few thousand remaining ended up making a stand at the end of the Western fork.

The River Lords reluctantly agreed upon a fragile treaty only when threatened with a scorched earth policy if they continued their invasions. If the Dreeats were going to die, they would render the most fertile lands in Otomoria uninhabitable. Now it appeared the treaty was crumbling.

"What about the lancers? I believe the Fifth Lancers are to keep the peace in your area."

Sobek shook her head. "The governor and her lancers have turned a blind eye to our plight. Therefore we, as lawful banner holders of House Eldor, now seek royal protection."

Shom was now scowling. "Thank you for bringing this to my attention. Of course, we will afford you protection. I won't sit idly by while they wipe out a whole segment of my subjects."

"But your majesty, with the lancers unwilling to help, what will you do?"

Shom gave a knowing smile. "As Sovereign I can wield a pretty big stick. I've got the perfect people for the job."

The Kan fog was rising more slowly than usual this evening in Makatooa. With his shift nearly over, private Jenning de Zor felt restless. For a boring guard mission, this had turned out to be quite eventful. Not to mention they had lost six good men, brave men, brothers-in-arms. Two had their brains fried on the very porch he now guarded and four had just up and disappeared. This had made the rest of the guys jumpy.

Staring out into the emptying city streets, he saw the lights coming on through the storefront windows. As rustic as it was, this was just too much civilization to suit him. He couldn't wait to get out of this town and back into the jungle where he belonged.

The fog was now thigh high on the few passersby still out and about when he saw four men in Forsvara uniforms, carrying lit torches, exit a side street and head toward the bank. Sweeping back a strand of blond hair from his forehead, he did a double take. There were sergeant stripes on one of those uniforms.

The missing men had returned! What happened?

"Sarge?" he said, coming down the porch stairs.

The men said nothing and kept their heads down. The torch light above their heads cast long shadows across their faces. Something was wrong.

He was about to call out again when the man on the far right looked up. It was a face he didn't recognize. Jenning was about to challenge the imposter when the advancing man tossed a dagger at the startled private. The double-edged blade plunged into the young man's lower neck, puncturing his windpipe. Jenning gasped, then gurgled blood as he dropped into the fog and out of sight.

Retrieving his knife, the assailant peered around the side of the bank. There it was, just where the boss said it would be. A large bale of hay rested against the side of the building. According to Serobini, he had placed bales all throughout central Makatooa. Pressing the head of the burning torch against the closely packed straw ignited the dry bundle. He then calmly exited the alley, joining the three others beginning their calamitous rampage.

On the opposite side of the street, the man with the sergeant stripes ran through a mother with her young child. The little girl screamed in horror as her mother's bleeding corpse slumped to the ground. The girl continued screaming while the sergeant wrenched her from the dead woman's grasp. He then threw her by the arm through the plate-glass window they were in front of. The transparent barrier shattered and the little girl's wailing changed from fright to pain. Pulling one of three unlit torches from his belt, he lit it and tossed the old one through the broken window. Fabric in the shop caught fire immediately, and within moments, flames engulfed the interior, licking out the now open window into the cool Kan fog. The young girl's screams echoed above the blaze. Her burning body appeared briefly, flailing through the broken window before the inferno engulfed it.

The other three Forsvara imposters calmly walked down the main street, cutting down any in their way, setting fires and destroying anything in their path.

By the time the first few Calden city guards arrived, much of the shops along the street were burning and people were running around and screaming in panic.

When the real Forsvara guards streamed out of the burning bank, the Calden forces began attacking them, thinking they were involved. The sound of clashing swords and shouts of battle joined the anarchistic din.

When Calden reinforcements entered the fray, it was a full riot, with street fights, looting and vandalism spreading quickly outward, engulfing more of the city. The upheaval was progressing rapidly toward the docks and the uniformed agents of mayhem continued their destructive route toward the bay.

Alto, who was standing next to Jullinar on the docks, heard the screams and crashing. His eyes narrowed when he saw the flames causing the city's skyline to glow.

"Get to safety," he said, when the first of the frenzied mob came into view. "Into the water!"

Jullinar stood frozen in terror when Serobini's men spotted them. Seeing the mermaid paralyzed with fear, Alto gave her a quick shove, plunging her beneath the fog. Her body made a loud splash and the swordmaster knew she would be reasonably safe.

Three men dressed as the Aramos army now charged the lone swordsman, a screaming frenzied horde behind them. The fire had now spread down to the wharf, smoke and flames adding to the thickening fog.

When the first of the charging Aramos men got to Alto, he dropped to one knee, avoiding a swing at his head. He simultaneously drew his sword and slashed upward while rising to his feet. Defari howled when she left the scabbard, then growled viciously when the diamond Etheria blade diagonally slashed the attacker from groin to upper chest. The massive wound sent his bowels and blood spilling out before he dropped to the deck.

Allowing the sword to travel in an arc, the swordmaster spun and fell to one knee again, slashing low against the next assailant's legs.

Defari continued her menacing growl when the sword severed both legs mid-ankle. The running man plunged forward, his lifeblood pumping out of detached stumps.

The third got off a crude overhanded strike that Alto easily parried while coming to his feet. Raising the man's arms exposed his entire torso. In a single fluid motion, Alto drew the short sword with his free hand, driving the tip through the attacker's sternum until it erupted out his back. Slashing sideways, the entire blade exited the body on the side, just below the ribs. The look of shock on the man's face faded into a vacant stare. He toppled over and joined his companions on the blood slick dock.

The frenzied mob fell upon him, with fighting, flames and destruction. Alto now faced a serious dilemma. The throng of clashing bodies weren't directly targeting at him and most of the rioters were unarmed. His code forced him to consider less lethal means to defend himself.

Serobini was beside himself with joy. Head tilted back rapturously, he waltzed in slow motion through the turmoil ridden streets of Makatooa. All around him people fought each other and wantonly destroyed property while a good portion of the surrounding buildings burned. Occasionally he would stop dancing to allow a violent act to pass by, all the while surveying the chaos with a serene smile. Pirouetting onto the burning wharf, he could hear the shrill whistles of the city guards attempting to restore order.

He stopped and placed his hands on his hips when he saw Alto. A berserk throng engulfed the swordmaster as the flames raged around him. Serobini noticed he subdued any who came near with the pummel and flat of the blade, as well as kicks and throws.

"Always with the fucking code," he said, shaking his head.

Standing amidst the fiery tempest raging around him, he remained transfixed on Alto's martial ability. The black robed swordmaster flowed in graceful circular patterns, deftly deflecting the mob's undisciplined attacks. His eyes twinkled in delight when he saw a partially burning beam over Alto give way. It plummeted in a shower of sparks, striking the unaware Alto on his head and back. He fell to the ground and Defari clattered to the deck beside him.

"Woo Hoo!" Serobini rejoiced, a single celebratory hop before skipping over to the unconscious swordmaster.

"Ya see," Serobini said, standing over him and looking down victoriously. "Ya never can account for random shit just happening."

He then reached down and picked up Defari.

The sword immediately lurched in his hands and he fought to hang on. Much like a dog that doesn't want to be held, the blade growled as it flailed and lurched in his grasp. In a final roll, it pulled itself free of his grip. Serobini gasped in astonishment when it briefly levitated in front of him. The emissary of chaos had no time to cry out when Defari spun in the air of its own volition. He heard the growling Etheria blade whistling above the roar of the insurrection. Its sheer velocity smoothly severed Serobini's head from his lanky torso. It bounced several times on the bloody dock and came to rest several feet away, propped against a small keg. It stared lifelessly outward at the mayhem with a lipless smile.

Serobini's headless torso teetered and flashes of blue flames and lightning erupted from the open neck.

The magical fireworks quickly dimmed, then went out and the lifeless body dropped.

Defari floated over to Alto and levitated by her master's head, growling at any who came near.

"WHAT THE FUCK!" Mal was on her feet, leaning on the console, staring out the windshield at the burning chaos below. The entire center of Makatooa was on fire, with people running about hysterically.

"Alto's down there! Kumo, get us in for a closer look!"

"Yes Captain."

The *Haraka* slowly descended toward the maelstrom, with everyone gathering around the command chairs to witness the chaos that enveloped their friend.

"So how are we supposed to find him in all that?" Zau asked, watching complete sections of buildings collapse in flames.

Zaad glanced down at the Singa in the navigator's chair. "With a fight of that size going on, if Mora's involved, all we have to do is look for the biggest pile of bodies."

"We'll start at the docks and work our way into town," Mal said, not taking her eyes off the calamitous spectacle.

Kumo took the airship down to fifty feet off the bay and swept along the piers. The fire had completely engulfed the Southern docks along with several ships. It was rapidly spreading to the Northern wharf, which up until now had only a few hot spots.

"What the—" Wostera said, leaning over Zau's shoulder. "Is that sword... floating?"

"Where?!" Mal's head snapped around to where the Bowmistress was looking. She gasped in dread when she saw Alto's body laying beneath a smoldering wooden beam. True to Zaad's speculation, there was a ring of twenty corpses littered around the unconscious swordmaster. He, however, appeared not to be the author of their demise.

Mal was about to give the order to get close when the blade, which hovered a foot over Alto's head, rotated upward. Two sailors were running down the dock toward the ship. Without hesitation or warning, the sword swept through the air, cutting down both when they got too close. The dead mariners dropped to the ground, hemorrhaging blood, adding to the growing pile of unfortunate innocents littering the decking around Alto.

"Defari!" Mal said, shaking her head in frustration. "She's protecting Alto."

Wostera continued to stare in wonder at the sword which acted on its own. "What is that?"

"The essence of Mora's dog is in that sword," Zaad replied. "Very protective."

"How?"

"It's a long story," Mal said, watching Defari strike down a Picean who was attempting to make his escape into the water. "It can't tell the fucking difference between innocent and foe."

"That dock is going to give way," Zaad said, pointing to several burning pilings. "We've got to get him outta there!"

Zau huffed loudly. "Does it look like that sword is going to let anyone get near him?"

Mal still had not looked away from her lover's perilous situation. "I've got an idea."

"Make it a good one Captain," Zaad replied, watching the very end of the dock buckle and drop a foot lower. "Because that section of pier is coming down."

Mal bounded out of her seat and stood by the side hatch. "Okay, we gotta work fast. Zaad, it's going to be mostly you and me. We're the ones she's used to. Kumo, pull up alongside the dock as close as you can to Alto then drop the side hatch. I just hope she recognizes the *Haraka*. Zaad, I want you and me to be the first sentients she sees. Everyone she doesn't know, that's Wostera and Kumo, you stay out of sight. Once we're on the docks, I'll get the sword. Zaad, get that fucking beam off Alto then get him in the ship."

"Right captain," the EEtah growled.

"All right folks, let's do this!"

Zaad got up and stood beside Mal. Kumo slid the airship next to the dock, hovering just above the water.

The side hatch dropped with a loud crunch as it came down on the edge of the strained wooden planks. A wave of heat and smoke rushed into the craft's interior as did the roar of pandemonium.

Mal cautiously walked down the ramp, never taking her eyes off the sword floating fifteen feet away.

"Hey girl," Mal said in a soothing tone while she extended her arms out in front of her, keeping her hands palms up. "Remember me?"

Mal drew closer, maintaining a simple placating dialogue and a calming tone. When the growling diminished, Zaad started out of the ship.

"Remember Zaad?" Mal asked. "You used to chow down together."

Defari had now completely stopped growling and whimpered.

"Don't worry girl," she said, slowly reaching up to the sword's hilt. "We're gonna take care of him." The blade continued to whimper when Mal gently wrapped her hands around the handle and began moving toward the ship. "Okay Zaad, now."

Zaad bent down and grabbed the end of the broken beam while Mal paused on the ramp, keeping a direct line of sight between the sword and its master.

The EEtah easily lifted the beam and tossed it aside, gently picking up the unresponsive Alto. He made it a few steps back to the *Haraka's* ramp where Mal stood when the end of the dock finally gave way, plunging into the water. The rest of the wharf now listed badly. Dead bodies and debris began sliding down the thirty-degree angle into the water.

Zaad was struggling to keep his balance and Defari whined loudly and lurched in Mal's hands when Zaad stumbled. The EEtah gave another labored step up the inclined dock when a plank gave way beneath his foot, trapping him. The entire dock creaked and shuttered under the strain. Zaad's yanking at his trapped appendage caused Alto to sway wildly in his arms.

"Come on Zaad," Mal nervously muttered. "Come on, get the fuck out of there!"

The dock suddenly shook and began groaning in protest when the fallen burnt end slowly rose from the water.

Mal felt a slight tingle behind and to her right. Cocking her head, she saw Wostera standing just inside the open hatchway with her brow furrowed in deep concentration. The bowmistress extended both her arms and blue sparkles danced across the palms of her open hands.

The dock continued to moan and pop as it settled back into its original position. With the pressure now released, Zaad could pull his foot free.

"Come on Zaad!" Mal heartened. "I don't know how long she can hold that thing up!"

The EEtah glanced quickly back over his shoulder then took off running as fast as his stubby legs would allow. When he stepped back onto the ship's ramp, Wostera lowered her arms and came out of her trance. Loud snapping sounds preceded the whole dock breaking away and crashing into the harbor with a thunderous splash.

Mal, still holding Defari at arm's length, followed Zaad into the ship.

"Kumo, get us the fuck outta here!"

"Yes Captain," she replied, spinning the wheel while Mal closed the hatch.

Zaad took Alto back to the cargo area and laid him out on the floor. Mal paused and looked over at Zau. "Is there anything you can do for him?"

The Singa navigator and mage got up from her command chair and turned over one shell on her belt.

"I can try," she said, passing her captain on the way to the rear of the ship.

The first thing Alto saw when he opened his eyes was a kneeling Wostera, staring down at him with a warm smile.

"I, I know you," he said groggily.

"It's good to see you again my friend," she said, gently patting his shoulder.

Lifting his head, the swordmaster took in his surroundings. "The *Haraka*?"

Wostera nodded. "You gave us quite a fright back there."

Alto slowly sat up looking perplexed. "Back there. Makatooa, What... Where are we?"

"We're just now coming off the Southwestern coast of Goya," Mal said, kneeling beside him. "You know, you gotta quit scaring the shit out of me like that."

"What happened?" he asked, touching the back of his neck and recoiling in pain.

"Wostera held up that burning dock you were on while Zaad pulled you off to safety."

"The last thing I remember was fighting off the crowd and trying not to seriously hurt anyone."

"Yeah, well, Defari wasn't nearly so discriminating," Mal said, motioning toward the sword propped up by his seat. "She killed anyone that got close to you."

"Yeah, there was a ring of bodies around you," Zaad said. "Good to have you back Mora."

Alto peered up at the man-shark. "Among the bodies, was there by any chance a tall…"

"Ugly, lipless bastard in a top hat?" Zaad finished.

Alto nodded.

"Yep," the EEtah confirmed. "Looks like Defari took care of him too. His head was laying nearby."

"That was some major shit going on back there." Mal said, helping him to his feet. "What the fuck happened?"

"In the end, it turned out to be the clash of two evil entities. One representing law, the other chaos." Alto replied lowering himself into his usual chair while Defari began a happy pant beside him.

"And the whole damn city paid the price," Zaad lamented.

A look of panicked realization swept over Alto and he bolted upright. "The city, riot, fire, my school?!"

Mal, who had sat down next to him, reached up and softly touched his cheek. "I'm afraid it's gone. When we left, the entire center of town was on fire. The city guards were just getting a handle on the riot."

The swordmaster stared blankly into space with a look of stunned disbelief. "Gone?"

Mal sadly nodded. "Between the rioters and the fire, I can't imagine there's much left."

"Gone…" Alto lamented, plopping against the back of his chair.

"I'm sorry Mora," Zaad said, settling into his seat. "I know it was your dream."

Alto remained silent and a lost look slowly overtook him.

"I was coming to get you anyway," Mal said, to distract him. "We're going to need your help on this next job and I was initially hoping I could convince you to tag along. You know, like the old days."

Alto finally looked over at her. "It would seem my schedule has been cleared," he said, his voice hollow. "And seeing how I just lost everything, I imagine I will need some funds."

"Don't you want to know what the job is?" Mal asked when he turned away.

"Does it matter?"

Mal paused at Alto's reaction. "Well, uh, sure, I guess. Shommy pulled us a gig down in Otomoria. Looks like we're going to be preventing a genocide."

There was no reaction from the swordmaster and Mal peered nervously at her team.

With a serene demeanor, Wostera stepped over and offered Alto her hand. Staring blankly back up at her, he took it.

"Come, join me," she tenderly said.

The swordmaster nodded weakly, then stood.

"Bring Defari," she said, leading him back to her meditation area just before the cargo bay.

Everyone watched as the bowmistress directed Alto into a kneeling position with Defari resting in front of him. She then knelt in the same position and closed her eyes.

"Breathe," was her only instruction.

"All right, we're approaching Otomoria," Zau announced, gazing down at the coastline ahead.

"Plot a course following the river upstream to the mountains," Mal ordered. "there'll be a set of hamlets around a lake and waterfall. Put her down there. The capital Toriss is inside the mountain. We'll have to walk."

Order given, Mal gave an irritated glance back at Alto and Wostera who were deep in a meditative trance, eyes closed.

"They've been at it for almost two deci," Mal muttered.

Zau glanced over at her captain, amused by the jealousy in her voice. "Lighten up, don't be such a schmuck."

Mal snapped an irritated glance back at the Singa.

"He just lost everything, his possessions, his money, his dream. And he almost lost his life. She's helping him heal better than you or anyone else could. I know you can't feel it but I can. But there's a lot more than just healing going on back there. Do you see the way they're sitting?"

Mal turned back to see what Zau was referencing.

"They're seated at an angle," Zau pointed out. "Their feet underneath them are touching. So are their weapons in front of them. I can feel the energy stinking up the entire cabin."

The Singa grinned when she saw Mal sniffing.

"They're bonding into what I'm going to guess will be a very formidable fighting team."

Mal's look softened but there remained a touch of skepticism.

"You said it yourself, we may be up against an army," Zau said, returning her attention out the windshield. "Those two are probably going to come in handy."

ACT TWO

The Peril Abroad

Toren de Upsala loved these kinds of mornings and this time of year. The frigid winds that swept across the fields of Southern Otomoria were finally gone, replaced by a gentle cool breeze from the West. The welcome change of seasons allowed him and his family to reap the harvest of winter wheat that the cold weather had afforded them.

Standing on the nearly full small barge, Toren looked out and watched his two teenage sons preparing to unload the last wagon into the ship's hold.

On the horizon, just moving out of sight, his third son drove the wagon full of tribute tax grain to the Sorbornef plantation of Staghorn.

Catching a whiff of roasting bacon made his stomach grumble and brought his attention to his wife, Gwen, and their daughter, who were milling around the cook fire they set up beside the river.

He enjoyed watching her gracefully move about. She had pulled back her long blonde hair into a ponytail because she was always afraid of it catching fire. He chuckled at how their nine-year-old, Marci, now mimicked her mother's style. Thankfully, she and her brothers favored their mother, instead of his ruddy complexion and head of unmanageable black curls. He wasn't sure what Gwen ever saw in him; he was just glad she did.

"We're just about ready to eat," Gwen called out.

"Good timing," Toren replied, wiping the sweat from his brow. "We're almost done here."

The stocky farmer peered down at his sons, who were digging their pitchforks into the shafts of grain. "Best hurry boys. The way your ma loves bacon, there won't be none left for us."

The two young men laughed as they tossed the wheat from the cart into the boat. Their dad was always joking around, which made the day go faster and work seem easier.

"Sure thing, Pa," said Bret, the oldest.

The sudden flare of the fire and the women's screams pierced the good-natured moment.

Toren gasped in terror. A Dreeat had Marcie's leg tightly in its mouth. She was being drug kicking and screaming into the river. The commotion had knocked the morning meal into the fire. The bacon grease accelerated the flames, catching the hem of Gwen's dress alight. Making matters worse, four other Dreeats, armed with machetes, scrambled up the bank.

Toren was about to cry out an alarm when he felt something heavy strike the middle of his back. He stared down in shock at the spear tip which had just exploded from his chest.

Teetering, he saw his boys charging the Dreeats, their pitchforks pointed at the attacking crocs. His vision was cloudy as he watched Marci drug under the water. His wife's dress was now completely on fire and the downward slash from the crocodile-men's blade silenced her screams.

The last thing Toren saw before toppling into the river was a Dreeat grabbing the end of a burning log and tossing it into the barge, setting the grain ablaze.

The *Drakin* had passed the lumina Nocturn border a short while ago. Okawa watched the towering peaks of the Os'Ani Mountains race past on their left. Down below, the narrow scrub laden foothills gave way to the vast expanse of the Dark Waste Desert.

"You're cutting it kind of close to those mountains, aren't you?" Okawa asked with a touch of concern.

Demetrius gave the Valdurian agent an amused side glance. "I don't tell you how to snoop around and kick butt, you don't tell me how to fly."

Okawa rolled her eyes and stared out at the sand dunes which stretched to the horizon.

"Right now, we need the cover those mountains provide," Demetrius said. "The moon will be setting soon, which means we can operate a little more in the open. We can't afford to be spotted."

"I thought the Shrouding Stone makes us invisible?"

"Mostly yes, but there's two problems. One, it won't work on some creatures we may encounter. And two, that Obsidian battery only holds so much PSI. We can't use it all on being invisible. We may need to shoot our way out of some less than hospitable place."

"Let's hope we can get in and out without shooting at anything," Okawa optimistically said. "But I wouldn't bet on it."

"We'll be okay. We just can't go frivolously spending PSI when good old sneakiness will do."

"I honestly don't know how you got used to this place."

"You don't get used to it," Demetrius replied, checking the controls. "You put up with it, do what you must, then get out. Nocturn is hardly a people friendly place."

"I'll say."

"All right," Demetrius said, slowing the craft. "We're coming up on the So'Let Rise."

Demetrius brought the airship to a complete stop against the wall of a low oblong mesa that blocked their path.

"Just beyond this pile of rocks is Gar-Yesh Point. The official end of the Twilight Lands and probably one of the most dangerous strips of land in the whole Annigan."

Okawa watched Demetrius reach up and press a blue disk on the overhead console, which activated the shroud.

"Just to be on the safe side," Demetrius casually said, locking eyes with Okawa.

Bringing the *Drakin* slowly up the face of the mesa, Okawa caught a glint of light off to their left.

"Demetrius!"

The pilot nodded and moved the craft even closer to the wall, slowing their ascent even more. When they reached the summit, both saw what was causing the unusual glimmer. Twenty yards away, near the mesa's lip, was a small temporary domed structure. Sitting on the edge were two orange Tiikeri. One of them was scanning the landscape before them with a spyglass.

"Tiikeri spotters," Okawa said, studying the man-tigers.

"Yeah, we caught the moon's reflection in that glass."

Okawa shook her head. "Well, I'm pretty sure they're not here for a picnic. Something's going on."

Demetrius remained silent, cautiously bringing the *Drakin* over the summit's lip, creeping across the mesa's flat top. The trek seemed like an eternity to Okawa, who never took her eyes off the oblivious Tiikeri.

When they slipped down the other side, the mountains completely obscured the moon. The absence of it bathed the land in a blanket of darkness, while up above, the sky exploded in a thick patchwork of stars.

Demetrius and Okawa flipped down the orange lenses on their glasses. Both could now clearly see the heat outlines of anything living.

"Well, that's one field test complete," Demetrius said, pointing the ship West. "Those lookouts never saw us. Let's just hope it keeps working."

Gar-Yesh point was a twenty-mile-wide, fifty-mile-long flat strip of land made of scrub and sand, with occasional outcroppings of rock. Keeping the *Drakin* at a height of a hundred feet afforded the two humans a bird's-eye view of the peninsula. There was activity all around.

On the ground, a small army of mongrel workers led by Tiikeri supervisors were constructing a large encampment of open-sided structures.

"What are they building?" Okawa asked, staring at the industrious bustle.

"Those look like Singa huts. What in the name of the gods are they doing that for?"

"Maybe it's for them?"

"Nah, Tiikeri prefer enclosed dens. Singas prefer the open."

"If you think that's something, check that out," Okawa said, pointing to the coast.

Demetrius peered out Okawa's side window to see construction on a massive series of docks.

"Well, it looks like something is definitely going on." Demetrius noted before something in the Western sky caught his attention. "I don't like the looks of that."

"What is that?" Okawa asked, squinting at the dark shape blacking out the stars and moving their way.

Demetrius performed a hard bank to port and began a quick descent toward a huge pile of large boulders. "Ash-Ta, Chiro clan, if I had to guess by the size of that group."

The airship slipped between two huge stones which dwarfed it. Demetrius gently nuzzled the ship next to one of the gigantic rocks with a gentle bump, then set the controls to hover.

"What are you doing? I thought we were invisible."

"Not to them," he answered. "Remember I mentioned about certain creatures?"

Okawa nodded.

"Those are some of the ones I was talking about. Ash-Tah eyes aren't that great. They rely on bouncing sound off objects to navigate. They mostly notice movement, so we're just going to make like we're part of the rock."

Okawa's hand automatically rested on the grip of her pistol when she heard the beating of wings. She relaxed when Demetrius rested his hand on her shoulder.

They could see the erratic flight patterns of the humanoid bats filling the surrounding sky. She marveled at their small size. Each one was only two feet tall, with an abnormally large head and jaw.

Demetrius raised a finger to his lips when several fluttered right in front of them. One briefly perched on a nearby boulder and looked straight at them.

Okawa felt her mouth go dry and her pulse quicken when it let out a series of high-pitched squeals. Both breathed a sigh of relief when it took off, following the group heading South over the Frozen Sea.

"That was close," Demetrius said, once at a safe distance.

"I take it they would have attacked us?"

Demetrius nodded. "If they were hungry enough and Chiro are always hungry."

"Why didn't they attack the Mawl workers?"

"Ash-Ta and Tiikeri are allies," Demetrius replied, steering the craft upward. "Mostly against the Do-Tarr."

They cleared the top of the crag, and Demetrius paused. "Okay, I know Joc' said to take the conventional route to gather information and we've got it. One thing's for sure, we won't make it past the Spine of the World without being spotted. The skies around the Ash-Ta's home are just teeming with them. We don't really have a choice. I'm taking us upstairs."

163

Nikki Sorbornef's eyes flashed with anger and her lips drew taut. "Father, mother, I am not marrying Adrik Targoff!"

Matka Sorbornef gave a rare, understanding smile. "Come now, dear, be reasonable. He's handsome and since his parents' drowning accident last grand, he is the new lord of House Targoff. We need this alliance."

"You mean father needs it for his war!"

Matka looked away for a moment and sighed. "We need this alliance to keep the family strong."

"But I don't want to get married. I've never even met him, much less love him!"

"You will grow to love him, dear."

"No, I won't because I'm not doing it. I'm not marrying him!"

"I'm afraid you don't have a choice, dear. Your father and I are well within our rights, and it *is* our duty to find you a suitable husband."

"I don't want a husband!" Nikki said, her shrill voice filling the room. "My place is here, helping you run Staghorn!"

Don Sorbornef pounded a fist on the table and pointed at his daughter. "Your place is where we say it is, young lady! You have always said you serve the family! Well, this is how you serve! You marry into a good family and produce children. Peace babies keep the peace between the river lords."

A spiteful look crossed the Sorbornef daughter's face. "I thought the Dreeat were river lords too."

"The human ones," Don said, in an icy tone. "And we'll be rid of those damn crocs soon enough."

"Dear, try to see the good side of this," Matka reasoned. "You'll be the lady of Targoff Manor, a very prestigious position."

Nikki was about to protest when her father cut in. "It's settled. Adrik Targoff and his men will arrive later today.

This evening we hold a greeting feast where we will properly introduce you. The wedding will be tomorrow."

The front door flying open and Paz bounding into the room cut short any further objections.

"Father!" he cried out, pointing out the door.

Everyone rushed out to the front of the manor. All the servants who had been preparing for the event were now standing and staring southward at the trail of smoke on the horizon.

"It's coming from the river," Don said, his voice a mixture of anger and alarm. "Quick, get the horses."

They could see the cloud of water vapor and spray the moment Mount Otoman came into view.

"Would you look at that!" Zau said in wonder, gazing out at the massive waterfall rushing out of an equally impressive cavern on the mountainside. The aquatic avalanche plummeted a hundred and fifty feet downward, where it thundered into Lake Otoman.

Sitting on the Southwestern shore of the lake, the small city of Bakuu sat just beside the very spot where the raging torrent of water collided with the lake. The immense brume of mist enveloped the entire city. The collected dew caused the community and surrounding area to glisten in Lumina's morning sun. Just to the right of the rushing water, a wide staircase, heavy with foot traffic, stretched from the city upward into the mouth of the cave.

"No airfield," Zau noted as the *Haraka* circled the community.

"I didn't expect one," Mal said, surveying the scene below. "Besides, that's where we're going." The Spice Rat pointed toward the cave and another entire urban expanse inside. "The hidden city of Toriss," Mal continued. "Central seat of power for the continent. The governor is supposedly expecting us."

Toward the rear of the craft, Alto and Wostera opened their eyes at the same time. The swordmaster looked over at the Amarenian and smiled.

"How do you feel Mora?" Wostera empathetically asked.

Alto took a moment to assess his condition. "Refreshed."

"Glad you two are back with us," Mal said, spinning in her seat. "We're here, and I have absolutely no idea how we're going to be received."

"You would think they'd welcome the help," Zau said with a touch of disbelief.

"You never can tell. Sometimes these regional leaders can get real fucking territorial. They don't like anyone from the outside telling them how to run things."

The Singa nodded. "I'm betting that goes double for having to tell them they're doing a crappy job."

"Captain, I don't see enough room for me to get us in that cave," Kumo meekly said.

Mal sighed and scanned the area. "Yeah, okay, put her down in that plaza by the base of the stairs. Zaad, you and Wostera oversee getting provisions. While you're at it, see if you can get a sense of what the locals feel. Zau, you and Alto get to come with me when I give the governor the bad news."

Zau eyed the busy staircase. "That's an awful lot of stairs."

Mal gave her navigator an amused look. "Set us down Kumo."

"Yes captain."

Mal kept a wary eye on the ground while they slowly descended. The predominantly human population paused from their industrious bustle and stared at the *Haraka* gently settling into the small courtyard, hovering a few inches above the cobblestones.

When the side hatch dropped, Mal felt the cool misty air and heard the constant roar of the waterfall. It surprised her to find that a small crowd had gathered. All stood staring, oblivious to the damp conditions surrounding them. They murmured curiously when Zau exited the ship behind Mal. A gasp went through the crowd when Zaad's imposing frame sauntered down the ramp, with Wostera by his side.

"I get the impression they don't see many of your kind around here," the Bowmistress playfully said.

The EEtah scanned the crowd of stunned faces. "It's far enough away from the coast. You're probably right."

The novelty of the new arrivals quickly wore off and the citizens resumed their morning activities.

"This dampness is miserable," Zau said, watching the crowd disperse and revert to random passing stares.

"This isn't so bad," Zaad said, obviously enjoying the thick dampness.

"The smell of wet fur doesn't do a whole fucking lot for me either," Mal said.

She stared up the fifty-foot-wide expanse of stairs sloped gradually upward to the mouth of the cave. The shallow risers and wide treads easily accommodated the steady foot traffic between the cities.

"All right, this is where we part ways," Mal said, glancing back into the city. "We'll meet back at the ship in a few deci. Remember, don't buy any stupid shit!"

Alto snickered at the reference to Shom's impetuousness and turned away.

Zaad chuckled. "Yeah, I miss the funny little man too."

Mal and Zau watched the mismatched duo disappear into the crowd before joining the swordmaster.

"That's an awful lot of stairs," Zau moaned.

"Then we best get to it," Mal said, taking a first step up.

Zau felt relieved the mist was gone once inside the mouth of the cave, but an ever-present metallic odor and taste replaced it.

The trio stood staring at the towering stone buildings of Toriss. They had constructed most of the architecture from hollowed out giant stalagmites and stalactites. Up ahead, on their left, a bridge spanned the river and led to a rectangular mine shaft in the far wall. Off to the right of the city, a large roughhewn slit running up the wall led to another chamber.

"What's that smell?" Zau asked in disgust.

Alto's face also soured. "I imagine it is coming from the mine over there. By the way, have either of you noticed that all the people around here are…"

"Bald," Zau said, finishing his thought.

"Yes, it is quite unusual."

"I bet it has something to do with that fucking smell. Come on, the sooner we're outta here, the better."

After a few inquiries, they located the Governor's office and residence located inside one of the many huge stalactites suspended from the cave's roof.

Governor Darga Shaheen was small in stature and carried a stern demeanor. Her bald head set off her full, pouty lips and pale white skin. She sat motionless at her desk, reading Shom's letter of introduction. Standing behind her and reading over her shoulder was her spymaster, Heddlu.

His eyes were narrow slits, and he looked back up at Mal frequently as he read.

Sighing, she put the letter down. "Well, everything appears to be in order. Our new sovereign has a lot of confidence in you. According to this, I am to provide you complete cooperation and every courtesy. I'm still unsure what the problem is."

"It would seem that some of your subjects are attempting to kill off the Dreeat," Mal said, glancing out the window at the busy cave floor.

"Ah, the lords of the Western fork," she said, nodding in realization. "They can be a rowdy bunch, but they pay their taxes. For the most part, they keep their skirmishes small and localized. What have you heard, Heddlu?"

The spymaster was now standing on the side of the desk and staring intently at the strangers.

"There was an incident several cycles ago," he explained. "The Dreeats caught the oldest Sorbornef boy poaching Caskels and executed him."

The Governor threw her head back and whistled. "I bet *that* went over well. Don Sorbornef has quite the temper."

"There's been some back and forth. Word is, Lord Sorbornef already has House Kenyev on board and is trying to rally the other neighboring houses."

"Has he been successful?"

Heddlu gave a shallow shrug. "He's marrying his middle daughter off to Adrik Targoff."

Darga closed her eyes and rubbed the bridge of her nose. "This just keeps getting better. Why have I not heard about this and why aren't the lancers keeping the peace?"

"Until recently, this was a small local affair. The lancers generally let the river lords settle their own squabbles."

"I apologize," Alto said, taking a short step forward. "I am not sure I understand how a wedding plays into all this?"

"Lord Sorbornef is sealing alliances by marriage," the spymaster curtly replied. "A Sorbornef, Kenyev, Targoff coalition can potentially rally a thousand men at arms."

"And suddenly this doesn't sound like a small fucking matter anymore," Mal said with a grimace. "Looks like we've got our work cut out for us, as usual."

"Well, your directive came straight from the king, so that entitles you to one of these," Darga said, reaching into a drawer. She pulled out a five inch long, thin golden rectangle and set it on the desk. Mal could see the governor's seal stamped on its face. "This will allow you unmolested travel anywhere in Otomoria. It also affords you complete assistance from any you might call on."

Mal gave an impressed nod as she picked up the pass. "Thanks, Your Honor. This will make things a little easier."

Darga gave a sad smile. "I hope so. I don't know how much help the Fifth Eldorian Lancers are going to be."

"If they won't help, they better at least get the fuck out of our way."

"What size of a force did you bring?"

"Five, not counting my pilot," she answered.

The governor and spymaster traded shocked, skeptical looks.

"It sounds to me like they'll vastly outnumber you."

Mal smiled confidently. "It won't be the first time. We've faced worse odds in a lot shittier places than this."

The governor sat back and studied the brash young woman. "In that case, I wish you luck."

Mal nodded her thanks and the trio left.

"I don't like it," Heddlu said once the door closed.

"You never like anything," Darga replied. "That's what makes you a good spymaster."

"I'll tell you someone else who won't like it, Aza! He's got his own thing going with the Fifth Lancers and doesn't like interference."

The governor chuckled wryly. "Something tells me that little fireball there can handle Commander Aza. Look, this is a winning situation for us no matter what. If they succeed, they'll restore the peace. If they fail, it will finally resolve the Dreeat issue. Either outcome is acceptable and, in both cases, we will not have to commit any of our forces or funds."

"She still struck me as a loose wheel, a real wild card."

"I'm counting on it Heddlu. Just keep a close eye on the situation. I want constant updates."

The turine from Makatooa rang out across the Shallow Sea, cutting through the thick Kan fog. From the Vedette boat slicing through the water toward the harbor, Gavin counted sixteen chimes. The city was asleep and their arrival should go undetected.

They caught the odor of burnt charred wood long before any of the shapes of the buildings came into view.

"Smell that?" Gavin said with an evil smirk. "That's the reason I requested a change from Aris to here. I caught some chatter on the docks back in Tannimore. Makatooa's gonna be much better for us."

"All I smell is burnt," Aurek said, gingerly rubbing his fused knees. "This dampness is killing my knees."

"Be glad she didn't cave your head in," Tabor said, slicking back his damp hair. "The way you were smarting off to the mayor."

The outline of the decimated wharf came into view when they passed the turine in mid harbor.

"Shit, that must have been some fire!" Tabor said when they came up on the burnt-out docks.

"They say it took a quarter of the city," Gavin said. "Which should be perfect for us."

"How Gavin?" Orn asked, baffled.

"This place is still reeling in shock," Gavin replied, addressing everyone. "General lawlessness, with the city guards stretched thin. Then you got all those homeless people. They won't be missed. That makes them perfect slaves for our new employers back in Tannimore. Yep, I feel hunting is going to be good."

The *Drakin* silently dropped from a dark, moonless, Nocturn sky. Demetrius quickly leveled off just above the rainforest canopy of the Dasos region, in the Land of Mists. Checking his position out the windshield, the pilot did a few tight circles inches above the dense, multicolored foliage.

"We are here and not far off the mark," Demetrius triumphantly announced. "If my calculations are correct, Hai-Darr should be about ten miles in that direction."

Demetrius indicated the starboard window, with a nod and a large, satisfied grin.

"Wow, that was good," Okawa said, listening to the leaves of the tree's upper canopy gently brush against the bottom of the hull.

Demetrius gave her a wink. "I aim to please."

"Yes, you do," Okawa breathlessly acknowledged, placing a hand on his shoulder.

Demetrius's eyes twinkled. "I meant about my flying."

"That too."

Demetrius returned a salacious grin. "Okay, how do you want to work this?"

"The way I figure it, the Yagurs are the key. You need Yagurs to make Worrgs. We just need to position ourselves to intercept our jaguar friends and follow."

"Makes sense to me. Now all we have to do is… okay, what in the name of the gods is this?"

Demetrius flipped down his orange lenses and inhaled sharply. "Okay, this isn't good!" he said, reaching for the flap's control lever.

"What?" asked Okawa.

The *Drakin* began a vertical descent into the foliage.

"The sky's alive," Demetrius replied, nodding out the windshield.

Okawa looked out to see small, neatly separated heat blooms performing erratic circles across the horizon.

"More Ash-Ta," Demetrius reported, listening to the crunch of branches and rustle of leaves against the hull.

The airship slipped below the vegetation and the star filled sky disappeared from view. "They look nothing like the others," Okawa said quizzically.

Demetrius adjusted the controls to hover and the *Drakin* settled into its makeshift camouflaged nest. "They're not. These are from clan Acero. They usually travel in mated pairs. The good news is they're vegetarian."

"That is good news."

"Yeah, the bad news is in addition to the natural sonic abilities, their eyes are better than most other of their kind, so they can spot us easier. They're also larger than the other Ash-Ta clans. Some get as big as outer clan EEtah. They're strong enough to pull this craft apart."

"But you said they're vegetarian."

"This ship looks enough like a seed casing to interest them. Besides, I thought the whole idea of this was not to get spotted."

Okawa nodded and quickly glanced to her left when the nearby branches bent and swayed. Demetrius held a finger to his lips when a furry arm reached through the thick blanket of leaves mere feet from the nose of the Drakin. It grasped about blindly several times while squeaking and sniffing. Both humans held their breath as the grasping claws came within inches of the invisible hull twice.

Finally, it latched onto its intended target; a large bunch of fruit hanging nearby. With a squeal of victory, it yanked it back up through the outer canopy. Soon, the squawks of protest and squabbling over the prize reverberated through the treetops.

They silently stared through the branches for what seemed like an eternity while the man-bats devoured their meal. Then, without warning, the leaves violently fluttered again and the Ash-Ta took off.

Okawa heaved a sigh of relief and she locked eyes with Demetrius. Both had the same relieved smile.

"That was a little too close," Demetrius said, searching Okawa's face.

His relief was short lived when he saw her eyes widen at something just behind him.

"What?!" he asked, spinning about.

Stretching across the lower corner of the windshield, several inches thick, succulent type vines were creeping across the glass. The thousands of minute hairs which propelled them left viscous smoking trails.

Demetrius could now see a network of the invading flora covered the entire bow of the *Drakin*. Wherever the pale blue vine with dark blue leaves covered, the area beneath smoldered. Some of the creepers were already burrowing into the Ukko Wood hull.

"What are they!?" Okawa gasped, automatically reaching for her pistol.

"Don't know," Demetrius replied, spinning back to the controls. "They must have snuck up on us while we were distracted by our flying friends. We gotta get out of here!"

Demetrius quickly adjusted the controls and the airship lurched several times but refused to budge.

Okawa pulled her pistol and looked nervously about while a grim-faced Demetrius futilely tried to free the craft.

When he heard the stern of the ship crack, he glanced back at Okawa.

"Forget the pistol. Get your knife out," he said, getting up from his seat. "We gotta get out of this ship before it's too late."

Okawa traded the pistol for the dagger on her ankle while staring anxiously at the pilot.

"Pry out those Etheria disks from the overhead control panel. We're probably gonna need them."

174

"What about the rest of the Etheria on the ship?" Okawa asked, popping out the crystals and putting them in her shoulder bag. "We can't let it fall into anyone's hands."

The *Drakin* lurched turbulently when vines tore the stern completely off of the craft, exposing the cabin to the stifling humidity of the rainforest. The network of vines pulled the tail end away and begin to envelope it.

"There'll be nothing left to worry about," Demetrius said, watching the blue ramblers invade the open end of the ship.

Okawa finished retrieving the last Etheria Disk when the bow of the craft groaned in protest.

"What now?" she asked, dropping the gem into her bag.

"I'm working on it," Demetrius replied, just before the nose of the *Drakin* snapped.

Okawa watched the tendrils burn through the windshield, shattering it in several places. "Better make it fast!"

Demetrius was desperately peering around the compromised cabin, frantically searching for an answer to their perilous dilemma, when the Valdurian agent swept past him.

"Out of the way fly-boy. I've got an idea."

Rushing over to two small crates just inside the open stern, she pulled the canvas coverings off.

Tossing one over to Demetrius, she started making a three-inch slit near each corner. "Just do as I do."

The bow gave way, pulled creaking and groaning into the foliage, and quickly squelched any questions arising in the pilot's head. Cracks appeared in the upper hull when the tendrils crept inside and began ripping the airship in two.

Okawa slipped her hands through the slits, making a crude parachute.

"Okay, we're going out the back," she yelled as the craft rocked once more. "Jump through the middle of the vines. Open this up above you and aim for the small branches on the way down. They'll help break your fall!"

"That's got to be a hundred feet down!" Demetrius protested.

"Go!" Okawa barked before diving out of the opening and vanishing from view.

"This is crazy, this is crazy, this is crazy!" Demetrius repeated as he bolted out into the forest.

Demetrius felt the jerk on his arms when the canvas filled with air. Leaves rubbed against his face, making vision impossible. Branches and limbs snapped and broke in his rapid descent. The airship pilot landed with a clatter in the crown of a large bush twenty feet from Okawa.

Both stared helplessly, heaving with adrenalin, watching the forest noisily rend apart and devour the remains of the *Drakin*. They caught their breath while the sounds of nature around them slowly returned to normal.

"My ship!" Demetrius lamented, climbing to the ground on shaky legs.

"Worry about your ship later," Okawa said, checking her gear then pulling back the bolt on her pistol. "We're thousands of miles inside hostile territory, on foot and on our own."

"So, what's your read on the governor?" Mal asked when she and Alto stepped out onto the streets of Toriss.

"She struck me as a typical politician, who is not fond of rocking boats," Alto replied with a tilt of his head. "Her spymaster, now there is someone who bears watching."

Mal chuckled. "Spymasters always bear watching. At least we've got the pass," she said, patting the token inside her vest. "Hey, this didn't take nearly as long as I thought it would. We've got a little while before we meet back at the ship. What say we find us a drinking establishment?"

"I would very much like you buying me a drink." Alto said, nodding.

"Me!? I thought you were buying."

"Well, it was your idea and my recent dilemma has left me devoid of funds."

The sound of children approaching from behind interrupted any further playful banter between the two. Both peeked around to see a dozen boys and girls between the ages of eight and fifteen boisterously horsing around with one another while they walked. They dressed shabbily and—as with the rest of the populous—were completely bald. One of the young girls squealed in delight when she saw the strangers and the group ran over and surrounded them.

"I really don't do well with kids," Mal confided in a low voice when the children playfully swarmed, each trying to touch their hair.

"You were one once," Alto said in an amused tone while he gently reached out, touching their heads.

As soon as all had rubbed their hair and clothing, the crowd quickly moved off, their curiosity satisfied.

"It would seem that our hair fascinated them," Alto said, touching his shoulder length locks.

"Well, considering it's a rarity here, I can see why," Mal said. "They also seemed taken by our clothing."

"Given the way they dressed, I can understand."

After mentioning clothing, Mal reached up and stroked her vest. A look of wide-eyed shock descended on her face and she began frantically patting herself.

"THE PASS!" It's gone!" she shrieked. "Those little fuckers picked my pocket!"

Alto quickly checked himself. "They got nothing from me."

Mal didn't hear him. She had already taken off in the direction the crowd of juvenile thieves had gone, cursing all the way. Huffing in frustration, Alto followed.

The trail led them to the far wall of the cavern, to the large vertical slit which led to another grotto. There were two city guards standing at the opening.

"Did you just see a group of kids go in there?" Mal asked, out of breath.

"Yeah, we just chased a dozen Pappia in there."

"Why the fuck did you stop?!"

"They made it into the narrows, they're gone."

"What the fuck are you talking about?!"

"Slums, too easy for the people you're chasing to disappear. No one in there will talk to us much less help us, just the opposite. You take your life in your hands any time you go in there."

"Of all the fucking places that's where we've got to go. Without that pass we can expect zero cooperation from the river lords."

"I would also mention it is probably not a good idea to have a gang of thieves running around with the governor's pass."

Mal gave a resolved sigh and started for the opening. "All right, let's do this. Why is it all these types of places smell like someone just took a giant dump?"

Demetrius was miserable. The misty, humid air had plastered his clothing and hair against his skin. Were it not for his exertion crossing rough terrain, he would have been shivering in the cool temperature. The inconvenient fact remained that the vines destroyed his beloved *Drakin* right before his very eyes.

He and Okawa had been slogging through a dense rainforest of mostly blue and yellow plant life. No starlight penetrated the triple canopy above them, making the use of their Etheria laced spectacles essential.

Glancing down at the clear Calicite Etheria disk in his hand, he noticed they had veered off course by a few degrees. Pointing slightly to his right, Okawa, who was right behind him, pistol drawn, nodded.

They froze when they heard the fluttering of wings just ahead. After a brief assessment they determined the source was not Ash-Ta. Demetrius drew a deep breath steadying himself, then pocketed the Etheria navigation disk and drew his pistol.

Both looked questioningly at each other when they spotted a multi-colored light source through the trees and several heat signatures around it. Approaching cautiously, the sound of fluttering wings grew louder with each step.

Crouching behind a low bush, they peered into a small clearing. In the center was a large outcropping of boulders with a glowing field of raw Etheria Crystals in its center. The light filled the clearing in the jungle and both humans had to raise their orange lenses so as not to overwhelm their eyes.

Now they could clearly see the source of the flapping. Eight humanoid moths darted about the clearing in midair. Large, gently sloped, moth wings folded flat onto their back of their humanoid frames. Two compound eyes and antenna dominated each side of their insectoid head and a mouth lined with hairs cut vertically down the lower half of their face.

The five-foot-tall sentients tittered and squeaked in delight as they took turns alighting on the glowing crystals and licking the accumulated dew off them.

The Larimar disk in Okawa's bag was having a difficult time keeping up with translating and Demetrius shook his head, straining to understand what they were saying. He had encountered nothing like it before. Their high-pitched noises first appeared in his mind as complex three-dimensional geometric shapes before transforming into a language that the pilot recognized.

Demetrius now understood what was going on. This was a mating ritual. The solitary female with a large, distended belly occasionally left the Etheria mound only to fly around the clearing, enticing her seven potential suitors. With each pass, their several foot-long penises would undulate furiously.

When the female landed on the crystal and began licking it, each male would fly up behind her and slip their weeping protuberances between her legs while still airborne.

Giving a silent, knowing chuckle Demetrius motioned for them to move off, leaving the moth-men to their lusty pursuits. From the other side of the clearing came a sharp clack which startled everyone. With a loud whooshing sound, several large nets dropped down from the trees and ensnared the copulating sentients.

The once ecstatic squeaks and squeals coming from the moth-men, were now of panic and terror. A victory roar preceded two orange Tiikeri and three mongrels entering the clearing.

"What did I tell ya," said one Tiikeri to the other. "They're easy to catch when they're horny."

The other gave a salacious laugh stepping over to the female.

"Not only is she a meaty one," he assessed. "Look at that egg sack on her. It's full."

"Yeah, this was a good haul."

Demetrius's mouth dropped open in shock when a man-tiger produced a short sword and calmly cut the female's wings off.

The amputated female screeched in agony, flailing against her entanglements.

"She won't get away now," the Tiikeri said, looking around at the others. "Let's get the rest of these clipped and bagged we..."

The Tiikeri didn't get the next word out. Okawa looked on in helpless surprise. Demetrius suddenly stood, shouted and shot the assaulting Tiikeri.

The special bolt thundered out of the barrel with a deafening report and struck him squarely in the back. The velocity, torque and Na-Kab carbon tip caused the man-tiger's entire upper torso to explode, showering his companions in a fine red mist while his detached head flew into the nearby bushes.

Demetrius was pulling back the bolt to load another round when Okawa stood and shot the other with the same results.

The startled, blood-sprayed mongrels let out a panicked yelp and bolted into the jungle.

"Nice stealth there, Demetrius," Okawa said, putting away her pistol.

"Hey, I wasn't going to just stand by and let them slaughter these innocent sentients."

The moth people stared around in relieved shock as the humans cut them free. Upon release, all the males rushed around the female who was writhing in agony.

One reached down and gently touched her belly. "The eggs appear unharmed," he reported. "Quickly, get her back to Cocoonessa. We can still save the children."

Two gently took the moaning female by each arm and lifted off, vanishing into the moonless sky. The remaining males circled curiously around the humans.

"We thank you for saving us," one said, stepping up to them. "You are not from here."

"I have not seen your kind before either," Demetrius said with his best diplomatic smile. "But I didn't think you wanted to be a Tiikeri meal."

"We are called Tinian. Our kind is a favorite food for the tiger people. How is it you speak our language?"

"We have a talking crystal," Demetrius explained. "But even it is having a hard time keeping up. Your language is so complex."

"Coxeter, the language of the cocoon. Where is it you are bound?"

"It's going to sound strange, but we're headed for the city of the tigers."

This caused the moth-men to look around at each other in surprise.

"Much danger there!"

"Yeah, and it didn't help that we just splashed a couple of their hunters," Okawa said.

"We're specifically looking for their breeding place," Demetrius clarified.

"We know of this place. Lately Yagurs from the Northern Forest have been there often."

"Do tell," Okawa said, her voice trailing off.

"It is many miles away. A most dangerous journey on foot."

"We didn't start on foot," Demetrius woefully replied. "It just kinda worked out that way."

"Let us help you. It is the least we can do for you saving us."

Demetrius shrugged. "Sure, we could use a little help right about now."

"How?" Okawa asked, a touch of skepticism in her voice.

"Let us fly you there."

Both humans stared quizzically at each other.

Suddenly Okawa's eyes narrowed as an idea danced across her mind. "We shouldn't be there long; can you fly us out?"

"Yes."

"This mission might just be salvageable," the Valdurian agent said when Tinians stepped up on either side of her and took hold of her arms.

The cavern was narrow, tall and stretched as far as the eye could see. Openings of various sizes dotted both flanking walls. Beginning with the third level up, some entrances had wooden walkways spanning across the fifty-foot-wide main room. Mal could see the filthy faces of women, children, and the elderly all staring suspiciously as they entered.

"The Narrows huh," Mal said, gazing upward at the vast network of tunnels and catwalks. "From what I understand this was the old iron mines. Now it's home for the miners and any other undesirables the good folks of Toriss don't want to look at."

"Aptly named," Alto noted. "I can see why the city guards don't bother to follow. I fear we might never find our thieves."

"We don't need to find them," Mal said, cautiously scanning the surrounding squalor. "We only need to find one person."

"Oh?"

"Those kids were working as a gang. Gangs have leaders. That's who we need to find."

"Most astute, how do you propose we do that?"

"Oh, I've got a feeling with a little prompting they'll find us."

"Perhaps it was unwise to send Zau back to the ship?"

Mal shook her head. "This could get dicey. I want nothing to happen to my navigator."

Just ahead Mal could hear yelling followed by commotion. From one of the side-tunnels a bald young girl in a badly soiled tunic came rushing out, colliding into people. Four older teenage boys followed her, two of which held large knives.

"You fucking little bitch!" one screamed. "I'll cut your fucking hands off!"

The girl rushed past with a look of both excitement and fear. Mal and Alto traded amused glances.

"You're not going to leave that alone, are you?" Mal asked with a resigned tone.

Alto's face crinkled into a mischievous smile and he nonchalantly stuck his foot out at the exact moment the lead boy attempted to go by. The youngster tripped, plunging to the floor, dropping the knife. Right behind him, his three companions had no time to stop and they tumbled over their friend, screaming and cursing.

The swordmaster playfully shrugged. "You said you needed a prompt, and the girl *was* unarmed."

Mal and Alto calmly watched the thugs get to their feet. The young men were in their late teens, tall and muscular. Their bald heads stressed the look of rage on their faces. All wore simple dirty tunics and were barefoot.

"YOU MOTHERFUCKERS!" the lead boy screamed, picking up his fallen knife and brandishing it in their direction.

The others were instantly leery of Mal and Alto's calm demeanor.

"Is this on me?" Mal coolly asked Alto, ignoring the irate teens.

"The prompting was your idea," Alto replied in an equally serene voice.

Mal nodded and faced the angry group. "Sorry to disturb your little run there, but we need to talk. Besides, my boy here wouldn't let you do anything to the girl. See, she was unarmed and he's kinda got a thing about that."

"COCKY BITCH! I'LL FUCKING GUT YOU!"

The others had now completely dropped their aggressive attitude and seemed unnerved by the strangers.

Mal remained confidently tranquil with her arms at her side. "Yeah, you probably don't want to do that. See, I'm the only thing standing in the way of my boy here carving up you jerkoffs like a holiday roast. I'm also the one that can keep all of you from being slaughtered by the city guards."

"We'll see about that!" the young man growled before lunging at Mal.

Alto drew Defari and sliced upward in one stroke. The blade growled, severing the arm at the elbow. It dropped to the floor with a dull thud and the knife clattered harmlessly beside it.

The now one-armed youth was screaming, blood pumping from his severed limb. Stepping back, the others froze in shock, unsure whether to run. A stunned murmur went through the small crowd that had gathered.

"I'd get that looked at," the Spice Rat nonchalantly said.

The wounded thug spun to face his friends, painting the front of their tunics with crimson spray. Finally, shock set in and he fell to the floor beside his severed appendage.

"All right, looky here jerkoffs," Mal said to the remaining three. Her tone was now hard and decisive. "Believe it or not I'm here to save your miserable asses. So, what say we quit fucking around and you get me in to see the head jerkoff before shit really gets ugly."

Mal peered into the cup of cloudy liquid then back up at Alto. "I sure hope this shit tastes better than it looks."

Alto chuckled. "You were not specific when you ordered ale."

"Something tells me it wouldn't have made any difference."

"Probably not," Alto replied before taking a sip. "Actually, this is not bad."

Mal glanced around the small pub, hewn from solid rock. It was only thirty-square-feet with half a dozen tables and benches also carved from the floor. There were only a few elderly patrons this early in the day and being the only ones with hair, the two strangers received quite a few stares.

"I sure hope they find this Lord of Thieves soon," Mal said, shifting on the hard stone bench. "The furniture around here is killing my ass."

When she looked back at Alto, he was staring at the open door and smiling. There, peeking around the corner was the young girl they had seen chased earlier. With a reassuring nod of his head, he waved her over. She smiled and blushed but remained just outside the opening.

"Uh, I really don't do well with kids," Mal said, lifting the glass to her lips.

Alto ignored the statement and continued to beckon to the child. "It's all right, we won't hurt you."

Keeping her shy smile, she slowly approached. Mal guessed her age to be about nine. She was thin and wiry, with golden brown skin. Her bald head and filthy appearance did not diminish her beauty. Her face was perfectly symmetrical, with full lips and dark almond-shaped eyes.

"What is your name?" the swordmaster asked in an overly friendly voice.

She bashfully glanced back and forth from Alto to Mal. "Taleeka."

"That's a pretty name. My name is Alto and this is Mal."

"I, I just wanted to thank you."

"You are very welcome. I am at your service. Would you care to sit down?"

She didn't reply but climbed up on the bench next to Alto.

"You sure can run fast. Why were those boys chasing you?"

Pausing, she looked down and fidgeted with her hands. "They caught me stealing food."

"Are you still hungry?"

She nodded.

"Well now, before we leave, we will have to make sure you get a decent meal," Alto offered.

Mal threw Alto an irritated glance for making the promise.

"You are strangers. Why are you here? No one ever visits the Narrows, at least not on purpose."

"Something was stolen from us and we're here to get it back," Mal said, finally speaking up.

"Lots of stolen things find their way here. The Narrows is a big and dangerous place. How are you going to find it?"

"We're not. Your Lord of Thieves is going to give it up."

A startled look crossed Taleeka's face. "You actually sought out Pangeran, the Lord of Thieves?"

Mal downed the rest of her drink. "Yep, the ones that were chasing you will bring us to him any time now."

Taleeka's eyes darted about nervously. "That is very dangerous."

"We don't have the time to go searching for it. We'll just have to persuade him to turn it over."

"What is it?"

"It's a golden card about this big," Mal said, showing the dimensions with her hands.

"I know of this. I don't think you're going to be able to convince him."

Mal chuckled. "We're gonna give it a try. How did you hear about it?"

"News travels fast around here. The word is Pangeran really took a liking to it, so much that he claimed it for his own."

"No honor among thieves," Alto said.

"As Thief lord it is his right."

"Yeah well, I hope he hasn't gotten too attached to it, cuz he's gonna have to cough it up. Fuck, he probably doesn't even know what it is."

"It's gold. That's all he cares about."

Mal disdainfully shook her head and scoffed.

"I can help!" Taleeka said enthusiastically.

Mal gave a placating smile. "Thanks, but…"

"No, I really can! I know my way around and I can do stuff."

Her zeal genuinely impressed Mal. "I don't think…"

"I know Pangeran. He's stubborn. Now that he's claimed it, he won't give it to you."

"How could you help?" Alto gently asked.

"I told you, I can do stuff. I only want one thing."

"Here it comes," Mal quipped.

Taleeka took on a pleading look. "When you leave, take me with you."

The request completely took Mal aback. "Out of the question! No!"

"I won't be any bother," she pleaded. "You can drop me off in the next city you visit. Please!"

"No, look if you think it's dangerous around here, traveling with us is *really* dangerous."

"Not so fast," Alto said.

"Are you fucking kidding me? Like our job won't be hard enough!"

"I'm sure there is some place we…"

There was a sudden commotion at the door. Mal and Alto looked over to see six scowling thugs enter and head their way. Out of the corner of his eye Alto could see Taleeka was gone.

"I believe our welcoming committee has arrived," Alto said, standing up.

The young men formed a semicircle around the table and one with an acne scarred complexion stepped forward.

"You killed my friend," he sneered at Alto.

The swordmaster gave a shallow bow. "I am truly sorry for your loss."

"Yeah, fuck you. We'll settle up later, right now the lord wants to see you."

Alto was unfazed by the open hostility. "That is most fortunate, because we too wish to speak with him."

The young ruffian eyed him contemptuously up and down. "You talk funny. Come on, let's go."

They led them down a series of tunnels, each one getting narrower and less populated. They halted in front of a wide double doorway.

The size of the room surprised Alto. It had probably served as a mine staging area. There were two wide tunnels in the wall to his left. On the far wall was a smaller single room. Running along all the walls, carved just below the tall ceiling were rows of rectangular air shafts. In the center of the room was a foot-tall circular riser.

There were a dozen shabby looking bald children of all ages lounging around the riser's edge. A young man the swordmaster estimated to be in his late teens occupied the lone chair in the center of the stage. His robe was open, revealing a chiseled naked frame. Kneeling before him were two fully clothed girls, who were giving him an enthusiastic double blowjob. The girls worked expertly as a team, up and down the saliva-soaked shaft. Other children around the chair—as well as the twenty standing about the room—completely ignored the lewd spectacle, instead concentrating on them leading Mal and Alto before the Thief Lord's throne.

The pair traded a quick disbelieving glance at the traditionally intimate moment on display for all to see.

A normally private act, not so private, Alto thought, catching himself fidgeting on the hilt of his sword.

Pangeran, head thrown back and eyes closed, was panting hard. With a grunt, his hips convulsed, and he began ejaculating into one of the girl's mouths. The other, who was down by his balls, quickly joined her partner at the head, greedily devouring their leader's seed. They could barely swallow the fountain of creamy white liquid which now coated all around their mouths and chins. He finally looked up with a lustfully savage smile. Putting his hands on both their heads he shoved their faces forcefully down on his still erupting member.

The girls, despite their young age, were undaunted in their oral assault. Finally, with a loud cry of pleasure the geyser slowed to a trickle and the prince relaxed. Catching his breath, he watched the girls clean off his shrinking organ and each other's faces with their mouths.

A look of cold cruelty descended on him when he focused on Alto and Mal. Roughly shoving the girls aside, he stood and closed his robe.

"You killed one of my men this morning," he said with a calm contempt.

"We were defending ourselves," Mal defiantly replied.

"Normally I would have you killed on the spot, but I just got my knob polished and that always puts me in a better mood."

"I can't stop you from trying to kill us," Mal said, tone icy.

"My people tell me your friend there is pretty handy with a blade. But I doubt if he could kill us all before we overtook you."

Mal scoffed and glanced around at their youthful captors. "Wanna bet?"

Pangeran paused, and all eyes were now on the brash strangers. Alto stood silently. From the corner of his eye, he spotted movement near the ceiling behind the Thief Lord and his entourage.

Alto discreetly watched Taleeka silently exit an air vent to his right and shimmy along the sheer wall toward the door behind them.

'*I can do stuff,*' he silently reflected on her plea. *Indeed.*

Pangeran gave a superior smile. "Like I said, I'm in a much calmer mood. My people also said you wanted to talk to me, so talk."

Mal now spotted the young girl slip into the shaft above the door. She remained focused on the prince so as not to give her away.

"Your people stole something from me and I want it back."

This caused the Thief Lord to laugh. "I'm not in the habit of returning items my people might come across. What was it?"

"A golden card."

"Ah yes, beautifully engraved," he recalled. "I liked it so much I claimed it for myself."

"You don't even fucking know what it is!"

"It's gold and it pleases me. That's all I need to know."

"Not quite, there's one more important thing you need to know."

"And what would that be?"

"That card was on loan to me from the governor. She's going to want it back."

The lord of thieves sorrowfully shook his head. "It sounds important. You should have been more careful."

Mal gave a frustrated sigh. "Look numbnuts, you and your kiddy gang are way out of your league on this one. It is important. Too important for the governor to let you keep it."

From above the door Mal watched Taleeka climbing out of the air vent. Gripped between her teeth was the Governor's Golden Pass.

"Let the city guards try to find it."

Mal shook her head. "You don't get it do you? This isn't just some expensive bauble you pilfered. This is enough for the governor to take his spymaster and city guards off their leash. They will clear out the Narrows and take it back over all your dead bodies."

Pangeran laughed again, thoroughly unconvinced. "The governor doesn't have it in her."

"The governor might not, but her spymaster sure does. He will have no problem killing all you greedy little fuckers. And because it's the governor, they'll have plenty of muscle and steel for the job."

Off to the right a young girl squealed in alarm and pointed to the wall behind them.

All turned to see Taleeka scrambling across the wall back to the opening she arrived from.

"MY PRIZE!" Pangeran screamed, watching Taleeka disappear into the air vent. "GET IT!"

The opening was much too small for the larger youths. Several in their late teens handed their knives to two small boys and boosted them up to the shaft.

"Bring me back my prize, and her head!"

The young boys nodded, their faces hardened and cruel beyond their years. They scrambled off after the thief.

Alto cleared his throat above the chaos. "Well, it would appear you are no longer in possession of that which we came for. We shall take our leave."

"The fuck you will!" the Thief Lord yelled, pointing at them. "You're involved in this!"

Alto locked eyes with the irate leader and drew his blade.

"We are leaving," he said, in a commanding voice over Defari's low growl. "Your people can either get out of our way or we will remove them."

"Get 'em!" the Thief Lord ordered and three large youths immediately charged.

Defari loudly howled slashing across the first two. A trail of blood arced outward following the blade. It painted a gruesome red stripe across several nearby children.

The third young man was unarmed and froze when he saw his two companions fall. Trembling, he stared down a growling Etheria blade and the man wielding it.

"I have no wish to harm an unarmed man," Alto's tone was calm and confident. "Stand aside."

Mal had now drawn her weapon and was pointing it toward the crowd steadily creeping up on them.

"They just killed two of your brothers right before your eyes!" Pangeran screamed and pointed. "Are you going to let them get away with it?!"

The leader's rallying cry emboldened all but the one facing Alto. Stepping aside, his fear laden stare never left the tip of the blade.

The advancing mob was growing more aggressive by the moment. While Alto opened the door, Mal kept the tip of her thin bladed rapier pointed at several who led the hostile group near.

When one began slashing, Mal lunged, plunging the tip of her blade into the assaulting shoulder socket. The attacker screamed, dropped his knife and clutched the bleeding wound. The one beside him didn't move quick enough. He froze when he felt the bloody tip press against his throat.

"Back off, ass wipe!" Mal growled.

The latest round of violence had a sobering effect on the youthful throng, allowing Alto and Mal to back out the doors.

They looked on in stunned silence when Alto lingered in the doorway, holding his sword out in front of him, tip facing down. Releasing his grip on the hilt the blade stayed aloft, hovering in mid-air, growling.

"Guard," was Alto's solitary command before he and Mal sprinted down the hall. He heard Defari's howl and knew some attempted to follow.

Once they made it around the corner, both froze. Taleeka crouched in a nearby doorway. She clutched the pass tightly to her chest while she quaked in fear. Two young boys were taunting her as they crept closer. The knives they brandished were too large for their hands and looked deadly yet out of place.

"Come on," one taunted. "We ain't gonna hurt ya."

"Taleeka!" Mal cried out.

They turned to face the escaping pair. Taleeka's face brightened with hope but fell again when a sharp knife edge pressed against her neck.

"Come any closer and I'll fucking kill her!"

Alto held out his hand and whistled. Defari flew into his grip with a bark and a growl.

The swordmaster stared down the startled youths. "Then there will be three corpses on the floor here today."

The growling sword proved too intimidating and the boys broke and ran.

"Come on!" Mal said, turning to run. "The others can't be far behind."

"This way," Taleeka said, opening the door she had been cowering against. "I know a quicker way."

Mal's warning proved correct. They had just enough time to step inside and close the door when they heard the angry mob pass.

Taleeka heaved a sigh of relief and pointed down the hall they were standing in. "This will get us back to the city."

"Uh," Mal expectantly said, pointing to the pass in her hands. "I believe that's mine."

"Oh yeah," Taleeka said, blushing and placing it into Mal's outstretched hands.

Mal slipped the pass back into her vest. "Well kid I gotta admit, you got skills."

"I told you I could do stuff."

"You sure did."

"So, does this mean I can come along?"

"Well, we sure can't leave you here. Not with the Lord of Thieves as an enemy."

Taleeka's face lit up. "Yay!"

"Before you get on *my* ship, you're gonna get a bath and some new clothes."

"I'm still hungry too."

"Don't worry kid. We'll scare you up something to eat."

Blood in the water.
Rippled sand of the Shallow Sea below.
Mother swimming off, never to meet again
The nurses from House Nur swimming behind her, devouring the afterbirth and the remains of his brother he'd consumed in the womb.
Then arguing while examining him.
"Too small, too weak. Banish to the outer clans."
"No, he has proved himself before being born. His brother was twice his size."
"What Sunal will have him? He is too small."
"It will be difficult for him but he has a fierce heart. You will see."

Fassee, of Adad Sunal came to. He had drifted with the current along the Zerian Reef since falling asleep. The best he could judge he was closer to his original destination, the seaport of Makatooa.

Righting himself, he felt his feet sink into the sandy bottom and he took off at a steady pace through the water.

The charred, floating debris was the first thing that told the EEtah investigator something was amiss, the broken pilings of docks burnt down to the waterline was the next.

Something bad had happened here and he wondered if it had anything to do with his assignment.

"So how come you like theatre so much?" Kem asked as they turned the corner and headed for the docks.

A placid look of recollection came across Velitel's face. "About twenty grands ago when I was with the Maritime Legion, we got shore leave in Dryden. I remember there were some street performers putting on a skit from a play debuting that very Kan. I liked what I saw so much, while my comrades spent their money getting drunk and arrested, I spent mine on a ticket to the play. It was called 'Kulla e Qelqit, The Glass Tower!' The entire thing was in Valdur-Ya, I couldn't understand a word of it! But the production, absolutely glorious! They held it in The Grand Dryden Theatre! The Dryden Orchestra provided the score!"

Velitel was now shaking his head in ecstasy at the remembrance. "And of course, there I was, a sixteen-year-old Legionnaire who's fresh off fighting Yupik in the Narrow Lands and I'm watching this, this... spectacle of the gods, right there on stage! I was a changed man after that. When I mustered out and came back, I actually tried to open a theatre company here."

Kem smiled in surprise. "Really?! What happened?"

"Well, let's just say that Makatooa isn't as sophisticated as Dryden. And I had never run a theatre before."

They stopped when they turned the last corner and saw the bodies on the partially burnt dock.

"Time to go to work," Velitel said with a sigh.

"This is gonna get a lot worse before it gets better," Kem said rubbing the back of her neck walking amongst the six dead bodies. "It looks like some of Javoko's goons had a run in with a few of Asad's Wharfies during the Kan," Kem continued, studying the grisly scene.

Velitel shook his head in dismay looking out over the scorched remnants of Makatooa's wharf. "They're fighting over charred remains. Unbelievable."

"My guess is Javoko is trying to take advantage of Asad's territory being destroyed." Kem said, kneeling over one body.

An EEtah's head emerged from the water interrupting the inspection of the crime scene. They curiously watched the humanoid shark wade ashore between a row of scorched pilings.

"That's the smallest EEtah I've ever seen," Velitel said, watching Fassee emerge from the sea and head their way.

Standing, Kem grunted in agreement.

"What in the name of the gods happened here?" Fassee asked, surveying the destruction and bodies.

"Nobody can say we don't know how to put on an exciting show in Makatooa," Velitel said, eyeing the EEtah who was only as tall as him.

"So I see," Fassee said, before catching himself under Velitel's questioning gaze. "Oh, sorry, Fassee from Adad Sunal. I'm here looking into the death of one of our boys a few cycles ago. I've got to check the body before it's turned over to House Nur for immersion."

"Hmm, I'm not familiar with that Sunal," Velitel quizzically said.

Fassee chuckled. "I'm not surprised. There aren't many of us. We handle the policing for House Bran. And I'm betting you two are with the city guards."

"I'm Velitel," he said, clasping forearms with the man-shark, "they tell me I'm in charge. This is Kem, she knows things."

Fassee nodded at the petite female. "Commander and spymaster, just the people I need to see."

A young guard walking over to them interrupted the pleasantries. "Commander, you're going to want to have a look at this."

Velitel gave a heavy sigh and exchanged a troubled glance with Kem.

"Mind if I tag along?" Fassee asked, noting the looks on their faces.

"Suit yourself," Velitel said, starting off behind the young man. "We can probably use another pair of eyes."

They led them a short distance to the burnt-out shell of Asad's main warehouse. Fire reduced the front of the building to ashes and charred the interior walls black. Several guards stared at the back wall.

The remains of a body leaned against the burnt partition, with both arms and legs severed and stacked in a neat pile beside the propped-up torso. Dried blood covered the surrounding floor. Painted on the wall above the corpse was a crude drawing of what appeared to be wings. The crimson artwork contrasted eerily against the black wall.

"What the..." Velitel muttered, taking in the grisly spectacle.

"That's one of Asad's men," Kem said, staring at the body's face, frozen in a silent and horrified scream.

"Is this some new gang ritual?" Velitel asked, examining the pile of limbs. "They've never dismembered before."

"I wonder what that symbol means?" Kem said, studying the drawing.

"Don't ask me," Fassee said, shaking his head. "I just got here. One thing though, look at his right hand."

"His pinkie's gone." Kem noted, bewildered. "And it's not with the rest of the body parts."

"Maybe someone is taking souvenirs," Fassee offered.

"None of the others had it done to them." Velitel said.

"None of the others were chopped up either," Fassee replied.

"The bodies outside were the result of a gang squabble," Kem said, gazing over at Velitel. "This is something else."

Velitel nodded then waved over two of his city guards. "I want Javoko and Asad in my office before the end of the cycle. Take as many men as you need."

The guards left and Fassee surveyed the scene one more time.

"Well, this has been fun, but if you can have someone take me to the city's municipal center, I can start my own investigation."

"Sure, but there's not much left," Velitel remorsefully said. "The whole area around the administrative buildings burned."

"I'd still like to see it."

"One of my men will escort you. I'd take you myself, but it looks like I'm going to be babysitting a couple of gang leaders today."

Matka Sorbornef gazed out the second-story window down onto the sprawling grounds of her family's Staghorn estate. The South lawn was ready, guests were arriving and her daughter had finally stopped crying.

Across the room, Nikki Sorbornef examined herself in the full-length mirror. Her mother's royal blue, lace wedding dress fit perfectly and the makeup covered her puffy eyes.

"You look beautiful Mz. Nikki," Alpin said, collecting the ends of the waist sash behind her.

Nikki gave a sad smile but said nothing while the houseslave tied it.

"We must make this knot just right," the servant continued. "Just tight enough to show off your shape, but loose enough that your new husband can quickly undo it for the consummation."

The suggestiveness of Alpin's last comment almost started a new wave of tears. The thought of having sex with a man she didn't know, in front of a crowd of people, terrified her.

"And now the veil," Alpin said before draping the blue lace covering over her. "There! Now you are ready to step into your new life."

"That will be all Alpin," Matka said, joining her daughter at the mirror.

The servant nodded and left.

"This is a great day for both you and our family," Matka said, peering over her daughter's shoulder into the mirror. "This marriage and alliance will secure our house as one of the most powerful of all the river lords."

Nikki remained silent and her mother continued. "Then, if the gods smile upon us, Adrik Targoff will put a baby in that belly of yours."

Nikki still said nothing when her father poked his head into the room.

"It's time," he said, beaming.

"Do yourself and all of us a favor," Matka sternly said, "When your father lifts the veil, be smiling."

Nikki continued her silence and followed her parents downstairs. She paused at the open door to the South lawn and took in the scene unfolding before her.

There were easily fifty people of all ages standing on either side of an unfurled strip of gold colored linen. The temporary pathway crossed the lawn and ended just before an archway—created by two tall saplings ten feet apart—bowed over and connected at the top.

Standing just under the arch was a priest of the earth god Toma. He was completely nude and long thin sprigs of vegetation hanging down to his waist replaced his hair.

Standing to his right was Adrik Targoff.

This was the first time Nikki had ever laid eyes on the young head of House Targoff. She was relieved that he was handsome, with his short black hair and beard. His eyes radiated intensity and a formal blue wedding robe covered his six-foot frame. She noticed the beard part and the corners of his mouth pull upward in a smile when he saw her.

Walking down the aisle, the faces of the people on either side were a blur. Several times she had to fight the urge to flee, so she kept her eyes straight ahead. Realizing her heart was pounding when they finally came to a stop before the arch, she took in a deep breath.

This was it.

Nikki vaguely heard her father giving the declaration of her identity and she forced a smile before he lifted the head covering and veil. Both parents then gave her a peck on each cheek before they joined her brothers and sisters on the side.

The young Targoff clearly liked what he saw and his face changed from a warm smile into a lecherous grin.

The priest had them face each other as he spoke. Nikki could barely discern what he was saying over the roaring in her ears. She heard herself reply in the affirmative when prompted but was unsure what he asked.

Then came the dagger, a thin bladed ceremonial one. With their right wrists together, the priest passed it between. She saw the blood but didn't feel any pain. Now, holding their bleeding wounds together, she knew she had reached the point of no return. She was now bound by blood to this man she had just met.

The binding of their wrists to each other immediately followed. It signified their bond, as well as aiding in stopping the bleeding.

Next came the white bird, long a symbol of purity and love. Using the same dagger, she watched him cut open the bird's chest. A flood of crimson flowed, staining its beautiful white feathers. The priest then sprinkled blood on both their heads before removing its heart.

Offering up the small bloody object, Nikki was too numb to feel revulsion as Adrik took a bite. When the priest placed the remainder in her mouth, she almost gagged at the slick salty morsel. It was chewy and she quickly swallowed to get it out of her mouth.

The priest then stepped back, raised his hands and face to the heavens and declared them man and wife.

Their first kiss, with bloody lips, was hard and rough. Not at all what she expected. His beard scratched her face and she wondered if she would ever grow used to it.

The crowd broke into applause and Adrik gruffly turned her so they both faced the audience. With one arm firmly around her waist he raised his other fist in victory.

Once the clapping and cheering waned a voice in the crowd called out "consummate." The guests quickly picked up the demand and began enthusiastically chanting it. A dozen of the guests then surrounded the couple and escorted them down the aisle while disrobing them. The rest of the cheering group followed. By the time they reached the feast tables both were completely naked.

Nikki trembled, she began nervously perspiring and her mouth felt dry. Surely all could see her anxiety. Being a tomboy, she had never entertained the idea of having sex before, especially in such a public manner. Tradition held they must consummate the marriage before witnesses for it to be considered legitimate.

Spreading her legs, he bent Nikki over the table.

"Don't worry wife," he whispered in her ear. "This is just for show. After the feast I'll give you a proper fucking."

Nikki felt the cool smoothness of the wood on her chest and cheek as he held her firmly down.

Tears flowed and she cried out when she felt the searing pain of penetration.

The guests were cheering and chanting wildly as Adrik Targoff pumped away with furious abandon. No one paid attention to the bride, who was now sobbing openly. An approving cheer rang out when they saw the blood trickle down the back of her legs.

Don and Matka Sorbornef stood side by side. Don was glowing with pride and accomplishment. On this day he had delivered his daughter, pure and untainted, into the hand of marriage.

And he now had his army.

Sitting on the side of a low hill, Demetrius and Okawa peered through the thick foliage onto the mist covered trail below. To the South was the Tiikeri capital of Hai-Darr, to the North lay the Great Northern Forest of the Arboro region.

"Ouch!" Demetrius said, swatting a small black and red bug on his arm.

Okawa gave a knowing smile. "I've pulled a few jungle operations before. The bad part about spending any time in the bush, is that everything is trying to eat you. And I'm not just talking about the big predators."

"I'd much rather be flying over the jungle," Demetrius confessed. "Of course, I don't have a ship anymore, so that's out."

"I wouldn't be too worried about that. If we make it out of here, I'm sure the Valdurian crown will secure you another ship. I just hope the Tinians will make good on their promise."

"That's the one thing I wouldn't worry about," Demetrius replied. "All the races I've encountered, except for humans and Tiikeri, are pretty good at keeping their word."

A noise down the trail caused Okawa to shush the chatty pilot.

They saw the standard first. The open triangle surrounding a single paw print fluttered atop a tall pole carried by a fawn-colored mongrel. Okawa's eyes narrowed suspiciously at the procession when it came into view.

An orange Tiikeri led the small group, followed by the mongrel standard bearer. Male Singa guards surrounded the four robed Yagurs, one on either side and one bringing up the rear.

They passed silently by the camouflaged humans and disappeared into the mist, marching steadily Southward.

"Well, the Tinians were right about the Yagurs," Demetrius noted.

"Yep," Okawa replied, standing. "And at their pace it shouldn't be hard to keep up."

They followed at a distance, always keeping the Tiikeri standard in view. The passing regular foot traffic forced them to seek cover several times, but the trek proved uneventful overall.

The moon was setting when the party arrived at a U-shaped building on the outskirts of Hai-Darr. A manicured garden surrounded the entrance and extended to a grotto below.

Crouching in the jungle, they watched as the Yagurs disappeared into the cave mouth. The lone Tiikeri went into the building while the Singas stood guard outside.

"The Kharry Institute," Okawa said, studying the grounds. "This is where it all happens. I gotta figure a way to get in there."

"Wait!" Demetrius hurriedly whispered. "I thought we were just supposed to spy on the place?"

"Your mission was to get me here. Mine is a little more complicated."

"How are you going to do it?"

"I'm thinking."

Under a late morning sun, the *Haraka* followed the mighty Otoman River Southward.

"Would you look at all that river traffic!" Zau marveled, peering out the side window.

Mal did a quick confirming glance out her side of the cockpit. "Yep, Otomoria provides a good portion of the grain for the whole Goyan Islands. Most of those barges head for the port of Locian."

"So, we're headed for some kind of fort?"

"Yeah, Fort Erod is on the Western side of the upper delta. Home of the Fifth Eldorian Lancers. I'm going to have a little chat with their commander and find out why they're not doing their fucking job."

Taleeka's laughter cut through the cabin.

"Do it again! Do it again!" she joyously squealed.

Both turned back to see the bald nine-year-old bouncing on Zaad's knees as Alto and Wostera looked on with broad grins.

"Cute kid," Zau said, with an amused chuckle.

"We're gonna be dropping her off in the next big city." Mal declared, a touch of uncertainty creeping into her voice.

"I don't know. Looks like everyone's getting kind of attached back there."

"We cannot keep a kid around. It's just too fucking dangerous."

"I thought you said she had skills?"

"She does, but this is still no place for a child."

"I'm hungry," Taleeka said when her laughter died down.

"And besides that," Mal whispered. "She hasn't stopped eating."

"Poor kid, this is probably the most food she's had maybe in her whole life."

"Yeah well, the first big city and we're kicking her loose."

"Uh-huh," Zau replied, thoroughly unconvinced.

"I'm serious!"

"Uh-huh."

"All right, we're here," Mal announced, happy to get away from the conversation.

The circular walled compound sat beside the spot where the river broke into dozens of watery fingers which would become the Otoman Bayou. Eventually each of the tributaries would empty into the Shallow Sea. Surrounding agricultural fields stretched to the horizon, with horse pens and stables just outside the North wall.

"There are a few small plazas but not enough room to put down inside. Set us beside the front gate Kumo."

"Yes Captain."

The airship circled the fort while it slowly descended and Mal could see they were drawing attention from the curious inhabitance. Doors were opening and people were coming out of the half a dozen buildings to look.

By the time the craft settled into a spot hovering inches above the ground, a small crowd of uniformed men had gathered.

"Okay let's go get some questions answered," Mal said, getting to her feet. "Alto and Wostera, you're with me. Zau, you and Zaad are going to be a novelty in these parts. Engage with the troops and see if you can find anything out. Kumo, you and Taleeka stay with the ship."

"I wanna go!" Taleeka whined between bites of the meat stick in her hand.

"No!"

With a huff and a pout Taleeka took another bite.

"Perhaps it might be beneficial if she were to stretch her legs?" Alto said, slipping his blades into his sash.

"I can keep an eye on her Captain," Zaad offered.

"What are you guys, a fucking comedy team? A military base is no place for a young girl. No!"

"Sorry kid," Zaad said, patting her head.

Kumo popped the side hatch and it became a ramp, extending out to a small sea of inquisitive faces.

Mal went out first, raising her hand in salutation. "Greetings Lancers, is your commander about?"

Her question remained unanswered. Just as she thought, all were gasping in astonishment at the female Singa and man-shark.

The inquisitive lancers quickly gathered around and Mal noticed a disturbance at the rear of the crowd.

"Get out of the damn way," a gruff voice bellowed.

The men parted and a uniformed man in his early fifties with a closely cropped gray beard and beret pushed his way through.

"What in the name of the gods is going on out here?!" he yelled.

He halted suddenly and his mouth dropped open when he saw Zaad.

"Are you the commander?" Mal asked.

"This is an active military base," he growled, stepping up antagonistically to the Spice Rat. "State your business!"

With a superior smirk Mal reached into her vest, retrieved the Governor's Golden Pass and held it up.

"If you're the commander I'm here to talk with you," she smugly said.

The commander's demeanor went from irate to begrudgingly annoyed upon seeing the golden card.

"This way," he spat.

Not waiting for a reply, he spun and took off at a brisk pace. "Sergeant, you're with me," he barked to a young lancer without breaking stride.

Mal, Alto and Wostera followed the two Lancers into one of the central buildings and into a spacious office with walls decorated with military regalia.

The commander pivoted and faced them the moment the door closed.

"I'm Commander Aza and that's my Lead Patrol Sergeant Cavus.

Mal introduced the group, noticing that Aza wouldn't look her in the eye and bristled when the Spice Rat identified the women.

"Very well," he curtly began, staring at Alto. "You came here to talk to me. What do you want to talk to me about?"

"The Dreeats and the River Lords," Mal said.

Aza threw Mal an irritated side glance before concentrating back on Alto. "What about them?"

Mal scowled at the commander's rudeness.

"Unless something is done, the Dreeats are going to be slaughtered."

Aza kept his gaze fixed on Alto. "There are skirmishes between those…"

Mal finally had enough. "Hey pal, I'm over here!"

The Lancer Commander abruptly stopped and slowly faced the Spice Rat with beady eyes and a tensely clenched jaw.

"We are not used to having those of your gender in our midst." He growled.

"Yeah, well tough shit, because your king and governor have sent me!" Mal snapped. "We're here to make sure a genocide doesn't happen."

"My *men* can handle the situation around here! We don't need you!"

"With all due respect Commander," Alto said, taking a step forward. "If you were handling the situation, our presence would be unnecessary."

Aza eyed the swordmaster with contempt.

"I don't think I like you very much," he sneered.

Alto shrugged. "Then it is fortunate that I am neither under your command nor seek your approval."

Both men's eyes locked in a tense moment.

"Look Commander," Mal said, to get the meeting on a more productive footing. "I'm not here to piss in anyone's pond, but I've got a job to do and I might need your assistance."

Aza finally broke his death stare at Alto. "The situation with the Dreeat and the Lords of the Western Fork is delicate. I don't need outsiders bumbling around making the situation worse."

"The situation is already worse. The powers-that-be have had it with delicate. I and my team are the blunt instrument of the crown."

"I don't know what you can do. The conflict between human and Dreeat has been going on a long time."

Mal gave a confident smile. "I can be very persuasive. You just make sure you've got some of your Lancers ready to go on a moment's notice. If something's going to happen, it will be in the next few cycles."

"Yeah, I'll do just that," Aza's voice dripped with sarcasm.

"Commander, I don't need to remind you what this means," Mal said, waving the golden card. "Just have them ready. Now, if there's nothing else."

"Yes, I've got work to do. The sergeant will show you out."

Sergeant Cavus opened the door and led them down a short hall to the front entrance.

"The Commander is taking money from the River Lords," Cavus said in a low voice after looking around. "He has had me deliberately keeping patrols away from Dreeat territory."

Mal scoffed and gave Cavus a determined stare. "Luckily, my authority supersedes his right now. Make sure you have a decent size contingent of Lancers in the area."

"The Commander will do everything in his power to try to stop that from happening."

"Just quietly reroute them. It's only for a few cycles."

Cavus shook his head and exhaled loudly.

"Use me as an excuse if he finds out. Right now, I technically out rank him and I'm giving you a direct order."

"Yes ma'am."

"If he fucks us on this, I will personally shove one of those lances so far up his wrinkled ass you'll think he's a Bailian meat stick!"

Cavus chuckled. "I'm sure a number of us would like to watch that. He's despised by the men."

They all could hear Taleeka's peals of laughter beyond the door.

Mal closed her eyes and sighed. "Give me strength." She glanced back at Cavus. "Thank you, Sergeant. I hope we won't need you."

Mal opened the door to find Zau and Zaad standing by the *Haraka* casually chatting with a small group of Lancers. With the swooping motion of Zau's arms she was no doubt regaling the curious troops about the wonders of flight. Taleeka was running around the courtyard playing tag with one of the younger soldiers. Right now, he had caught her and had lifted her off the ground in an enthusiastic hug. Taleeka squealed in delight.

"HEY!" Mal's stern voice reverberated across the plaza.

Everyone froze, then turned to look at the annoyed Spice Rat, glaring with hands on her hips.

The young Lancer quickly put Taleeka down with a sheepish look. "Sorry ma'am, we were just fooling around. She reminds me of my little sister."

Mal ignored the explanation. "I thought I told you to stay in the ship young lady."

Taleeka looked down at the ground, fidgeting. "It was such a nice day and... I'm sorry."

"Zaad was right there," Alto said. "I seriously doubt if he would allow any harm to befall her."

Walking over to the ship, Mal gave him an unamused look. "You know, between the two of you, you're going to drive me fucking crazy."

Once airborne Mal spun in her chair and saw Taleeka fiddling with something in her hands.

"What's that?"

The nine-year-old immediately shielded it from view. "Nothing."

"Taleeka..."

Begrudgingly, she held up a small folding, multi-function utility knife. She'd managed to open half a dozen various fine tools.

"A knife! Where did you get that?"

"One of the soldiers," she innocently said.

"You lifted it from one of those Lancers?!" Mal sputtered.

Taleeka meekly nodded, unsure if she had done something wrong.

Alto's laughter broke the tension. Reaching over he rubbed the top of her head.

"You indeed can-do *stuff*. You climb walls. You pick pockets. Pray tell what else can you do?"

"Locks!" Taleeka exclaimed, holding the small knife in front of her and smiling proudly.

The *Haraka* silently skimmed just above a field of gently waving wheat. To the right the western fork of the Otoman River surged eastward. Just ahead the central pyramid of the Dreeat city of Hasteen peeked above the horizon.

"Alright, we're coming up on Hasteen," Mal said spinning in her command chair facing the cabin. "This is where we split up. "Alto, you and Wostera get the Dreeat's side of the story. Alto this is where you use that silver tongue of yours to calm things at this end."

"I will do my best."

"Zaad, you're with me. After we drop them off, I'm going to have a little chat with Lord Sorbornef. Everyone else stay with the ship."

The Spice Rat pointed to a series of low tree covered hills a quarter mile away in between Sorbornef and Dreeat territories. "Kumo park the *Haraka* out of sight in those trees and set up a perimeter. We should be able to keep an eye on both parties from there. We'll rendezvous back at the ship when we're done."

Everyone nodded that they understood and Kumo took the ship up and circled. The city was situated in between a fork at the river's end. Smaller tributaries continued on, snaking outward into immense fields of sugar cane. The metropolis itself consisted of a massive step pyramid, surrounded by an intricate network of canals carved into the land at precise right angles. Interspersed along the canals, were hundreds of individual home ponds of different sizes. All about were humanoid crocodiles harvesting fish and chopping away at stalks of sugar cane. They stopped what they were doing and watched the *Haraka* descend to within inches of the ground and let two humans out before rapidly speeding away.

The half mile trip to Staghorn Plantation was a short one. Mal could see the south lawn of the estate bustling with a large celebration.

"Looks like a feast," Zau said noting the dozen occupied long tables. "And check out the tent city on the north lawn. Are you sure you want to go down there? You're going to be really outnumbered."

Mal watched everyone staring at the airship settling to the ground. "On second thought, Kumo, when you let us out, take her up to about thirty feet and hover. Be ready with the ballistas. Zau's right and I have a feeling Lord Sorbornef isn't going to take the news very well."

"Yes Captain."

Everyone gasped and began chattering when they saw Mal and Zaad exit the ship.

"It's a pretty solid bet almost none of these people have seen an EEtah before," Mal said, watching several scruffy looking men-at-arms get up from the table and stand in their way.

"Probably not an airship either Captain. Hey, I've seen those before," Zaad said, nodding toward several extremely cute, miniature mawls who kept the children amused. "They showed up in Immor-Onn shortly before I left with you. The queen even had one as a pet."

"What the fuck are they doing here?"

"Beats me Captain."

"That's far enough," one of the approaching men said.

Mal stopped and addressed the crowd.

"I'm looking for Don Sorbornef."

"Lord Sorbornef is busy," the other sneered. "So, get back in that flying contraption and get out of here!"

Mal looked them in the eye and gave a bored sigh.

The man threateningly put his hand on the hilt of his sword. "I said beat it!"

Reaching into her vest she pulled out the golden pass and held it up. The two men's faces fell when they recognized the token.

"Don Sorbornef, now!"

A large, robust bearded man and someone who Mal assumed was his son, got up from the head table and warily approached.

"I'm Don Sorbornef," he said, stepping past his men. "Who are you to interrupt my daughter's wedding feast?"

"I apologize for the interruption," Mal calmly replied. "I'll be brief. My name doesn't matter, my message does."

"Message! What message could be important enough for you to darken this happy day?!"

"Yeah, it's about to get a lot darker. This message comes straight from your king and governor. It's a simple one. You *will* stand down on any aggression towards the Dreeat."

Lord Sorbornef's eyes flashed with anger.

"Those filthy creatures killed my son!"

"I'm sorry for your loss but this order comes straight from the top."

A contemptuous sneer contorted the beard around his mouth. "Ah yes, the *new* sovereign. I've heard he's weak, with a *woman's* heart."

"Yeah, he can be a softy," Mal said, letting the insult slide. "That's where I come in. My team and I are the ones charged with handing out the spankings."

Sorbornef's eyes briefly darted up to the hovering *Haraka*. "How dare you come onto my land and dictate to me!"

"You're forgetting this land belongs to House Eldor. You're just the caretakers, and I just delivered a direct order from your king."

"*Fine*, you've delivered your message. Now go!"

"I'm not just the messenger. I'm the enforcer."

"And if I refuse?!"

"I told you. I hand out the spankings."

"You threaten me as if I were a child!" Sorbornef bellowed. "I've killed for less!"

Zaad roared and drew Bowbreaker when the seated men got up and drew their weapons. Mal raised her arm and clenched her fist. Lowering it, she pointed in front of the advancing mob.

A dull thump came from the stationary airship and a three-foot-long ballista bolt shot into the ground just in front of them. The men froze in their tracks, their attention bouncing from the EEtah with the enormous sword, to the projectile which just missed them, then up to the airship.

"Like I said, I'm the enforcer,"

With another wave of her hand the craft settled to the ground behind her and the side hatch lowered. They slowly backed into the craft not taking their eyes off the angry throng.

"Your order is to stand down!" Mal authoritatively said. Her demeanor then softened a bit before entering the ship. "Congratulations to your daughter."

Don Sorbornef vibrated with anger watching the *Haraka* take off and speed Southward.

Also keeping a wary eye on the fleeing airship, Adrik Targoff stepped up beside his new father-in-law.

"With what just happened, has anything changed?"

"No," Lord Sorbornef said, watching the craft move out of sight.

"Good," Adrik said with a sadistic grin. "I leave at the lifting of the Kan to take my bride to her new home and return with more than enough men for the job."

It wasn't the dozen or so humanoid crocodiles headed their way that concerned Alto. It was the barely visible eyes and snouts peeking out of the water on either side of him that gave the swordmaster pause. Much like non sentient crocodiles, Dreeat were ambush killers which struck from the water. Approaching the pyramid on a series of narrow berms, water was all around them.

"I must admit Mora, this is quite unnerving," Wostera said, eyeing the various individual ponds they passed. "These are their homes and I don't think I've ever felt so out of place."

"Caution is not unwise," Alto said, eyeing the approaching Dreeat. "Human and Dreeat relations are rather strained right now."

"Why are you here, humans?" asked the lead Dreeat, a twelve-foot-tall female with a machete at her side. The others appeared to be smaller males carrying barbed spears.

"Hardly the greeting one would expect as people who have come to help."

"You are from the far away king?"

"Indeed, we are. Alto de Gom, at your service," he said, with a slight bow. "This is Wostera and we would very much like an audience with your queen."

The female paused while she assessed the request.

"This way," she finally said. She then spun to the male workers behind her. "Return to your work," she ordered.

The males quickly went back to the wide main moat around the pyramid. Following the female, Alto noted the males resumed using their spears to gig fish and toss them into large baskets.

They led them to the far side of the pyramid and a large pond surrounded by lush vegetation. There was a path leading through the foliage which gave way to a sandy beach extending around the circumference of the pond.

There, half reclining on her back in a dug-out furrow, was the Dreeat queen. Alto guessed her around fifteen-feet-long although this was hard to calculate because part of her tail remained submerged. She threw her head back with eyes closed, basking in the sun's warmth. Beside her was a metal platter with several of the fish he had seen the male workers spearing.

Casually reaching over, she took one by the tail and tossed it into the air over her head. It fell, and she quickly lashed out, snapping her powerful jaws around it. Keeping her head raised, swallowing her treat, both the humans could see the telltale lump move down her throat.

"Wait here," the female said, before approaching her monarch.

Kneeling beside the ruler she whispered something. The Dreeat queen opened her eyes and looked over at the two humans. With a wave of her hand, she summoned them.

Both quickly approached and immediately went down on one knee.

"Your majesty," Alto began, with his head bowed. "Thank you for receiving us. I apologize for arriving unannounced, but we were told the situation was urgent."

"Sit," she said, indicating a spot in the sand next to her.

Alto and Wostera sat cross-legged, watching the Dreeat queen lean back and close her eyes again.

"I am glad the new Eldorian Sovereign is taking my people's plight seriously. His predecessor would have let us parish."

"King Shom is concerned with all his subjects," Alto said. "Even the ones that do not look like him."

The queen opened her eyes and stared wistfully into space. "My people once lived along the entire river before the humans came. The river sustained us. For the river is magical. Humans only used it for a waterway. They are so short sighted. After thousands of grands of bloody fighting, they took our lands little by little. Finally pushing us back to here, the farthest point in the Western fork. This is where we made our stand. There were several treaties. The humans broke them all. It was only when we threatened that our last act as a people would be to poison the land so none could use it, they stopped." Pausing she finally looked over at the two humans. "And now they have begun again. They seek our sugar cane and Caskel fish."

"When did the hostilities resume?"

"Ten cycles ago they stole our entire stores of Arapa skins and killed the guard. Then four cycles ago, they raided one of our hatcheries, killing dozens of babies."

"Arapa skins?" Wostera asked.

"Arapas are giant fish that can breathe above and below the water. Their skin is very tough and makes good, lightweight armor."

"If they haven't gotten rid of it, I will see it returned to you," Alto pledged.

"How big of an army did you bring?"

"There are five of us," Alto said.

The queen's eyes widened at the news. "What good is five against an army?!"

"It has been my experience, that quality always prevails over quantity."

"Brave or foolhardy I cannot tell," the queen said in disbelief. "Seeing how your numbers are so few I have a gift that may prove useful."

Smacking her tail in the water a male servant appeared.

"Confection," she said.

The servant nodded his head and slipped away. He quickly returned with a small leather bag tied at the top. The queen nodded toward Alto and he handed it to him.

"Thank you, your majesty."

"Open it."

He did as requested and discovered twenty small, brown balls filled the sack.

"This is our greatest achievement. Our candy."

"Thank you, your majesty."

"These are not just simple sweets. As I told you before, the river is magical. The silt that accumulates on our flood plain effects the sugar cane. These sweets have healing properties. Use them sparingly."

"Is there anything else you can tell us your majesty?" Wostera asked.

"No, for anything more you must consult the Oracle of the River."

There was a distinct chill in the early Kan fog. Commander Truden de Tonck watched his six remaining Forsvara Guards huddle together, attempting to stay warm. As ordered, they had positioned themselves at the extraction point, just off the beach to the North of Makatooa.

Truden stared out at the fog shrouded water, lost in deep melancholy. The mission had been a complete failure. He had lost fourteen good men, including his beloved lieutenant Doosara. The money and bank they'd tasked the guards to protect was gone. Aramos and Calden relations were at an all-time low because some entity who impersonated six of his men had set off a murderous riot which burned a quarter of the city.

Now, defeated, demoralized and compromised, they could do nothing but wait.

"All right lads, on your feet," Truden said when he saw the bow of a small open-top Nolton Boat emerge from the mist.

When the driver maneuvered it parallel to the shore, the commander could see a single passenger hop over the side into the ankle high water. The figure made his way to shore and crouched down on the beach.

His extraction order had said nothing of a contact, but Truden took a chance. He had to get his men out.

"Come on let's go," he said, stepping out of the jungle onto the soft sand.

When he saw the men emerging from the dense foliage, the mysterious passenger went over to meet them.

Something looked familiar to Truden as the figure rapidly approached. He was just under six feet tall, with a thin muscular physic, and a head full of wavy black hair set atop an intense, youthful face.

"Mathas?" Truden said in surprise when he finally got close enough.

"Truden," he acknowledged, with a nod of his head. "This one really went sideways on you."

"A total shit storm, right from the beginning." Truden replied. "Well, I guess it's your problem now."

"Best of luck," Mathas said, before disappearing into the thick jungle.

Mathas de Sury, Truden silently mused, getting into the boat. He was as tight lipped as ever. The Forsvara Guard commander had worked with the young Black Talon several times before. If they were calling him in, it was probably because of his fluency in the Calden dialects spoken in Makatooa. That, and he was as cultured as he was ruthless. He would be a perfect deep cover wraith. What he'd be monitoring however, was way above Truden's pay grade.

Moving through the hastily constructed tent city on the outskirts of Makatooa, Gavin felt his heart racing with excitement. The quartet of slave hunters warily searched the multitude of inhabitants for any unsuspecting prey. He had been right about things being easy pickings. They'd stolen the wagon Aurek drove earlier that day. Its owner now appeased the ravenous ghouls of the Old City beneath them.

He knew if they kept the creatures fed, he and the rest of his crew could operate out of their abandoned subterranean abode.

The Turine in the harbor had long since rang eleven times. The Kan was about to set in and the smell of the cookfires accentuated the pervasive smoky smell emanating from the charred remains of the burnt-out section of the city. All around, people sat staring blankly into space, still reeling in shock at their homes and lives turned upside down.

We're doing these poor fuckers a favor, he thought, turning right at the main intersection heading toward the jungle. *Most are going to starve to death.*

The outskirts of the encampment were in worse disarray. This was where the new arrivals hastily staked out a claim and territorial fights broke out over whatever small patch of ground remained.

Gavin motioned for them to stop when he spotted a family of four away from the others on the very edge of the massive bivouac. The mother and sixteen-year-old daughter were watching the father and thirteen-year-old son struggle with putting up a crude tent.

"Wait for my signal," Gavin whispered to Aurik. With a nod of his head toward the jungle, Tabor and Ornn silently slipped into the woods.

"Here, let me help you," Gavin cheerfully said, approaching them.

The family stopped and watched him walk up. The father looked relieved and gave a weak smile.

"Thanks," he said, with a frustrated sigh. "This thing is giving me fits!"

"I'll steady it from here. You push the pole upright," Gavin said, kneeling by the base of the pole.

The man and his son pushed up on the rod when Gavin torqued the base, snapping off a foot-long section of the support.

The loose edge of the simple tarp slowly fluttered to the ground, obscuring Gavin and the family from their neighbors.

"Dammit!" the father shouted in exasperation.

Gavin came up out of his crouch and drove the end of the broken stick into the man's solar plexus. He groaned and doubled over; the wind driven from his lungs. Another blow to the back of his head sent the man toppling at his feet, unconscious. The son—a tall gangly teen—charged.

Lashing out quickly, Gavin punched the rushing youth in the forehead. His eyes crossed and he dropped to the ground.

The mother and daughter got out a single scream before Tabor and Ord stepped out from the jungle and grabbed them from behind. Putting their hands across their mouths muffled the women's cries.

Gavin drew his knife and waved it menacingly in front of their terrified faces.

"Shh," he softly said with an evil grin. "We wouldn't want to disturb the neighbors."

Reaching out from behind the dangling tarp, Gavin waved to Aurek who pulled up behind the partition.

They quickly gagged the four, tied them up and placed a bag over their heads.

After positioning them in the wagon's bed, Gavin covered them with a tarp and leaned over the concealed bodies.

"If you stay quiet, you just might live through this," he warned in a low growl. He then turned his attention to Aurek on the buckboard.

"Get them to the boat," he ordered. "All except the boy, he's mine."

Zau had lost count of how many times Mal checked out the windshield.

"Dammit, the Kans starting. Where the fuck's Alto and Wostera?"

"Now you're the one who needs to relax," the Singa said, looking around the cabin.

Taleeka was fast asleep on Zaad's lap and didn't seem to mind his snoring. Kumo stood motionless at the ship's wheel. Even though her six eyes couldn't close, Zau knew she was sleeping too. There were three strands of silk attached to one of her rear legs. They ran out the partially open side hatch and connected to the perimeter of webbing she had set up around the ship.

"We should all try to get some rest," Zau advised.

"There you go again," Mal said, nervously watching the fog enveloping the surrounding landscape. "Doing your best fucking imitation of my mother!"

"With a mouth like that I bet she beat your ass on a regular basis!"

"My parents didn't believe in hitting me."

"Well maybe they should have."

"Trying to rest." Kumo's meek voice ended the bickering and the two looked away from each other in a huff.

Zau, finally decided to take her own advice, slumped back in her seat, closing her eye.

Mal continued her vigil, but the fog only allowed about twenty yards of visibility.

Suddenly, one strand on Kumo's leg began vigorously vibrating. The Makara came to life, snapping out of her slumber.

"The alarm!" she said, her docile voice fraught with anxiety.

"Heads up kids," Mal called out. "We got company!" She reached beside her chair and grabbed her pistol crossbow.

Zaad gently lifted Taleeka off his lap and set her in the seat beside him before grabbing Bowbreaker.

"What is it?" Taleeka asked, rubbing her eyes.

"I don't know," Mal replied, cocking the pistol. "But we're gonna find out."

Everyone apprehensively watched the single strand, still pulsating wildly on Kumo's leg.

"It's coming from the rear of the ship," the spider woman reported.

Mal searched the faces of her comrades. All appeared ready. "Okay Kumo, drop the hatches. I'll go out the side. Zaad, you're out the back. Zau, you and Taleeka stay put."

The EEtah drew the large blade from its sheath and grinned. "Yes Captain!"

Mal heaved a deep sigh, then gave a resolute nod. "Now!"

The hatches opened and Mal cautiously exited the ship. Seeing nothing, she started for the rear of the craft when she heard Zaad's laughter echoing off the surrounding trees.

She stopped and lowered her pistol, exhaling in relief. Zaad was standing just outside the rear cargo hatch and leaning on his great sword, watching three deer in a futile, panicked attempt to free themselves.

"Looks like we got a late dinner," Zaad said. "I was getting kinda tired of those rations we packed."

The others were now standing at the open portal watching their next meal tire themselves out.

"Good, I'm hungry!" Taleeka said.

Zau leaned toward Kumo, shaking her head admiringly. "I gotta say, that's some neat trick."

Kumo humbly lowered her head and blushed. "Thank you."

Mal smiled at Zau's thawing attitude towards Kumo and Taleeka's voracious appetite. "All right kid you just named your own poison. Get me a fire started. We don't eat the way any of these characters do."

The young girl's face lit up and she eagerly bounded out of the ship.

Uncocking her pistol, the Spice Rat anxiously surveyed her surroundings as far as the fog would permit.

"Where the fuck are Alto and Wostera?" she wondered, her voice little more than a whisper.

Instructor Jaag's face, so close you could smell the fish from his last meal... screaming!

The Sunal is all!

No special treatment because of size!

Running on the seabed, paralleling the shore.

Then up on the beach for the run back.

The Sunal is all.

Into the circle, feeling the sun's warmth as the blows landed. Brutally punched and kicked.

Falling, almost unconscious into the soft sand.

Instructor Jaag. "GET UP! GET UP!

No special treatment because of size.

Delivering the same kind of punishment to the next trainee to enter the circle.

The Sunal is all...

Fassee shook his head, clearing it from the daydream. He almost walked past his destination. Up ahead he could see several city guards milling about. Towering over them was their commander, Velitel.

Drawing closer, he spotted the diminutive form of his spymaster Kem. She was kneeling over something he couldn't quite make out.

"This looks awfully familiar," Kem said.

"Too familiar," Velitel replied.

"What's familiar?" Fassee innocently asked, coming up on the pair. "Oh…"

Laying on the ground in front of them was a pair of human arms and legs, separated at the ankles and knees and the four parts arranged into a square shape. The killer arranged the arms, severed at the wrists and elbows, within the boundary of the leg parts. They extended the forefingers to touch the top of the circle. Despite the horrific nature of the scene, there was no blood. They had neatly cauterized all the open ends of the extremities.

"Looks like you've got an artist on your hands," Fassee noted.

Velitel shot him an unamused glance. "Don't you have your own investigation?"

"Yeah, I was just on my way."

"These belonged to a male, in his teens." Kem said, studying the gruesome spectacle.

"Where's the body?" Fassee asked, looking around.

"Unknown," Velitel said, not bothering to look up.

"The killer removed the pinky on the right hand," Kem said, pointing, "just like yesterday in the burnt warehouse."

"If it's the same person, they're honing their craft," Velitel said, stroking his beard.

"Ramu," Kem said, coming to her feet.

Fassee gave the spymaster an inquisitive glance. "What's that?"

"A particularly brutal gambling dismemberment game. They have outlawed it in the Goyan Islands." Kem gave an ironic chuckle. "One of the few things the great houses can agree on. Word is, it's still legal in Tannimore."

Fassee winced in surprise. "Wow, and they say EEtahs are savage."

"Nothing beats humans as far as sheer ingenuity when it comes to killing."

"I guess," Fassee conceded. "On a completely different subject; I passed this mansion on my way here. On the shore just outside of town. They actually built part of it out over the water?"

"Ah, the Hanara estate," Velitel said, a touch of familiarity in his voice. "Lord Hanara is the richest sentient in the Spice Islands for sure. He owns the Spice Island Trading Company."

"Sentient you say?"

"Yes, he's an EEtah."

"Really?!"

"Yep, but unlike you, he's got a hammerhead."

"Palu EEtah's are rare." Fassee said, before descending deep in thought.

"He's a real recluse," Kem added. "He's got a human staff that interacts with us townsfolk."

Fassee remained silent while Velitel continued.

"Recluse is right. The mayor hasn't even met him yet. One thing's for sure, he was one of the sentients responsible for making Makatooa's docks what they are today. Or rather, *were*."

"A story I would love to hear," Fassee said, stepping back. "But that will have to be another time. I've got a body to check out."

The ground beneath Alto's feet grew progressively soggier. He and Wostera, along with one of the male workers as a guide, had left Hasteen with the lifting of the Kan. They followed the narrowing river Westward until it broke into dozens of small streams fanning outward into the vast fields of sugar cane. The terrain eventually gave way to a small swamp and their guide stopped just before the towering cypress trees.

"I am not permitted to enter the sacred woods," he said, pointing to the expanse of partially submerged trees. "Continue in this direction. The moment you enter the water, the oracle will know of your presence."

Without waiting for comments, the male Dreeat scampered away back down the river toward his home.

"This is where the whole affair becomes interesting," Alto said, stepping into the ankle-deep water.

Having to slog through the stagnant swamp slowed their progress. Algae and floating flora collected around their legs while snakes and small aquatic creatures scurried and slithered out of the way.

"I can't help but get the feeling we're being watched and evaluated," Wostera said, studying the surrounding wilderness. "The feeling grows stronger with each step we take."

"I only hope this oracle can divulge something useful," Alto replied.

Eventually the trees gave way to a submerged clearing. Both humans paused, staring in wonder. On the opposite side of the dell were two twelve-foot-high totems carved from dead cypress trees. The figures were of Dreeat warriors armed with spears.

In-between the towering wooden figures was an immense, partially submerged catfish. The creature was easily twenty feet long. Its body was four feet across and equally tall. It gazed at its two visitors with eyes that bespoke of ages of wisdom. From both sides of its snout, dozens of whiskers penetrated the surrounding water.

"I believe we have reached our destination," Alto said scanning the clearing.

"We were being watched the whole time," Wostera added. "The feeling emanated from here."

The water rippled on either side of the creature's snout and two long whiskers rose from the swamp and slowly undulated toward them.

"It wants to talk," she said, unslinging her bow.

"Are you sure?"

"Yes," she said, handing the bow and her single arrow to the swordmaster.

Untying the sash around her waist, she removed her robe and hung it on a nearby limb.

Alto marveled at her porcelain white skin, watching her nude body glide gracefully through the water toward the mysterious creature.

She stopped directly in front of it and placed both her hands on its snout. The two gently waving whiskers found their way to the naked human before them. One gently caressed her face while the other stroked the front of her body. With slow, deliberate motion one entered her mouth while the other disappeared between her legs, penetrating her from below.

A brief wave of concern swept over Alto when Wostera shuttered, then seemed to go into a trance. He calmed when he saw no deleterious effects on the bowmistress.

She stood, intimately connected to the oracle until late morning. When the being finally untethered its human subject, she teetered and the whiskers immediately returned to their watery element. Alto rushed to her side and caught her before falling.

"Thank you, Mora," she weakly said, attempting to get her footing.

"Are you alright?" Alto asked, assisting her back to where her robe was hanging.

"Yes, just overwhelmed."

"What were you shown?"

Reaching for her garment, a look of profound sadness crossed Wostera's face. "This creature is thousands of grands old. It can perceive any activity on or around the entire river."

Alto's eyes widened in astonishment. "This river extends across the entire lower half of the continent!"

"Yes, and it has seen it all. First the history of the land passed before my eyes. It was just as the queen said. The Dreeat used to inhabit the entire river until the humans began their conquest. They returned the atrocities committed on them and there has been constant conflict. Then it showed me recent history. The Lords of the Western Fork are gathering their men into one large host under House Sorbornef. Three have already joined and the army of the prancing fox draws near as we speak. There is also something from afar here. The danger stands just outside the oracle's perception."

Now fully dressed, Wostera's balance had returned.

"Time is of the essence," she said, accepting her weaponry from Alto. "We must return to the ship and warn the others."

What remained of Makatooa's municipal complex was a short walk from the docks.

Fassee stood outside the open gate and stared at the charred remains. From where he was standing, he could clearly see the blackened body of the EEtah laying just inside the gate. It had been three cycles since the riot and fire. Lying under the constant sun, he began to smell and draw flies.

Fassee hated this part of his job, but thankfully he didn't have to deal with the body. He only had to examine it. With a resigned sigh, he stepped through the gate and looked around.

Two things about the scene bothered him. First was the open grate in the ground to the city jail. The guard's key was still in the lock.

Next was the condition of the EEtah's corpse, despite its charred state, Fassee could see hundreds of tiny bites and claw marks covering the body. They'd also gouged the eyes out and chewed off the gills on both sides of the neck.

Could the devastation inflicted on this city have been an elaborate ruse for a jailbreak?

"This place is as busy as the Zorian Market," Demetrius said, watching the steady flow of Mawls going in and out of the Kharry Institute grounds. "How the heck are we going to get into there?"

"Not we," Okawa corrected. "Me."

"You're not thinking about going in there by yourself?"

"Yep, I may have to move fast and you'll just get in the way."

"I feel pretty useless without a ship. Speaking of which how in the name of the gods are we going to get home?"

"One thing at a time. You just stay put and be ready to cover my exit in case things get hot."

"Fair enough, have *you* even figured out *how* you're going to get in there?"

"Partly," she said, reaching into her bag. "You'll notice hardly anyone is going down in that grotto. That's where I'm headed."

Okawa retrieved a knife, two magazines of crossbow bolts, the round Shrouding and Talking Stones and a multicolored Etheria shard from her bag.

"What's that?" Demetrius asked, eyeing the unusual crystal.

"A little Etheria cocktail for our feline friends," she said, holding up the shrouding disk. "This is going to get me in and that guard over there is going to help."

Demetrius looked over at the lone Pomaku guard walking the far perimeter. All he could make out above the mist was the head and shoulders of the man-leopard tracing his route back and forth in front of the fence.

"How?"

"Be right back," she said, before slipping off into the dense undergrowth.

Demetrius watched the lone sentry on his solitary trek. The pilot gasped when he saw the humanoid leopard silently and violently yanked beneath the mist, then out of sight.

Long, tense moments later, Okawa emerged from the jungle in a crouch. Blood streaked her face and Ghost Suit and she smelled awful.

"You smell like a cat just went on you."

"It did," she replied, surveying the grounds. "Now, they won't be able to see or smell me."

"I didn't even consider smell."

"Humans have a pretty distinct odor that can single us out in a flash. Our late leopard friend over there just took care of that."

She then reached down and picked up one of the Etheria disks and partially unbuttoned the front of her Ghost Suit.

Demetrius gave a satirical grin. "Uh, as much as I enjoy looking. I don't think this is the time."

Throwing Demetrius a bored glance, the Valdurian agent placed the disk on her upper chest and buttoned the suit back up.

"Okay, nothing left to it, but to do it." She then pointed at a water tower with a single wide base off the side of the central plaza. "If it looks like I'm in trouble, the first thing you do is shoot at the base of that tower. Bring it down."

"Got it, then what?"

"Run like the wind to where we're supposed to meet the Tinians."

"I'm not leaving without you."

"Just do it. I can take care of myself. We'll meet at the rendezvous point and the Tinians will get us to a safe distance."

Without another word she was off, sprinting toward the fence. When she was halfway across the narrow clearing, the air around her wavered and she disappeared.

Heaving a nervous sigh, Demetrius checked to make sure he'd chambered a bolt in his pistol for the tenth time. Now all he could do was watch and anxiously wait.

He was surrounded.

Six of them, his supposed Sunal brothers.

Taunting, cursing, attempting to bully,

all because of his size.

Quit, they chanted, retreat to the outer clans!

Determine and assess the leader.

Easy to do. He was the biggest. The one doing most of the talking.

Take out his legs.

Bring him to the ground.

Blood, on his hands and jaws,

A flurry of punches and bites.

*The bully underneath him, bleeding and whimpering
while the others stand around, in stunned shock.*
"You wanted to see me?"

Velitel's voice snapped Fassee back to reality.

He stood outside a huge, multi-room tent, the temporary
home to the temple and offices of EEtah House Nur.
Traditionally, House Nur's inverted shark fin arch was a
fixture on every wharf in the Goyan Islands. The fire which
devastated a quarter of Makatooa, and a majority of the
docks, also destroyed their former location.

"Yes, thank you for seeing me on such short notice
Commander. I have some news to share."

"Good news I hope."

"More informative than anything."

Velitel gave a forlorn sigh. "I guess to those in our line of
work, good news is a rarity. What ya got?"

"I examined the EEtah guard Kaaza and found some
disturbing irregularities at the scene."

"Like?"

"Hundreds of tiny bite and claw marks covered the entire
body. I believe that was the cause of death. The burning
came after. They left the door to the jail open with the key
still in it. The jail was empty, no bodies."

"Cul-Ta," Velitel said, with a frustrated frown. "We
arrested their leader earlier that cycle. Sounds like they broke
him out."

"You don't think they staged the fire to cover up the jail
break?"

"Nah, they're not that smart. Besides, we know who
started the fire. It was a handful of rogue Aramos Forsvara
Guards sent to guard the new bank. The others disappeared.
We're looking for them now."

"Why in the name of the gods would they do that?"

"That's a question for the politicians and believe me I've
never seen tensions this high between House Calden and
Aramos. Say, I'd like to get a look at that body."

"You're going to need to hurry. I'm about to authorize the charming ladies of House Nur to pick up the body for immersion."

"I'm on my way. Thanks for the heads up."

Fassee watched Velitel head off into the city then pulled open the flaps and entered the tent.

Much like all the establishments run by House Nur, the main area was a large open temple with a circular pool at its center. They'd hastily constructed this one out of wood and hanged an inverted wooden shark fin arch over it.

Standing beside the pool, a female EEtah in purple robes ceremoniously dipped an ornate ladle into the water then poured it over the heads of two human who were facing her.

"Can I help you?" came a voice from behind.

Fassee turned to see a very young and attractive priestess and it took him a moment to realize he was staring.

"Uh yes," he said, collecting himself. "I'm Investigator Fassee of Adad Sunal. I'm here to authorize the release of the body of Kazza for Immersion. You can find it over at the municipal complex."

The female smiled and shyly nodded. "I will inform the High Priestess."

He hesitated for an instant and the priestess started off. "Uh..."

She paused and gazed expectantly.

"I need to invoke Protocol Thirteen," he said, trying to sound as official as possible.

The look on the young female EEtah's face went from serene to serious. "You were expected, this way."

She led him to one of the smaller rooms which lined the rear of the tent.

She poked her head through the flap. From where he stood, he could hear her say, "He's here."

Stepping back, she held the flap open for him.

The room was twelve-foot square with two long parallel benches in the center. Seated on the one to his right was a large female EEtah wearing long purple robes with gold trim.

"Hello, I'm invest..."

"I know who you are," she cut him off. "Have a seat and keep your voice down. The walls in our new location are thin."

Fassee warily sat down and studied the stern-faced high priestess across from him.

"Investigator Fassee, my name is Gopana. You will report to me while on assignment here. Have they briefed you?"

"Only that it had something to do with a Palu. Because of their rarity I imagine Lord Hanara is involved."

"That is correct. A short while ago a Calden scout ship spotted an unknown vessel coming from out of the Kusonga Ice Field from Nocturn. They trailed them across the Northern coast of the Narrow Lands to the Goyan Islands where they parked off the edge of the Western Goyan Rise until the Kan. Once sure they were unseen, they made their way here where they unloaded at the Hanara estate. They then returned to Nocturn by the same route."

"And you want me to figure out what Lord Hanara is up to?"

Gopana nodded. "You are an investigator. Investigate."

Okawa easily made it over the fence unseen, pleased how the Shrouding Stone's bending light cloaked her. What she hadn't taken into consideration was the concept of perceived spatial placement. After two near missed collisions with rushing Mawls, she realized that the detriment of being invisible was that anyone or anything would naturally assume they could occupy the same space.

Her trek across the main courtyard and garden was a nerve-racking dance to avoid bumping into anyone. By the time she made it to the cave entrance she was breathing hard.

The solitary guard standing to one side briefly sniffed the air when she passed but didn't give it any further consideration.

Now inside, she felt the cave's cool dampness and under the orange glow of crystals set into the ceiling, she saw a wide staircase just ahead.

Descending slowly, she could hear a chorus of Mawls chattering away in their language.

The stairs emptied into a large chamber fifty feet tall and several hundred feet across. The chattering had grown louder with each step and was now a raucous cacophony.

Okawa knew she was in the right place, known as the Worrg Pits of Hai-Darr, but wasn't sure what to expect. The seasoned Valdurian agent was unprepared for what she discovered. She froze in position and gave out a shocked low gasp which was more than drowned out by the constant caterwauling.

Suspended mongrel Mawls draped three of the four walls, arranged one just above the other in dozens of vertical rows from floor to ceiling. A pale fleshy tentacle from the floor impaled each row of humanoid cats, entering the anus and exiting the mouth, extending upward to the next one above it. A blank white color glazed over their eyes and they constantly babbled even though their mouths were full. Every so often, a thick yellowish-brown liquid escaped the side of their mouths and drip to the floor below, now covered in the excretions.

She guessed the ones at the top had been here the longest because their limbs had withered from lack of use.

The tentacles stretched across the floor and connected to a large flesh monolith in front of the fourth wall. It stood ten feet tall with the same horizontal dimensions. It had no discernible features, but it appeared to be pulsing with life.

Four Yagurs stood directly in front of the living edifice and several orange Tiikeri were behind them.

The flesh wall rippled slightly just in front of a Yagur. The skin parted and a vertical orifice opened. A trail of the yellowish fluid escaped when the Yagur gripped both sides of the oozing fissure and pulled it open wider. He then leaned forward and pushed his head completely inside the soggy cleft. A few moments later the humanoid jaguar pulled his head out, dripping with the viscous fluid.

He faced one of the other Tiikeri.

"That was from a pet Cheepa of the Bailian ambassador in Zor," he said. "I overheard a most interesting conversation…"

Okawa reeled in revelation. The Cheepas, those adorable miniature mongrels which everyone loved to have as pets, were Tiikeri spies. This was a remote viewing center. The Worrgs hanging on the walls could see and hear through them.

Okawa was still processing her discovery when the Tiikeri rushed up the stairs with the information. The wound then closed, resuming its original shape. After a short period, another opened and one of the other Yagurs repeated the process.

Careful to avoid stepping on any of the tentacles, she made her way across the floor to the living monolith. Removing the Etheria shard from her pocket, Okawa began navigating past the Mawls when a commotion erupted, drawing their attention away to the stairs.

An agitated white Tiikeri rushed onto the top landing followed by two orange Tiikeri guards who bounded down the stairs.

"There's been a security breach along the perimeter," he yelled. "This compound is now on lock-down!"

The spear wielding man-tigers herded the confused Yagurs into a corner.

Okawa, now eager to take advantage of the distraction, edged closer to the viscid tower. She could hear the shamans concerned chatter as she passed them when a loud explosion drowned them out. The thunderous crash of streams of water rushing down the stairs followed the detonation.

Demetrius! The water tower! she thought, gripping the Etheria tighter and moving closer to the somatic pillar.

Water was now flooding the room when she saw the fleshy surface gently undulate, then open.

In a flicking motion, the Valdurian agent shoved the shard into the orifice and stepped back.

The opening snapped shut with a wet plopping sound and the obelisk immediately began trembling. From the shard's insertion point black striations crawled across the pink fleshy surface. The dark rivers of rot quickly spread, covering the rapidly dying organism.

Okawa headed for the stairs, moving carefully so as not to slip.

When she reached the top landing, she saw that the entire edifice was now black and it toppled to the wet floor in a dark amorphic heap. The decay spread down the tentacles, turning them the same shadowy color. When it reached the mongrel Worrgs on the wall, they thrashed about wildly, their screams muffled by the blackened tendrils lodged in their mouths.

The water had stopped rushing by now and Okawa headed for the cave's mouth. She paused when she saw the white tiger giving orders to the guard by the opening, but there appeared to be plenty of room for her to pass them.

She was only a few feet away from them when the white tiger gestured toward the fallen water tower in the plaza. His hand made contact square in the middle of Okawa's back pitching her forward to the ground.

She landed with a loud splash. The shallow pool she was lying in now betrayed her shape.

The white Tiikeri bellowed in rage, snatching the spear from the guard. Okawa had just enough time to roll away before the spear tip plunged into the ground where she had been laying.

The water was still giving away her position and she dodged two more attempts before bounding to her feet.

No longer worrying about stealth, she sprinted toward the fence.

"The footprints in the water!" the white Tiikeri screamed, taking off after her.

Halfway to her destination Okawa saw two Pomaku perimeter guards just beyond the fence. Unable to see her, they held their spears at the ready, nervously trying to make out the source of the disturbance.

Okawa made it to the fence, wondering how she was going to get past the two Pomaku guards in her path. With peril directly on her tail, there was clearly no time to fight them.

One finally heard the leader's warning and looked down at the splashing headed their way.

He was about to notify his companion when a deafening crack split the darkness and his torso exploded, showering his friend with the remains of his vaporized body. The lone guard now looked around, panicked.

Staring down at his comrade's dismembered legs, he raised his spear with trembling hands and vainly attempted defending himself against an unseen foe. With all the commotion, he couldn't hear Demetrius chambering another bolt.

The white Tiikeri saw the splashing foot falls stop at the fence.

"They're climbing the fence!" the Tiikeri leader shouted, pointing to the area where the splashing stopped. "Don't let them get away!"

Still seeing nothing, the guard peered wildly around until another resounding boom echoed off the trees and his torso burst apart, bathing the white tiger in crimson just as he approached the wrought iron boundary.

Cursing, he unlocked the gate and threw it open. More guards streamed into the courtyard.

"They're going that way," he screamed, pointing at the sound of crashing through the jungle. "All of you, come with me!"

Okawa heard the Tiikeri's orders just as she came upon Demetrius crouching behind a bush, pistol still drawn.

"I thought I told you to run after you took down the tower!" Okawa admonished still running, removing the crystal from under her jumpsuit and reappearing.

"You're welcome," Demetrius said with labored breath, taking off after her.

Rushing through the jungle the pilot nervously kept glancing behind them.

"They're catching up!" he direly reported.

"We're almost there!" Okawa said, bounding over a low bush.

Demetrius suddenly stopped and held his arm out to block Okawa's advance. There was a break in the forest. The ground in front of them was steeply sloping and he felt the rocks beneath his feet give way. He could see the tops of the trees resume fifty yards in the distance, but the mist rendered the ground invisible.

"Woah! Who put a gosh darn ravine here?"

Okawa glanced back toward the sound of their approaching pursuers. Reaching into her pocket, she retrieved a small orange crystal.

"I sure hope they're paying attention," she said, giving it a solid smack.

The white Tiikeri could hear his troops breathing heavily behind him.

"Come on," he rallied. "We're gaining on them!"

Just ahead a small, bright orange light penetrated the misty darkness.

"That's them!" the leader roared. "Come on!"

The Tiikeri rushed into the clearing just in time to see four Tinians flying away, carrying Okawa and Demetrius by each of their arms.

"Humans, aided by Tinians," he spat, watching them fly off. "They will pay!"

"Should we try to follow on the ground Lord To-Nok?"

The white Tiikeri spymaster shook his head, watching the moth creatures disappear. "No need, I know where they're going."

The small, two-person wagon hit a hole in the wide, hard-packed dirt road, jarring Nikki out of her trance. She had been staring wistfully at the fields of grain as they sped by., Nikki scowled and shifted uncomfortably on the seat. The soreness between her legs aided in fueling the now burning hatred for her parents for having put her through this. Even though she would soon be the lady of the house and a powerful figure, it was a poor consolation for having to put up with her brutish new husband.

Adrik snapped the reins and cursed. "The Kan will start soon," he said. "And I intend to be home before that happens!"

Nikki remained silent and adjusted the hem of her dress which was starting to ride up her legs. She hated wearing dresses. She much preferred the freedom a good pair of riding pants afforded. Now, in her new role of Lady Targoff, the reluctant bride figured she better get used to them.

She could see the steeples of the Targoff estate peeking over the horizon when the first wisps of mist appeared.

"The entire staff will be there to greet you," he said, slowing the buggy down. "I'm sure they will all take to you. I wanted to warn you of the head houseslave. She's used to doing things a certain way. I suppose that was my mother's fault. She was not a very ambitious woman and let Tsaara run the house as she saw fit. Remember, you are now the lady of the house. Set things up the way you want them. She will probably resist. Be firm."

"How many servants do you have?" Nikki finally asked.

"We," he replied. "How many staff do *we* have?"

Nikki glanced down at her lap and blushed. "How many do we have?"

"Fifty for our personal estate. Forty field hands and ten house staff which you will oversee. This doesn't include the vassal farms with their own staffs."

Nearing Targoff manor, she saw it was slightly larger than her prior home. The mansion was three stories tall with a wide columned porch and portico. Behind the main house, were the kitchen and the slave's quarters. The Northern grounds next to the barn was a massive bivouac.

"They're arriving already," Adrik grinned. "Excellent!"

Pulling up under the portico she saw the line of people out in front of the manor. At the beginning of the line were scruffy looking males which were obviously the field hands. The ten better presented, mostly women, were clearly domestics. Standing at the end of the line was an older woman and a young boy.

"Welcome back sir," one greeted when Adrik climbed down. "Congratulations on your wedding."

"Thank you, Perci," he replied, helping Nikki down.

He then positioned his wife at the head of the line and addressed the staff. "Everyone, this is the new Lady Targoff. Obey her as you would me!"

Nikki felt a touch self-conscious when everyone bowed but she managed a smile and nod.

Adrik then paraded her down the line where she got a good look at each. Most managed a weak smile then averted her gaze. You could see the uncertainty on their faces at having someone new to answer to.

Near the end of the domestic line, she saw someone she recognized. A young woman in her early twenties with shoulder length black hair and a beautiful light coffee brown complexion. Her mother had traded her to the Targoff's three grands ago.

"Jassusa!? I'm so glad to see you!" Nikki said, happy to encounter a familiar face.

"Thank you for remembering me ma'am," she said, blushing.

"Jassusa is a member of our kitchen staff," the older woman at the end of the line said, friendly, yet commanding. She was Nikki's height, in her mid-forties with bags under her eyes and gray streaks in her hair. "My name is Tsarra and I am the lead domestic."

"It's good to meet you Tsaara and who might this handsome lad be?"

The woman brightened and smiled.

"This is my son Erzi," she said, putting an arm around his shoulder and drawing him close. "And he is a huge help around here, aren't you?"

"Yes," he meekly agreed.

"Now don't be rude Erzi. Say hello to Lady Targoff!"

His greeting was just as weak as before.

"I look forward to working under you ma'am," Tsaara said, attempting to take charge of the conversation.

Nikki didn't let her.

"I'm happy to hear that. I would like to meet with you right after the lifting of the Kan. You can get me up to speed. Then we'll call a meeting of all the domestics and I can go over any changes I wish to make."

Tsaara's face flashed with indignation but quickly returned to a placating smile. Adrik's booming voice interrupted any reply the head domestic might have offered. "Excellent! I'm glad to see you're jumping right in as lady of the house."

Lord Targoff then looked around at the waist high fog.

"The Kan is here," he said to Nikki. "My men and I leave before the Kan lifts to join your father, so we better turn in. We had our wedding night, but you know, there's nothing like fucking in your own bed!"

Tsaara's face turned dour at the ribald comment, but she remained silent.

"That's it!" Adrik said, officially dismissing the servants. "Everybody get some rest. Tomorrow is going to be a big day."

Pride.
Graduation day.
Instructor Jaag actually smiling
as he presents the Yudon harpoon.
A badge of honor and respect,
The Sunal is all.

Makatooa Harbor's Turine rang twelve bells, snapping Fassee back and he shook his head to clear it. The Kan was setting in and he would have to get closer to monitor the Hanara estate.

So far, things in and around the seaside mansion had been uneventful. He mostly remained submerged just offshore since he'd left House Nur. The only activity had been a steady stream of gulls flying in and out. Business was clearly being conducted and he was racking his brain trying to figure out what that business was.

When fourteen bells rang, he saw the front door open and a human female with an oversized shoulder bag step out. A cloaked male, obviously some sort of bodyguard, accompanied her.

The EEtah investigator pondered that it was probably nothing, but it was the only real activity he had seen this cycle, so he followed.

The streets were all but empty, forcing Fassee to hang back at the edge of visibility through the fog. They travelled across the burnt area to the North side of town by the waterfront. They paused in front of a small freestanding building. Above the door was a sign containing three shells and the words' SPICE ISLANDS TRADING COMPANY. ' There were no lights on in the single window of the unassuming structure. The woman unlocked the door and both entered. Shortly after, the lights appeared, cutting outward into the fog.

Quickly scanning the street for anyone coming, Fassee crept over to the window.

The room was a small office with a desk, several chairs and a bookcase. The woman had placed her bag on the desk and opened it. He could finally get a good look at her. She was barely five feet tall with a triangular shaped head and almond-shaped eyes slanted upward at the sides. Dark hair swooped across her forehead and her pouty mouth seemed etched in a permanent scowl.

The man, however, was nowhere to be seen.

She pulled a smaller leather pouch from the bag. Undoing the restraints, she poured its contents out onto the desktop. Fassee instantly reassessed his original thought of this as a wasted trip when he saw the large pile of glittering, cut gems.

The woman walked over to the bookcase and slid it aside. Behind it was a three-foot square safe door. Producing a key, she turned the lock, slid the bolt aside and opened it.

Her back was blocking his view of the safe's interior, but she pulled out three locked boxes and placed them beside the gems.

Another key opened the boxes and Fassee could see they also contained gems. The woman then divided the pile on the desk into thirds and added them to each box's contents.

Fassee was about to back away from the window when he felt a sword tip in his back, just above where he strapped his Yudon harpoon. He silently cursed his carelessness. By getting so wrapped up in watching the jewels, he allowed someone to sneak up on him from behind.

"Who are you?" a male voice growled. "Why are you spying on us? What business are we to the Sunals?"

"Which one do you want me to answer first?" Fassee asked, slowly raising his hands.

"Maybe I just run you through and be done with it."

"It'll be hard to answer questions if I'm dead."

The swordsman paused.

"May I turn?"

"Slowly," the man warned.

Fassee began his turn and the man backed off with the blade. The moment Fassee felt the pressure of the tip release, he pivoted quickly. With his already upraised arms he swatted the flat of the blade with his forearm.

The force of the blow sent the arm and sword swinging wildly to the side. By the time the man recovered Fassee had his Yudon firmly in hand.

Fassee knew this was an experienced swordsman when he attempted to deliver an immediate slice to his midsection. The EEtah had barely enough time to parry it when another strike rained down from above.

He raised his harpoon horizontally over his head, stopping the blow and the sound of clashing metal echoed through the empty streets.

The man snarled in frustration. While Fassee's arms were still in the air, the assailant delivered a kick to the midsection.

The blow wasn't strong enough to knock over the stout man-shark, but it shoved him back and off balance.

Another swing of the sword followed.

Fassee grimaced when this attack struck, severing half of his dorsal fin. Fassee grimaced when this attack struck, severing half of his dorsal fin. With the blow striking home, the next attack was slower and Fassee was ready. Catching the blade in the barb of his harpoon, a savage yank he sent it flying. It clattered noisily on the other side of the street.

The man's face went pale in panic and his cape fluttered when he spun and ran.

"You aren't going anywhere!" Fassee growled in a rage.

Fassee, like all EEtahs in extended combat, had entered a blood frenzy and needed a kill.

Leaning back, he wound up and hurled the Yudon at the fleeing man.

The harpoon struck him in his upper back with such force that it catapulted him face first onto the street. The shaft of the harpoon completely impaled him and stuck six inches out of the front of his chest.

Fassee pulled on the lanyard, dragging the oozing corpse toward him. The tip made an ominous scraping sound on the cobblestones below the body and a swath of blood painted its trail.

When the body was finally at his feet, he put a boot in the small of the back and yanked the Yudon out of the carcass.

The barbed spear made cracking sounds, breaking bones on its way out.

With a final raging snarl at the dead gangster, he wiped the blood off on his cape before securing his weapon and slipping off into the fog.

The boat was late and Gavin was growing anxious. All around him the Kan fog hung like a blanket of obscurity. Vague shapes seemed to move and dance just outside the limits of perception, all timed to the gentle lapping of the waves on the shore.

They'd nestled the wagon with the bound prisoners in the jungle, just out of sight off the beach.

"I don't like this," Aurek said, walking stiff-legged onto the sand. "He was supposed to be waiting."

"Are you sure we've got the right spot?" Tabor asked, standing on the buckboard.

"Yes, I'm sure," Gavin said, pointing to a misshapen palm tree. "This is the spot where they dropped us off."

"Gavin knows what he's doing," Orn said, coming up beside Aurek. "Gavin's smart."

"All right knock it off," Gavin said, watching several figures moving their way from further down the beach. As they drew closer Gavin could make out a human and two outer clan EEtahs calmly emerging from the Kan fog.

The man stood just under six feet tall, with slicked back, short, greying black hair. His face contained deep furrows and there were scars running along his right cheek bone across the bridge of his nose. A neatly trimmed mustache twisted upward at the corners, created a sinister smile and his eyes radiated intensity.

Stopping just in front of Gavin, he kept the smile while raising a crossbow pistol and shooting Aurek in the chest.

The force of the bolt knocked him onto his back and the surrounding sand seeped red.

The three remaining slavers stood paralyzed in shock.

"That was an attention getter," he said, still smiling.

"Gavin, what's going on?" Orn asked.

The man cocked the pistol. "I'm afraid your friend on the boat has been unavoidably, and dare I say, permanently detained."

"What do you want?" Gavin asked, finally able to find his voice.

"It pains me to say that you gentlemen have violated the natural order of things here in the Goyan Islands. You see, House Whitmar has a lock on the slave trade. Oh, where are my manners? My name is Wolff, Merin Wolff and House Whitmar has tasked me with cleaning up these kinds of irregularities. I take it the people are in the wagon? Where were they bound?"

Tabor's nostrils flared. "You expect us to just hand our catch over to you!?"

Marin, still smiling at Gavin, coolly raised the pistol once more, aimed without looking at Tabor and fired.

The projectile embedded deep in Tabor's chest, knocking him from the wagon's buckboard and into the underbrush.

"Tannimore," Gavin quickly offered. "They were going to Tannimore. Mister, we're sorry. We knew nothing about House Whitmar being the only ones allowed. It's our first time doing this."

Merin gave an understanding nod. "These kinds of things are best left to professionals. You know, I believe you. I really do. I killed your friends because they were insolent and unrepentant. You, on the other hand, have apologized and seem genuinely remorseful. However, being in my line of work, trust doesn't come easily. I'm still going to need a token of your sincerity."

"Gavin, what's going on?" Orn innocently inquired again.

"I'm going to allow you to dispatch your dim friend over there. That should be sufficient proof."

Gavin looked over at Orn's perplexed face. "You want me to…"

"We will then consider the fine paid in full."

Gavin swallowed and gazed back at Orn's still smiling face. "Sure, but not here and not now. I want to do it my way."

"Very well, but I will require proof."

"Oh, you'll have your proof."

"Splendid," he said, putting away the pistol and drawing his knife. With a nod of his head one EEtah lashed out, striking Orn on the back of his skull. The childlike brute dropped to the beach, unconscious.

Marin then pulled back the tarp covering the wagon bed. Three gagged, terrified faces of the kidnapped family gazed up, first at him then at the knife.

"Please allow me to apologize for this terrible inconvenience," he said, cutting their bonds. "I'm afraid I'm going to have to ask you to get out of the wagon. It's needed elsewhere."

"Where's our son?!" the father frightfully asked once his gag came off.

"I don't know, you see I just arrived," Merin replied. With a sweep of his arm one EEtah picked up Orn's motionless body and carried it over to the wagon.

"But our son!" the wife wailed.

Merin gave a deep sigh. "Please don't make me repeat myself. I hate repeating myself. Your question is one best taken up with the city guards. Now if you want some sage advice, I'd seek shelter from the Kan. It's simply not safe out here."

The traumatized family, now free, ran toward town.

"I want those other bodies too," Gavin blurted out when they loaded Orn in the wagon.

"I suppose there is something to be said for properly disposing any loose ends," Merin replied, directing the EEtahs to load the corpses.

"Nah, I don't give a shit about that. I've got hungry mouths to feed."

A look of genuine amusement crossed the Whitmar agent's face. "You know, I'm almost curious enough to ask." He paused reflectively. "But no, I don't believe I will."

It was early. The Kan fog would recede soon, giving way to a new and, likely, very violent day.

Nikki Targoff watched her husband rally the mounted men under his command and considered how her life had dramatically changed in the last three cycles.

This was her new home, but she wondered if she would ever consider it as such. The estate was larger than Staghorn, but it lacked warmth and vitality. She also felt a twinge of guilt from being thrusted upon the house staff so abruptly.

He had taken her last Kan, as promised. She shivered in revulsion at the memory of his clumsy, harsh advances. She scowled reliving him on top of her, pumping away with inept, selfish abandon. Thankfully, the humiliating act was over quickly, followed by him grunting in satisfaction, rolling off her and dropping off to sleep. The tears she shed listening to him snoring beside her was at the thought of this being her new life.

Now, watching the undulating sea of men and horses through the fog, she felt a touch of sadness in the thought that some would not be coming back. All to answer her father's misguided call for vengeance against a race of sentients.

A shout from Adrik Targoff brought Nikki out of her melancholy musings and she watched the mounted army thunder off, vanishing into the fog.

Sighing, she headed back to the main house. There were two potentially contentious meetings with the house staff she wasn't looking forward to. Passing the kitchen, she could smell the cooking fires and see the aromatic smoke billowing out the chimney, blending with the now receding fog. The oblong building was a flurry of activity as the kitchen staff prepared the morning meal.

"Lady Targoff, could I have a word?" Jasusa said, stepping out from the throng of workers.

"Of course, Jasusa."

"In private if you don't mind," Jasusa said, wiping her greasy hands on her apron.

Nikki motioned her off to a corner of the building.

"So, what's going on?"

"Ma'am, I just wanted to warn you that your life is in danger."

The statement hit her like a cold slap in the face.

"What, how?!"

"During the Kan when I was closing down and cleaning up the kitchen, I overheard Tsarra plotting with Kasap the butcher. Something about chopping you up and throwing your parts in the river."

This news took Nikki completely aback and she felt a twinge of fear rise from the pit of her stomach. She had expected resistance and intrigue, but hardly this level of treachery so soon after arriving.

"In the name of the goddess, why?"

"Lord Targoff is the father of her son Erzi. She has always held out the hope that he would inherit the Targoff name and become lord of the manor. She was quite upset at the news of his marriage. It happened so suddenly. She cannot allow you to birth an heir."

Nikki reflected for a moment on the grim news and found her trepidation waning, replaced by a calculated loathing.

"Tsarra is unaware you overheard them?"

"Yes ma'am."

"Good, I've got a piece of information I want you to drop in casual conversation today. Make absolutely sure she can hear it."

We have got to stop meeting like this," Fassee jovially said, working his way through the crowd of onlookers toward Velitel's towering frame.

"Wow, we really do," the EEtah investigator said, entering the area secured by three city guards.

Kem was kneeling over Orn's muscular arms and legs arranged in a diamond pattern on the side of the road. In the center of the macabre design the brute's head sat on its cleanly severed neck, staring outward in a silent scream. Like the others the killer had neatly cauterized the wounds, leaving the area devoid of blood.

"You know him?" Fassee asked.

"No idea," Velitel replied, shaking his head.

"Here's something," Kem said, taking out her dagger. She ran the tip under the nail of the big toe. The spymaster stared intently as a small line of packed white sand came out on the blade.

"I don't know who he is," Kem said, rubbing the powdery grains between her fingers. "But he was recently on a beach."

"Put together two teams," Velitel told one guard. "Search the shoreline to the North and South of town."

"What are we looking for sir?"

"I don't exactly know. But if this is a sample of his handiwork, you'll know it when you see it."

"Yes sir," the guard replied before wading through the crowd.

"Three bodies in three cycles," Kem said. "Looks like our boy's got a real taste for it."

"And like the others, the right pinkie's gone," Fassee said, pointing down at the body parts.

"The killer's definitely taking trophies," Velitel said with a touch of exasperation.

"At this rate they're gonna have quite the collection by the time we catch up to them," Kem grimly assessed.

"You mean *if* we catch up to them," Velitel countered. "Whoever's doing this isn't leaving us much to go on."

Kem shook her head resolutely. "Eventually, they're going to make a mistake. The killer must keep their lucky streak going. We only need to get lucky once."

"We'll increase the Kan patrols around here; they seem to like this area."

"Hey, while I've got the two of you here," Fassee began. "Have there been reports of stolen gems? Or maybe a bunch of gems hitting the street?"

Velitel and Kem searched each other's faces, then shook their heads.

"I've heard nothing," Velitel said.

"Me neither," Kem agreed. "Why?"

"Nothing firm. Just some faint chatter."

"Is that the reason you're sticking around?"

"Partly," Fassee coyly said.

Passing through the dispersing crowd, Merin Wolff glanced down dispassionately at the body parts.

Interesting, he thought. *Well, he said he wanted to do it his way.*

The Whitmar agent quickly moved on. He had no time to linger and marvel at the killer's gruesome handiwork. There were pressing matters in Zor that needed his attention. In his profession, pressing matters could turn deadly in the blink of an eye.

Raising the spyglass, Wostera looked down on the sea of men encamped on the grounds of the Sorbornef estate. She and Alto had arrived just after the Targoff forces thundered onto the scene.

The massive bivouac split in three separate encampments beneath their family standards, the Leaping Stag of House Sorbornef, the Boar's Head of House Kenyev, and the Dancing Fox of House Targoff flying above the largest numbered force by far.

"The dancing fox," she muttered. "Just like the oracle said."

The Bowmistress then handed back Mal's optical device.

"There is well over a thousand men down there," Alto noted.

"Not good odds," Zau said, looking out her window.

"There's got to be something down there to tilt the odds a bit in our favor," Mal said, peering through the spyglass.

"That's gotta be some tilt," Zau said bleakly.

Mal ignored the complaint and continued to scan the grounds.

"And we might just have something here," Mal said, stopping her sweep. Behind the barn was a smaller building with a lock and guard standing outside. The Spice Rat watched as several men went in and out. With each passage, they always secured the door.

"That building," Mal said, handing the glass to Alto. "Security's pretty tight. I wonder what could be so important?"

"Perhaps something that may aid our endeavor." Alto offered, looking through the glass.

"Yeah, and maybe not!" Zau fired back. "In case you didn't notice there's a freakin' army down there guarding it!"

"I disagree," Alto calmly said, lowering the glass. "There is only one guard. Everyone else is preparing for battle both physically and mentally. Most will be in their own little world. We can deal with one guard."

"Yeah, but the lock!" Zau countered. "You can't go breaking in the door. Someone's gonna notice!"

"Those locks are easy," came a small feminine voice between lip smacks.

Everyone turned to see Taleeka chewing on a dried meat stick, staring out the windshield at the building.

"You can get me in there?" Alto asked.

Taleeka nodded confidently and took another bite.

"The Kan will be starting soon," the swordmaster reasoned aloud. "It will give us adequate cover."

"NO!" Mal snapped in a matronly tone. "Are you fucking kidding me?! You're actually considering taking a young girl into an armed enemy encampment?!"

"But those locks are easy," Taleeka said innocently, wiping her hands on the front of her tunic.

"Look, this was not in the plan. We're supposed to be dropping her off in the next city. She's not supposed to be taking part in a risky as fuck operation!"

Zaad's boisterous laughter interrupted the argument. "The captain sounds more and more like a mother each cycle!"

257

Mal spun in frustration and pointed a finger at the amused EEtah. "Yeah, and when I want your fucking opinion, I'll carve it out of you!"

Bringing her attention immediately back to Alto, she missed the amused look that passed between Zaad and Wostera.

"I think someone did a little poky-poky on a nerve just then," Zau said, suppressing a chuckle.

"There was no fucking nerve!" Mal futilely defended. "It just wasn't part of..."

"Please my love," Alto serenely said. "Neither I, nor Defari would allow any harm to befall the young one."

At the mention of the sword, Mal's resolve melted. She recalled the ring of corpses around an unconscious Alto, laying on the burning Makatooa docks. Just above him, a growling Defari, hovering, allowing none to come near.

Mal sighed and her shoulders slumped. "You say it won't take long?"

With the Spice Rat's concession Taleeka's face lit up and the crew all traded knowing glances.

Mal reached out and gently held Taleeka by her shoulders. "I want you to do everything Alto says. Understand?"

Taleeka nodded, still keeping a broad smile for them including her in the mission.

"And I want you to be careful."

"I will."

"Don't take any unnecessary risks."

"I won't."

Mal sighed deeply. "Okay, give me a hug."

The young woman fell into a warm embrace. Mal closed her eyes as she held her tight and rocked her back and forth.

Watching the tender moment, Wostera leaned over to Zaad. "You spoke in jest, but your observation was an accurate one my aquatic friend."

It had begun raining the moment Fassee left Kem and Velitel to deal with the mysterious body parts. The EEtah figured he better get used to it. With the cold weather gone, the rainy season was upon the Goyan Islands.

Stepping up to the front door of the Spice Island Trading Company he could see that the rainwater had washed away the blood from the streets from last Kan's altercation.

Knocking on the door, he didn't wait for a reply before entering.

Asad de Mak's short, portly frame filled the chair at the lone desk. On the wall to his left was the bookcase with the safe behind it.

"My friend Asad!" Fassee boisterously greeted.

The gangster spun in the chair and gave a wide, welcoming smile.

"Inspector Fassee," he beamed. "What can this humble shipping merchant do for the good sentients over at Adad Sunal?"

Fassee paused, almost flattered. "I'm surprised you've heard of me."

"Inspector, I think you're going to find that there is very little that happens on my docks that I don't know about."

"Fair enough," Fassee said. "Actually, I was hoping to ask you a few questions?"

Asad continued his pleasant demeanor. "Of course, I apologize for the cramped conditions, but we had to move to these temporary quarters since my warehouse burned."

"Yes, it's quite a mess down there," Fassee agreed.

"I hate being away from my docks during the Kan," Asad bemoaned. "This neighborhood is *especially* unsafe. Just last Kan, someone killed an associate of mine in front of this very building!"

"Really?!"

"Yes," Asad answered with a frown. "Run through with some sort of spear, according to the city guards."

Fassee watched Asad's eyes linger on his Yudon harpoon strapped to his back.

"It's a shame," Asad added with a slight forlorn look. "Quldur was a good man, he will be difficult to replace."

In an instant, Asad returned to his jolly baring. "But, enough about my problems, you said you had questions?"

"Yes, I was wondering what you knew about the 'Mama's Boys' gang."

This genuinely surprised Asad. Keeping his broad smile, he stared away thoughtfully for a moment.

"Now there's a name I haven't heard in at least twenty grands. What would you like to know?"

"Well, anything, but more specifically, what part Lord Hanara had to do with it?"

The air was still and heavy. The Kan fog, which had risen quickly, clung its dampness to everything. Alto and Taleeka moved in a silent crouch between rows of wheat. They could smell the campfires and hear the men talking.

The grain field stopped twenty feet from the side of the buildings. From this angle, Alto could now see the smaller building attached to the rear of the barn.

A lone guard, armed with a sword, leaned against the wall, looking very bored. Judging that there was no way he could cover the distance without the guard sounding the alarm, Alto slid his knife from its scabbard, prepared to make his move, when Taleeka's head suddenly snapped to the right and she grabbed his arm. He had no sooner given her a questioning look when he heard men approaching.

There were two of them and they walked directly over to the guard, talking loudly and passing a wine skin between them. The sentry perked up when they approached. All three talked and laughed while passing around the skin. Alto was a bit surprised that the guard was drinking on duty until he remembered that these were undisciplined farmers turned men-at-arms at their lord's command, not professional soldiers.

After a short, lively conversation, the two wandered off and left the wineskin with the guard. He resumed leaning against the wall, this time taking in gulps of liquid.

Alto waited until the vessel was almost empty. The man was tilting his head back and lifting the skin to get the last few drops.

When the guard exposed his throat, and with his vision obscured, the swordmaster hurled the knife at his target.

The foot long Etheria blade plunged into the unsuspecting sentry at the base of the neck. It severed the windpipe and major blood vessels before exiting just to the right of the spine. The tip lodged in the wall behind him, pinning the startled guard.

Dropping the skin, he could only gurgle while clawing at the handle of the knife. When he finally went limp, gravity pulled him downward on the blade. It easily sliced through the soft tissue, opening the throat vertically until the jawbone halted the bloody progression to the ground.

After a quick check to make sure they were alone, the duo bolted to the door. Alto removed the blade, allowing the body to fall. The swordmaster wasn't sure whether to be relieved or concerned at Taleeka's nonchalant attitude at the man's violent death.

With no time to ponder, he dragged the oozing corpse into the wheat field. Taleeka retrieved her recently acquired multi-use pocketknife, selected the proper tool and went to work on the keyhole.

Alto returned just in time to hear the soft click of the lock opening.

The young girl looked back at Alto, beaming with accomplishment.

"See, easy," she whispered.

Checking around one more time and finding nothing, they cracked the door just wide enough to enter. Slipping inside, Taleeka quietly closed the door while Alto pulled out an orange gem from his pocket and tapped it on the wall. The room immediately filled with the gem's warm orange glow.

The enclosure was about thirty feet deep with a door on the far end; Alto assumed it led to the barn's interior. In the center was a small anvil, forge and tool rack. Weapons of every type lined the walls, both hanging and on stands. Directly beside the far door was a table and a small cask sitting beside it.

"I believe we have found their armory," Alto said, walking over to a stand.

Taleeka made her way over to the table and cask. There was a large stack of skins at one end of the table.

"Scratchy," she said, running her hand across them.

"Those must be the stolen Arapa skins the Dreeat queen told me about." Alto said, joining her.

Gazing down at the partially open cask beside the table, Alto plucked the top off and discovered arrowheads filled the container.

Alto picked one up and held it aloft, examining it. These were not like the crudely forged weapons on display along the walls. They'd crafted these arrowheads out of finely honed red Etheria Crystal.

Alto was about to mention the oddity when the door crashed open.

They spun to see Don Sorbornef standing in the threshold with half a dozen men. The door to their left opened and Paz

Sorbornef stood with as many men behind him in the barn. The trapped duo leapt to the center of the room by the forge.

"I don't know who the fuck you are," Don said, stepping into the room. "But I'd be willing to bet you got something to do with that mouthy bitch who crashed my daughter's wedding the other cycle."

Taleeka grabbed a dagger off the weapons rack when Paz entered, causing him to chuckle.

Alto appeared calm and raised an eyebrow at the lord of the manor. "Actually, I am here to retrieve these stolen skins and return them to their rightful owners."

Don let out a wry laugh. "The fucking crocks don't have any use for them; besides, I need them for trading with my new friends."

"The arrowheads for the skins, I imagine."

"That's right. Isn't it Bo-Lah?"

"The beginning of a long and beautiful friendship," came a booming voice from outside.

Alto drew Defari when a seven-foot-tall orange Tiikeri stepped into the room.

"I like your blade," Don said, eyeing the growling sword. "It'll look good in my collection. We'll put your head on a pike to inspire my army. As for the girl, my men can have her too, for a different kind of inspiration."

"I want the girl first!" Bo-Lah demanded.

Don gave a salacious chuckle. "Well, there you go. He is my guest and I wouldn't want to be inhospitable."

By the time the Tinians set down in the small clearing Okawa and Demetrius were shivering uncontrollably, but at least they were alive.

The area was a forty-foot diameter break in the multi-colored rainforest of the Dasos region. All around them, large cocoons hung from the lowest branches. Most of them were hatched and broken open at one end. Others contained Tinian larva waiting to be reborn. Six of the humanoid moths lovingly tended to the unhatched cocoons swinging about in the waist-deep mist.

Just off center, surrounded by wild stalks of yellow grass was a small outcropping of orange, purple and green Etheria crystals.

One of the Tinians who helped carry Demetrius tapped one of the orange crystals and it glowed. He then beckoned the two frigid humans over.

Once they were standing by the ardent gem, their trembling subsided in the wake of its radiant heat.

"That little trip gave me a whole new appreciation for the warmth the ground gives off," Demetris said when the trembling subsided.

"I thought you were used to flying around Nocturn?" Okawa questioned, rubbing her upper arms as she crouched over their natural heater.

"Not outside an airship," Demetrius replied.

"Your bodies are not equipped for spending long periods here," the Tinian said.

"Believe me," Demetrius said, finally warming up. "I try to spend the least amount of time in the Land of Mists as possible. Though now that I've hooked up with her, I seem to spend more and more time here."

Okawa rolled her eyes at the pilot's assessment.

"So, what was that all about back there?" Demetrius asked.

"Let's just say we set the Tiikeri spying and communication operations back at least five grands, maybe more," Okawa said, looking upward through the clearing at the sky. "Now all we have to do is find a way home. The moon's rising. We're going to be easier to spot."

"Yeah, that's a little more difficult without my ship," Demetrius said, glancing over at the Tinian. "Speaking of no ship, thanks for saving us back there. Those Tiikeri were pretty sore at us."

"To the cat peoples we are food," the Tinian said. "We strike back any way we can."

"So how are we going to get back?" Okawa pensively asked.

"That's a good darn question."

"Well, we better think of something fairly quickly. I'm betting those Tiikeri are looking for us. Hey, what about those mantis creatures? What did you call them, Do-Tarr?"

Demetrius shook his head. "There are tunnels below us but they're empty right now. That was the home of the Na-Kab until recently. Besides, the Do-Tarr wouldn't have a way to get us home."

"Yeah, but we wouldn't be sitting ducks up here waiting for the Tiikeri to catch up to us."

"The Do-Tarr are neutral. They really don't care about our problems. And trust me, being down in the Do-Tarr hive is only trading one set of problems for another."

A frustrating moment passed as both humans struggled to think of a solution.

"Hey!" Demetrius said with a grin of revelation. "Does that purple Etheria crystal look familiar?"

"Hard to say."

"I mean it's not the same size or shape, but I could swear that looks like that big purple crystal we encountered in that ice city out on the Frozen Sea."

"The one that swallowed those ice clans?" Okawa's face lit up. "Portal!"

"Just maybe."

"So how do we open one?"

"We probably can't, but given the nature of the Tinian's language, they might."

Demetrius brought his attention back to the moth-man who was staring intently at them.

"Do your people have names?"

"Yes, once we emerge from the cocoon, we may call ourselves anything we wish. I am called Sitsa."

Demetrius pointed to the purple crystal. "Sitsa, this gem has special powers. Is it possible for your shamans to use it and open a portal?"

Sitsa appeared perplexed. "What is 'portal?'"

Demetrius sighed and organized his thoughts. "A portal is an opening to travel great distances in this world or even to other worlds."

Sitsa faced her companions. Demetrius heard her say the term and the basic description he had just conveyed. The Tinians paused for a moment, glancing around at each other while contemplating the foreign concept.

Suddenly, one blurted out an idea. The vision appeared in the two humans' heads much like the other conversations began, with a three-dimensional ball with lines and points across its surface and advanced mathematical notations surrounding it. As other voices joined the conversation, the math changed and the ball morphed. The conversation now moved too quickly for the talking stone in Okawa's bag to keep up. Its amorphous shape soon transmuted into a pyramid which then inverted, all the while the mathematics surrounding it were fluctuating at such a rate that even if the humans understood what they were looking at, they couldn't have read them. Eventually, the evolving shape in their heads transformed into a hyperboloid funnel, and the math glyphs slowed to a stop.

"We think we can do it." Sitsa confidently said.

"Think?" Okawa replied, her voice laced with concern.

"My people have not attempted it before. However, the concept seems logical."

"Hey, it's that or deal with the Tiikeri." Demetrius countered. "I'll take my chances in the Middle Realms thank you very much!"

Okawa gave a resigned sigh. "Okay, how do we do this?"

"It would be best if we sealed both of you up in one of our cocoons," one of the other Tinians said.

"I don't know…" Demetrius started, staring at the empty shells hanging all around them.

"This will prevent you from being separated in the Middle Realms," Sitsa explained. "Your destination is determined by concentration. You must be single minded in envisioning your destination. Disregard anything you see or hear. Think only about where you want to go."

"Zor?" Demetrius offered.

Okawa nodded. "There's one of these crystals in the Valley of Chains."

Demetrius exhaled loudly. "Looks like that's where we're going, I hope."

Sitsa motioned to four of her fellow Tinians. She accompanied them into the trees when they lifted the two humans. They positioned Okawa and Demetrius so that they were facing each other just above an empty cocoon. The silken enclosure hung directly over the outcropping of crystals and was large enough to accommodate them both. In a mid-air ballet, the Tinians brought Okawa and Demetrius face-to-face. Embracing so they could fit, the moth-men lowered them into the hanging sheath.

"Hey, I kinda like this," Demetrius said, snuggling up against Okawa's warm, voluptuous body.

"Concentrate fly-boy, concentrate," the Valdurian agent playfully admonished.

The interior of the cocoon was soft and smooth but only came to their necks, leaving their heads completely exposed.

Sitsa landed on the branch above where a three-foot-long stem held the now occupied swaddle aloft. Crouching, she gave out a shrill call while tapping the branch.

The foliage above them immediately came to life and six, foot long larva advanced down the branches. Slithering quickly, they moved down the tendril to the open top of the encasement. Three Tinians on the ground positioned themselves around the crystal and began a soft buzzing.

The Tinian larva circled the opening, excreting layer after layer of silk, sealing the cocoon inches from the human's heads. Okawa winced at the smell of rotting vegetation they emitted while inch by inch their view disappeared.

Directly below them, the Tinian's buzzing increased in tempo and the purple crystal started glowing. The Etheria field swirled into a blue vortex around them.

Okawa leaned forward and kissed Demetrius. Caught by surprise, he barely had time to return it.

"For luck," she purred.

"We're gonna need it," he softly replied.

One of the Tinians interrupted the intimate moment shouting, "Tiikeri!"

The sound of arrows whistling around them immediately followed the warning. Sitsa watched a dozen Tiikeri crashed through the jungle, rushing their way. Every so often one would stop to release an arrow. So far, the trees provided cover from the missiles, but they struck one of her companions on the ground.

The larvae didn't have time to seal the whole cocoon, but Sitsa could only see the tops of the human's heads and bolts of blue lightning were erupting from the vortex below them.

"We are out of time. We must go now!"

Fluttering off the limb, she chewed furiously on the tether.

The Tiikeri entered the clearing with a roar and a fresh volley of arrows. Sitsa heard and felt two just miss; one lodged in the limb just above but the other embedded in the middle of the cocoon.

Panic was setting in all around the clearing. Sitsa watched one shaman fall and the portal flickered.

He wasn't chewing fast enough, and if they got another one of the three shamans, the portal would close, ensuring their doom. Reaching up, she yanked the arrow from the limb above. When she looked back at the cocoon, she saw the red stain around the lodged arrow.

Raking the barbed tip of the Tiikeri arrow against the partially chewed tendril it broke free. Seeing the silky envelope begin to drop, she tried to fly backward, only to have the base of her right wing become entangled in the falling cocoon's wildly undulating chord.

The trapped Tinian plunged with the partially sealed cocoon into the rapidly closing Flavian Portal. It disappeared into the cyclonic blue field just as the humanoid tigers overran the clearing. The last Tinian shaman held the portal open until a Tiikeri spear ran him through.

To-Nok entered the glade last and surveyed the carnage. An orange Tiikeri approached and saluted.

"Lord To-Nok the humans and one of the Tinians got away."

The Tiikeri spymaster was seething. "How?!" he growled.

"They disappeared into some sort of energy field."

Closing his eyes and gripping his hands into fists To-Nok let out a roar of frustration.

This injustice would not stand. There would be a day of reckoning. One that he would be the architect of.

Alto counted a dozen men and one Tiikeri. In this case, being inside gave the swordmaster the advantage. Even though technically trapped and outnumbered, his adversaries would still have to come to him. Because of the close quarters it would be difficult for them to gang-up on him.

"Kill him, take the girl," Don ordered.

When the first of Sorbornef's men entered the room, Alto tossed Defari in the air in front of Taleeka.

"Guard!" was the swordmaster's solitary command.

The sword floated; tip pointing upward in front of the wide-eyed girl holding the knife, hands trembling.

Simultaneously drawing his short sword and knife Alto slashed upward across the chest of the first, then ran through the second.

Paz and three men closed in on Taleeka. The Sorbornef son quickly reached for a wall rack and retrieved a weighted fighting net. In a single motion, he tossed the net over the hovering sword, successfully entangling it. The sword twisted and growled under its restraints.

Paz grabbed Taleeka by her throat and lifted her off the ground, holding her out at arm's length.

The young girl slashed through the air in vain; Paz was well out of her reach.

"Grab her!" Paz gruffly ordered, and two men clutched each arm, keeping her aloft.

Paz sneered at the brash youngster. Releasing her throat, he punched her in the stomach.

Taleeka's cries of pain distracted Alto. He quickly glanced her way just long enough for a mace to strike him from behind. The impact threw the swordmaster to the floor and he dropped his short sword.

The man raised the mace for another strike when Alto rolled onto his back and threw his knife into the man's chest. He gasped once then dropped to the ground, while a growling Defari sliced free through its bonds.

Paz and his men, sensing an opening, dropped Taleeka and advanced on an unarmed Alto. Defari howled and before the enemy could attack her master, completed a wide arc, severing the Sorbornef son and three of his comrades completely in half. Their split torsos toppled to the ground, littering the floor with blood and internal organs.

The bloody sword righted itself for another strike, painting a gruesome stripe of crimson across the ceiling. Alto seized the opportunity, grabbing his short sword from the floor and pulling the knife out of the dead mace wielder.

The remaining men froze in shock; four of their numbers were already dead.

Bounding to his feet a blood-spattered Alto stood in ready position, blades in each hand. Defari levitated in front of a gasping Taleeka, growling and snarling.

Don stared in stunned disbelief at his son's detached body parts, then into his men's frightened and confused faces.

Lord Sorbornef's lips trembled with rage. "GET THEM! I SAID GET THEM!"

Two more rushed through the door from the outside and met the same fate. Alto stabbed one in the throat and kicked him in the stomach, sending the bleeding man toppling back into Sorbornef. Both lord and corpse tumbled to the ground.

When Defari howled and began another swing, Alto threw his knife at the remaining Sorbornef entering the doorway.

The diamond tipped Etheria blade plunged into the charging man's forehead and protruded out the back of his skull, catapulting him backward onto the ground.

The door was now clear.

"RUN!" Alto ordered.

Taleeka didn't need a second prompt. She bolted out the door at full speed and disappeared into the fog.

Defari had just finished cutting down another attacker when Alto ran to the door. There were only two men-at-arms left. The elder Sorbornef was getting to his feet and the Tiikeri stood off to the side of the room, calmly watching the altercation.

All attention was now on the swordmaster defiantly standing in the doorway. Whistling, he pointed at the door's threshold.

"Guard!" he commanded, before rushing off.

Defari flew over to the open entrance and blocked it.

The remaining men started for the door but halted when the blood stained Etheria blade resumed its ominous growling.

Don stared at his dead son and felt the hot tears of rage coursing down his cheeks. Kneeling by his head, he gently brushed back the matted hair and closed his son's eyes.

He heard a whistle in the distance, and the sword flew off in the direction Alto had gone.

"I noticed you didn't get involved," Don bitterly spat at the Tiikeri.

"I'm here to trade, not to fight," the man-tiger replied, walking over and looking out the door. "Besides, it was twelve against one."

"Aren't you going to give chase?" The Tiikeri asked, staring into the Kan fog. "You do have an army at your disposal."

Don shook his head while staring at the face of his dead son. "They've got too much of a head start. We'll never find them in the fog. Besides, they're headed out across Horsefly Marsh. Why waste men when nature will take care of things?"

Don then looked up at Bo-Lah, his face streaked with tears. "I need all those men. We ride on Hasteen at the lifting of the Kan. We're gonna kill every one of those fucking crocs! Every single one!"

Alto had run about a hundred yards when he felt the ground soften under his feet. He could make out a small lake bordered by a few large trees off to his right. Up ahead he could hear Taleeka's footfalls which had slowed considerably.

He heard her cry out a moment before he felt the first searing sting on the back of his neck.

He swatted it, then examined his kill. It was a fly the size of his thumb.

He could now hear the buzzing and see the swarms rising from the marshy ground. Just ahead, he could hear Taleeka screaming and the swatting smacks against her skin.

His own body burned in pain as the vermin swarmed around him. They crawled under his robes and into uncomfortable recesses of his body. The swordmaster ironically reminisced on the recurrence of his situation before he spotted Taleeka through the fog.

The young girl was on her knees, frantically smacking at a swarm around her. She winced in pain and cried out with every bite. Hungry insects covered her bald head and they swarmed like an ominous cloud around her.

Alto reached down and snatched her up under his arm without breaking stride. He tried in vain to keep the swarm away from her head with his other hand.

Between fatigue and the unending bites, Alto felt searing pain coursing down his legs. Focusing on his breathing and the foothills ahead, the swordmaster diverted his attention away from the pain, running steadily—but ever slower—forward.

The ground grew firmer when the foothills came into view, but the flies were relentless. With firmer ground, he could make better time.

Alto still couldn't see the *Haraka*. By now his legs felt like lead weights, as did Taleeka, who was now completely comatose in his arms. Through pain and labored breath, the realization that they might not make it flashed across the swordmaster's mind.

Overwhelming waves of guilt stabbed at him. Mal's warning about placing Taleeka into danger's path had come true.

Alto stumbled, then caught himself and wondered how much longer he could last. His pace slowed with each step. A feeling of light-headedness swept across the swordmaster and he felt unconsciousness looming, when he suddenly jerked to a stop, and a force he couldn't make out through the thick mist held him firmly.

Almost immediately, the side hatch of the *Haraka* opened and light from the inside of the craft streamed out into the fog. With labored vision he could make out Mal's silhouette, holding her pistol crossbow.

"Holy shit! It's Alto and Tally!" he heard her say through the buzzing.

The Spice Rat rushed over and everyone piled out of the airship behind her.

She halted when she saw the flies. "What the fuck!"

Fighting back anger at being right, Mal quickly slipped into commander mode.

"Kumo, get them down off the web. Zaad bring me a smoking stick from the fire."

"Right captain," he confirmed, trotting to the campfire on the far side of the craft.

"All right you two, hang on," she consoled, swatting furiously at the flies. "We got ya now, it's gonna be okay. Zau, you got anything on that belt of yours that can help?"

"Yes, once we get them down," the Singa replied, not taking her eyes off her beleaguered crew mates. "We've also got that bag full of Dreeat candy the queen gave Alto."

"Here ya go captain," Zaad said, handing her a foot long stick that was smoldering at one end.

She stepped up to the webbing where Kumo was wiping a handful of insects off Taleeka's head and scooping them into her mouth while lifting her to safety.

Mal set the burning stick on the ground beside them and the billowing smoke slowly drove the insects away.

"Let's get them in the cabin," Mal ordered.

Taleeka was twitching uncontrollably when they laid her out on the floor of the cargo area. Eyes swollen shut from insect bites, she whimpered in pain from dozens of tiny bleeding wounds.

"I knew something bad was going to happen!" Mal admonished Alto. "I told you! Didn't I fucking tell you?!"

Alto slumped in a chair and wearily put his head in his hand. "Is this really the time to discuss this?"

Mal furiously snapped her head away from Alto and back down to Taleeka.

Wostera came back from the front of the ship, opening a leather bag. She pulled out a small brown ball and handed it to her captain. Mal accepted it and gave Zau a worried glance.

"I sure hope this works," the Singa said, turning over one shell on her belt.

"Here sweetie," Mal gently comforted, placing the candy on Taleeka's lips. "Put this under your tongue."

She then nodded at Zau, who placed a hand on the wounded head, rubbed the rune on the shell and began a low chant.

Wostera offered a confection to Alto and sat down beside him.

"So, what happened Mora?"

"Sorbornef is trading with the Tiikeri," Alto said, popping the ball into his mouth. "They discovered us but we escaped. The flies attacked us when we crossed a marsh."

"Mora I'm far from an expert on politics outside of Amarenia but I must ask; what are the Tiikeri doing so far from Nocturn?"

"An excellent question Valorous," Alto replied, astounded at how much better he already felt.

In the cargo bay, Taleeka had stopped whimpering and stirred from her agonizing trance.

"Excuse me," he said, getting to his feet.

He knelt beside Taleeka and opposite Mal who flashed him a fiery glance.

Between the healing candy and Zau's rune work the swelling was all but gone. The bites quickly scabbed over then dropped off.

Zau removed her furry hands from the top of Taleeka's bald head and Mal gave her a smile of thanks.

When Taleeka opened her eyes, she broke into a broad grin. Reaching up with both hands she hugged Mal and Alto's necks simultaneously. With the girl's reaction, Mal felt the anger slipping away, replaced by a sense of relief and affection.

"I love you," Taleeka said. "Both of you."

In the forward cabin, Wostera was watching the touching scene and closing the bag when Zaad stepped up beside her.

"I think whether or not they like it, Mora and the captain are now parents," he whispered.

The Bowmistress smiled as she cinched the bag closed and watched the three embrace. "I believe you're right Zaad. I also don't think they're going to be 'dropping her off' anytime soon."

"Me neither bow lady, me neither."

First assignment
The look of fear and respect on the other EEtah's faces

So different from when he was in training
Adad Sunal, the internal police
No one wants to see them
They caught the sentry stealing
His investigation was conclusive.
The House's reputation was on the line
Unstrapping his Yudon
Terminate with extreme prejudice.

Fassee snapped out of his bored trance and wasn't at all sure what he was looking at. They appeared to be miniature humanoid cats, the likes of which he had never seen before.

He had swum in under the overhang to get in close to the Hanara estate and a better look around. It had double glass doors leading out onto the narrow beach and trap doors overhead, perfect for unloading shipboard contraband or a quick getaway.

The water below the overhang was shallow. He could stand on the bottom with just his eyes and snout above the surface. Peering through the glass doors, he watched the woman with the gems from last Kan dote and play with two of the curious animals.

He could see how they would enamor humans. They were cute, fuzzy and loveable. To the EEtah they looked like a great snack more than anything else.

When the Turine in Makatooa's harbor rang sixteen bells, he realized he had been there quite a while, and it was shaping up to be a very boring surveillance watch.

Kicking off her slippers, Nikki Targoff sighed deeply and stepped out onto the garden's cool damp grass. It had been a very stressful day breaking in the house staff and a calming Kan walk amongst the flowers was just what she needed. She had admired the garden since her arrival but had no chance to inspect it. Now, the diffused light of the Kan fog softened the flower's vivid colors and beckoned her to wander amongst them.

She moved out of sight from the main house and happened upon a narrow path. It wound through neatly manicured bushes and trees until it ended with an arbor and wide stairs leading down to the river road.

She was deciding whether to continue or turn back when she heard a twig snap behind her.

Spinning in surprise, she saw nothing.

A wave of apprehension suddenly swept over her and she turned back. She had gotten another fifty feet when she heard the bushes on her left rustle. Glancing over and seeing nothing, Nikki quickened her pace as she felt her anxiety rise.

Leaving the trail, she had no time to enjoy the cool grass on the bottom of her feet because she was now certain she heard footsteps behind her.

Nikki could now make out the shape of the house through the fog. Up ahead was a small clearing with several benches and a low table. When the bushes rustled again, she broke out in a run.

A sense of relief washed over her upon entering the dell, but her respite was short lived. Gasping in surprise, she cried out when she found Tsara sitting on a bench, staring menacingly at her.

Nikki's heart started pounding in her chest when she saw Kasap, the butcher, stepping up beside the bench holding a large meat cleaver.

She considered turning to run when she heard someone coming up behind her.

"Did you really think I would let you come into our home and turn it upside down?" Tsara said, getting to her feet.

"Next thing you know you'll be popping babies out of that belly of yours!"

Glancing back, Nikki saw one of the male kitchen staff with a large carving knife, barring any escape.

"You see, there already *is* an heir," Tsara hissed. "That means there's just no room for you."

"The lord of the manor will never marry a slave," Nikki countered. "Your son will always be a bastard!"

"My son *will* be lord of the manor one day," she confidently said, stepping toward her. "As for *you*, you're going to be fish food shortly."

Tsara halted when a devious smile replaced Nikki's look of fear.

"Thank you for this little chat, it lets me know exactly where we stand," Nikki said. "And I also want to thank you for making this easy on me. I was really afraid we were going to play a lengthy game of cat and mouse."

Craning her head to the side, Nikki let out a loud whistle and the clearing quickly filled with armed Targoff men.

Tsara and her two cohorts glanced around in a panic at the dozen swords aimed in their direction.

"Drop your weapons," Nikki ordered.

The two kitchen workers hesitated.

"Drop your weapons or they'll run you through right here and now."

Staring at Nikki, Tsara's face was a mask of rage and hatred. The weapons fell silently on the soft ground and they gruffly seized the three of them.

"Take them to the root cellar," she ordered. "Strip them down then bind them in really uncomfortable positions. Put the boy down there too. *My* husband, the lord of the manor, can decide what to do with them when he returns."

The Kan had just lifted and Mz. Lau, along with a rather large bodyguard, was on the move across the busy streets of Makatooa.

Fassee followed at a discreet distance and watched as she interacted with street vendors and shop owners. This trip was more than just morning errands. Witnessing the diminutive assistant leave her guardian on the street, peer cautiously around, then enter the city's limited sewer system, decidedly piqued the EEtah investigator's interest.

Pausing at a nearby street vendor, he ordered a raw fish. Fassee bit the fish in half and was crunching away while pondering this strange activity when he heard a familiar female voice behind him.

"Yeah, that's pretty weird," Kem said, coming up beside him.

"My breakfast, or the fact a well-dressed woman just climbed down into the sewers?" Fassee asked, not taking his eyes off the bull-necked bodyguard.

"The latter."

"Why Mz. Aleki, are you following me?"

"Sort of, I was kinda wondering about a few things."

"Ask away."

"So, you already know who killed your Sunal brother, right?"

"Right."

"That means your beef is with the Cul-Ta. But that's not why you're still here, is it?"

"Very clever, Mz. Aleki. You are correct."

"Anything you can share?"

"With you yes, but it's not to be made public knowledge."

"Secrets are my business investigator Fassee."

The EEtah finally looked away from his surveillance and popped the rest of the fish in his mouth.

"The good sisters over at House Nur asked me to keep an eye on Lord Hanara. It seems he received a rather mysterious shipment from Nocturn a little while ago and they're curious what he's up to."

"Any idea so far?"

"None."

"I also hear that you've been asking around about the Mama's Boys."

"Yeah, Asad wasn't very helpful."

"He usually isn't. There is someone else you could talk to who will probably be more forthcoming."

"Oh, who?"

"Velitel."

The Kan fog had receded and Mal watched the sun glisten off the dew-covered pyramid of Hasteen.

The Dreeat city had been on high alert for quite some time with everyone preparing for an imminent attack.

Inside the *Haraka*, Mal went over final instructions to Zau and Kumo while Taleeka looked on.

"Okay, everything's ready, right?"

"Yes captain," they said in unison.

"Kumo, take her up to about fifty feet. Zau, watch for my hand signals for ballista targets. If you see a juicy target, feel free to take a shot. Just don't waste ammo, we've only got so much. If any of us looks like we're in the shit, open the bottom cargo bay doors and come in on top of us. Got it?"

"Yes captain."

Mal then turned her attention to Taleeka.

"All right miss Tally, I want you to keep your head down and do what they tell you. I'll be back in a bit as soon as I'm finished killing me some assholes."

Taleeka gave a nervous grin and the two embraced. Mal sighed deeply and kissed the young girl on the top of her head before releasing her.

"All right kids let's do this," she said, exiting the hatch.

Standing in the field just in front of the giant pyramid, Alto, Wostera and Zaad stood amongst several hundred Dreeat warriors armed with heavy bladed machetes.

The Spice Rat walked over to Alto when she heard the loud Dreeat honking coming from upriver. Nearby, Zaad was talking to several of the humanoid crocodiles and all looked in the alarm's direction.

"That's from our sisters tending the oracle," one of the Dreeat's who had been talking to Zaad announced. "They're coming."

"All right!" Mal rallied at the top of her voice. "Let's kick some ass!"

A rousing cheer went up from the Dreeats while they waved their weapons over their heads.

Mal gave Zau the signal and the *Haraka* lifted off. It leveled off at the proper altitude and hovered menacingly over their heads.

Mal looked over at Alto when horsemen appeared on the crest of the foothills to the South. A thick cloud of dust gathered around the horse's legs when they paused.

"You know it's a fucking shame so many horses are going to die today." she said, watching the hill tops fill with riders.

"And what of those on the horses?" Alto inquired.

"Fuck em!" Mal's tone was hard and unforgiving. "They're willing to kill off a whole race of innocent sentients, for no other reason than they look and act different. Those motherfuckers get no sympathy from me. The horses, they got no say in the matter."

In the *Haraka's* cockpit, Zau stared out the windshield at the gathering cavalry.

"So, we're ready?" Zau nervously asked.

"Yes," Kumo replied.

"You replaced the single bolts with the chain shot in the ballista pods?"

"Yes."

"Wait, something's wrong," she said, her eye sweeping over the ever-growing throng of mounted attackers.

"What is it?"

"The numbers aren't right," she said, shaking her head. "I mean, don't get me wrong, there are a lot of schmucks on horseback down there. But from what I've already seen, there should be more."

The Singa's brow suddenly furrowed. "Kumo, bubby, turn the ship around for a moment. Let's get a look behind us."

The *Haraka* pivoted mid-air, now facing North.

"I knew it!" Zau called out when she saw the force advancing toward them across the plain.

"Are they sneaking up?" Taleeka asked, slipping into Mal's command chair next to the Singa.

"No, they're going to try to take the cane fields before the Dreeats poison the ground. Hey! Are you supposed to be up here?"

"All she said was to keep my head down," Taleeka replied.

Zau didn't have time to debate. She flipped over a shell on her belt then reached into her pocket and gripped her Larimar talking stone. Closing her eyes, she held the stone and gently rubbed the rune.

Mal's eyes suddenly went wide when Zau's voice filled her head.

Captain, behind you, the cane fields!

"How could I have been so fucking stupid!" Mal admonished herself aloud. She then pointed to a group of fifty Dreeats. "The cane fields! All of you, with me!"

Not waiting for a response, she spun and took off running with a small contingency of Dreeats following.

They made it to the fields just ahead of the horde.

"Go in low," she said, crouching over as she ran. "They have us outnumbered so we'll use the cane to cover our attacks. Stick and move, don't let them know where you'll attack from."

The Dreeats immediately went down on all fours and easily overtook and passed the Spice Rat.

Alto heard the shout from the hills and watched the horsemen charging down onto the river's flood plain.

"Steady," Alto said above the thundering hooves closing in on them. "Hold."

The swordmaster could see the scowling faces of the attackers when the first two lines of horses collided with the spider silk Kumo had suspended between the sparse tree trunks. The single, all but invisible strand caught the horses just below the knees. It sent them and their riders toppling forward with a deafening roar and screams of pain.

The two waves directly behind them, with no time to stop or turn, toppled over their comrades and suffered the same fate.

The charge, given the attacker's sheer numbers, which would have certainly overrun their position, was now in complete disarray. Confused and panicked horsemen circled on their mounts, uncertain what happened or where they could ride.

On the ground between the two forces a hundred men and their mounts lay dead or badly wounded.

"NOW!" Alto screamed, leading the Dreeat charge.

Crouching down amongst the rows of sugarcane, Mal noticed the warm moist dirt beneath her boots. She heard the charging mass slow when they saw the empty agricultural field.

"They're all fighting our main force," she heard the leader shout. "Ain't no one here. let's catch 'em from behind! We'll cut through the field here. Boy, are we gonna surprise those crocks!"

Unable to see where their horses would step, the cavalry entered the towering stalks of sugarcane cautiously. Once the company of three hundred riders fully entered the field, a horse at the rear of the pack whinnied in pain when something yanked it and the rider out of sight below the stalks, followed by human cries and loud crunching sounds.

Everyone stopped and turned to see the disturbance.

With everybody now facing backward, Mal sprung to her feet and drove the tip of her rapier under the chin of the leader. The thin bladed weapon punctured cleanly through the skull and poked out the top of his head. He toppled from his mount with an astonished grunt.

From the far-left side of the group, a twelve-foot Dreeat rose above the cane tops with a roar and struck an unsuspecting rider with his machete. The force generated by the powerful creature, along with the heavy blade, cleaved both horse and rider in two. Both halves crashed to the ground, showering the riders on either side in blood. Before anyone around the victim could cry out, the crocodile-man dropped to the ground and out of sight.

"They're in the cane, they're in the cane!" one shouted in terror.

No sooner did they sound the alarm, when something pulled another horse and rider from the center of the group under the stalks. They heard the man's screams piercing through the neighing and confusion.

The now leaderless unit panicked, riding their horses around in frantic circles, slashing wildly at the sugar cane surrounding them.

The charging Dreeats closed the gap quickly and engaged the now disorganized attack. Alto heard a round of chain shot whistling over his head. The long bolt with four spiked chains on its tip, spun swiftly from the *Haraka's* ballista pod. It struck squarely in the middle of the charging throng, chewing up a dozen riders and their mounts in its path.

Off to his right the swordmaster could hear Zaad bellowing as he swung Bowbreaker in a deadly arc.

When Alto reached the bodies of the first wave of attackers, he vaulted off the body of a dead horse, drawing long and short sword mid-air. Defari howled upon release and continued to growl as it slashed across the chest of an attacker.

Immediately after, the swordmaster engaged two horse-borne sword wielders. He was unsuccessfully trying to keep one in front of the other but found it impossible because of the close quarters.

He had just finished a double simultaneous parry, and prepared to strike back, when the attacker to his left exploded. The blue sparkle that followed told him it was Wostera's arrow that came to his defense.

The remaining swordsman froze in shock when the remnants of his comrade's torso sprayed across his body.

Alto, already in position to strike, continued Defari on her deadly path. The man shifted in the saddle and the Etheria blade missed its original mark but severed the man's sword arm at the socket. Screaming, he tumbled from his steed, blood pumping from the open wound.

There was a brief lull in the fighting around Alto, and Wostera joined him at his side.

"There are too many," she direly assessed. "We need to cut the head off this serpent before it overwhelms us."

Panting, Alto nodded in agreement.

"I caught a glimpse of their leader over there," he said, motioning to a cluster of fighting mounts off to his right.

"All we need to do is get me close enough for a shot," she said surveying the area Alto mentioned.

"Let's go!"

Zau watched the battle unfolding and marveled at Wostera and Alto as they moved with deadly precision through the conflict.

She felt their synergy and bonding when they meditated in unison and knew they would be formidable, but to watch them together was a wonder to behold. They fought, circling back-to-back. The bowmistress took out any threats at a distance. Her arrow flew and returned to her hand in a shower of blue sparks. Alto dealt with any that got too close and the Singa could hear Defari's howls.

Zaad was standing by himself, deep within a blood frenzy, his chest peppered with a dozen arrows. Zau knew from experience that the arrows protruding from his chest only annoyed the EEtah. Surrounding his constantly slashing frame were the bodies of men and beasts, giving him a distinct advantage. The bleeding barrier was tall enough to prevent the mounted horsemen from getting close to the man-shark with their long swords, while allowing plenty of reach for the EEtah's great sword.

"There are so many of them," Taleeka sadly noted, looking over at Zau with wide, worried eyes.

"Too many," Zau replied, pointing to a force of about fifty who were attempting to outflank the Dreeats and come up behind them.

"Kumo, put one over there!" Zau said, continuing to point.

The spider-woman pulled back the lever with one of her eight legs and let another bolt fly.

The chain shot chewed up the first ten men attempting the flanking maneuver, but it did nothing to stop their numbers from growing or the path they were pursuing.

Peering out the side window she saw the riders had made it out of the cane field and were lighting torches to set it ablaze.

"That's not good," Zau anxiously said. "The captain's still in that field. Kumo, can you get us over there?"

Out of the corner of his eye Alto saw the chain shot destroy the first line of those attempting to sneak around behind them, but he realized its effects would be minimal.

He and Wostera were moving away from the main body of Dreeat warriors, slowly making their way across the battlefield searching for the river lord's leader. His men would soon surround the crocodile people and they could do nothing to prevent it.

Already the Sorbornef led enemies had lost hundreds of men to the Dreeat's considerably smaller force, but the tide of attackers was relentless.

Alto's breath grew ragged and his limbs felt made of lead. He had to come to grips with the idea that the situation was dire.

"I see him!" Wostera suddenly shouted over the din of combat.

Zau pointed toward the three mounted men lighting their torches. "Aim for the fire!"

Kumo lowered the *Haraka's* nose slightly and let the projectile fly.

The spider-woman's aim proved true. The spinning bolt collided where the torches met, causing an explosion of flames. All the men lost arms and their tunics started burning. Some of the destroyed torches fell to the ground, igniting the grass and the edge of the cane field.

"Yikes!" Zau lamented. "Just what I didn't want to happen."

Reaching down, she flipped over another seashell on her belt. The rune etched into the underside of the shell connected the bearer to the powerful elemental forces of water magic. Chanting softly, she rubbed her thumb over the rune.

From the moist soil, groundwater began to rise, saturating the area. Slowly, the flames started flickering out.

"Look, the flames!" Taleeka cried out.

Zau felt completely drained and her eyelids became heavy. With an exhausted huff, she plopped down in her navigator's chair.

"Are you alright?" Taleeka asked, placing a tiny hand on the lioness' shoulder.

Zau managed a weak smile. "Yes, little cub. Commanding even a small part of the universe is tiring work. I need to rest."

Don Sorbornef was fifty yards away toward the rear of his charging men under a lone tree. He was a commanding figure on the back of his horse, waving his sword in the air and rallying his troops. To his immediate right was a scowling man in a black tunic that Alto assumed was his bodyguard. Directly behind him was a boy of twelve, seated atop a horse, holding a pennant bearing the family standard atop a tall staff.

Wostera nocked her arrow and aimed when a rider waving his sword screamed and headed her way.

Alto bounded forward and dropped to his knees. A single swipe of Defari severed the horse's front legs, plunging man and beast forward just in front of the aiming bowmistress. The crashing cavalryman bumped into her extended bow arm on the way to the ground.

The shot went high, crashing into the limbs of the tree above them.

All three ducked from the small explosion of blue sparks and the rain of foliage.

Exhaling in frustration, Wostera remained calm and extended her drawing hand. Blue sparkles immediately appeared just before the arrow.

She nocked and fired the second shot in one motion.

In an instant, the entire top of Don Sorbornef detonated in a shower of blood that completely drenched the boy behind him as well as the standard he carried. The bottom half of the river lord remained macabrely seated in the saddle.

The young standard bearer screamed in horror when the bodyguard's torso erupted, splattering the tree trunk behind him.

Wostera was nocking the arrow again when Alto touched her arm.

"Valorous, the boy is unarmed and no threat," he kindly rebuked.

"Fair enough," she conceded, before pivoting and firing at another rider who was charging Zaad.

The arrow struck at the same time Bowbreaker connected. The subsequent bloody disintegration of the attacker caused even the frenzied EEtah to reel in surprise.

Alto wondered how long it would take before the troops found out their leader was dead, and what affect it would have on them. The swooshing sound of a passing sword indicated a near miss, but the force of the passing horses knocked Alto to the ground and sent Wostera staggering around in confusion.

291

By the time she regained her footing and perspective, the men had turned their mounts and all three were engaging Alto, still on his back.

Quickly firing, the man raising his sword to strike exploded in a crimson shower.

Alto swung Defari low to the ground, severing the lead horse's legs just below the knees. Beast and rider tumbled forward, allowing him a moment to get to his feet.

He fully expected an attack from the third man armed with a small battle axe. When it didn't come, he looked up to see the Sorbornef soldier heave the weapon.

Across from Alto, Wostera extended her arm from her side. Blue sparkles emanated from her outstretched palm, signifying her arrow's imminent return. The battle axe struck and buried its head deep in her exposed chest. The sparkles immediately ceased and Wostera dropped to the ground.

"NO!" Alto screamed.

He quickly pulled his knife and hurled it at Wostera's killer with deadly precision.

The blade struck the man directly on his nose, catapulting him backward from his saddle onto the blood-soaked ground.

Unbridled rage coursed through the swordmaster.

The man whose mount Alto had just brought down was trying to recover his senses and get up.

Alto unceremoniously ran him through as he walked past.

Now using both long and short swords, Alto began slashing his way across the battlefield in a blinding fury, unconcerned for his own safety or his next target.

The flurry of Alto's next kills became a blur, until a trumpet blast resounded across the flood plain, finally breaking his murderous trance. The swordmaster looked up to see a line of lancers galloping down from the ridge of the foothills.

They plunged through the Sorbornef lines, impaling combatants as they passed. The leaderless Sorbornef forces put up a brief fight, but eventually succumbed to the fresh reinforcements and fled the field in small groupings The lancers didn't interfere with the retreat or give chase.

Alto's shoulders slumped wearily as the defeated horsemen galloped away, leaving the ground littered with bodies.

A small contingency of lancers led by Sergeant Cavus came to a halt in front of Alto. The swordmaster sheathed Defari and gave Cavus an exhausted smile.

"Many thanks for your help, sergeant," Alto said. "They almost had us."

"That's commander," Cavus corrected. "And you're welcome. Aza has been relieved, permanently. This is going to be a perpetual patrol route from now on."

"Oh," Alto replied, clearly surprised.

"Like I said before, the men despised him."

Everyone stopped to watch the *Haraka* slowly descend behind them, hovering inches off the ground.

The side hatch opened and Taleeka rushed down the ramp. She ran toward Alto at full speed, colliding in an enthusiastic hug around his waist.

"I was so scared," she said, looking up at him, her eyes filling with tears. "I'm so glad you didn't get hurt."

"As am I." Alto replied, patting her gently on top of her head. He looked over at Wostera's body. "Unfortunately, one of our numbers was not so lucky."

Taleeka glanced over at the Bowmistress' impaled body and buried her face in Alto's pant leg, sobbing.

Mal was leading the company of Dreeats from the cane field when she heard Zaad's labored screams.

Several lancers were watching the EEtah roaring and hacking with wild abandon at the fresh corpses around him.

Mal smiled knowingly at the lancers shocked expressions.

293

"I wouldn't get too close," she casually warned. "It usually takes him a little while to come down off a blood frenzy."

Her mood turned solemn when she saw Taleeka and Alto standing over Wostera's prone body. Walking over to them, she felt a lone tear inching its way down her cheek.

Kneeling over the body, Mal reverently closed her eyes then retrieved the Samikort from the pocket of her blood-soaked robes.

Standing, she stared for a moment at the engraved green disk, silently vowing to see it returned to Amarenia.

"She died saving my life," Alto mumbled.

"Now at least she can be at peace with Klatka." Mal said, in a resigned tone, pocketing the Samikort.

Gavin casually strolled through Makatooa's tent city, eyeing its displaced citizens. The recent rains had turned the ground around the various shelters into a muddy mess. Filthy children splashed around the soggy area, squealing as they played. He ignored the kids and women, concentrating on the young men instead.

He realized his choice of patrons was one of the most important parts in the process of his evolving. The arms and legs needed to be long enough to notice the sign from above; the body had to be substantial enough to appease his hungry friends below. Gavin knew the gods of the air would look for sincerity, and he knew his signs to them would convey his understanding of their ancient culture. He could feel his pinkie fingers shrinking, and when they were finally gone, he would be one of the Avions, a pure, original race. Yes, he would soon have his wings.

"You are the one called Gavin?" A feminine voice from behind pulled him from his fantastical reflections.

He spun to face a diminutive, well-dressed woman with jet black hair which swooped across her forehead and up swept eyes.

Gavin despised her at first glance. She reminded him of a whore back in Aris. The one he couldn't get it up for. The one that brought him to the realization of how much disdain he harbored for women.

"Maybe. Who the fuck are you and what do you want?"

Madame Lau stood motionless, her expression dour.

"You are the one called Gavin?" she repeated in the same tone.

"Beat it *quim!*" he said, with a sneer, turning away.

"Lord Hanara wishes to see you," the voice persisted.

At the mentioning of the richest man in town, Gavin turned back around and eyed Lau suspiciously.

"Yeah, what about?"

"This way," she coolly said, then turned and set off down the muddy street.

Gavin hated dealing with a woman, but she had raised his curiosity.

He grew excited when they stepped onto the well-manicured grounds and into the opulent mansion.

"Please wait here," she asked, just before stepping through a set of two large ornate white doors.

Gavin stared around in awe at the massive foyer. To his left, a wide intricately carved staircase curved upward to the next floor. On his right, a sizeable archway revealed an expansive dining room with a long-polished table lined with high-backed chairs.

He had just enough time to survey the surroundings before Lau reappeared through the doors.

"Lord Hanara will see you now," she droned, before stepping back through the door.

She led Gavin through the central living room. He trailed humbly behind, staring at everything, never experiencing such exposure to wealth.

The room had a comfortable looking seating area in the center and an enormous fireplace. The most impressive part was that the far wall was composed completely of large glass panels that looked out over the water.

Opening a door on the right wall near the massive windows, she extended her hand toward the room's interior.

The glass wall extended into the spacious office and there was a formatively wide desk set diagonally in the far corner.

It was the sentient seated behind the desk that caused Gavin to pause in astonishment.

The seven-foot-tall hammer head EEtah rose to his feet and gave a welcoming smile.

"You must be Gavin," he said. "Welcome! You'll have to pardon me, but I don't shake hands."

"That's all right," Gavin said, taking in the room. "Nice place you got here."

Hanara looked around with a self-satisfied grin. "It keeps the rain off us. Please have a seat."

Gavin lowered himself into one of the four chairs facing the desk. For the first time, he was self-conscious at his shabby clothing on such expensive furniture.

"Gavin, I'm busy so I'll cut straight to the point," he said, sitting back down. "We've been watching and you have quite the reputation on the street of… oh how do I put this delicately?"

"I don't take shit from people."

Hanara nodded. "That will do. Gavin I would like to offer you a position in my employ."

This stunned the former dock worker. "Doing what? I can't imagine I'm qualified for doing much of anything except working on your docks, which ain't there no more."

"Well, I wouldn't sell myself short. And you have just mentioned the very thing that I will require your services for."

Hanara gave a cunning smile at the befuddled look on Gavin's face. "We have to get this city moving again. I am about to embark on a very aggressive rebuilding project. Your job, in part, would be removing stubborn obstacles in my way."

"I don't know nothin' about the law or dealing with the city."

This caused Hanara to chuckle. "I have barristers for that. Your job would be more, security, in nature."

"Security?"

"Yes, you see I lost my fixer the other Kan. Someone ran him through with a spear outside one of my offices."

"Fixer, huh? So, you're telling me the job is dangerous?"

"Somewhat, that's why it pays well. You'll stay here because you'll be on call any time, I may need you."

"I can still do my thing, can't I?"

Hanara's smile turned licentious. "Oh yes, I would never stand in the way of a man and his, *needs*."

Gavin's throat tightened at the thought of him being aware of his transcending activities in the Old City.

"Yeah, I think we can work something out," he gruffly said.

"Splendid, you start immediately. In addition to your lodging, we'll also provide your meals and... some new appropriate attire. You'll be working closely with Madame Lau."

Gavin cleared his throat and shifted nervously. "Uh, sir, I really don't work well with the quims."

A displeased look quickly overtook the EEtah's face and Gavin felt a shiver go down his spine.

"Madame Lau is a valuable and trusted person in my organization. The key word here is, *trusted*. We will pay and treat you well. However, we will have your replacement harshly deal with any disloyalty on your part. Do we have an understanding?"

"Yeah, sure."

"Splendid, now Madame Lau will show you to your room, get you settled and see that you are fitted with decent clothes. One more thing, I would also like to see a new attitude along with those new garments. You're going to be operating in a much higher arena now."

With that rebuke, Hanara went back to reading one of the many papers on the top of his desk.

"Yes sir," Gavin docilely said, getting to his feet and leaving.

Gavin was ecstatic. This promotion to a higher station in life was confirmation that he was pleasing the gods. This new position would afford him new and even better ways to draw their attention and approval.

Yes, he was sure of it, soon he would have his wings.

"Such a fucking waste," Mal said, gazing out the window of the *Haraka*, watching the remains of the defeated Sorbornef forces slowly return to Staghorn Plantation. Weary, defeated men slumped down in their saddles, eyes staring vacantly downward or into the distance. The Spice Rat almost felt sorry for them. They had felt duty bound to follow one man's vision of hate and vengeance. Now they were paying the price, one that would extend far beyond the lives lost. These were not professional soldiers; they were ranchers and farmhands that someone had shoved a sword in their hands and told them to kill.

With the casualties from those no longer in the work force, food production would be down. This dip in agricultural productivity not only affected the individual plantations, but the entire Goyan Islands.

"Put her down in the front yard Kumo," Mal said when the manor house came into view. "I want them to see us coming."

"Yes captain."

There was a small group of people gathered on the lawn in front of Staghorn Manor when the *Haraka* landed. They mostly consisted of women tending to men's wounds while they rested on the ground. The main bulk of people gathered around the barn and corral.

Standing, Mal put on her sword belt. "All right, I'm going to go deliver the bad news personally."

"Do you wish any of us to accompany you?" Alto asked, reaching for Defari.

"Nah, I got this. It shouldn't take long."

"Emotions are still high my love."

Mal nodded and picked up her pistol crossbow and cocked it. "Then I'll make sure I'm extra careful," she said, sticking it in her belt.

"Okay Kumo, drop the side hatch."

Alto watched her exit the craft and stand in front of the stairs leading up to the front porch. A dozen fearful hate filled gazes fixed on her and the swordmaster anxiously picked up a still sheathed Defari.

"YOU IN THE HOUSE. MATKA, MATKA SORBORNEF, COME OUT. WE NEED TO TALK."

A few moments passed before the front door opened and lady Sorbornef stepped out. She wore a long black dress accentuating a pale, frigid face twisted in anger. Two young men in their early twenties accompanied her. Their clothes were torn and bloodstained.

One saw Mal and reached for his sword.

"YOU KILLED MY FATHER IN THE CANE FIELDS!" he screamed, stepping forward. "I SAW YOU DO IT YOU FUCKING BITCH!"

"Elam no," Matka pleaded to no avail.

The man continued forward to the edge of the porch. "YOU COULDN'T FIGHT HIM FAIRLY! YOU HAD TO JUMP HIM."

"Don't do it kid. Don't do it," Zau said aloud, watching the enraged young man step onto the stairs, the sword in his hand trembling.

When he reached the second step Mal calmly pulled the pistol crossbow and fired. The bolt struck mid-chest and propelled him backward onto the porch at Lady Sorbornef's feet.

Several of the women tending wounds screamed. Matka's stare at Mal's blood-streaked face was a mask of bridled rage.

Mal shook her head in disbelief. "I swear to the goddess, you people never fucking learn!"

Matka continued her silent glower and Mal looked away in frustration. When she turned back her determined stare bore into Lady Sorbornef.

"Here's the way it's going to be," she said. "All the river lords are going to stop harassing the Dreeat. They get to stay! You're also going to honor any treaties you have with them."

"It was my husband that had the vendetta against the crocks, not me."

"That's good, because if I have to fucking come back here, I swear to the goddess I will reduce this plantation to rubble! Now, I'm going to go back and report to your king and my friend, that we've resolved the situation. Don't make me a fucking liar. But before I go, I've got one more promise to keep. You need to give up those Arapa skins your people stole. We're returning them to their rightful owners."

300

The moon would soon rise over Hai-Darr and already the Tiikeri capital city was coming to life. Mongrel slaves bustled about the sprawling expanse of single-story wooden buildings on their morning errands.

Spymaster To-Nok hurried along the corridors of the royal palace. The king liked to have his moonrise briefings and he had no intention of being late. Last Luna's meeting, as expected, did not go well because he had to tell the king about losing the Worrg pits. The royal tantrum resulted in the death of several mongrel slaves and he had no wish to repeat it. The white man-tiger hoped this morning would be better.

He arrived outside the receiving hall just as a young Yagur in clerical robes arrived from the opposite direction.

"Why are you here *priest*?" To-Nok said, eying the humanoid jaguar with disdain.

Ra-Jaa, priest of Pa-Waga halted in front of the Singa door guard and returned the condescending look.

"I was invited," he said, voice dripping with scorn.

The spymaster's tone became icy. "I see."

The guard opening the wide double doors cut short any further contentious banter. Unaware of the king's mood, both entered watchfully.

Kar-Gor, the once-a-generation black Tiikeri, formerly known as the Cub Prince, appeared tired, reclining on his wide throne. He had obviously been visiting a prospective queen last moonless. The time was upon him to birth a successor. All the prominent Tiikeri families from across the land of Mists would bring their daughters to mate with the king. Only one would produce a Tiikeri with black fur and dark grey stripes, the new Cub Prince. The process, as pleasurable as it may be, was exhausting and the king's mood reflected it.

Both mawls entered the bare room and briskly approached the throne. The Yagur went down on one knee and the white Tiikeri bowed.

With a wave of his hand, both resumed regular respectful stances.

"What news do you have about the Worrgs?"

"Your majesty the Kharry Institute has given the replacement of the Worrgs their top priority."

"Allowing the humans to destroy what took my clerics many lunas to make should be unforgivable!" Ra-Jaa spat.

"You speak as if your cult has always found favor with the crown," To-Nok countered. "May I remind you that you have only recently gained his majesty's ear!"

The spymaster watched his king silently observe their tense exchange. Normally, the king would intervene in such bickering between advisors, but he knew Kar-Gor wanted to keep friction between the two of them. There were few things more detrimental to a king's reign than the spymaster and head cleric getting too chummy.

The king's attention went to his high cleric. "Ra-Jaa, I would also remind *you* that the manifestation of your god in Lumina was banished. Both of you have failed me."

"Your majesty," Raa-Jaa apologetically said. "I have a plan to remedy that situation, ready for immediate implementation."

"Go on."

"A group of religious pilgrims are ready to journey to Lumina. All I require is our ambassador in Zor to clear the way."

"Your majesty, I would like one of my men embedded in that group."

"Granted!" the king said, cutting off a protest from Ra-Jaa. "And what of the Dark Waste operation?"

To-Nok brightened at the prospect of delivering good news. The king had been in a foul mood since learning of the loss of the Worrg network. The prospect of bringing in a large load of Trinilic from the Dark Waste would go a long way in appeasing the cranky sovereign. Not to mention the Etheria fire crystals would be an enormous boost to the empire's military might.

"Sire, one of my best agents and his team are en route as we speak."

Kar-Gor nodded his approval. "Very well, we must recover these losses quickly if any of our plans are going to succeed. I need not remind you how important this is to the empire. Do not fail me again."

Blyth Calden had to admit he was a bit nervous at the news and he eyed Madam Lau with some apprehension.

"Lord Hanara is here to meet with me?"

Lau gave a rare smile. "Yes, if you have the time to see him."

"Of course. Would you mind if one of my people is present?"

"Lord Hanara has no objection."

Pulling a lever on his desk, a small bell rang outside the door and the young boy in the blue tunic who had been squatting beneath it, soon appeared.

"Fetch Kem immediately. Tell her it's urgent."

The boy nodded enthusiastically and scurried out the door. Lau followed him out into the hall and returned with the Palu EEtah.

Blyth smiled and offered his hand to the seven-foot-tall hammerhead EEtah with bluish gray skin. He dressed in expensive blue silk robes with gold trim and Blyth noted the single gold signet ring on his forefinger.

"Your honor," Hanara said, withholding his hand. "Please forgive me. I don't shake hands. I mean no disrespect."

The mayor pulled his hand back and gave an understanding smile. "Quite all right."

"Thank you for seeing me without an appointment."

"Not at all," Blyth said, offering him a seat. "I've been mayor for the past four grands and this is our first time meeting."

A knock on the door interrupted the pleasantries and the Calden spymaster entered the room.

"Lord Hanara this is…"

"Oh, I'm familiar with Mz. Aleke," Hanara said, grinning.

"I usually deal with Madam Lau." Kem replied, returning the smile and nodding at his assistant. "This is an honor your lordship."

"Not at all, not at all!" Hanara said.

"So, to what do we owe the honor of a visit from our most prominent and reclusive citizen?" Blyth asked, finally sitting down.

"I've come to make you an offer Your Honor."

"I'm intrigued."

"We must get the docks and the city operating again. I am prepared to purchase the destroyed areas and rebuild them at my expense."

Blyth and Kem shared a momentary stunned glance.

Seeing he had their attention, Hanara continued. "Right now, the only way you can generate the revenue necessary for such a monumental project would be to raise taxes or institute new ones. This city is ill equipped for that."

"Pardon my cynicism Lord Hanara," Kem spoke up. "But why? What's in it for you?"

This caused Hanara to laugh. "Mz. Aleke you are an Intelligencer; I would expect nothing less. As for my motives, they are both altruistic and mercenary. I pick up cheap land, the city rebounds better than before. I even have an associate of mine meeting with the Valdurians about building an air station."

Blyth could not contain his curiosity. "How would it work?"

"After the purchase, I would provide the manpower and materials to rebuild, to your specifications of course. After construction is complete and the displaced businesses and people are situated, I would be the recipient of all rents. The city would still take in the appropriate taxes. In short, this is an opportunity for both our interests to flourish."

Blyth sat silently, assessing the proposition.

"I think I would be a fool to turn down such a proposal," Makatooa's mayor finally said. "I guess everything hinges on your offer."

Nikki Targoff reeled in shock and felt lightheaded. Her father, brothers and husband were all dead. Now she, and her accursed mother, were the only ones left. With no chance of an heir, Nikki knew she would become desperate. She didn't know what the old bitch would attempt, but she knew she must be prepared to strike first.

Jassusa took hold of her arm to help steady her while they watched the rider who delivered the tragic news gallop out of the compound.

"My lady, I am truly sorry!"

Nikki swallowed hard and stared into space while she collected herself. After a few moments, she stood up with a stern look on her face.

"My brothers I'll miss. I'm just sorry my mother wasn't among the dead."

The statement shocked Lady Targoff's new assistant, but she kept a kindly look about her.

"My lady, this means you are now the head of House Targoff."

A thin, cruel smile crept across Nikki's face. If her mother were out of the picture, she could unite the two estates under her banner.

"The prisoners in the root cellar," she said in a cold, hard voice. "Hang them immediately."

It took a moment for the order to resonate in Jassusa's mind. "Even the boy my lady?"

"Yes, especially the boy."

Wind buffeted the *Haraka* slightly and drops pelted the windshield when it passed into a rain cloud on Goya's Eastern coast.

"The rainy season's definitely here," Mal noted.

Down below, a bustling seaport appeared when they exited the rain maker.

"Hey, Ovora's down there," Mal teasingly said to Taleeka who was standing between the command chairs, staring wide-eyed at the scenery. "It's the next big city you were talking about. We can drop you there?"

Taleeka's face fell and tears welled up in her eyes. "No! I want to stay with you and Alto and Zau and Zaad and Kumo! Why can't I stay?!"

"It's okay," Mal conceded with a matronly smile. "You're my little Tally and you can stay as long as you want."

Taleeka was still sniffling when she fell into Mal's arms.

Zau, who was sitting in the navigator's chair next to them reached out and gently swatted Mal on the back of her shoulder.

"Look what you did," she admonished. "Scaring her like that!"

Mal ignored the rebuke, broke the embrace and held the girl out at arm's length. "All right, if you're going to be traveling with us, I need to give you something."

The Spice Rat reached around and pulled her pack off the back of the seat.

Opening the top, she reached in and pulled out a sheathed knife with a foot long blade and intricately woven cords and silk covering the handle.

"You need to get rid of that piece of shit steel you picked up in the Sorbornef armory," she said, handing it to Taleeka. "That will just get you hurt."

The boot knife appeared as large as a sword in the young child's hands and Taleeka broke into a broad grin as she rubbed her hand over the polished black scabbard.

"That was Alto's old knife, before he picked up the fancy set he's got now. It's sharp, so make sure Alto shows you how to use it before you get yourself hurt."

"I will!" she enthusiastically agreed, before skipping back into the cabin gripping the knife in front of her.

"Alto, Alto," she gleefully cried out, "look what I got!"

"All right kids, first we check in with Shom and get paid. Then, it's back to Zor. Tally and Alto, you'll be staying with me."

Alto stared at Mal with a surprised expression. "Really?!"

Mal scoffed. "Sure, what do you have back in Makatooa?"

"Nothing that isn't singed," the swordmaster admitted.

"My place is huge and it's got a great view. How does that sound to you Mz. Tally?"

Taleeka looked up from the knife in her lap with a broad grin. "I get to come live with you?!"

"If you want to."

The girl bound to her feet, rushed over and wrapped her arms around Mal.

"I'll take that as a yes."

Taleeka nodded, still holding on tight. "That would be nice," she said, her face buried in Mal's chest. "Uh, Mal."

"Yes?"

"I'm hungry."

ACT THREE

The Tiikeri Objective

"I fear there could be dark times ahead my friend," Jo-Rakk ominously said, staring out the window of Kai's apartment suite in the Bailian palace.

The Bailian spymaster and priestess of Orad paused and looked up from her evening meal. The petite, one armed human put down her fork and peered inquisitively at the white Tiikeri. "Well, that's a rather dire prediction if ever I heard one. Are you sure you don't want any of this roasted elk? I've got plenty."

"Thank you, no. Cooked meat turns my stomach," the Tiikeri ambassador said, leaning on the windowsill.

Down below, the wind blustered through the covered streets of Immor-Onn, blowing about the garments of the passing citizens.

"My beloved Cub Prince, the very one we risked our lives to put on the throne, is changing. He has allowed Ra-Jaa, the high priest of Pa-Waga, into the palace and listens to his council."

"Your government has always considered that a dangerous cult. What changed?"

Jo-Rakk shook his head and walked over to the crackling fireplace. "King Kar-Gor has changed. Pa-Waga can be very tempting. Greed and power are formidable motivators."

Kai speared another morsel and looked over at the Tiikeri warming himself. "Come on, he's king. You would think he has all the wealth and power he could handle."

"Under the influence of Pa-Waga, too much is never enough. That's what's so dangerous about it. It's the very reason we outlawed it for so long. It's an insatiable hunger, because once you get what you desire, you automatically want more."

"What could Kar-Gor possibly want?" Kai asked, finishing her meal and sliding her plate away. "I mean, he's up to his neck in gems and if I'm not mistaken, it's time for him to be breeding a successor. So, that means he's drowning in pussy. You would think that would calm his ass down."

The humanoid tiger chuckled at the assessment. "Never enough, and I fear he may turn his voracious gaze toward this continent. I've been getting rumblings that my people have begun open conscription among the Singa Prides."

"You do realize the Bailian Empire has no direct claim to any of the Twilight Lands except for what's around the city state of Immor-Onn."

"And the Bailian's have no standing army," Jo-Rakk noted.

Kai sighed and stared past the Tiikeri into the flickering flames.

"So, Singas huh?"

"Yes, the empire uses them as foot soldiers in any large conflict. The males are fighters, the females are scouts and hunter-killers.

"I'm not sure what's to be done, if anything," Kai frustratingly said.

The statement was only partially true. She had already made up her mind to step up her surveillance on the western end of the continent. What she revealed to her Tiikeri friend would be guarded from now on. The sad fact was that, if her former comrade-in-arm's message was accurate, sooner or later they may very well be at odds with one another.

Blyth Calden pulled the lever and reveled in the torrent of cool water that poured down over his naked body. Now that the winter chill had passed, he could finally resume his coveted morning showers. Ever since experiencing them in the Zorian Baths some time ago, he had become addicted. The new mayor loved the morning ritual so much that he had one built outside his home upon assignment to Makatooa.

Reaching for a towel, he watched Velitel approach his front door at a brisk pace.

"Over here," Blyth called out, directing him to the side of the house.

The commander of the city guards looked around for the direction the voice was coming from, then beat a direct path toward the partially obscured shower stall.

"Your honor, you've got to come see this!" he said, his voice containing a rare, agitated edge.

Wrapping a towel around his waist, the mayor eyed his top constable warily. Velitel was not prone to excited outbursts.

"All right," Blyth said, moving to the mansion's back door. "What is it?"

"Sir, you just need to see it for yourself." Velitel replied, following close behind.

"Just let me get some clothes on," he said, opening the door and stepping in. "Am I going to hate this?"

"Hard to say sir," Velitel said, stepping in behind him. "But this little addition to our drama is definitely unexpected."

Both halted when a familiar voice resonated from down the hall. "Blyth, do you know where my…"

From around the corner, a frustrated Kem, wet hair, with only a towel wrapped around her petite frame, stepped into the room, then froze.

An awkward moment passed as all three stared at each other.

"Morning Velitel," she greeted in an embarrassed tone. "I better finish getting dressed."

Spinning, she quickly slipped back around the corner.

Velitel nervously cleared his throat and gazed down at the floor.

"I better finish getting dressed too," Blyth said, following Kem toward the bedroom.

"Sir, I'll meet you down at the docks," Velitel said, heading for the back door.

"I'll be right there," Velitel heard Blyth call out from the other room.

Velitel stood with his hands on his hips, surrounded by the sounds of hammers and saws, when the mayor finally joined him.

"I thought you said you were going to be right behind me?"

Blyth blushed slightly. "I was unavoidably detained. Who knew getting caught would be so, stimulating?"

"Yes, well, life can be both a comedy and a tragedy."

"Okay, now what was so all important... oh."

Mayor Blyth Calden of Makatooa stared in disbelief, mouth agape. The entire wharf swarmed with Cul-Ta demolishing the burnt docks and busily constructing the replacement structures. They chattered to each other constantly and, because of their diminutive size, people found the construction scenes comical. The rat-men displayed a stubborn dexterity and clever inventiveness along with their incredible feats of practical acrobatics. The humor of the scene had the mayor grinning despite his revulsion.

"Well, Hanara said he would provide the manpower," Blyth said, watching three of the rat-men standing on each other's shoulders while wrestling with a wooden beam.

"Yeah, but all this?!" Velitel protested.

"This seems out of the ordinary," Blyth agreed. "Let's go have a little chat with Lord Hanara. See what other surprises he may have planned."

Arriving at the ornate front doors of the stately manor, Madam Lau answered the door promptly.

"Your Honor, Commander," she welcomed them with a slight bow. "Lord Hanara is expecting you."

Both city officials paused, taken by surprise at the greeting.

"Do come in," she said, bidding them enter.

She led them back to Hanara's spacious office with the window wall overlooking the water.

"Gentlemen, come in, have a seat!" he boisterously greeted from behind his desk. "I had a feeling you would drop by."

"Yes, Lord Hanara," Blyth said, settling into one chair facing the desk. "I'm certainly glad you could get such a robust and early start, but it's about your workforce."

"The Cul-Ta," Hanara acknowledged with a bob of his head. "Industrious little bastards, and they work cheap!"

Velitel sat forward with an apprehensive expression. "Lord Hanara, surely you're aware the Cul-Ta are a criminal nuisance in the eyes of the citizens."

"Perhaps if they treated them more like citizens, they would start acting like it," Hanara offered.

"Lord Hanara, I don't think you fully grasp the hatred and distrust the people have for these creatures," Blyth retorted.

The hammerhead EEtah sat back and smiled. "Gentlemen, the good people of Makatooa will just have to get over themselves. I didn't rise to the position I hold by being naïve. The people will feel differently once they have a beautiful new waterfront and rebuilt city, completed on

313

time, perhaps even early, and under budget. Speaking of budget…"

Reaching into a desk drawer, he pulled out a stack of five one-thousand-secor gold commodity notes and set them down on the far edge of the desk. "As agreed, five million gold. It arrived by courier earlier this morning."

"Lord Hanara, we thank you," Blyth said, taking possession of the five wooden tokens. "I just wish you would reconsider your choice of laborers."

The EEtah's tone became conciliatory. "Your honor, let me assure you I will assume full responsibility for any misconduct my workers may engage in. They were well paid… I mean, well paid for *them*, and I have always found gold to be an excellent motivator."

"I would have to agree," Blyth said, holding up and examining one of the commodity notes.

Mal sat back in her chair, took a sip of Argel tea and gave a contented sigh. The view from her balcony afforded a sweeping panorama of the Zorian cityscape cascading down the hillside where it joined with the tranquil waters of Narian bay.

Just inside the open glass doors to her spacious apartment, Taleeka sat on the floor with their Picean seneschal, Peshk, who was giving the girl her morning lessons.

The combination of warm sun and a cool breeze felt good on the Spice Rat's face and she got the feeling that she could get used to this kind of tranquil lifestyle. It had been eight cycles since they had returned from Otomoria. Alto and

Taleeka had settled in nicely and she could finally sample some of the fruits of her labors.

Mal's gaze settled on little Taleeka and she automatically broke into a satisfied grin. Her hair was growing out now that she was not subject to the vapors of the Toriss mines. She was also proving to be one sharp kid. She was pondering how the nine-year-old stayed so thin with the volume of food she could put away. A knock on the front door broke her from the contemplative trance.

Setting her teacup down, she padded through the living room, past teacher and student. Just before the door, she stopped by a small table. Opening the solitary drawer, she removed a pistol crossbow and cocked it.

Slipping quietly up to the door, she peered through the peephole and visibly relaxed.

Turning the lock, she opened the door and came face to face with Joc' Valdur, along with a mountain of a man in the traditional green jumpsuit of the Valdurian Air Service.

"Hello Maluria, aren't you going to invite me in?"

Mal broke into a broad smile and stepped to the side.

"Stay by the door," he ordered the guard before entering.

"Wow, a bodyguard now. Did you piss someone off, or is this just a healthy dose of paranoia?"

Joc' gave an amused grin at Mal's appraisal and his conspicuous gaze traveled down to her loaded weapon.

Mal held up the pistol and shrugged. "Ya can't be too careful nowadays."

"True," Joc' agreed, looking around the lavish home. "Nice place!"

"Thanks, House Valdur paid for most of it."

"We *have* been keeping you busy of late," Joc' acknowledged.

"So, what brings you knocking on my door?" Mal asked, putting the pistol back in the drawer.

Joc' was about to answer when Taleeka bounded over.

"Hi my name's Taleeka but everybody calls me Tally I'm nine-years-old," she rattled off in a breathless, rapid-fire monologue. "I live here now with Mal and Alto and Peshk sleeps in a big water tank in her room She's teaching me EEtah Want to hear what I learned? Thayokraoy ryy anak slab haey, that means back off or you're dead."

Joc' stared down at the precocious young girl and couldn't help but return the smile.

"That's very good young lady," he praised. "My name is Joc'."

"EEtah's fun!" she beamed up at him.

"All right Mz. Tally," Mal intervened. "You are very smart. Now, you need to go back and finish your lesson while Joc' and I talk."

"Okay!" she cheerfully said, romping back and sitting beside her Picean tutor.

"That *is* the reason you're here?" Mal softly asked with a touch of uncertainty. "I mean, this isn't a social visit, is it?"

"Do you have a spot where we can talk?" Joc' asked.

"This way," Mal replied, leading him out to the balcony and closing the doors.

"Speaking of Alto, how is he?"

"He's got a gig as an instructor at the local Wouvian sword school under Master Keraso. It keeps his hand in it, given what happened to his school back in Makatooa."

Mal sat back down in front of her teacup and offered Joc' a seat across the small table.

"And you're teaching her all the language essentials I see," Joc' said, settling into the chair.

"I tell you what, she's got a mind like a sponge and she remembers everything. So be careful what you say around her. It just might come back to haunt you at the worst possible moment."

Both shared a chuckle and Mal looked down at the half-filled cup. "Where are my manners? You want some tea?"

"Argel or Baul?"

"Argel, of course."

"I thought I smelt it."

"Half a dozen grands ago, old man Argel found himself a little strapped for cash. He finally made a big sale to get his plantation out of the hole and didn't want to pay tax on it. I got the whole shipment past the Quartermasters for him."

"If he was out of money, how did he pay you?"

Mal raised her cup and took a sip. "Tea for life. Every quinte a box arrives. I love this shit. It's even good cold."

Joc' shook his head. "Anyway…"

"Anyway," Mal said, catching herself. "What's going on?"

"I just got out of a meeting with Rafel," he began.

"Oh, I can tell this is going to be fucking hilarious already."

"Anyway… he just got word from his people in Immor-Onn. A large shipment of Trinilic just arrived by caravan to the Asaro-He Oasis in the Dark Waste. Its destination was the compound of lapidarist Master Istan-Le."

"Those are the Etheria fire crystals, right?"

Joc nodded.

"So, what's the big deal? Send a transport over and pick them up."

"It's not that simple."

Mal chuckled wryly. "Okay, here comes the hilarious part."

"The same sources also say that Tiikeri agents in Immor-Onn have been inquiring about Trinilic."

"And you want us to beat the Tiikeri to the Trinilic?"

"We sure can use the stuff, and the idea of the Tiikeri with that much fire magic is unsettling."

"What's going on with the Tiikeri? I thought we were friends. I mean, we traded ambassadors and everything."

"I'm really not at liberty to discuss any of that."

"Does it have something to do with your new bodyguard?"

"So, you'll take the job?"

"I'm pretty sure I can put a team together. What's it pay?"

Captain Sandor de Nier watched the Northwestern coast of Goya go by off the port side of the Whitmar slaver *Vergas*. They were just finishing an easy run from the Spice Islands. Down in the hold were fifty indentures bound for the auction block in Neir.

Sandor liked easy runs. A load of indentured servants was always the most profitable. They required less security, which meant less crew, and that equaled a bigger cut of the profits for everyone. Besides, indentures didn't attempt to escape like punishment slaves.

"Captain, what in the name of the gods is that?" The first mate Mutal asked, pointing off the stern.

Sandor stepped past his driver and joined his subordinate at the rear of the quarter deck. He squinted at the tiny object in the distance, closing in fast.

"Glass!" he ordered, keeping his eyes on the object and holding out his hand.

Mutal quickly handed him a long spyglass. Sandor opened it to its full length of three feet and put it up to his eye.

"It's fairly small, about twenty feet long and open top," the captain said, straining to look at the distant object. "Looks like she's slave powered. I count six oarsmen per side. Still too far away to get a good look at them. I can't spot any identifying marks or writing on the hull. Wow, she's moving fast!"

Sandor continued to monitor the nautical anomaly. Suddenly, he lowered the spyglass. His eyes were wide and his face ashen.

"GET ALL THE SHEETS IN THE WIND! OPEN THE ARMORY! ISSUE A WEAPON TO EVERY CREWMEMBER!"

The first mate's youthful, clean-shaven face was a mask of worry. "Captain, what is it?"

Sandor locked eyes with Mutal, then silently handed him the glass. Peering through the powerful optical device, Mutal stared in disbelief.

"Cat people?"

"And they're gaining on us. Did you get a look at the loaded ballista on the bow?"

He handed back the glass. "Hard to miss, sir."

"Get down to the armory. Arm everyone with bows and arrows, as well as a sword. Hopefully, we can keep them at a distance."

Mutal nodded and raced down the stairs.

Sandor put the glass back up to his eye and inspected the fast-approaching vessel. The dozen rowers were some sort of lion hybrid with thickly muscled arms, shoulders and chests. There were two orange tiger-men amidship and one at the ready behind the ballista.

Mutal soon returned with half a dozen of the twenty-man crew, armed with a bow and arrows. Sandor lined them up along the stern's railing.

"Fire the instant they come into range," he gruffly ordered.

The archers anxiously nodded.

It only took moments for the archers to release the first volley of arrows. Sandor watched the missiles pepper the ship and strike one of the tiger-men in the arm.

The loud thump of the firing ballista answered the barrage of arrows. All saw the chain shot hurtling toward them. They heard the ominous whistling of the balls rapidly rotating.

The deadly missile clipped the edge of the quarter deck on its way upward into the second mast and sails.

The explosion of metal colliding with wood took out the entire back half of the quarter deck. It shredded a good portion of the sails and snapped off the top ten feet of mast.

Captain Sandor was barely conscious and found he couldn't move, because the demolished deck railing crushed his legs and sprayed wooden shrapnel across the bottom half of his body.

Moving his arms, he felt the oozing body of Mutal lying next to him. Through a descending curtain of darkness, he could see a foot long section of railing protruding from his chest.

The last thing Sandor heard before losing consciousness was the clank of grappling hooks over the side.

They were about to be boarded.

Despite her calm, confident exterior, Matka Sorbornef was a wavering mass of uncertainty. She coped with her anxiety the way she always did, by presenting a hard and domineering demeanor.

It had been eight cycles since the crocs and the king's strangers decimated her family. Six cycles ago, hundreds of funeral pyres burned up and down the Western fork of the Otoman River.

Now was the time for consolidation of their fragmented houses.

It was time to face her daughter.

The ride from Staghorn Manor to the Targoff estate was a short one given the size of the individual house's land holdings. All the while, Matka kept a stoic watch out the window of her carriage.

She found her hands fidgeting in her lap when the buggy entered the Targoff compound. For the first time since leaving her home, she looked down at her bony white hands, contrasting them against her black lace dress.

Several people gathered to greet the carriage and she recognized one of them.

When the driver opened the door and helped her out, Matka looked around, coldly eyeing her welcoming committee.

"Lady Sorbornef," Jasusa bowed.

"Hello Jasusa," Matka's tone was cold and condescending. "I see you made it out of the kitchen."

"Yes ma'am. I'm Lady Targoff's personal assistant."

"I see," Matka said, eyeing the former kitchen slave. "Run along then and inform Lady Targoff that her mother is here to see her."

"Yes ma'am," she said, before rushing off into the house. She returned a few moments later. "Lady Targoff will see you now."

They led her to a sun-drenched parlor with tall oblong windows lining the Western wall. Nikki Targoff, wearing a somber black dress, sat stiffly on a narrow sofa, warily watching her mother enter.

"Lady Sorbornef," she said, not getting to her feet. "So good of you to grace us with your presence."

The antagonistic formality in her daughter's deportment shocked Matka.

"Lady Sor... Nikki! I'm your mother! We're family!"

"Wrong! We *were* family. You gave me away, remember?"

"Nikki, that was for the good of the family. And look at you now. You're the head of one of the most powerful houses of all the Otoman River Lords."

"Ah, so the ends justify the means. That's easy to say if you didn't have to experience the means. Shall I tell you about the means? Forced to marry someone I could never love! My first sexual experience, a painful one, was in front of an audience. My skin crawled every time he touched me with those dirty, brutish hands. I could go on!"

"That's not necessary."

"And kindly refer to me as Lady Targoff. Nikki is for friends and family."

Matka stood in stunned silence. She had expected her to be in shock over her husband and father's death, but not like this.

Nikki was unrelenting. "Why are you here, Lady Sorbornef?"

Matka cleared her throat and composed herself. "As you wish, *Lady* Targoff. I had hoped to propose a plan of unity and cooperation between our two houses. I see now that idea was premature."

"Yes, premature."

The two stared at each other for a long, tense moment. Inside, Matka was seething at her daughter's disrespect and her inability to control the situation.

"Well," Matka began, breaking the silence.

"Yes, you may go, Lady Sorbornef," Nikki said in a last act of dominance.

The new Lady Targoff knew by not allowing her visitor to take her own leave, but dismissing her instead, constituted a slap in the face of civility to the Sorbornef matriarch.

Outraged, infuriated and demoralized, Matka gave a slight bow of the head and an angry, thin smile, before turning to go.

"Oh, one more thing, Lady Sorbornef."

Matka paused and peered apprehensively back over her shoulder.

"Never come by unannounced again."

Mal felt her boots sink into the sand when she stepped off the cobblestones of Beach Drive in Zor. The water was calm in Narian Bay and the small fishing boats which littered the sand during the Kan, had long since disembarked.

She trudged past the cave opening, which led down to the Temple of the Golden Avatar. From deep within its recesses, she could hear the high-pitched wailing and lamenting of the Otick Clerics, living in their grief and pride at the sacrifice of their god in saving Lumina during the recent War in the Darkness. They now spent their days scouring the oyster beds of the three great Otick houses for signs of the forming of the next pearl avatar. They now tended to the temple, preparing for its return.

The Spice Rat's destination, however, was the cave further down the beach on the far side of the city. This interconnected network of volcanic grottos contained the domains of the city's more aquatic citizens who could function on land but needed a watery home to return to.

Like Zaad.

Mal had many fond memories of the outer clan EEtah. Ever since they found him floating, left for dead off the Zerian coast, he'd proved to be a valuable and loyal member of her smuggling crew. She didn't blame him for wanting security and stability; smuggling was a dangerous business in the Goyan Islands. She had lost contact when he joined the Valdurian Marines just after the Unification War. It wasn't until her first trip to Immor-Onn that they reconnected and their wild ride picked right back up as if never interrupted.

"ZAAD!" she yelled from the cave mouth. The Spice Rat knew the perils of entering an EEtah's abode unannounced, even if they were a friend.

The greeting reverberated down the tunnel extending twenty feet and ended in a "T." The EEtahs had sanded and polished its roughhewn volcanic rock walls smooth.

Zaad's voice came from the tunnel leading to the right. "Back here, captain."

The apartment consisted of two connected rooms. A smaller one, where he ate, containing the stench of dead and rotting carcasses; and the larger of the two housed a twenty-foot diameter pool with a ten-foot lip around it leading to the walls. Carved from the floor of that lip were several stone benches for any of his less aquatic guests. All the stone surfaces were smoothly polished. In typical austere EEtah fashion, the walls were bare, except for the great sword Bowbreaker mounted within easy reach.

A nude Zaad was at the opposite end of the pool in chest high water. Several small lamprey fish slogged their way across his body, cleansing it.

The surrounding water swirled from a dozen miniature dolphins, who nibbled sensuously on the body parts cleaned by the lampreys. Mal could make out his massive, engorged erection, which measured over a foot and a half, being attended to by several of the tiny porpoises. By the considerable grin on the EEtah's face, he was enjoying himself immensely.

"Come on in captain, the water's great."

"That's okay, Zaad," Mal said, unable to stop staring at the bizarrely ribald spectacle under the water. "I'm good right here."

"Suit yourself. You can have a seat. Where's Tally? She's almost always with you."

"Back home with her tutor and studies. She's got quite a bit of catching up to do."

"Heh, she'll catch on. That's one smart kid."

"Yeah, sometimes too smart for her own good. The other day we were walking past an alley and there was this whore getting nailed against the wall. She looks up at me and says,

Look Mal, they're wrestling just like you and Alto. She even makes the same sounds as you.'"

The EEtah erupted in boisterous laughter, which echoed off the bare walls. "From the mouths of babes!"

"Yeah, well..."

"Oh, come on, captain! She loves you and Mora. A blind Ash-Ta can see that. And you two feel the same way. Don't try to deny it. Moving in together was the best thing for all of you, especially her. Anyway, I'm sure you didn't come here to discuss your new family life. What's going on?"

Mal paused, considering Zaad's term of family. She had lost her parents at about the same age as Tally was now. Privateers killed both her mother and father for settling on a disputed island. To the Spice Rat, the memory of a family unit was an alien concept.

"Joc' Valdur paid me a visit yesterday," she said. "He's got a job for us over in the Dark Waste."

"We just got back from Otomoria," Zaad reminded. "You sure we've had enough time to rest?"

"Looks like you got the recreation part covered."

The EEtah chuckled. "I try. So, the dark Waste, huh? I hated that place. Not enough water to suit me."

"They don't call it a desert for nothing."

"What's it pay?"

"A shit load. More than enough for you to finish your interior decorating."

The EEtah surveyed the bare walls. "What do you mean finish? I was done."

Rafel hated giving bad news to people he liked. Standing outside Tate Whitmar's office door, he gave a resigned sigh, then knocked.

"Come in!"

Opening the door, he stuck his head in. "Ambassador, have you got a moment?"

Tate looked up from behind his desk, where he was reading some papers. "Sure Rafel, come on in."

The Whitmar ambassador stood when the spymaster entered and extended his hand.

Rafel always got a little tongue-tied around the ruggedly handsome Whitmar. He had fantasized about him frequently and he always felt as if his looks would betray his lustful longings.

A tingle went up his arm when they shook hands and he returned Tate's smile.

"Would you care for a seat?"

"No, thank you. My visit will be brief and I wish it were under better circumstances."

Tate scowled. "Well, that certainly sounds unpromising. So, what can I do for the Society of Whispers?"

"I'm afraid I've got some bad news, ambassador," Rafel hesitantly said.

Returning to his seat, Tate kept the scowl. "Oh?"

"I just got the report that one of your slavers, the *Vergas*, is adrift off the Northwestern coast of Goya. It appears badly damaged and there is no one onboard."

Tate exhaled loudly. "Did anybody see what happened?"

Rafel shook his head. "Unknown, I just got this. It happened close to shore. That may hold some hope of a witness."

Tate nodded. "Okay, thanks Rafel. I'll put some people on it."

Rafel gave a conciliatory smile and headed for the door. "Like I said, I wish the circumstances were different."

When the Zorian spymaster left, Tate reached into his desk and retrieved a small piece of paper and a leather sleeve. Quickly jotting a note, he slipped it into the sleeve and sealed it.

Reaching over to the far corner of his desk, he pulled a lever and heard the bell outside his door ring.

Moments later, a young boy in a bright blue tunic entered.

"Get this to a gull station," he said, handing the boy the sleeve and two copper coins. "It goes to Merin Wolff."

Merin Wolff was a city boy through and through. He loved the sights, the sounds, the smells, and the bustle of a large cosmopolitan community.

He hated it when he had to chase a runner into the bush. Unfortunately, ninety-five percent of the time, people escaping Whitmar servitude headed right for the countryside.

Thankfully, this one was different. He had pulled an assignment in his favorite urban hunting grounds, the high holy city of Zor.

His quarry was a former clerk in the Zorian tax office. They'd caught her skimming money and offered her a choice: five years of punishment slavery or lose a hand. She did the time, right until she decided to run.

The Whitmar agent had a hunch about this runner. She had a husband and two small girls in the Tuath Plat in Zor. He only had to stake out the two-bedroom apartment for a day. Sure enough, her plan had obviously been to return home and lie low until the heat died down. Unfortunately for her, the heat never died down with Wolff. He always caught up, eventually.

He spotted her a few cycles ago, through the open front door, when she greeted her husband returning from work.

Today looked like it was shaping up to be the same. The Whitmar agent loved creatures of habit. Merin saw him turn the corner. Popping the last bite of a mutton roll in his mouth, he fell in behind him.

When the man approached the apartment's stairs that led up to the second floor, the Whitmar agent pulled the pistol crossbow from under his tunic and stepped up behind him.

The man was only slightly taller than Wolff, with a slim build and was well-dressed.

"Easy does it," Wolff said, jamming the barrel into the small of the back. "Let's go check on the family."

"What! I... I..." the man stammered.

"You just keep quiet. Your wife is the only one that has anything to say that I want to hear."

Upon mentioning his wife, Wolff caught the odor of urine and all the way up the stairs tried to avoid the liquid trail flowing down the frightened man's leg.

When the front door opened, she was there. He could hear the girl's excited cries of "Daddy's home."

Her welcoming grin disappeared when Merin shoved him through the door and into her, thrusting both violently into the center of the room.

The girls squealed in fright when they saw Merin enter and close the door.

"Keep the kids quiet," he ordered. "You, over there," he commanded the husband, waving the pistol to his right.

The man meekly obeyed and the mother stood shushing the girls, who were sitting on the floor.

When she turned back to face him, Merin gave a friendly smile. "So, what's for dinner?"

Husband and wife exchanged quizzically terrified looks and remained silent.

"That's okay, I'm not hungry."

"Please, we don't have any money," the husband insisted.

"Shut up!" Wolff snapped. "You know why I'm here. It's the reason you pissed your pants when I mentioned your wife."

"You are Cora de Burgor?" Merin asked, returning his attention to the woman.

She stood in front of her children, silently shaking her head, trembling while tears streamed down her face.

"I asked you a question."

She wofully nodded, unable to speak.

Merin sighed. "All right take off your shirt and turn around."

Trembling hands fumbled at the buttons. She shyly covered her breasts and slowly turned her back to Wolff.

Merin gave a satisfied smile. There it was, in the center of her upper back, a Whitmar slave brand. The seared S was six inches tall, indicating the size of her crime.

"I don't suppose you have your 'Satisfaction of Servitude' papers handy?"

Sobbing, the woman shook her head.

"I knew that," Merin said. "But I believe in being thorough. I would hate to put anyone through such unpleasantries because of a mix up in paperwork." Wolff sighed in frustration. "You know, you have got to be a special kind of stupid," he admonished. "You had less than a grand left on your sentence and you decided to *run*!"

"I, I just couldn't take being away from my family anymore," she said through racking sobs.

"And you!" he said, looking over at the husband. "Harboring a runner carries a pretty stiff penalty."

With that statement, he raised the pistol and fired.

The bolt struck him in mid-chest, propelling him brutally back against the wall, smashing a small table and vase which rested against it. He sank to the floor, leaving a crimson trail across its pale blue surface.

Both mother and daughters screamed at the sudden violence.

Without waiting, Wolff pulled back the cocking lever which dropped another bolt into the chamber.

Aiming for the brand on her back, he pulled the trigger, silencing Cora's screams when the projectile plunged completely through her body and lodged into the far wall.

Merin could see her arms covering her breasts flail violently outward as her chest cavity exploded, showering the wall and her daughters in blood.

The two young girls were shrieking and crying hysterically when Merin calmly walked over to them.

He paused briefly, staring down at the inconsolable girls.

Keeping the pistol out, Merin kneeled in front of them. Blood spattered faces looked up to a stern expression.

"Kids, I'm afraid with your parents being gone, it's going to be up to you to repay their debt."

Without waiting for a response, he stood, put away the pistol and took the father's rope belt from off the body. Binding the two girl's hands to each other, he tied the other end to their dead mother's leg. "Some of my associates will be along in a bit to collect you. You are now property of House Whitmar."

The moment he stepped outside the door; the sound of a gull's squawking replaced the children's wailing.

At his feet, a lone gull circled on the ground. Picking it up, he removed the leather sleeve attached to its ankle and cast it into the air.

Merin didn't watch it fly off. He pulled open the narrow pouch and removed the note instead.

Reading the orders, an assured grin spread across his face.

Finally, a mission he could sink his teeth into.

Once he saw the tip of the needle glowing, Gavin removed it from the small orange chunk of Trinilic. Holding the pinkie by the tip, he sank the three-inch barb into the end of the amputated digit until it met the round weight on the end of the shaft.

With a satisfied smile, he dropped it into the long glass tank on the table in front of him. It plunged quickly to the bottom of the clear pickling solution and came to rest on the tank's pebbly floor.

Gavin stared with pride at the four human pinkie fingers sticking upright on the bottom like a macabre aquatic garden.

His collection was growing, but he couldn't help but feel a twinge of disappointment. After four attempts Modrick, Avion goddess of storms, had yet to acknowledge his signs. He was certain the patterns of the arms and legs were correct. The pinkie removed from one of the hands showed his intent, his desire for transformation. Did he need to display them more prominently to see his signs from the air? Yes, that had to be it. If the winged god of the air tested his patience, it was a test he was determined to pass.

Behind him, he could hear flesh tearing and bones breaking. The Zoande Clan was feasting on the body.

Kneeling beside his trophy table, he placed the severed arms and legs into a canvas bag.

He made sure he gave the feasting ghouls a wide berth on his way out. Blood was everywhere. Already they had completely opened the body and were gorging on the internal organs and stripping the bones with their sharpened teeth. He wasn't worried about the mess. Ghoul's insatiable appetite for all things flesh meant they would leave nothing left except cleanly gnawed bones. They would even lick clean the dismembering table where they now fed, as well as the surrounding floor.

Heading up the stairs, carrying the bag over his shoulder, the idea came to Gavin.

331

He now knew where he must place them. It was so simple. For him to ascend to an elevated state of being, he must place his sign in an elevated location. A spot where Modrick could easily see as she soared aloft.

There was a spring in Gavin's step when he walked out into Makatooa's cool Kan fog. He felt confident, worthy; certain they would grant him his wings and purify him.

Are you certain he will keep the appointment?" Alto asked, taking a sip of ale.

"I expect so," Mal replied, peering over at the beaded curtain in the doorway. "He's the one that wanted it."

"Do you trust him?"

Mal chuckled. "About as much as I trust anyone. Merin Wolff is one cold, ruthless motherfucker, but he plays by the rules and he's the best fixer House Whitmar has."

Alto listened to the Grand Turine ring seven bells out in the Zorian harbor. "And he seems to be running a bit late. Would you like to order some food? I'm growing a bit peckish."

"Maybe after. Dealing with guys like Wolff kills my appetite."

"I sincerely hope it returns. Pronari has assured me he has made an oyster stew some would murder for."

Mal all but smacked her lips. Even though Pronari de Bogat was the owner of the Dokana Pub, he insisted on personally supervising every evening's special. They always afforded Mal preferential treatment because she was the one who had loaned him the money to open the place.

The beads rattled and Pronari parted them. Owner and Spice Rat nodded at each other before he stepped aside and Wolff entered the room.

"I'll take an ale," Wolff said, not bothering to look at the owner as he passed.

The short man with the intense, scarred face looked around the room suspiciously before sitting across the table from Mal and Alto.

"Hello Wolff."

"Well, well, Maluria, you sure have come a long way. Private dining room and the run of the nicest pub in Zor."

"I'm doing all right."

"You know I always figured it was just a matter of time before our paths crossed. Who's your friend with the fancy cutlery?"

Alto smiled and nodded. "Alto de Gom, at your service."

Wolff's face soured and he looked over at Mal. "Does he always talk like that?"

"You get used to it."

"I heard about your pardon and commendation. I've been able to catch bits and pieces of your exploits. You can't imagine how sad that makes me. I kinda enjoyed chasing you."

"Yeah, well that's just tough shit for you and every Ironmark in the Goyan Islands. So, what do you want Wolff? I'm sure you didn't call me here to waltz down memory lane."

"I had a meeting with Tate Whitmar earlier today. He suggested I contact you."

"About what?"

"Two cycles ago one of our slavers was apparently attacked on their way to Nier. The ship is adrift off Goya's Northwest coast. It looks like they killed the slavers and stole fifty slaves."

"How do you know they were stolen and it wasn't an onboard slave revolt?"

"These were indentured conscripts, not punishment slaves. We have reason to believe the Tiikeri might be involved. I'm heading there tomorrow to check things out. The word running around the Society of Whispers is that you and your team are the resident experts on all things Nocturn."

"We've pulled a few jobs over there, but we've had relatively little contact with them. All I know is that suddenly, those devious fuckers, or their influence, are turning up more and more in Lumina. You should talk to Okawa over at House Valdur. Her and her pilot Demetrius have had more dealings with them."

"They're next on my list."

"Sorry I couldn't be more help."

"Had to try," Wolff said, accepting a tankard from a server. "Hey, wouldn't it be a strange twist if we were stuck working together?"

"Yeah, a million fucking laughs," Mal said, sitting back in her chair.

"Would you care to join us for dinner?" Alto offered. "I'm hungry and it sounds as if you have quite a few amusing antidotes about Maluria's past you can regale us with."

The swordmaster smiled warmly at Merin, ignoring Mal who angrily squeezed his thigh under the table. "I have it on good authority the owner has made a wonderful oyster stew."

It started raining long before the Kan fog lifted over the streets of Zor. Fassee finished huffing up the last few stairs before stepping out onto the rooftop where a barrage of cool droplets immediately pelted him. Velitel was there with two other city guards at his side. Kem was standing under an umbrella held by a guard, sketching furiously on a large piece of paper.

"His routine has changed," the EEtah said, coming up on the crime scene. "Why roofs?"

"The pattern's changed slightly too" Velitel said, indicating the arms and legs arranged in a diamond pattern.

"This means something," Kem said, not looking up from her artistic endeavors.

"I agree," Fassee said, pointing to the fingers. The killer removed the pinkies as usual, but folded the remaining digits into a fist, with the thumb and forefinger of each hand extended and touching, creating a triangle. "I've seen something like that before. I'm pretty sure it's Avion in nature."

"You remember any details?" Velitel asked, futilely wiping rainwater off his face.

Fassee shook his head. "It was early in my career. It'll come to me."

"Let's hope it comes to you before the final curtain falls on another."

"I'll sleep on it."

"All right, I'm done," Kem announced. "I'm gonna get out of the rain before this drawing gets ruined."

"Any sign of the body?" Fassee asked on their way to the stairs.

"Nope, just like the others" Velitel said, stepping into the stairwell. "I sure would like to know what he does with the bodies."

"I'd almost be scared to find out," Fassee said and closed the door.

"Maybe you're right," Velitel replied. "Either way I'm going to get into some dry clothes."

"Hey, you mind if I ask you something?"

"Not at all, a detailed program enhances the play."

"What can you tell me about the Mama's Boys Gang?"

The question made the commander pause and cast a bewildered grin in the EEtah's direction.

"An odd question. I did not see coming."

"Kem suggested I speak with you about it."

"That makes sense because I was a member briefly before I joined the Legion. What's your interest?"

"Specifically, Lord Hanara's part in it."

"You gotta remember this was twenty grands ago, and the term gang is a little exaggerated. We were all in our early teens."

"We?"

"Yeah, there were two sisters and one sailor named Mitchell. Each sister had a number of kids by him, of which I was one."

"So, you're saying…"

"Yep, we were both siblings and cousins. Mama T had four and Mama J had six, of which I was the oldest.

"So where does the gang part come in?"

"We all stuck together and watched out for the people on the docks. After a while, the two mamas were running things on the docks, much to the displeasure of the Quartermasters Guild."

"I can imagine. Were they hard on your mothers?"

"They started to, but a distraction shifted their attention."

"What was that?"

"Preskot Nallor and his Silent Partner Cabal is what happened. For a while, the Mamas 'Boys and the Quartermaster's interests were actually aligned."

"That had to be weird."

"I can only imagine. I wasn't around to see any of this because I was in the service by then. Everything came to a head in four P.A. That's where Hanara enters the scene."

"I imagine things escalated quickly at that point."

"I'll say, the Nallor Cabal killed two of my brothers before Hanara killed a bunch of the cabal members and drove Preskot underground."

Velitel paused briefly, searching the EEtah's face.

"That was pretty much the end of the Nallor Cabal here on the Makatooa docks. Preskot still runs things on this side of the Zerian Reef, but from seclusion. No one's seen him since Hanara hooked him off the stage."

"How does Asad fit into the picture?" Fassee asked, genuinely curious. "He wasn't very forthcoming with information when I asked him about it."

Velitel chuckled. "Yeah, he wouldn't be. Asad was going out with my cousin Moreeta at the time. He exited stage left when things got tough. It broke her heart. When Hanara started the Spice Islands Trading Company in direct competition with the mama's, Asad went to work for him. Both mamas died a few grands later which left The Spice Island Trading Company the only game in town. With no competition, he turned it into a huge shipping operation. If you wanted your spices shipped quickly and efficiently out of the Spice Islands, the soon to be *Lord* Hanara was the sentient you dealt with. By the time I mustered out of the Legion and came back, the Makatooa docks were a very different place."

"Is Hanara's a legal operation?"

"The Quartermasters love him."

That wasn't necessarily a yes, the EEtah investigator silently assessed. *He's hiding something*.

These were desperate times, Matka repeated over and over to herself. If they couldn't produce an heir, the Sorbornef line would fade into the dustbin of history and the neighboring river lords would parcel off Staghorn Plantation amongst themselves.

The way she calculated her situation, she had one chance remaining, and it was a long shot.

Everything would fall to her youngest son, the only remaining male Sorbornef, Dobet.

She had seen him going toward the garden with a book in his hand and she knew he would head for his favorite bench.

It was a beautiful day. The sun shone brilliantly with only the hint of wispy clouds above. With the cold weather finally gone, the garden was erupting in a rainbow of colors and a bouquet of aromas.

Matka was in too solemn a mood to enjoy the blooming flowers lining the garden path. She paused at the arbored entrance to the garden's main plaza and sighed deeply when she saw Dobet sitting where he always did, quietly reading.

She knew her contingency plan was a long shot. Dobet had yet to show any sexual tendencies. She was sure however when they did, he would prefer males.

That really didn't matter. There were many noble lords and sovereigns which were married and had many children despite their predilection for cock.

This would have to be one of those arrangements.

"Hello dear," she said, stepping up in front of the effeminate young man.

"Hello mummy," he said, looking up.

She smiled and sat down next to him. "What are you reading?"

The boy's face brightened at the question. "It's called Ulirlyn Duu."

"Song of the Seasons," Matka said, trying to recall a passage.

"It's by the famous Eldorian poet Sair de Ovora," Dobet said. "I'm using it to teach myself Eldor-Ya."

"That's good dear. You're learning to better yourself and I'm proud of you."

Dobet beamed at the compliment and brushed away the bangs of brown hair which swept across his forehead.

"There's something I must talk with you about, it's for the betterment of the family."

"What is it mummy?"

"Your father and brothers are now gone."

Dobet pouted at the statement. "I miss Paz."

"Me too, but you know, it's now up to you to be the man of the house."

"I guess."

"It's not a guess Dobet. You're the one responsible for carrying on the family name."

"What do I have to do mummy?"

"Starting tomorrow, I want you to follow Kokua around and familiarize yourself with the way she runs things. After all, you'll be in charge one day. And you're a young man of fifteen. Of course, they'll expect you to father an heir. So, we need to find you a suitable wife."

"But mummy I don't like girls."

This caused Matka to chuckle. "Most men don't either, they just want to fuck them."

"But mummy…"

"But nothing!" Matka's voice grew stern. "This is your family duty. Now I've been in contact with House Annov. They have a lovely daughter named Nuvia. She's a little older than you, which is good. You'll be meeting her soon and we'll have a small private ceremony here in the great hall."

All Dobet could do was stare at his mother with a startled hush. This was all so sudden!

With an elated smile she took Dobet by both arms. "Isn't this exciting?! You're getting married!"

Ge-Wakk could hear Zu-Zu's panting over his own labored breaths. He knew it was dangerous to venture too close to the surface, but that was where the best food was. Now they were paying the price. There was still a bounty on his people's heads. One silver coin was all their lives were worth and the hairless ones from the surface were always trying to collect.

The two young Cul-Ta raced ever deeper into the sewers of Zor. After each turn and double back maneuver, their human pursuers fell further behind.

"I think we're losing them," Zu-Zu gasped.

Ge-Wakk didn't reply but felt a sense of relief that the human's noisy splashing footfalls seemed to fade.

Zu-Zu was about to make another comment when he saw Ge-Wakk trip and pitch forward. A loud whooshing sound echoed off the walls and the liquid around them rippled violently. A net laying hidden under the two inches of water covering the tunnel's floor swept them both up in it. Now suspended from the ceiling, their squawks of protest accompanied the ringing of a small alarm bell attached to one end. The more the rat-men struggled, the more the bell rang.

Finally, exhaustion set in and the two lay motionless, gasping for air, awaiting their inevitable death.

Both noticeably trembled when they heard the splashing of feet and voices approaching.

"Look Pa," came a youthful voice from the darkness. "We got them both!"

"Heh, heh, yep we sure did. Two silver pieces will feed the family for quite a few cycles."

When the father tapped a crystal on the wall it filled the intersection with orange light.

The man was of a medium build. Clean shaven with shoulder-length brown hair. His son was in his early teens and very much resembled his father.

"They're kinda scrawny, Pa."

The father chuckled again. "Good thing we only need their pelts. You gig them and I'll do the skinning."

They heard a quick growl and rapid splashing down the tunnel. The son raised his short spear and his father withdrew a knife.

They cried out when they saw two orange eyes, glowing out of the blackness at the edge of the gem's illumination, rushing straight for them. When the Tiikeri leapt into view, he rose from all fours to his seven-foot height. Roaring loudly, he raked a claw across the father's chest. The force of the blow sent the much smaller human hurtling into the nearby wall. He sank to the floor, still holding onto the knife while blood gushed from the wounds, mixing with the sewer water around him.

The boy cried out and clumsily poked at the man-tiger with his spear.

Swatting the gaff out of his hands, the Tiikeri grabbed the boy by the throat and lifted him up to his face.

The young man gurgled from the chokehold, his face frozen in terror. Studying him for a moment, the Tiikeri suddenly closed his grip, crushing the young man's neck. The spine cracked as it broke, eyes popped from their sockets and he spit out a viscous, reddish-brown fluid.

With a contemptuous sneer the Tiikeri casually tossed the boy's body on top of his father.

Staring up at the trapped Cul-Ta, the Tiikeri growled something the humanoid rats didn't understand and they chattered back.

"Perhaps the common tongue," he said, cutting open the net.

"Thank you for saving us," Ge-Wakk said, looking up at their rescuer in awe. "We have never seen your kind before. Who are you?"

The Tiikeri gave a superior smile. "Right now I'm your people's best friend and I really need to speak with your leader."

The wind whipped through the military hangar of Air Station Three, blowing everyone's hair about wildly and tugging at their clothing. Outside the broad open bay, Demetrius could see the rooftops of Zor sloping down the hillside toward Narian Bay.

Beside him, Sitsa fluttered his wings in nervous anticipation. Demetrius smiled at the Tinian's excitement. He had been practically giddy since they passed through the portal in the Valley of Chains. The constant sunlight of Lumina excited him to the point of distraction.

"Why the military hangar?" Demetrius asked.

"From now on you'll be using the military hangar of every air station," Joc' said, scanning the sky. "This new bird of yours is packed with proprietary equipment. That includes a bunch of Etheria based toys from our friends over in Landagar."

"Speaking of Landagar," Okawa said, joining Joc's vigil. "I thought they'd be here by now."

"You can't go anywhere till tomorrow anyway," Joc' replied, not looking away from the enormous opening. "The Kan will start soon."

"Go anywhere?" Demetrius repeated suspiciously.

"You got someplace in mind, boss?" Okawa asked.

"As a matter of fact, yes," Joc said, finally looking back at his two operatives. "Two cycles ago, someone attacked the *Vergas,* a Whitmar Slaver, and took fifty indentures. The initial reports mentioned Tiikeri activity. They've sent Merin Wolff to investigate."

"Well, that explains this morning," Okawa said, nodding at Demetrius.

The pilot returned the knowing glance piquing Joc's curiosity. "What?"

"Wolff caught us at breakfast this morning," Okawa replied. "He had a bunch of questions about the Tiikeri."

"Yeah, and he wouldn't say why," Demetrius added.

"I'm betting they don't want it to be common knowledge that they just had a bunch of slaves snatched from them," Joc' surmised. "I want you to head over to Nier. Poke around the slave markets. Maybe trace their route from the Spice Islands. If the Tiikeri are using the Northern coast of Goya for their new hunting grounds, we need to know."

Demetrius scratched his head. "I'm hardly a diplomat, but if it was the Tiikeri, isn't taking a ship considered an act of war?"

"Tate Whitmar is lodging a formal complaint with the Tiikeri ambassador tomorrow."

"It's going to be pretty hard doing any of that stuff without a method of transportation," Demetrius said, watching a transport ship gently lift off and glide out into the skies of Lumina.

"Ah, here we are," Joc' said when an airship sped through the opening and rapidly approached.

Demetrius nodded appreciatively. "Resistance Class, huh."

"Yeah," Joc' confirmed. "The *Drakin* was a bit too small for the operations you've been pulling lately."

The craft continued toward them at a dangerous pace for the local. At the last moment it swung to the side and came to a sudden stop only ten feet from them.

"Hey what do you know, someone flies just as crazy as you," Okawa quipped to Demetrius.

The pilot was about to comment when the side hatch dropped and a short, squat man in goggles and a green jumpsuit made his way down the ramp carrying two small boxes.

"Well, here she is!" Tresna de Warton, code name, The Dwarf, proudly declared. "Brand new and just packed with all kinds of fun toys."

"The same kind of toys you put in the *Drakin*?" Demetrius asked.

"Yep," the Dwarf replied, handing the boxes to Okawa and Demetrius. "The big change was moving the steering wheel onto the command console. The really new stuff is in those boxes."

Okawa opened hers and the Dwarf stepped over to her.

"Okay," he said, pointing to the various items inside. "You've got two new jumpsuits and a new Ghost Suit. They've got Ukko Wood fibers sewn throughout."

"Arrow and sword proof?!" Demetrius excitedly asked.

"Well, it won't stop something big and nasty, but it should keep the everyday weaponry off you. By the way, there's two blouses in your box."

He then pointed to six small oblong pockets sewn onto the outside of both upper sleeves.

"Those pockets are for these," he said, holding up an oblong Etheria shard. "These match the Etheria disks in your overhead panel. They worked so well in your latest adventure over in the Land of Mists we decided that having them on you is a good idea."

"They sure got a thorough field test," Demetrius remarked.

"Unintentional, but you're right. By the way, Okawa, that was smart thinking on your feet, taking those disks from the panel before we lost the *Drakin*."

He then held up a black Etheria rod, six inches long and two inches in diameter. It had a core of dark green crystal set into a metal clasp.

"This is your personal PSI battery. It clips right onto your belt, it's got a Vivante core which doubles the PSI in either strength or battery life."

"Wow, okay," Demetrius excitedly said, looking over the new ship.

"You got a name for her?" Joc' asked.

"The *Atilla*," the grateful pilot declared. He then glanced over to Okawa. "My dear, would you care to accompany me on a maiden voyage around the bay?"

Okawa lowered her head and blushed. "Sure."

"Sitsa, hang tight," he called out to the Tinian. "We'll be right back."

Climbing in the cockpit, Demetrius noted the additional seat between the two command chairs.

"Nice," he said, slipping behind the wheel. Once Okawa took her seat, he started the Etheria engine and took the craft airborne.

"She handles a lot better than your average Resistance Class," Demetrius noted when they shot into the sky.

He performed a few banking maneuvers over the city before heading out over the bay.

Seeing Demetrius 'broad grin and boyish exuberance, Okawa reached over and gently placed a hand on his shoulder. "Are you pleased?" she cooed.

"Golly yeah! Who wouldn't be?! I'm just sorry we don't have a bottle of wine to christen her with."

Okawa leaned over and took the lobe of his ear sensuously between her lips. "You know, there are other ways to christen things."

Demetrius stopped the craft, allowing it to hover over the water. "Oh, do tell?"

Standing, she unbuttoned the front of her jumpsuit. Her breasts tumbled free and Demetrius noted the patch on her side.

"You gonna be okay with that spot where the Tiikeri arrow grazed you?"

She gave him an amused grin and let the jumpsuit tumble around her feet.

"You weren't too worried about it last Kan," she purred, walking back to the cargo bay naked.

Matka had never dealt with their Tiikeri guest. That task always fell to her late husband. She especially had no desire to encounter an angry man-tiger.

Like now.

"We had a deal!" Bo-Lah growled. "I want those skins!"

He had stopped pacing the length of the small one room guest cottage and stood menacingly in front of her.

Matka stood her ground, arms folded tightly in front of her, glaring up at the seven-foot orange Tiikeri.

"That was before the king's forces took them. I don't see how I'm supposed to trade something I no longer have in my possession. May I remind you that you may have lost out on a transaction but I just lost most of my family!"

The Tiikeri's look softened. "I am sorry for your loss. Don Sorbornef was a true friend of the Tiikeri."

Matka sorrowfully lowered her head. "He was also ill-tempered and rash. He brought this on all of us." Lady Sorbornef's last statement was little more than a whisper.

346

"I am sorry to have lost my temper Lady Sorbornef. We will not forget your family's hospitality and cooperation. Perhaps I can offer a new bargain."

"You have my attention."

"My government is willing to make regular payments to you for the upkeep of Staghorn Plantation. However, you'll need to purchase new field slaves, and educate at least one of them enough to supervise."

Matka uncrossed her arms and gave a questioning look. "In exchange for what?"

"From time to time my associates may need a safe haven in your land. Staghorn could be that place."

"Associates like yourself?"

"Yes, and perhaps others."

"What others?"

"Mostly Singas, male and female and perhaps a Yagur or two."

"I don't know what those are."

"Singa's resemble lions and Yagur's resemble jaguars."

Matka stared at the floor while considering the proposition.

"The same arrangement as you?"

"Yes, food, shelter and privacy."

"Very well. The cost will be ten secors a Quinte whether or not you use us. Payable in either Eldorian Grain Notes or Imperial Gold Notes."

The Tiikeri flashed a satisfied smile. "We have a deal."

"One other thing."

Bo-Lah paused and eyed the human warily.

"Throw in those arrow heads," Matka slyly said.

The man-tiger chuckled. "Done."

Now it was Matka's turn to give a contented smile. Those Etheria arrow heads would give her people an advantage during their next skirmish.

Bo-Lah retrieved his pack from under the bed and pulled out a one-hundred-secor gold note and handed it to her.

"Here's the payment for the first grand, in advance."

The combination of cool sea spray and warm sun felt good on the face of Merin Wolff. Standing on the bow of the small Nolton Boat, the Whitmar agent watched the ghostly curtain of receding Kan fog ahead reveal the lifeless hull of the slaver *Vergas*.

Besides the Vedette driver on the stern, two Whitmar Roji, armed with light crossbows slung across their backs, sat amidship. These elite slave guards were Merin's first choice for muscle back up. They were smart, well-trained and experts at handling servitors.

"Circle the ship," Wolff yelled back at the driver, rotating his hand in the air.

The Brightstar captain nodded and complied.

When they came around to the badly damaged stern, Wolff held his hand up and the Ukko powered craft stopped.

Standing motionless, the Whitmar agent seemed oblivious to the pitching of the boat while silently staring up at the destroyed quarterdeck and second mast.

Chain shot, he assessed. *Fired from about this position.*

Signaling to resume, the Vedette slowly came around the far side of the drifting ship. When he saw gouges in the railing, Merin ordered the driver to stop again.

This is where they boarded, he noted with a sigh.

Wolff then glanced over at the two Roji.

"No one's been out here?"

"No sir, we've kept her quarantined since we found her."

"All right, let's see what they left us."

One man tossed the hooked end of a rope ladder over the railing and the three climbed aboard.

Coming over the side, all could hear the loud buzzing of flies over the creaking of the ship. The smell of death hung like an ominous cloud over the deck.

There were a dozen dead bodies lying about and drying blood coated the wooden planks of the surface. Clouds of flies clustered on and around the mutilated corpses.

The condition of the bodies astonished Wolff, and he was no stranger to savagery. Navigating amongst the carnage, he could hear one of the Roji vomiting. He noticed that all the bodies had massive gashes to their torsos and their weapons were laying nearby.

They put up a fight, he thought, coming across two partially eaten bodies. *But nobody deserves this.*

"How many in the crew?"

"Twenty-five sir."

I wonder where the rest are.

"I'm going to check below," Merin said, heading for the broken door. "You two put these bodies over the side."

There was one more dead sailor at the bottom of the stairs. Something had clawed out his throat with a single swipe, based on the wound and arterial spray on the wall.

Merin paused when he saw something small and white protruding from the post the body was laying against. Merin struggled prying the tightly lodged object out of the dark wood. When it finally gave way, he held a single claw aloft, larger and thicker than his thumb.

The Whitmar operative examined the lone barb and frowned. Wolff had never seen a Tiikeri attack before, but he would bet his entire pay he was looking at one now. Pocketing the claw, he continued searching.

The entire rest of the ship was empty, with only the splattering of blood on the walls indicating a conflict. The captain had entered the last entry in his logbook the cycle before the attack. It suggested nothing was amiss.

Merin made it back up to the deck as they heaved the last body over the side. It splashed into the water of the Shallow Sea and sharks immediately set upon it.

"Twelve crew missing presumed dead," Wolf grimly reported. "Fifty indentures missing, presumably stolen."

"Sir what did this?" one of the Roji asked.

Merin held up the claw for both to see. "Something we've never dealt with before." The Whitmar agent took another look around the blood-stained deck. "There's nothing more we can do here. Let's get back to Nier, they can get her towed in. The shipwrights have got their work cut out for them today."

Mal's knocking on Demetrius' apartment door matched the timing of the Grand Turine ringing seven bells in the Zorian harbor.

She was about to knock again when the door opened and Okawa's face appeared.

Mal's face betrayed mild surprise while Okawa's relaxed in relief.

"Oh, hi Mal," she said, opening the door. "Come on in."

The Valdurian agent stepped back and attempted to keep her flimsy silk robe closed with one hand, while holding a pistol crossbow in the other. She was naked under the thigh length garment and reeked of the musky aroma of recent sex.

"Sorry, I didn't mean to disturb you."

"It's okay, we were done," she said, putting down the weapon and securing her robe. "Demetrius is making us cocktails. Care to join us?"

"Uhh, sure," Mal replied, following Okawa into the modest living space.

Demetrius was standing in the food preparation corner, dressed in a matching robe, pouring a red colored liquid.

"One more for drinks," Okawa announced.

Demetrius looked up and smiled at their guest. "Hey Mal. Let me pour you one."

"Thanks, make it a small one, I can't stay long. We're heading out in the morning and this was the only chance I'm going to have."

"What's going on?" Demetrius asked, handing Mal and Okawa their drinks.

"You know I was the one that sent Wolff to talk to you?"

"He didn't mention it," Okawa said, taking a sip.

"Yeah, he came to me last cycle asking all kinds of questions about the Tiikeri. I told you two had more dealings with them and, after our little encounter down in Otomoria, we should probably compare notes."

"Otomoria?" Okawa asked, clearly puzzled. "What happened in Otomoria?"

"Those furry fuckers from Nocturn were there. They said it was for trading with the river lords, but they were stoking the flames between the humans and Dreeat."

"Really, did you report it to Joc'?"

Mal shook her head then took a long drink. "Hey, this is good!"

"Why didn't you say anything?"

"Because I was working for House Eldor on that job."

Okawa gave a worried tilt of her head. "Something tells me all the noble houses of Lumina should be sharing information about the Tiikeri."

"No argument there," Mal said, finishing her drink. "Especially now that Wolff's involved with the Whitmar slaver that was attacked."

"How did you know about that?"

"Joc'," Mal said, setting her empty glass down on the counter. "He filled me in when he hired us. Well, I gotta go. Thanks for the drink. We'll compare notes when we get back, but I'll tell ya one thing. Those devious motherfuckers are turning up everywhere. I got a bad feeling about this."

With the lifting of the Kan, the *Haraka* raced Eastward out of the Goyan Islands, leaving the sun to sink progressively lower in the Western sky.

"Is it time for my lesson?" Taleeka excitedly asked, her hands gripped tightly around the sheathed blade.

A grinning Alto nodded and motioned her back to the cargo area.

When the swordmaster made it back, he found the young girl already prepared with the knife tucked into her belt.

Approaching Taleeka, Alto's attitude took on a serious fatherly quality.

"All right, I have shown you the basic stances. Have you been practicing them?"

"Every cycle," she said, nodding.

"Good, this cycle we will begin with getting you used to the concept of facing an adversary."

Taleeka was wide-eyed, transfixed on Alto, eagerly absorbing every word and nuance.

"Every time you face off against someone, there are three enemies to overcome. The first and greatest enemy is fear. It clouds the mind and paralyzes limbs. The second enemy, nearly as dangerous, is anger. It blinds you and makes you act irrationally. And last, the least of the great enemies is the opponent you face, for if you have defeated the first two, your technique will flow, and you will be effective."

Zaad chuckled from his seat. "Ya never can go wrong quoting Tabak, Mora."

Alto nodded at the EEtah before turning his attention back to his student. "Today I will show you the most basic of attack openings. Most of the techniques you will learn in the future will build upon this, so your foundation must be solid. It is called Jawo Yajin, the drawing strike. Observe."

Using his short sword, Alto slowly drew the blade and continued the arc outward in a deliberate slashing motion until his arm extended upward over his head. The swordmaster repeated the motion again and Taleeka's eyes never left the demonstration.

"Now you."

Taleeka's first few attempts were clumsy and Alto patiently corrected her by moving and guiding her limbs.

"You must practice this technique until you can perform it in your sleep."

Mal watched the lesson from the captain's chair with a sense of relief. Her little Tally was taking the first steps in learning to protect herself.

"Let's bypass the stop in Immor-Onn and head straight to the oasis. We'll save some time and keep away from prying eyes," Mal said to Zau. "How long?"

The Singa lifted her eye patch and the ethereal globe projected out in front of her. She studied it for a moment before looking back at Mal.

"The way I figure it captain, we've got a full cycle in the air. That's provided the weather doesn't go kaput on us."

"Give us a little extra speed," Mal ordered. "We gotta beat the Tiikeri to the punch."

Standing on the Western docks of the port city of Nier, Merin Wolff watched them unload the slave ship *Granger's* human cargo. First came the indentures. These contracted servants were unrestrained and peered around wide-eyed at their strange surroundings. The manacled punishment slaves followed them, harassed by their handlers every step of the way. Wolff wondered how many would eventually try to run. No matter, both groups would be on the auction block by tomorrow.

Moving down the wharf, Merin glimpsed his childhood home in the distance. Ever since the slave revolt which killed his family and left him disfigured, the neighboring estates took over the Wolff plantation. The Whitmar fixer was ambivalent about his early years, he didn't miss the pastoral life; he certainly wasn't a farmer.

Pausing once again, he watched an empty slaver leave the port and wondered if it would make it back. The scene of the partially eaten bodies on the *Vergas*, as well as Mal's words, haunted him. If the Tiikeri were up to something, which he sensed they were, it was still a mystery. He wasn't even sure he would find anything about the missing slaves here in Nier. But it was a start.

"How ya doing Wolff?" a feminine voice from behind snapped him out of his contemplation.

"Okawa, what are you doing here?"

The Valdurian agent leaned on the railing beside him. "You know, your boss talks to my boss. My boss gets concerned and sends me."

Wolff scoffed and watched the departing slaver exit the bay and head West, out of sight. "I'm not even sure what I'm looking for here. I'm just going where my gut tells me."

"You've been doing it long enough. I'd trust your gut."

"What's your boss's interest in missing slaves?"

"It's not the slaves, it's the reports the Tiikeri might be involved."

Merin reached into his pocket, pulled out the single claw and laid it on the railing. "Not might; definitely involved."

Okawa picked up the large, barbed nail and gave a silent whistle while examining it.

"It wasn't pretty out there on that ship." Wolff said in a haunting tone.

Okawa shook her head and handed back the claw. "Tiikeri raids never are."

"I'm still not sure what I'm looking for here!" Wolff said, obviously frustrated. "I mean I feel like I should be out beating the bushes somewhere else."

"If it makes you feel any better, my pilot is out flying over the ship's route. He's hoping to find something from the air that will help."

"Help, huh?" he muttered before a long, thoughtful pause.

Merin finally stood up straight and gave a few resolute raps on the railing. "Well, I'd love to stay and chat, but I think I'm going to pay a visit to the Harbor Master's office. If you guys really want to *help*, just stay out of my way."

"Screw you too, Wolff," she said with a chuckle when he turned to go.

The moon had long since risen over the Dark Waste Desert. Its stark brilliance cast long shadows over the dunes and reflected off the hull of the *Haraka*. The airship was streaking Westward a mere twenty feet over the barren landscape, kicking up a trail of sand in its wake.

Zau's spectral globe bathed the cockpit in glowing blue light. She checked a point on its translucent surface and it dissipated back into her eye.

"All right, miss, I gotta secret," she said, lowering her eyepatch. "You wanna tell us exactly where we're headed and what's going on?"

"Yeah, it's about time," the Spice Rat said, spinning in her seat to face everyone.

"First, I just wanna say, sorry for all the cloak and dagger shit. I know I've always been up front about any kind of job we go on, but this was different. So, thanks for trusting me on this one."

"I gotta say captain, just telling us we were going to the Dark waste was a little thin," Zaad said with a good-natured smile.

"The Valdurian government wanted this to be hush hush, that's also the reason for the roundabout course we took."

"I was wondering about that," Zau said. "it was like going over your shoulder to scratch your backside."

"The fewer eyes on us the better," Mal replied. "So, the Valdurians want us to go to the Asaro-He Oasis. A lapidarist there by the name of Istan-Le received a large shipment of Trinilic a short while ago. The Valdurians want us to get it."

"What's a lapidarist?" Taleeka curiously asked.

Alto touched her shoulder and gently smiled. "That is a sentient that takes raw gems, cuts and polishes them so they are pretty. Some who are very skilled work with Etheria Crystals. One of them made my swords."

The answer satisfied the youngster because she settled back quietly in her seat.

"Wait a minute," Zau said. "Isn't Trinilic the Etheria crystal that deals with fire magic?"

"Yep."

"That's some pretty dicey stuff."

"Yep, that's why we get the big money."

"Speaking of money," Zau cautiously said. "How much is this paying? I don't think they're going to give us the Etheria for free. Who's footing the bill for that?"

"There's a thousand-secor Air Note waiting for each of us upon delivery of the Trinilic. They're also going to outfit the *Haraka* with some of it and that'll up our fucking firepower. As for payment, the Valdurians have been in secret negotiation with oasis leaders in Immor-Onn. They're getting an air station."

Alto quizzically cocked his head. "Doesn't that seem a bit excessive? I mean, an air station in a remote oasis?"

"According to Joc', this isn't like the two oases we recently visited. This is a small city on the shore of a vast lake you can barely see across. It's the biggest oasis in the Dark Waste. It's also the closest to Lumina and it sits at the end of the most extensive trade route in the desert."

"Captain, Trinilic can be tricky to deal with," Zaad added, sounding equally puzzled, "but why all the secrecy? What you've been describing is... well... commerce."

"Yeah, here comes the fun part," Mal said sarcastically. "They've spotted Tiikeri agents in Immor-Onn snooping around and fucking asking about... wait for it... Trinilic!"

A collective groaning swept through the cabin.

"The Valdurians are concerned, rightfully so I might add, about the Tiikeri getting their furry hands on that much fire magic."

"So, it's a race?" Zau said, raising her eyepatch. "Well, now that I've got a better idea of where we're going..."

The globe, once again projected out of her eye and she zoomed in on the oasis.

"His compound is on the Northern edge of the city. It's supposed to be a pretty extensive operation."

"There," Zau said to Kumo, pointing at a glowing dot. "We're almost on it captain."

The ground below them showed signs of life when they caught the moonlight shining off the domed rooftops in the distance.

"Well, I'll be fucked! Small city is right!"

Down below them the scrub and sand were turning into rows of well-manicured agricultural fields punctuated by frequent stands of trees.

"Kumo take us up over tree top level," Mal said when she saw them coming up on a group of farmers hard at work. "No sense freaking out the locals."

"If they're going to be putting an air station here, they better get used to it," Zau said, watching the Bailian farmers stop and stare at the ship whisking by.

"Baby steps," Mal said. She then pointed to the only walled compound in sight. "I'm betting this is the place. Kumo put her down on the other side of the compound away from the city."

"Yes, Captain."

The *Haraka* set down, kicking up a cloud of sand which quickly dissipated in the stiff breeze.

"All right," Mal said, getting to her feet. "Zaad and I will get the goods. Alto poke around town. Pick up some provisions but mostly keep an eye out for any hint of Tiikeri presence."

"I want to go!" Taleeka said, coming to her feet and sliding the knife into her belt.

"No, not a good idea!" Mal admonished. "Why don't you stay here and keep Kumo and Zau company? You can practice that move Alto showed you."

"I have been practicing!" she protested.

The young girl then stepped back and, in a blur, executed a flawless drawing strike. She paused at maximum extension, her face taunt and serious.

Mal and Alto stared at each other while she deftly sheathed the blade, both nodding approvingly.

"All right you can go," Mal agreed, holding her hands up. "I guess it's only fair. You do most of the eating around here. You should help out getting the provisions."

Upon hearing Mal's consent, Taleeka's intense happiness instantly replaced her martial seriousness.

"Thank you!" she squealed, running over and hugging Mal.

"All right, let's do this," Mal said, surveying her team to see if everyone was ready. "The sooner we get back the sooner we get paid."

"I heard that!" Zau enthusiastically said.

"All right, Kumo drop the hatch. Everyone get in and out of the ship quickly or that fucking sand will be everywhere."

The side hatch dropped and the team quickly disembarked. It surprised Mal to see that a small crowd had gathered about thirty feet from them. The curious group consisted of a few Bailians, several Gila and two On-Dara. All of them seemed harmless and quite taken by the strangers and their flying boat.

"Well, so much for stealth," Mal muttered under her breath.

Tate Whitmar was a big man, with a barrel chest and chiseled good looks, known for his plain talk and overall good nature. Now, the Whitmar Ambassador marched across the Zorian forum, and his eyes burned with intensity over a scowl etched across his face. Few things angered Tate to the point of violence more than interference with his family business of slavery.

Along his morning trek, he met anyone attempting to engage him in conversation with an up raised hand as he marched by them. Finally, coming to a stop in front of the Tiikeri ambassador's office and residence, he took a moment to compose himself before knocking vigorously. A hairless mongrel, with pale, wrinkled skin, opened the door.

"I need to see Ambassador Za-Tar immediately!"

"I'm sorry sir but the ambassador cannot be disturbed," the mongrel said in broken common.

"Looky here missy, I ain't playing around!"

"It's all right Wa-Ya," came a booming voice from within.

The mongrel opened the door and Tate stepped past her.

Immediately upon entering, Tate winced at the dank stench of ammonia. The orange Tiikeri was standing in the door leading to his residence in a bright blue robe.

"Ah, the sovereign hand of Whitmar," he greeted. "I must commend your people on their hospitality. Take this robe for instance. This is the finest silk I have ever felt. It makes the Tinian silk from my home feel like burlap. Now this could be a valuable trade item between our peoples."

"Ambassador I did not come here to talk about textiles!"

"Ambassador Whitmar, I see you're upset," the Tiikeri's tone was overly friendly to the point of condescension.

"Yer darn right I'm upset!"

"Nothing I've done, I hope."

"Not you, but your people apparently have been causing trouble with my people!"

"Oh, how so?"

"Three cycles ago, raiders attacked one of our slavers off the Northern coast of Goya. They killed the crew and took all the slaves."

"This is of course terrible, but why are you telling me?"

"Because I just got word from one of our operatives who inspected the ship and there is overwhelming evidence those raiders were *your* people."

Za-Tar appeared genuinely shocked. "I apologize for not having heard of this. My Worrg lost contact with Hai-Darr several cycles ago. What evidence are you referring to?"

"Claw and bite marks on the dead crew. Partially eaten bodies and a broken off claw. That's just some of it. They're towing the ship into port for repairs. Where they'll make a full inspection."

"Ambassador I share your frustration but there are other Mawl races. Perhaps..."

"The other Mawl races don't have seafaring capabilities and you know it! And I don't think you *do* share my frustration. You see, those taken weren't punishment slaves, they were indentures. That means they were under contract for a set number of grands. Now that they took the product, people on both sides of that contract are affected."

The Tiikeri gave a frustrated sigh. "Ambassador, even saying some of my people were behind this senseless action, surely you realize *we* have pirates too. Lawless attacks are an inevitable by-product of our two peoples finally encountering each other."

"Tate remained resolute. I'm on my way to file an official grievance against your government with the Zorian High Council."

Za-Tar's eyes widened and his mouth tightened. "Ambassador! I hardly think that is necessary."

Tate paused at the door; his face was grim. "It's a grievance now. If any of those indentures turn up in your slave markets. Well then, we'll have ourselves a genuine international incident on our hands."

Captain Lar-Ga hated diversions. He and his crew were raiders, not a delivery service. Still, he had his orders.

He checked back into the twenty-foot-long open top ship and shook his head. The three crates of Cheepas would soon be gone and he couldn't wait to reach Otomoria where he could get rid of the three female Singa passengers. The stone face hunter-killer squad made even the hardened privateers of his crew nervous.

Adjusting the fish skin eye covering, the Tiikeri captain raised his hand, ordering his Ves-Lari rowers to slow. The Kan fog was thick and he didn't want to take a chance of encountering some errant fishing boat as it bumbled about Narian Bay. Up ahead he could see the lights of Zor twinkling orange through the mist.

Navigating to the coastline just South of town, the ship slipped silently onto the soft sugar sand beach.

By the time his crew had placed the wooden boxes on the shore by the waterline, six Cul-Ta emerged from the foliage. The humanoid rats pulled the crates up further on the beach and opened them.

A dozen Cheepas immediately flooded out onto the sand. The cat creatures were slightly smaller than their rodent liberators and they swarmed around them, hugging and cooing.

Their Ves-Lari craft then slipped back into the bay waters. The Tiikeri captain watched as several of the Cul-Ta began fucking the adorable cat creatures right there on the beach, while the others were being guided toward the city. Disappearing into the fog, Lar-Ga was thankful the Grand Turine in the Zorian harbor blocked out the sounds of the Cul-Ta's lustful chattering and the compliant cat creatures cries of pleasure.

The setting moon over the Asaro-He Oasis bore witness to one of the frequent sandstorms in the Dark Waste Desert.

Clouds of swirling sand, combined with the weakened illumination of the celestial orb had reduced visibility to no more than twenty feet.

On a narrow side street near the edge of town, three Ky-Awat were chattering away angrily while playing a tug of war over a loaf of bread.

All the five-foot-tall rat-men stopped their squabbling when the swirling sand whipping around them became electric and the hairs on their bodies stood up. The rat-men stood paralyzed in shock when a swirling blue energy field appeared on a nearby wall. Bolts of azure lightning erupted from the portal, filling the alley in a ghostly light.

Moving away and cowering, the humanoid vermin squawked nervously when Da-Olman stepped out of the gateway and onto the street in front of them.

The lightning retracted into the shrinking blue energy field leaving the Gila/Bailian hybrid staring at the recoiling Ky-Awat. He surveyed the cringing desert denizens dispassionately, then reached into a pocket on his floor-length duster jacket. Pulling out several red gems he tossed them to the frightened rat-men who greedily snatched them from the air.

"Come with me," the Etheriat's voice rang out over the wind. "There's more where that came from."

Not waiting for a response, Da-Olman headed for the main street. The Ky-Awat rapidly assessed the potentially profitable opportunity that had befallen them. Tossing the contested loaf of bread aside, they eagerly followed.

He led them to a store front just around the corner that was ready to close.

"Wait here," he said, opening the door. "Allow no one to enter."

The Etheriat stepped inside his shop, leaving the rat-men to huddle together against the wind and sand.

Inside, a lone Gila clerk was replacing some bottles on a shelf behind the counter with his back to the door. Da-Olman couldn't help but notice Stryder's mark on the back of his neck.

"We're closing," Mazadoor said, not bothering to turn around.

"Good, that means we will be uninterrupted."

Upon hearing his employer's voice, the young Gila spun around with a broad grin.

"Sir, you're back. I'm so glad!"

Da-Olman nodded at the young man's enthusiasm and looked around the tidy well-stocked shop.

"I see that things are going well. That's good."

"Yes sir, all praise to the lord. Ever since Pa-Waga extended his mighty hand over us and bestowed his bounty, he greatly blessed us."

Da-Olman shook his head and loudly scoffed which prompted a confused look on the young acolyte.

"I don't understand, sir. You were a constant companion of Saint Stryder. How could you be in such proximity to the Vicar of Pa-Waga and not believe?"

"Don't fret young Mazadoor. It's not just you and Stryder's god that I deny. I don't believe in any god."

"But sir, after the things you have witnessed?"

"Yes, I have experienced many things, especially recently. There are a lot of *very* powerful entities out there in the multiverse. Primitive and ignorant sentients may choose to worship them as gods, but not me. In my mind, if *real* gods existed, they'd be made of much sterner stuff."

Mazadoor became quiet, unsure how to react to such a blasphemous statement.

"Anyway, enough talk of gods and religious nonsense. My visit will be brief. I'm here to discover why there has been a slowdown in the shipments of Etheria to Tannimore."

"Yes sir, the lapidarist we have been using, Istan-Le has had less to offer. It seems there are two other players vying for his Etheria."

"If he has become unreliable, why not secure another?"

"Sir, Istan-Le is the largest lapidary in the entire Dark Waste. The smaller ones couldn't begin to meet our demand."

Da-Olman paused, locked in contemplation.

"Two others, huh? Do you know who they are?"

Mazadoor nervously shook his head. "No sir, his clients are kept confidential."

"Well, we'll just see about that," the Etheriat said heading toward the door. "I've been his best client for a long time and of late, his biggest. I think it's time I had a talk with Istan-Le about loyalty and money."

Buttoning his coat, Da-Olman stepped out into the oasis' turbulent atmosphere, marching out of sight with the Ky-Awat following close behind.

As far as sandstorms were concerned, this was a mild one. Da-Olman could remember ones so bad they reduced visibility to zero.

Now, as he strained to watch the walled compound of Istan-Le across the street, he was becoming increasingly irritated with one rat-men's constant squeaking and chittering.

"Quiet!" he hissed.

"Sorry," one other said, placing a hand on the shoulder of his noisy companion. "He's young and nervous."

The Gila Etheriat ignored the explanation and continued observing two of the lapidarist's large cyclops workers load the last of the boxes into the lowered rear hatch of an airship parked just outside the gates of his walled complex.

By the type of crates, Da-Olman knew they contained Trinilic rods. The Etheria fire crystals could be potentially volatile and needed shipping in sectional boxes to avoid contact with each other.

When the hatch closed, the human female shook Istan-Le's hand and they appeared to be briefly exchanging pleasantries. Da-Olman had never seen an EEtah before and the nine-foot-tall man-shark standing beside her fascinated him.

With business concluded, the side hatch dropped just long enough for human and EEtah to enter. The airship rose a few feet off the ground and sped off, disappearing in swirling sand.

Da-Olman knew they weren't going far in this weather. They would be easy to find. He was about to leave when he saw four figures emerge from the murky air on foot. They dressed in desert protection garb, with head and face covered. Even with their identities concealed, the Gila could make out the furry faces of cat people.

The one leading the group had orange fur around his eyes and hand which pounded against the gate.

After prolonged loud knocking, a cyclops answered. Da-Olman could hear the leader become loud and insistent. The cyclops finally gave in and a few moments later the blue skinned Istan-Le appeared.

Da-Olman could barely hear them but the conversation was quickly becoming heated. The louder they got, the more their voices became discernible and Da-Olman strained to hear.

The argument was making the younger Ky-Awat anxious and he began pipping again. Without warning, Da-Olman seized the rat-man and effortlessly snapped his neck. Nonchalantly tossing the corpse to the ground, he returned his attention to the contentious conversation. The two remaining Ky-Awat stared down in shock at their dead companion.

The cloaked man-cat was having a meltdown, screaming, "they had a deal!" Istan-Le stood firm, stating how he promised the Trinilic to the first buyer with the best offer. Da-Olman realized that these were definitely the two other "players" his assistant had mentioned.

Istan-Le ended the conversation by shooing them away and slamming the gate in their faces.

The three other cloaked mawls watched the orange-furred leader stomp, shout and curse in the middle of the sand covered street. The surrounding sandstorm matched the Tiikeri's turbulent mood. Eventually the tantrum ended and they moved off into the sandy darkness.

Da-Olman quickly turned to his new henchmen.

"You, follow them. And you, find that airship, get as many of your little friends as you need to help. They couldn't go far. Report back to me at my shop."

Both rat-men nodded and scurried off.

The Gila knew all he had to do was bide his time and he had a feeling it wouldn't be long. The Tiikeri weren't the type of sentient to take no for an answer. The irate man-tiger was going to make a play for the Trinilic. When he did, the Etheriat would be there to take advantage of the confusion.

Fassee felt a deep sense of irony that he could be around so much water and still feel uneasy. He figured it must be the stench. The sewer system of Makatooa, limited as it was, smelled as bad as any, but it had rained constantly for the last ten cycles and the fecal-laced water rose to his thighs.

When he reached an intersection, the tunnel to his left sloped gently upward. A torrent of water rushed down toward him but it got progressively shallower and it additionally contained a relatively dry three-foot-wide ledge on either side. It also included something that led the EEtah investigator to believe he was on the right path; Cul-Ta droppings.

Following the incline upward Fassee noted crude shaft openings of various sizes on either side. Water was gushing out of all but the largest one.

Stepping out of the filthy torrent he allowed his eyes to adjust to the dim light, then pressed onward. He reached a large cave and paused.

There was movement in the shadows. He could feel multiple eyes upon him.

"Hello!" he called out into the darkness. "I want to talk."

The rustling just beyond his vision grew louder. Reaching into a pocket he retrieved a small gem. Tapping it caused an orange glow to fill the chamber.

Now illuminated, Fassee could see a dozen of the four-foot-tall rat creatures had surrounded him. They armed themselves with crude kitchen knives which looked like swords in their tiny hands. Hissing menacingly, they advanced.

Dropping the light on the ground, Fassee reached over his shoulder and removed his Yudon harpoon. He deftly spun and twirled it around his body. The rifled metal shaft made an ominous humming as it sliced through the air. The EEtah stopped the weapon directly in front of him, its barbed tip glinted menacingly from the orange light below.

"We can fight if you want, but I came to talk."

The rat-men, intimidated by the martial display, halted and stared apprehensively at each other.

"What you want to talk about?" one said, stepping forward.

"Not to you," Fassee said, lowering the harpoon. "None of you here are old enough. I need to speak with your clan elders."

This request set off a clammer amongst the Cul-Ta. They squeaked and yipped feverishly, each with their own opinion. Everyone went silent as the leader raised his hand.

"Why you want to talk with Nu-Ta?"

Fassee completely lowered his Yudon. "Let's save time. Why don't you take me to this Nu-Ta and listen in?"

The Cul-Ta hesitated then gave a curt nod. "This way."

They led him down several corridors which would occasionally open into a cavern punctuated by individual living areas burrowed into the wall.

All stopped when they entered the fourth grotto. The leader pointed to an elderly group, seated on the far side of the cavern.

"Thank you," Fassee said, then made his way over to the conversing Cul-Ta seniors with the younger escorts trailing behind him.

The group came to a stop directly in front of the seated elders who didn't look up nor stop their lively conversation. The young Cul-Ta around him did not try to interrupt, and the seniors completely ignored them. Several long moments passed until there was a lull in the conversation.

The young leader then stepped forward and reverently announced the EEtah.

A decrepit looking female stared up at Fassee with clouded eyes. She was small and hunched over. Large swatches of fur were missing across her body, revealing multiple scabbed wounds. Six shriveled, deflated breasts lay pendulously on her chest and she constantly licked her lips.

"What do you want fish-man?"

Fassee gave his best disarming smile and knelt so they were at eye level.

"I'd like to speak with you about something that happened long ago."

"Why should I talk to you? Your kind has always sided with the humans."

A twinkle appeared in Fassee's eyes and his warm smile transformed into a mischievous grin.

"From what I just saw up in the city, your people are siding with the humans too."

The Cul-Ta crone laughed, revealing many missing teeth. "Fish-man is right. What would you pay for such information?"

Fassee stood, reached into the pocket of his pants and pulled out a single silver piece.

"It's all I have," he said, handing it to her.

The woman stared off into space while she rolled the coin around in her hand.

"Imperial silver piece," she said, keeping her vacant stare. "I've been told this is the total value of my people's lives."

Fassee, unaware of what she was referencing, stood quietly.

"Very well fish-man, ask your questions," she finally said.

"Do you remember a long time ago, when the humans were fighting over control of the docks?"

The blind Cul-Ta peered upward in his direction. "Some say a long memory is like a curse," she sadly said. "I was young, but yes, I remember."

"What about the outsiders that tried to take over?"

The old Cul-Ta nodded her head. "Preskot Nallor."

"Yes, that's him!" Fassee said, his voice filled with hope.

"He was a cruel man," she recalled. "He divided my people. Some sided with him, others with the two sisters and their sons."

"Which side did you choose?"

"I was too young, but I remember the battle in the fog. That was when Hanara showed up."

Upon hearing the name, the detective became excited. This might fill in the missing pieces of the Nalor Cabal and Hanara's part in their ouster.

"Was that when Hanara drove Nallor out of Makatooa and forced him to go underground?"

A puzzled look crossed Nu-Ta's face just before she broke out in peals of laughter.

"Hanara didn't drive Nallor anywhere. Hanara killed Nallor and took over."

The news hit Fassee like a blow to the side of his head. All this time The Spice Island Trading Company had been a front for the Nallor Cabal of the Silent Partner.

The only real question now was how much of this Velitel knew.

The only people that looked happy during the ceremony were the members of a very small audience of twenty.

Both Dobet Sorbornef and his beautiful new bride Nuvia looked as if they might burst into tears at any moment. There was, however, nothing they could do; their hands were bound and their blood mingled. They were married, except for one last detail.

Matka Sorbornef beamed and nodded her approval to the bride's parents, Peutor and Mosi Annov. Both families would benefit from this union. House Annov had gained a powerful ally in House Sorbornef and Matka now had a strategic position to her rebellious daughter's estate.

The guests crowded around the couple in the Sorbornef great Hall and began moving them toward a nearby couch, all the while undressing them.

Both bride and groom looked mortified when they forced their naked bodies down on the sofa. With cheers and applause, they pulled Nuvia's legs apart and pushed Dobet down on top of her.

The bride's tears and the groom's flaccid penis effectively squelched the once festive, lubricious mood. When the guests saw the futility of the coupling, their cheering and clapping slowly waned, replaced by gasps and whispers.

Dobet looked down at the sobbing, naked woman beneath him with her eyes tightly closed. Then in a humiliated panic peered around at twenty shocked, judgmental faces.

"He's not a man!" Peutor Annov angrily blurted out.

The insult proved more than the sensitive Sorbornef youth could take. With tears streaming down his face, Dobet bolted to his feet and ran up the stairs. They could hear the door to his bedroom slamming over the crowd's murmurs.

For a moment that seemed to stretch into an eternity, Matka and her guests stared at each other with embarrassed, befuddled looks.

A disgraced Peutor Annov, his face pale and his mouth drawn taut was the first to break the silence.

"Nuvia, get dressed. We're leaving."

He then tugged on his wife's arm while glowering at Matka.

"I will not forget this!" he growled.

Screaming from outside interrupted the tense scene. Everyone rushed through the front door with Matka in the lead. They found a female field slave staring upward at the house screaming and crying.

They looked up, following the slave's gaze, and Matka shrieked in horror. The nude body of Dobet, the youngest Sorbornef, hung suspended by a bed cord around his neck from the open window to his third story bedroom. His tongue protruded from his mouth and his eyes stared lifelessly outward while he swayed gently against the house. The streaks of his tears stained his face and a trail of urine ran down his leg, trickling onto the lawn.

The guests panicked, running around and yelling. Matka stood there amongst the chaos, staring upward at her dead son and her family's last chance for dynasty, now gone.

Tate Whitmar trusted the Tiikeri ambassador about as far as he could throw him. It had only been two cycles since he filed a formal complaint against the tiger peoples. Now, Za-Tar requested, and the Zorian High Council granted, a special emergency audience before them. Tate didn't know what he was up to, but he was pretty sure he would not like it.

The acting chairperson, Donis, Avion emissary from House Eacher, gaveled the meeting to order. Tate liked the beautiful blonde-haired sentient because of her clear-headed sense of fairness. She also didn't seem to possess the usual Avion superiority complex.

With a slight flutter of her folded wings behind her, she consulted a piece of paper in her hand.

"The next order of business is a proposal from the Tiikeri ambassador. Si. Za-Tar, you have the floor.

The orange Tiikeri, dressed in yellow bureaucratic robes, stepped out onto the recently repaired floor of the amphitheater and gazed around at the three tiers of very diverse sentients.

"Madam chairperson and esteemed council members," he began. "Thank you for affording me this opportunity to speak. I have come before you today with a sense of urgency. I have just received distressing news from my homeland. Extremists have callously persecuted and exiled a small, peaceful, religious faction."

Tate's brow furrowed. The Tiikeri was lying. He couldn't have *just* found this out. The Tiikeri already admitted their Worrg communications network was down no more than two cycles ago during their contentious meeting.

Za-Tar gesticulated passionately while making eye contact with the members. "I would beseech the Zorian High Council, in the spirit of inclusiveness that this city was founded on, to offer this band of religious refugees asylum."

A murmur went through the chamber and Donis came to her feet.

"We have a proposal by the Tiikeri Ambassador," she said. "I will now open the floor for discussion."

The Otick Ambassador from House Sensu stood. The humanoid crab outstretched his two claws in a pleading gesture. "How many pilgrims are we talking about?"

"Less than a hundred," Za-Tar replied.

Tate caught Joc' Valdur and Rafel's eye. All three shared a concerned look.

"Do we have room for them?" asked the EEtah Ambassador from House Nur.

"There is a small area next to the Seven Sisters," the director of public works offered.

"What about feeding them?" another posed the question directly to Za-Tar. "I don't think your people survive on bread and water."

"My people are experts at breeding herd animals for our food. It will be difficult at first, but within a short period we should have enough extra to start selling them. This will mean more locally sourced food stores for the city."

"Madame chairperson," Tate said, standing. "Before we get all googly eyed at this proposal, I would remind the council that there's a formal complaint on file against these folks. With all that's going on, I just don't think that's a very good idea."

"A complaint that *you* filed Si, Ambassador!" Za-Tar said, throwing Tate an angry glance. "And may I remind the council he did not direct the complaint toward the individuals we are discussing?"

"The fact is, until our investigation is complete, we don't know that. Ya can't leave the barn door open in a storm hoping something good blows in."

The Tiikeri was now staring down the human with a menacing scowl. "And exactly what *storm* are you referring to ambassador?"

The sound of the gavel cut short the heated exchange.

"Is there any further discussion or questions from the rest of the council?" Donis asked.

The Otick stood back up. "Yes, Madame Chairperson. I would like to say that I stand in favor of this proposal. The High Holy City of Zor was founded on and has always been a beacon of inclusion throughout the Annigan. My people, being a pious race, stand in solidarity with the faithful of all sentients. It is our obligation as Zorians to welcome these refugees and give them shelter."

The speech drew a round of applause from all the delegates except the human ambassadors.

"Is there anything else?" Donis asked glancing around at the envoys.

Hearing nothing, she gaveled again. "All right then. I officially call for a vote."

The Avion recited the role and each representative announced their ballot. Tate was the only dissenting vote with the other three human houses abstaining.

"The motion is carried," Donis announced, bringing the gavel down. "Ambassador, tell your people they are welcome here in the High Holy City of Zor."

The Tiikeri bowed formally. "Thank you madame chairperson and council."

Returning to his seat, Za-Tar gave Tate a gloating smile while Tate returned an icy stare.

The Whitmar Ambassador barely remembered the rest of the meeting, which dealt with the mundane affairs of running the large city. He was too concerned about a potential threat just invited into their midst. Tate was going to have a word with Rafel after the meeting, but by the look on the spymaster's face, he knew they were thinking the same thing.

Zor's newest residents would need to be watched closely.

The sandstorm had abated with the rising of the moon. The *Haraka* sat nestled in a small dune which had collected around it over the course of the tempest.

Alto slid his blades into his waist sash when he noticed Mal and Zau in the cockpit. The Spice Rat had pulled back the panels under the console. She laid on her back with the upper half of her body tucked inside the inner workings of the airship's control center. Zau was sitting in her navigator's chair and Kumo was at the wheel. Both were moving levers and controls at Mal's command.

"There is fucking sand everywhere!" Mal said in a frustrated, muffled voice while she busily cleaned out the intricate mechanisms under the dash. "Okay try it again."

"How did all that sand get in there?" Zau asked, pulling on a lever in front of her.

"First time in a desert huh?" Mal sarcastically asked.

"As a matter of fact, no," the Singa replied. "Are you sure you're doing that right?"

"You wanna fucking come down here and do it?!"

"We've already established that I won't fit down there."

"Yeah, lucky fucking me!"

Taleeka studied the swordmaster meticulously place his swords in his waist sash. With awkward movements, she attempted to mimic his almost ceremonial outfitting.

He smiled at her narrow band of fabric, cinched high on her waist.

"Lower your sash," he advised. "It should sit just above your hips."

Taleeka complied and Alto smiled while playfully tussling her hair.

"Now the handle of your weapon is within your natural reach. Got it?"

Taleeka nodded with a broad grin.

"Well, all right, we should be off in search of provisions to sustain us."

"Like food?"

"Yes little one, like food. Kumo drop the side hatch please."

"Good because I'm kinda hungry."

The door opened, pushing the sand that had accumulated aside. Brilliant moonlight set atop a carpet of stars reflected off the white sand, illuminating the landscape as far as the eye could see. Just in front of them, the oasis bustled with life.

"Oh, I believe we will be able to procure some nourishment for you." Alto said, standing in the doorway and watching the mostly Gila and Bailian populace shuffle back and forth in the sandy streets.

"Good, I want to try something new. Something from around here."

"Then what are we waiting for?" he announced. "We'll return shortly."

"Wait a minute, wait a minute!" Mal said, shimming out from under the console, sitting up and extending her arms.

"Mz. Tally, you're not going anywhere without giving me a hug."

With a broad smirk the young girl ran into Mal's arms. The Spice Rat gently rocked Taleeka while they tightly embraced.

"Okay remember," Mal said, holding her at arm's length. "Be careful and…"

"I know, do what Alto says."

"Right," Mal confirmed, kissing her on the forehead.

"I'll bring you back something good to eat," Taleeka said joining Alto at the door.

Mal sat and watched the pair walk down the ramp, Alto's hand on Taleeka's shoulder.

Zau silently observed the tender scene from her seat.

"She's a good kid," the Singa said in a nostalgic voice. "And you two make great parents."

Mal spun toward her navigator, eyes wide in surprise. "Woah! Parents, what the fuck are you talking about?! Nobody said any fucking thing about parents!"

Zau gave her a pained look of disbelief. "What?! Are you kidding me?" the Singa then flashed back at Zaad who was oiling Bowbreaker. "Is she kidding me?"

Zaad chuckled and Zau faced Mal again. "It's as plain as the nose on your face! You two are acting so much like proud parents, you may as well have given birth to her!"

"She's not lying captain," Zaad spoke up. "It's kinda nice."

"Yeah, well I think you two are full of shit," Mal said, laying back down, inching toward the exposed console. "Hand me that small brush will ya?"

Taleeka's eyes were full of wonder surveying the strange domed architecture and different looking peoples of the Asaro-He Oasis.

They swept the streets of hard-packed sand following the sandstorm. Large docile lizards with long plumed tails finished with the last streets before handlers led them away.

In their wake, merchant shops and street vendors hocked their wares to the mostly Gila population. Occasionally a Bailian or Kretos, as well as a wide variety of multi-racial Gila and Bailian hybrids, would wander by. All foot traffic kept clear of the center of the street, which was a chaotic torrent of lizard drawn carts and carriages of all sizes, rushing about on their own specific errands.

"Why is there no sun around here Alto?" Taleeka asked, scanning the moonlit skyline.

"No one really knows little one. I only know that it allows for very different beings to exist."

"Why is everyone staring at us?"

"Because here, we are the ones that look different."

Content with the answer, Taleeka continued to watch the bustle of the cosmopolitan oasis until an odor ahead caught her attention.

"Ooh, what's that?" she asked, gravitating toward the smell.

They ended up at a roadside food vendor. The Bailian/Gila hybrid chef knelt on a large rug spread out in the sand. To his left ran a trough of glowing gems, popping with drippings from the roasting meat on the grill above. At the end of the trough was a hole filled with more glowing crystals which surrounded a tubular, open top oven.

Taleeka followed the cook's every move while he prepared a thin sheet of dough and slapped it on the wall of the oven.

She looked up at Alto with an excited expression. The swordmaster smiled and gestured they wanted one. The vendor grinned at the young girl and went to work. Reaching into the oven, he peeled the now baked shell off the oven's side with his bare hands. He then spread a layer of savory porridge on it, as well as some roasted meat from the grill. Deftly rolling it into a tube, he handed it to Taleeka with a tender smile.

"Thank you!" she said, accepting the treat with wide-eyed excitement.

The food merchant gave Alto an approving look when he paid with a small red gem. "You have raised a respectful daughter, something to be proud of."

The swordmaster fondly glanced down at the young girl chewing away ravenously. "She is indeed our little wonder."

"Please excuse me," the vendor said as they started off." I couldn't help but hear that you were in search of a wagon to hire."

"Indeed we are," Alto replied.

The vendor shook his head. "Unfortunately, there are very few around here." He then pointed to a nearby side street. "A short distance down that street is a more artisan area. There you will find wagons for rent."

Alto nodded and smiled. "Many thanks," he said, handing the vendor another gem.

The vendor watched the two move off. Reaching into the pocket of his tightly cinched pants, he pulled out an oblong white Etheria crystal. Holding it in the palm of his hand he faced away from the street.

A gruff voice resonated in his head. "What?!"

"I have located the ones you seek and have sent them your way."

Taleeka's hunger finally addressed, the pair moved off farther into the city of Asaro-He. Following the directions the food vendor gave them, the buildings shed their mercantile facade, taking on a more industrial appearance.

"If the cook is to be believed, this is where we should locate something," Alto said, looking around.

"There's one, over there," Taleeka said, pointing down a side street with the partially eaten roll-up. Squinting through the stark shadows, Alto could make out a lizard drawn wagon with a driver, loitering just outside a warehouse door.

"Good eyes," Alto said, impressed with her powers of observation.

"The light was always like this back in the Narrows," she replied between bites.

Approaching the wagon, Alto felt a wave of apprehension sweep over him when he saw the sharp angular features of the driver's ears, nose and chin. Moving closer confirmed his suspicions; it was a Kreetos. They had a reputation around the oasis as being unscrupulous and more than a little ruthless. The last time he had encountered one of their numbers he had to kill it.

"Hello," Alto said, stepping up to the wagon. "I was wondering if we might hire you and your wagon?"

The Kreetos stopped fidgeting with the reins and suspiciously scanned the swordmaster.

"We don't see many humans here in the desert," he said, his pointed ears twitching. "My language is not well known. How is it you speak it so well?"

Alto reached into his shirt and pulled out a small chunk of Larimar suspended from a chain necklace—its white crystal with blue striations fashioned into a teardrop shape.

"I see you know the ways of Etheria."

"I dabble. So, is your wagon for rent?"

"Maybe, for the right..."

The lizard suddenly hissed in panic and lurched forward. This interrupted the Kreetos mid-negotiation, knocking him off balance and almost throwing him off the buckboard. Alto's reflexes automatically kicked in and he reached up and grabbed the reins with both hands.

In the confusion, no one heard several bow strings being released, nor the swooshing sound of them driving toward their target.

Three arrows embedded in Alto's back. The swordmaster convulsed with each strike then dropped the reins and fell to the alley floor.

Through the fog of pain and shock, Alto saw a dozen Ky-Awat leaping from the rooftops to the street in front and behind, sealing off any escape. Taleeka shrieked in horror while seeing Alto fall. The swordmaster helplessly watched several of the rat-men, along with another Kreetos, muscling a kicking and screaming Taleeka into the bed of the wagon.

Alto blacked out to the sound of Taleeka's cries above the rumble of the wagon speeding away.

Matka could barely discern the people running about, crying and yelling all around her. She stood there in paralyzed shock, unable to take her eyes off her naked son, dangling by the neck out his bedroom window.

The swaying had now stopped and the young man hung motionless against the side of the house like a gruesome ornament.

Not taking her eyes off the horrific spectacle, the matriarch and now sole survivor of the Sorbornef name, fell to her knees shrieking. She didn't see the woman step up behind her from the panicked crowd.

"Your daughter wishes you well," she heard whispered in her ear before feeling the knife plunge into her side.

The mass confusion drowned out Matka's cry of pain. She turned to see a smiling woman she didn't recognize, rearing back to stab her again. Reaching out, she grabbed the blade of the dagger just before the tip entered her. Matka wrestled the blade away from her body and felt the dagger's edge slicing into her palm.

A man from the crowd attempted to intervene by grabbing the assaulting woman on the shoulder. She spun with a sneer and slashed the blade across his chest. He grasped the wound in shock, blood spilling from between his fingers.

The woman took off running while the man staggered and toppled forward, joining Matka on the lawn of Staghorn Manor.

When the man wouldn't stop screaming, Gavin's erection throbbed to the point of being painful. The nude killer tossed the freshly amputated leg onto the pile of limbs, then placed the saw back on the rack over the glowing gems.

He had to admit, this first contract kill for Hanara was a tough one. Normally, by the time he removed the second leg, shock would have set in and they would be as good as dead.

But not this one.

Staring down at the crown of his cock, glistening with a thick layer of pre-cum, he leaned in close to the man's ear.

"You're teasing me, aren't you?" he said in a whisper. "Seeing how long I can hold out."

The man didn't hear him. His cries of agony more than drowned out any conversation that might have occurred.

"Well, seeing as how you're still with us, what's next?" Gavin said, scanning the man's limbless torso.

He picked up a hooked bladed knife from the rack. Examining the blade glowing red hot, he nodded approvingly.

Perfect.

Gavin was pleased to see that by the time he made it back to the table, the man had stopped wailing and was now whimpering in pain. After all, this was a delicate procedure. He had to allow the victim to come down from the threshold of agony before ramping up again. Otherwise, it would be over too quickly.

Gavin held the glowing knife in front of the man's face and his eyes widened with dread.

"I think we need a little treat for my friends," he said with a maniacal smile.

Slowly, for effect, Gavin moved the blade down to the man's penis. Gavin almost giggled when he started screaming and pleading with him. Placing the hook around the base of the scrotum, he slowly cut upward. More shrieks and the smell of burning flesh filled the air. Gavin found himself breathing hard when he picked up the severed member by the tip.

"You're definitely not going to need this anymore," he said, holding up the severed manhood and clinically examining it. "But I don't know how much more of this you can take, and my hungry friends are growing impatient."

With a flick of his arm, he tossed the severed cock over to the dozen pale, transfixed faces of the Zoande clan. The ghouls lunged for the morsel and scuffled over it. The winner greedily stuffed it in his mouth then returned its attention back to the procedure.

Next came the ears. It pleased him how easily they separated from the head. Gavin tossed them to the undead group which resembled dogs straining at their collars.

The torturer could feel the man close to death and himself nearer to release when he started removing the nose. By the time he detached the olfactory appendage, the man shuddered and died.

Gavin groaned in pleasure and shot his load with the man's death rattle. The force of his orgasm sent streamers of ropy ejaculate exploding over the warm corpse.

It took a moment for Gavin to compose himself from such a powerful release. He leaned on the table, struggling to catch his breath while the ghouls moved ever closer. He finally stepped back and let the residents of the Old City feast.

Collecting the severed limbs, he watched the ghouls descend on the torso, rending it apart. Placing his treasures in a sack, Gavin made his way to the staircase leading upward to the city streets of Makatooa.

He paused at the doorway and looked out at the rain which had now been falling constantly for the last ten cycles. His efforts must be working. He felt like he had attracted the attention of the Avion goddess of storms. Soon she would make herself known to him. He could feel it every time a rumble of thunder shook the city and a bolt of lightning lit up the sky. He was also grateful his new employer took away the drudgery of having to choose a victim.

But the best part of the whole thing was, he was getting paid for it.

It had been a tumultuous day. Not wishing his presence to be known just yet, Bo-Lah observed it all from a safe distance at the window of the guest cottage.

There was no mistaking that Staghorn Plantation had undergone seismic changes in the recent past. All the family's misfortunes seemed to have culminated with the youngest cub hanging himself and the attack on the lady of the manor.

The Tiikeri wasn't sure how this would affect his plans, but they were too far along to stop now.

It was late in the Kan. The servants had all gone to bed, but he could see a lone light burning in the study. Creeping up to the window, he peered in.

Matka was sitting in an overstuffed chair drinking amber liquid from a crystal tumbler. He could see her bandaged left hand and the murderous scowl on her face.

She looked up from her vicious musings when he tapped on the glass.

"I'm sorry to disturb you," he softly said, when she let him in. "You've had quite the day and I just dropped by to see if there was anything I could do."

Matka scoffed and took a large gulp. "My own damn daughter tried to have me killed," she said, with a slur.

"I saw the commotion. Why does your daughter want you dead?"

"Any of a number of reasons, I'm sure," she said, wincing in pain and touching the bandage on her side. "She could hate me for forcing her into marriage. Or it could just be naked ambition. She is now the solitary head of House Targoff."

"What do you plan on doing? She's probably going to try again."

"Yeah, well you better hope she doesn't succeed. If I die, our deal dies with me."

With the ominous statement, the Tiikeri became pensive.

"Perhaps there is something I can do to help," he finally said.

"I'm listening."

"Any cycle now I'm expecting several of my associates to visit. Associates that are uniquely qualified to handle such situations."

Demetrius decided he liked the new design features for the Resistance Class Cruisers. Everything was within easy reach and the upgrades were proving to be useful.

"So, what do you think Sitsa?"

The Tinian stared out the windows from the navigator's seat of the *Atilla*. "I love this side of the world. It's always bright. I'm still assessing land masses and horizon line positions. It's going to take a little while before I am fully competent in my duties as navigator."

"Not to worry," Demetrius said, watching the Northern coast of Goya slip by beneath them. "I'm pretty familiar with this area. It's the less frequented regions I'm going to need help with."

"How big is the vessel we are looking for?"

"A lot smaller than the last one. A single mast ship, forty-two feet long called the *Praelar*. She was hauling twenty indentures and scheduled to be in port this morning."

"If they were being preyed upon, why was the ship not escorted?"

"House Whitmar has virtually no navy. Slavers almost exclusively comprised their fleet. Until now, no one preyed on slave ships."

Approaching a line of small barrier islands, Demetrius slowed the craft for a better look.

"Okay, this doesn't look good," he said, spotting a ship's mast and shredded sail floating in the Shallow Sea. At the top of the broken pole was the Whitmar flag, with its rose, chain and dagger. When he took the *Atilla* down to fifty feet off the water, he spotted the ship run aground, virtually hidden in the mangroves.

"Let's get a closer look," Demetrius said, slowly approaching the badly damaged vessel.

Demetrius set the airship to hover close to the ship's stern and both occupants grimly surveyed the wreckage of the *Praelar*.

"I wonder if it went aground or was forced aground?"

"Captain, the damage to the rudder gives it an eighty-six percent chance of being forced aground."

"Either way, it's time to hand out the bad news," Demetrius said, reaching up and touching the Larimar disk in the overhead console. Immediately he could feel Okawa's presence.

"Okay, we found it," he said aloud.

"What's the status?" Okawa's voice filled Demetrius' head.

"It's about a hundred-fifty miles East of Nier on one of the barrier islands. It's pretty beat up and there are bodies on the deck. From what I can see they look like someone really hacked them up."

"Understood, you heading back here?"

"Yeah, there's nothing I can do."

"All right, see you in a bit."

Okawa took her hand off the Larimar Etheria shard in her sleeve pocket and looked over at Wolff. "Demetrius found the *Praelar*. From what he described we're dealing with the same situation."

A scowl crossed Wolff's scarred face. "Damn it, now I gotta break off my tail and go examine the ship."

"You suspect someone?"

Wolff nodded his head in the office's direction across the square.

"See the guy sitting at that desk by the window?"

"The one with the trimmed beard and bad haircut?"

"That's him. His name is Xain de Barat and he's the Assistant Routing Director for the slave market. He's also the weak link in the chain of evidence. I checked and he was the one that arranged the route for the *Vergas*. I also checked the schedule and guess what his next routing assignment was?"

"The *Praelar*." Okawa knowingly ventured.

"You got it. He's dirty. I can feel it. I just got to catch him in the act."

Okawa gave a shallow shrug. "So, go look after your boat. I'll keep an eye on him."

"It's a ship, not a boat and I thought you agreed to stay out of it."

Okawa gave him an amused glance. "I didn't agree to anything. You ordered me to stay out of it. The thing is, I don't take orders from you. So, unless being in two places at once is in your skill set, you can quit being a jackass and accept my help."

Alto awoke screaming Taleeka's name and thrashing about as if he were still in combat.

It took Zaad's formidable strength to subdue the swordmaster until the panic passed.

Panting furiously and looking around wild-eyed, the swordmaster finally recognized his surroundings and slowly calmed.

There was a cloyingly sweet taste in his mouth and his back ached from where the arrows struck him.

Mal and Zau were kneeling directly over him. Everyone else was standing around the cargo bay of the *Haraka*. All had anxious looks on their face but none more than Mal.

"What happened?! Where's Tally?!"

Alto groaned and tried to sit up but Zau's furry hand kept him on his back.

"Don't try to move," she advised. "You need to rest. One of those arrows missed your heart by only a few inches."

Alto exhaled and relaxed. "We were securing a wagon when they attacked. The rat-men were jumping from the roofs on either side of us. I was trying to steady a panicked lizard when they shot me from behind. Before blacking out, I saw them carrying her off in the wagon. The driver was one of those Kreetos. I believe he was in on it. I, I failed her."

Mal scowled. "Kreetos, you can't trust those motherfuckers!"

"How did I get here?"

"The city guards found you and put two and two together. Zau used some of the Dreeat candy and a few of her tricks to patch you up. They found the knife you gave Tally next to a dead Ky-Awat."

The swordmaster managed a weak smile. "It would appear that she got one of them."

Mal was on the verge of tears. "Alto, what are we going to do?"

Alto slowly sat up. "I do not think their intention was to kill her or they would have done it on the spot."

"That's not very fucking comforting! Children go for a lot of money in the slave markets!"

Alto tenderly rubbed his shoulder, his mind racing for a solution when one strand of Kumo's alarm webbing vibrated.

Zaad grabbed Bowbreaker and Mal reached for her pistol crossbow. "When they brought you in, I had Kumo move us away from the city where she could set up a perimeter," she explained on her way out the back hatch.

Exiting the ship, Mal and Zaad saw a captured Kreetos thrashing about in an intricate network of webbing suspended between several trees.

It stopped struggling and looked up when Mal, Zaad and Zau approached.

"Release me," it hissed. "I have come to trade."

"You're in no position to demand anything," Zaad said, slinging a sheathed Bowbreaker onto his back.

"Trade what, dipshit?!" Mal snarled, stepping closer.

The Kreetos 'eyes were darting nervously from side to side, unsure whom he should address.

"You have certain items in your cargo area that the parties I represent desire. They have recently come into possession of something you might want."

Mal's face was a mask of pure rage and she cocked the pistol. "I've got a better idea shithead. You bring me back my kid and I won't hunt you down and kill you all slowly. And that goes for your rat buddies too. We're talking open season."

The Kreetos 'pointed ears were twitching nervously despite the air of authority he tried to project.

"I do not have the child, but she is somewhere safe, for now."

Waves of murderous fury radiated from the Spice Rat. Rapidly aiming the pistol, she shot the defiant Kreetos in the upper leg. The four-inch-long projectile punched cleanly through the thigh, blasting away a sizeable chunk.

"GIVE ME BACK MY KID, MOTHERFUCKER!"

The creature screamed in agony and Mal cocked the pistol again.

"I, I told you," it said between winces of pain, "I do not have the child. The tiger-men have her. It is the tigers!"

Mal screamed and fired once again. This time the bolt struck center mass with a dull thud, killing him instantly.

All three companions had seen their captain angry before. This, however, was vastly different. They could do nothing but stand, silently paralyzed in shock.

Tears were streaming down the Spice Rat's face while she shrieked, cocked and fired bolt after bolt into the suspended dead body.

"Uh, Captain," Zau meekly said.

Mal ignored the interruption and let another bolt fly.

"Mal," the Singa said, a little more insistently.

The Spice Rat stopped screaming and turned to face her navigator. The look of unbridled rage on the tear-stained face made the Singa shutter.

"I think he's dead."

Not breaking eye contact with the Singa, Mal fired again, adding to the projectiles protruding from the Kreetos 'corpse. The airship captain, still weeping, calmly turned back to her target and fired once more. When she cocked it again, the magazine was empty and no bolt dropped into place. Mal didn't seem to notice. She continued to cock and fire the empty weapon.

Alto slowly emerged from the rear of the ship carrying a three foot long, thin, piece of metal.

He weakly walked over to Mal, gently put his hand on her extended arm and slowly lowered the pistol.

She met his gaze, then completely broke down, falling into his arms.

"We will get her back my love," he comforted. "But we need help. It's time to call for some friends."

His breath finally returning to normal,

the blood frenzy finally over.
Pulling the Yudon from the renegade EEtah's corpse,
pausing, looking up at the two he saved.
Their beating wings suspending them just above the
ground.
The looks of gratitude on their beautiful faces...
and the salute:
Arms extended in front of them, hands together,
thumbs and forefingers forming a triangle.

Fassee jolted awake. He had moored himself to one of the new dock pilings so he wouldn't drift and now he was glad.

He had to get to Velitel quickly.

The scene was becoming all too familiar to Fassee. The rain, the roof, and the city guards milling about the artfully arranged body parts.

"Is it ever going to stop raining?" the EEtah investigator asked, stepping up to a very perplexed Velitel.

A bolt of lightning crashed down into the bay and a loud peal of thunder echoed from above. The commander cast a worried glance at the sky. "Not only that, it gets steadily worse every cycle."

Velitel then resumed staring at the arms and legs arranged just as before. "I wish I knew what this meant."

"It's the exact pattern as the one four cycles ago," Fassee confidently said. "I think your boy has found something that works for him."

"Yes, a repeat performance, if you will."

"I know what it is."

Velitel stared at the EEtah with an excited look and wiped away the rainwater dripping off his beard. "You remembered?!"

"I told you I needed to sleep on it." Fassee replied.

"So, what exactly is it?"

"It's an Avion salute, used by the priests of one of their storm gods."

"What about the missing pinkies?"

Fassee shrugged. "That, I can't help you with. Every Avion I've ever encountered had all their appendages."

Velitel peered back down at the artfully arranged limbs. "I wonder if our killer knows that?"

"I can't say for sure, but I'm guessing not."

"Well, it's certainly something to go on." Velitel said. "Thanks for making the trip to let me know."

"Actually, I came by to say goodbye. My investigation is complete and I'm leaving. It's been a pleasure working with you."

It genuinely surprised Velitel. He had gotten use to the EEtah's presence and insight. "Really? So, the curtain finally descends on our little play. Did you find anything of note?"

"Actually yes. I had an interesting conversation with a Cul-Ta elder a few cycles ago. It seems Preskot Nallor has been dead for quite a while. Lord Hanara killed him and took over the Nallor Cabal using the Spice Islands Trading Company as a front. And I'm pretty sure you've been looking the other way the entire time."

Velitel's pleasant demeanor vanished. "I don't know what you're talking about."

Fassee scoffed. "Commander, you are one terrible liar. Relax, the everyday goings on of you humans is none of my concern. No Sunal laws were broken. I'm done here."

Velitel visibly relaxed. "Preskot Nallor had to go. He was cruel and ruthless but worst of all, he was bad for business. Nature abhors a vacuum however, and we didn't want a full-on gang war. That would have been terrible for all the city's enterprises, especially those on the wharf. Hanara proved to be the perfect understudy. The story of Preskot Nallor going into seclusion seemed to satisfy everyone. Turns out, no one wanted him around, even his own people."

"My compliments on you being able to pull it off for so long. But I wouldn't be getting too buddy-buddy with Lord Hanara. He's up to something. From what I witnessed he's been getting secret gem shipments and who knows what else from Nocturn. I tell you this as a professional courtesy. It's officially not my problem." The EEtah started moving toward the waters of the bay. "Good luck finding your artist."

Tor-Maa was in a foul mood. The orange Tiikeri adjusted the covering over his eyes and cursed the endless sunshine of Lumina. He had been traveling for two full cycles in the cramped Ves-Lari ship with fifty religious pilgrims from The Land of Mists.

The Tiikeri operative was now of the opinion that the only thing worse than being cooped up with a bunch of religious nut jobs, was *pretending* to be one. He hated the constant blissed-out looks on their faces and their ceaseless babbling about how their mighty god delivered them to the land of prosperity. Their leader and priest of Pa-Waga, a Yagur by the name of Al-Zah, fueled all their pious prattling. The old fool had launched into loud rambling prayers multiple time per cycle, causing his parishioners to join in with joyous shouts of approval. If it wouldn't have blown his cover, he would have tossed the irritating zealot overboard soon after departing.

Their destination, the city of Zor, came into view when the vessel rowed into Narian Bay and the compliment of various Mawls on board swooned with excitement. Tor-Mah was just glad the voyage was almost over.

Their ambassador to Zor, Za-Tarr, would be there to greet them, along with various human bureaucrats. He would check in with their envoy and communicate his presence. His was to be a second set of eyes in the human capitol now that their Worrg network was not working.

The ship was nearing the dock and sure enough, the ambassador and a host of yellow robed human stood awaiting them. Tor-Maa wasn't sure why the Tiikeri high command was placing so many assets in Lumina. That was obviously on a need-to-know basis.

One thing was for sure. It was going to be big.

The turine in the Nerian harbor rang ten bells and the Kan fog quickly rose around Demetrius and Okawa's legs.

"This is my first trip to Nier," Demetrius said, looking around at lights coming on in windows and shop owners closing up. "It's got a strange, almost unsettling feel to it. I don't know…"

Okawa pulled him closer and snuggled against the fog's chill while they walked at a leisurely pace.

"It's a slaver city," she somberly replied. "A lot of misery has passed through this port."

"Even the food here is weird."

Okawa chuckled. "I couldn't help but notice you ate all of yours and part of mine."

"Hey, I didn't say it was bad." Demetrius said, then indicated the man they were following with a tilt of his head. "Besides, we didn't choose the place, he did."

"Yeah, well when in doubt go where the locals go."

Demetrius adjusted his arm around her shoulder and smiled when he caught the scent of lavender in her hair. "So, Wolff's sure about this guy?"

Okawa caught him sniffing and gave a smile. "He seems to think this is the leak. His name is Xain de Barat and he's the assistant routing director for the slave markets."

"So, shouldn't Wolff be doing this?"

"Relax, it's just until Wolff gets back from checking out that ship you found this morning."

"You mean what is left of it."

They followed Xain across the bridge leading into the Northwest Ward of the city. The Kan fog was now so thick you could only hear the rushing water of the Saruso River below.

Once in the Northwest Ward the amount of street traffic thinned considerably. Street walking prostitutes and boisterous bar goers were the remaining residents, interspersed by the occasional carriage rumbling by on the cobblestone streets.

Okawa stopped and put on her blue Etheria glasses and flipped down the orange lens.

"Good idea," Demetrius said, following suit.

Unbeknownst to the pair of pursuers, two sets of eyes had locked in on them from the shadows of a nearby alley.

The two female Singas silently followed, unaffected by the Kan or urban terrain, drawing ever closer with each street traversed.

The followers paused when their quarry reached Xain's abode, a small apartment on the third floor. While Demetrius and Okawa watched Xain climb the stairs, one of the Singas slipped off to the side in a flanking maneuver.

Demetrius watched Xain's heat outline step inside the door of his apartment and disappear.

"Well, all right," he said with a sigh. "We've got him tucked in for the evening." He then turned and put his arms around Okawa's waist. "Now what say we find a nice comfy bed to tuck ourselves into?"

"Not so fast fly-boy," she said, gently pushing him back. "As much as I would love to rub body parts with you, someone's got to hang out here and make sure he stays tucked in."

"Aww," Demetrius said with a pout. "I was really looking forward to rubbing…"

The sound of objects whistling by their heads cut Demetrius' amorous protest short.

"What the…" was all the pilot could get out before Okawa tackled him to the ground. Just above them, they saw two small sickle shaped throwing blades embedded in the wall.

"Come on," Okawa said, drawing her pistol and scrambling toward a nearby pillar on her hands and knees.

"Who do you think it is?" Demetrius asked when he finally joined her crouching behind cover.

"I don't know," she said, looking around warily. "I didn't recognize those blades and I didn't see a heat signature anywhere."

"So, what do we do?"

"Well, right now, I say we enjoy this lovely cover," Okawa said, checking to make sure her spare magazine was handy.

From the corner of her eye, she caught the briefest flash of orange. "Look out!" she said, shoving him onto his stomach while she dove in the other direction. Two more throwing blades immediately struck the pillar where they had just been.

"This way!" she said, bolting to her feet and sprinting toward a nearby side street.

They rounded the corner to the sound of another blade ricocheting off the wall.

"This is not how I envisioned working off dinner," Demetrius said, flattening himself against the wall.

"I count two of them," Okawa said, assessing the alley which was open at both ends. "And they're fast. Come on!"

The Valdurian agent took off toward the other end of the alley with an agitated Demetrius behind her.

She stopped abruptly, halting a short distance later when the alley crossed a wider street. Holding out her arm and signaling Demetrius to stop, she peered cautiously around the corner.

"Shouldn't we be hiding behind something substantial?" he asked, nervously checking the direction they'd just come from.

Okawa shook her head. "Moving targets are harder to hit. Go!"

Okawa darted across the major thoroughfare to the alley entrance on the opposite side, pistol poised at the ready. Demetrius followed and another blade bounced off the corner right beside his head, clattering noisily in the street.

"I thought they were back the other way!" Demetrius anxiously said.

"Like I said, there's two of them. They're working as a team to box us in. This way."

Rushing down the narrow side road they passed three large crates stacked pyramid style.

"Cover," Demetrius gasped when they passed them.

Okawa ignored the suggestion and continued running.

From behind they heard the rattle of the wooden boxes followed by a thud when a sickle struck the back of Demetrius' thigh. The pilot cried out in pain and dropped to the alley floor.

Okawa spun to see a female Singa crouched on the top crate. She was immediately joined by a second one who was vaulting over one of the bottom crates. In her hand was another of the throwing blades, poised for release.

There was no time to aim. Okawa raised her M3 pistol crossbow and fired.

A thunderous roar echoed off the narrow walls when the bolt left the barrel. The custom projectile struck the leaping Singa mid-jump. The top half of her body exploded, spraying everything in the area with the remnants of her spattered torso. All that remained of the Mawl assassin were two furry legs, which dropped lifelessly to the ground.

The remaining one on the top crate was reaching for another knife off the bandolier across her chest. She froze and glanced around with a shocked expression. Crimson covered her entire body, as well as the flanking walls. Her gaze lingered on her partner's legs oozing red onto the street. She looked back into Okawa's defiant stare, hissed malevolently, then bolted off in the opposite direction.

"What in the name of the gods was that?" Demetrius asked through waves of pain shooting down his leg.

Okawa kneeled over him and assessed his wound. "I'm not sure what role female Singas play in this little game, but they seem to be quite effective."

"Do you think that had anything to do with retaliation for us taking out the Worrgs?"

"Maybe, or they're keeping an eye on our boy we just tucked in back there. No matter, ultimately the Tiikeri are calling the shots. Let's get you back to the ship. I've got a small first aid kit in my bag. We've got whisky, right?"

"Yeah, and boy could I use a jolt!"

"I meant for the wound," Okawa said, helping him to his feet.

"You use it your way and I'll use it mine."

Mal wasn't sure how, but at some point, during the moonless, she dropped off to sleep. She woke with the rising moon to find Zau seated in her navigator's chair staring out the window at Alto.

"He's been out there this entire time," she said when her yawning captain made her way into the cockpit. "Just sitting there, tapping out the same rhythm on that metal piece he stuck in the sand."

"He says he's calling for help," Mal said, peering out at the swordmaster sitting cross-legged beside the ship. "We should do something instead of just fucking sitting around."

"We *are* doing something. Calling for help is doing something."

Mal gave her an irritated look.

"I mean it," Zau defensively said. ,So"Whataya think we should be doing? We don't know where they took her and we're not familiar with the area. Not to mention that's one big desert out there and you shot our only contact to where she might be!"

Mal fumed, staring out the window. She knew Zau was right.

The Spice Rat sat up in her seat, staring intensely when she saw the sand shift and swirl a short distance from where Alto sat.

Three humanoid figures rose from what was once empty desert. They were wearing tan one-piece outfits, cinched tight around their arms and legs, which perfectly matched the surrounding sand. The material covered their noses and mouths, but Mal could see the enormous eyes and scaly, dark green skin of the Gila race.

"I recognize these guys!" Mal said when they pulled back their face coverings. "Jangwa!"

Zau curiously peered out at Alto and one of the Jangwa clasping forearms, then over to Mal who was bounding to the side hatch.

"It is good to see you Alto de Gom," the lead Jangwa said with a smile. "I did not think it would be this soon."

"I wish it were under better circumstances Voda-Mon," Alto grimly replied.

Mal interrupted the greeting by rushing down the side ramp—followed much more slowly by the rest of the *Haraka's* occupants.

"Voda, am I ever glad to see you!"

The Gila gave a shallow bow. "Maluria."

When she reached Alto's side, the Gila addressed them both. "What circumstances were you referring to and how can I help?"

"It was those fucking rats!" Mal blurted out before Alto gently squeezed her arm.

"The Ky-Awat and Kreetos have abducted our daughter and we need your assistance in finding her."

"I was unaware that you had a daughter."

"It's a long story," Mal said, a tremble in her voice. "Can you help us Voda?"

"Of course, but frankly I'm amazed the Ky-Awat found the ambition or intelligence to abduct someone."

"They're not the ones behind it," Alto replied. "Cat people from another land put them up to it."

"Why?"

"Because they want what we have in our cargo bay," Mal sneered.

Voda gave an understanding nod. "We will find your daughter. But we will need assistance." He then pointed to Alto's metal strip still embedded in the sand. "May I?"

"By all means."

Voda kneeled by the exposed metal and retrieved his dagger. Using the flat of the blade he began tapping on the top edge of the metal strip. This pattern, unlike the one Alto made, was sharp and staccato.

Voda kept repeating the sequence for several long moments until the sand for twenty yards surrounding the *Haraka* shifted and rippled. Slowly, dozens of small, human like heads rose from the agitated ground. They were scaly and angular with long feather-like plumes for hair. Slender, gangly arms emerged next, pushing a humanoid frame and snake's lower bodies from the fine white powder. Several slithered over to Voda, their serpentine tongues flicking out of their mouths.

One with feminine features approached Alto. She coiled her tail and used it to bring her head even with his.

"I know you," she hissed. "From before, we hid in the grotto with Voda. You were injured."

"I apologize for not remembering you. Alto de Gom, at your service."

"No need for apologies, you were all but unconscious at the time."

Lowering herself, she and three others turned their attention to Voda. "How may the Mai-Gai serve the Jangwa?"

While Voda was giving them their instructions, Alto turned back to Mal. "When they find her, we will need to be ready to go at a moment's notice."

Mal rested her hands on Alto's chest and gave him a sorrowful but appreciative look. "*When* they find her—I like the way you think blade slinger."

Gre-Norr stood in Hanara's office at the large picture window and watched the Kan fog slowly rolling into Makatooa harbor. The orange Tiikeri gave a troubled sigh while pondering his options.

"If this Fassee character knows everything, shouldn't he be dealt with?"

The hammerhead EEtah got up from behind his desk. "He found out the details of my past, as well as Velitel's intentional ignoring of my business deals, but he doesn't know about us, nor do I think it would make any difference if he did."

The Tiikeri operative peered at him with a quizzical look. "Oh really?"

Hanara shrugged. "According to Fassee, we violated no Nurian Edicts or specific Sunal Laws. He's already gone home, wherever that is. Besides, killing him would bring down a Sunal vendetta and trust me, you don't want any part of that."

"A rather odd arrangement don't you think? I mean, I'm not complaining."

Hanara chuckled. "It's worked for thousands of grands. The only way the EEtah race cares about human activities is when it directly affects them or when they're paid to."

"And you're certain this won't disturb our business dealing?"

Hanara shook his head. "Not in the least. The funds you provide will go a long way in this city's reconstruction, and your people will have a discreet, safe harbor here in Lumina."

Gre-Norr stared back at the advancing fog and smiled at having successfully completed his mission.

"This really is quite a view you've got here."

Xain de Barat stared down at the dispatch laying on his desk. He quickly read it with both greedy anticipation and unease over the lack of prior notice. According to the notification, the slaver *Basha* made a requested unscheduled stop in Amarenia where they picked up a haul of no less than fifty indentures. That was good. The Tiikeri paid double for women and he was going to be handing them a ship full. The bad part was they were due into Nier in just two cycles.

There was no time to lose.

Looking around and finding no one paying attention, he quickly scribbled out the course and other pertinent information on a small piece of paper.

"I'll be back in a centi," he called out to his three co-workers who were toiling away at their desks.

"A break already?" a smartly dressed woman with tired features asked when he reached the door. "You just got here."

"A quick errand I forgot about," he apologetically said. "Back in a jiffy."

It was a short walk to the docks and the gull station. The blind old man sat before a single long perch of squawking gulls. Droppings were everywhere, including all down his dirty tunic.

Xain handed him a silver piece and the note. The old man reached back without looking and grabbed a bird from its perch. He deftly attached the paper to the bird's leg then held the creature up for Xain's direction.

Xain reached down and touched the bird, envisioning its destination. When the creature started squirming in its handler's grip, he knew it was eager to fly. Tossing it up in the air, the gull swiftly winged away.

Xain heaved a sigh of relief. He was certain the message would arrive in time.

Halfway back to the office, he felt the pressure on his bladder from the three cups of tea he had that morning. Seeing no public privy handy, he stepped into the nearest alley and picked a location not visible from the street.

He had just unbuttoned his pants and started pissing on the wall in front of him, when he heard a ratcheted click behind him.

"Hello traitor," Wolff said, pointing his pistol crossbow at the back of Xain's head. "I see you passed along my message, thank you."

Xain's throat went dry in panic and his scrotum tightened. He could barely hear the Whitmar agent's words over the pounding of his heart.

"Don't you worry," Wolff menacingly continued. "I'll make sure we warmly welcome your tiger buddies."

"Wait, I..." was all he was able to get out before Wolff pulled the trigger.

The bolt punched through the back of Xai's skull with such force that it blew his entire face onto the wall in front of him.

The lifeless young man dropped to the alley floor with most of his brains dripping down the wall and urine still flowing from his exposed penis.

Slipping the pistol back under his jacket, Merin Wolff calmly strode back out into the Nerian streets.

Maybe an early lunch, he thought after feeling his stomach grumble.

The Kan fog hung like a thick blanket over the fertile fields of Otomoria. Targoff manor was dark, save for a lone lit window on the second floor. The limited activity on the estate left armed guards on only the wall and at the manor's double front doors. Both alternated patrols around the wall and grounds so that the inner estate remained always watched.

Bantay was standing on the wide porch, directly in front of the doors awaiting the return of his counterpart, Vagt, from the wall. The field hand and Targoff man-at-arms was daydreaming of the kitchen slave Lady Targoff just purchased. She was a beauty, with flowing red hair, wide hips and large breasts. Just his type. He had seen the looks she gave him—and all the men for that matter. It didn't matter if she turned out to be the biggest whore on the plantation as long as he got some of the action.

To Bantay, loneliness was the hardest part of the job. It wasn't the back breaking labor and long hours; it was the lack of female company.

Adrik Targoff was a good boss; he knew what it was like for his men. Twice a grand he always threw a big party for his people with lots of food and liquor. He would bring in a couple of wagon loads of whores, both women and men, from the brothels of Locian.

Even though he could be a stern taskmaster, Bantay missed Adrik Targoff. He hoped the new lady of the manor kept the much-loved tradition going, but in the meantime, there was the new cooking wench.

The guard's lustful musings dampened when he noticed he'd been standing there longer than normal, and Vagt had not returned to his station above the gate. He drew his sword and cautiously made his way around the large manor house, scanning the grounds for anything amiss.

Bantay made a complete circumambulation of the property and found nothing inappropriate nor any sign of his missing comrade. Standing on the North side between the estate and the kitchen building, he lowered his sword and scratched his head.

High-pitched whistles from behind him drew his attention just before two crescent shaped blades struck. One pierced the back of his skull and protruded upward like a miniature horn. The other sliced cleanly through the back of his neck lodging in his spine with a crack.

Bantay groaned once, let the weapon slip from his hands, then toppled over. From out of the fog, two female Singas crept over to him and dragged his body back into the shadows laying him beside an equally dead Vagt. Then, crouching low on all fours, slipped toward the house.

On the second floor, Jasusa gently knocked on Lady Targoff's bedroom door.

Nikki Targoff was sitting by the fireplace reading. She looked up and smiled when her lady-in-waiting entered.

"How is the cook slave working out?" Nikki asked, setting the book down in her lap.

"She's sure turning heads," Jasusa replied with a smirk. "Red heads are a novelty."

"As long as she can handle her kitchen duties, she can spread her legs as much as she wants."

Both chuckled, then looked over at the door when they heard a rustling in the hall.

"I thought everyone was in bed," Nikki quizzically said.

Jasusa nodded in confirmation. "They were. I just got back from securing…"

The bedroom door flew open with a crash that broke the hinge.

Both women cried out in terror as two female Singas rushed into the room.

Entering quickly, the first one hurled her sickle blades at Jasusa.

The throwing knife struck her squarely over the heart. Jasusa stared down in disbelief at the crescent object protruding from her chest and the spreading red spot. When she looked back over at her assailant, she mouthed, "Why?" before toppling to the floor.

Nikki tried in vain to fend off the two much more powerful creatures. They easily seized her with taloned fingers that dug into her flesh. She screamed, kicked and punched, all to no avail.

One had positioned herself behind the struggling human, securely gripping her upper arms. The other stepped so close to her face she could smell the Singa's mangy fur and dried blood caked around her mouth.

With a single swipe of her claws the Singa shredded Nikki's night gown. Now, naked and terrorized, a quaking

Nikki cried and babbled at two creatures she had never seen the likes of before.

The one in front of her glowered menacingly and held up a hand. In a single flicking motion, a two-inch-long claw popped out of her forefinger.

The Singa examined the deadly protrusion then gave an evil smile at Nikki's panicked expression.

"A gift from your mother," the Singa growled in broken common.

The humanoid lioness then reached down and hooked the claw between Nikki's legs and began a slow slice up the front of her body.

Nikki cried out at the initial puncture but quickly went into shock as her blood gushed out onto the floor. By the time the Singa made it to Nikki's sternum, her bowels were spilling out. The lacerated human began convulsing, mouth and eyes wide in a vacant stare.

Jasusa could feel her life slipping away with her own blood, which collected in a pool around her. The last thing the Targoff assistant saw before losing consciousness was the sight of the two female Singas violently rubbing their crotches on her mistress 'corpse, spraying their fresh kill and howling wildly.

Beden de Vidus stared out the window from his spartan third story room. The receding Kan fog slowly unveiled the abject squalor that was the Seven Sisters Slums. Off in the Zorian Harbor, the Grand Turine rang out sixteen bells making the end of the Kan official. The other event, equally significant, was the sight of old Mz. Prabina leaving her room on the first floor, heading for the fish market. Every day without fail she made the trek, following the fog as it receded into the bay and again in the evening when she discarded her rubbish.

The beloved neighborhood matriarch roamed the dangerous streets of the Vidas Plat with impunity. No one dared touch the woman who was constantly feeding and helping everyone. He, as well as most of the inhabitance of this incredibly poor neighborhood, had grown up with her loving presence and he marveled at how she always looked the same. These days she walked a little slower, a little more hunched over and with a cane. However, you could set a turine by her twice-a-day walks.

Watching her hobble out of sight, a cool breeze wafted in from Narian bay. It blew about his long dark hair. Some locks flew into his badly scarred face and he irritatingly brushed them aside.

The breeze also brought something else, the smell.

Not the normal odors he'd become used to; born and raised in one of the poorest areas of the slums. This was a distinct aroma, an ammonia laced stench from the far side of the world: Mawls.

Locals were already calling it Tiger Town. He had watched the tent city go up and the humanoid cat refugees arrive four cycles ago. Already there were problems, the smell and the noise. Two different cultures colliding always caused friction. Eventually, that kind of tension always led to violence.

Bedin never thought twice, nor lost sleep over resorting to brutality. As a low-level strong arm and thief for a guy named Boka, hostility was his constant companion. Even though Boka ran most of the action in the Seven Sisters from the slightly more prosperous Karo Plat, every criminal had to stay low level in Zor, lest they attract the attention of the city's spymaster, Rafel. That almost always resulted in a fatal visit from Red Division.

Beden was certain the tigers would have their own criminal elements, eager for new territory. He also knew Boka would have none of that. The Sisters may have been a shithole, but at least it was *their* shithole. If conflict was inevitable, then Beden wanted to know what he was going to be up against.

So, he watched and listened from his perch overlooking the Mawl encampment.

So far, he counted fifty of them, all had bandanas covering their eyes. Most looked like mixed breed mongrels, but there was also half a dozen tiger people as well as male and female lions. The leader looked like a humanoid jaguar and he was always holding gatherings in the large circular common area in the center of Tiger Town.

From the far edge of the slum's recent addition, a rapidly escalating screech went up, and another immediately joined it. The two cries reached a crescendo with the sound of mutual howls and colliding bodies.

Another fight, Beden noted. There was always at least a handful every cycle, mostly during the Kan.

They were extremely aggressive, that was obvious, but they were also industrious. Already, several were turning their tents into more permanent structures from materials scavenged from around town. A few were spreading out beyond the boundaries of their assigned area, infringing into neighboring plats and other's territories.

Yep, he thought, spitting into the street below. *Trouble's coming.*

Taleeka was shivering from the chill when they finally took the blindfold off. Blinking her eyes, she slowly became accustomed to the low orange light.

She sat against a wall, hands and feet bound, in a large room with a high ceiling and multiple arched doorways. Sand covered the stone floor, piling up against everything.

The orange Tiikeri who removed her covering stood up and stared down at her. It surprised him that even though the cub showed wide-eyed concern for her surroundings and situation, there was a distinct lack of fear on her childish face.

"I'm hungry," she calmly said.

The Tiikeri gave a low unamused chuckle. "If your traveling companions don't give me what I want, I'm going to feed you to my friends over there. How's that for hungry?"

Taleeka peered around the man-tiger. A short distance away, a group of ten Ky-Awat and three Kreetos chattered quietly in their own languages.

"Oh, you're going to get it all right. When they find me, you're going to get it good!"

"No one is going to find you unless I want them to. And you need to watch that insolent mouth of yours!"

"What does insolent mean?"

The Tiikeri snarled and then spun when a large blue flash illuminated one of the doorways.

"I thought you said no one could find us." Taleeka chided.

Zo-Dah gave the youngster an angry, frustrated look then pointed to one of the Kreetos. "Watch her. Gag her if necessary. The rest of you, come with me!"

Stepping out into the cool of the moonless, a clear sky full of stars illuminated a vast array of rooflines peeking out above massive sand dunes. They could make out movement just beyond where they held the wagon and riding lizards.

The Ky-Awat quickly raised their weapons and chittered angrily. When a tall, blue-green Gila hybrid in a floor length duster jacket strolled confidently toward them, the Tiikeri motioned for some of the rat creatures to flank around to the side.

"The Buried City of Nof-Salom," the stranger said in a friendly tone, ignoring the raised weapons. "An excellent hiding spot. Just one problem…"

"Kill him," Zo-Dah growled, and the armed desert vermin aggressively advanced.

Reaching into the pocket of his jacket, Da-Olman pulled out a small glass ball filled with glittery orange powder.

Throwing it at the feet of the lead rat-man, the orb exploded on contact. Etheria fire instantly enveloped the Ky-Awat's legs. The magical flames quickly spread upward, igniting his tunic.

The creatures froze in shock while their comrade, now completely ablaze, shrieked in agony. When the fire rapidly subsided, the smell of burnt fur and flesh filled the air. His charred body teetered and then pitched forward into the sand.

Da-Olman opened his palm to reveal a handful of glass globes.

"Plenty more where that came from," he said with a superior smile. "You all need to relax, we're on the same side. Well, sort of."

"What do you want?" Zo-Dah angrily asked.

"Same as you, the Trinilic. I'm here to help you get it, for a cut."

"Thanks," the Tiikeri sneered. "We've got the situation covered."

Da-Olman looked around at the Ky-Awat and scoffed loudly. "Not with this crew you don't. Remember that one problem I mentioned before your boys here got all hostile? The Mai-Gai have already spotted you and are reporting back right now. Pretty soon, some very serious folks are going to be coming to take back your bargaining chip. I know who they are, if only by reputation, and these lightweights don't stand a chance."

Zo-Dah glared at the Gila, considering his ominous warning.

"What do you suggest?" he finally asked with a much more softened tone.

"So, do we have a deal? I mean, I only want twenty-five percent."

"Fine!" Zo-Dah said with a clenched jaw.

Da-Olman's face lit up with a satisfied smile. "Now we're talking."

From another pocket, the Etheriat produced three Etheria disks each two inches in diameter. He placed the amber one on the ground in front of him and held the other two iridescent Aur-Quaz in the palm of each hand.

Clapping his hands together caused the Etheria to give off a shower of sparks, which lit up the area and rained down onto the amber disk.

He repeated the action several more times in a slow, deliberate manner until the ground around them rumbled and shifted.

The rat creatures looked around in panic when humanoid torsos began digging themselves out from the sand.

They were tall and gaunt, with greenish-brown mummified skin. Some even had ribs and organs peeking out from large gashes in their rotted, petrified flesh. Pointed ears and noses along with blue glowing eyes cast an eerie, menacing appearance. All one hundred of the summoned creatures' mouths were sown shut with gold thread. The mindless beings shuffled forward and stood before Da-Olman, awaiting instructions.

The Etheriat extended his arm dramatically toward the zombies.

"Presenting, the Elders of Nof-Salom! At least now we stand a chance."

As much as Captain Lar-Gaa loved a fight, easy plunder was the next best thing.

The Whitmar slave ship was exactly what and where their informant said it would be. As reported, the *Kamin* was heading back to Nier from Amarenia with a load of twenty female slaves. To the Tiikeri captain's utter delight, upon spotting their approach, the *Kamin* went dead in the water.

"She's running up the white flag Captain!"

"So I see," Lar-Gaa said, guardedly optimistic. "All the same, keep that ballista trained on them."

"Yes sir."

The mongrel oarsmen increased the pace of their strokes, driving the open topped Ves-Lari craft rapidly toward the slaver's port side.

"BOARDERS!" the captain shouted. With that order, half the rowers left their posts and began preparing the hooks and ropes.

"It's awful quiet up there captain," the first mate said, studying the ship's deck from his station on the bow.

"If they know what's good for them, they're on their knees with their hands raised," Lar-Gaa replied.

"Looks like the captain's up there to welcome us," the first mate said when he saw Merin Wolff peering over the railing, smiling down at them.

"He looks happy," the captain direly noted. "I don't like it."

"We're too close for the ballista!" the first mate cautioned.

Lar-Gaa was about to order the boarders to toss their grappling hooks when he gasped in shock. Twenty archers had joined Wolff at the railing with arrows nocked.

"IT'S A TRAP! DISENGAGE! GET OUT OF HERE!" the captain shouted.

The raider was pulling away when the first volley of arrows took down half his boarding party. Impaled bodies peppered with arrows toppled into the Shallow Sea and floated lifelessly.

The raider moved quickly away from the *Kamin* when the next round of arrows struck, taking out two more crew.

"MOVE! PUT YOUR BACKS INTO IT!" Lar-Gaa screamed to the frantically rowing mongrels.

When he turned back to order his first mate to take a shot to cover their retreat, he found him slumped over the weapon with several arrows in him.

Pulling the dead Tiikeri off the ballista, he was about to spin the weapon and take the shot himself when he saw a shimmering in the sky a hundred feet ahead of them.

The glittering gave way to ripples of opaque air and the *Atilla* appeared from out of the turbulence.

On the deck of the *Kamin*, Merin Wolff and the Whitmar archers stared in disbelief.

The Tiikeri were also watching in astonishment when the tip of one of two thick rods on either side of the Atilla's hull glowed red.

A collective gasp went up from the archers on the slaver ship when a single ball of fire shot from the glowing end. The fireball impacted the Tiikeri raider amidship with a thunderous explosion and a column of flame that shot high into the air. The eruption quickly subsided, leaving the burning hull floating aimlessly on the waters of the Shallow Sea.

Looks like the Valdurians have a few new tricks, Merin noted. He then looked over at his astonished archers still staring at the burning craft.

"Keep an eye on the water," he said, watching the *Atilla* fly off. "Take out any survivors, if any made it through *that*."

Mal hadn't felt this kind of anxiety since she lost Alto to the sands of the Dark Waste several grands ago. She found it ironic, that throughout a career of being known as a hardened loner, she could become so attached to a man and now a small child. It had been four cycles since they'd taken her little Tally, and now the Spice Rat felt ready to jump out of her skin. Watching her pace the length of the *Haraka*, the faces of her crew grew worried. Outside the craft, Alto squatted in the sand by the side hatch, keeping a lonely vigil as he absentmindedly twirled Tally's knife from hand to hand.

From the corner of his eye the swordmaster saw the ground shift off to his right and Voda rose from the sand.

Quickly standing, Alto rapped the side hatch then went over to greet him. Almost immediately, the doorway opened. Zau, and Zaad with Mal leading the way, streamed out of the airship.

"We found her," the Gila desert commando reported. "She appears to be unharmed."

A look of relief crossed everyone's face and the Jangwa continued. "She is being held about a hundred and fifty miles to the South of here in the Buried City of Nof-Salom."

Zau perked up at the mention of the name. "I know that place!"

Mal reeled in surprise. "By the goddess, how?"

"I spent several grands there under the tutelage of a very prominent mage. He taught me to read the Tanem Charts. He's also the one that gave me my eye."

"This person sounds like a powerful ally," Alto said with a touch of optimism.

"I wouldn't exactly call Master Garak an ally." Zau replied. "Like all who deal in magic, he's out for himself.

He's always looking to increase his knowledge and power. If you want his help, you better have something to trade."

"It matters not," Alto resolutely said. "If Taleeka is there, we are going to get her back."

"There is a complication," Voda hesitantly said. "Someone has raised the Elders of Nof-Salom."

Zau heaved a deep sigh and closed her eye while shaking her head in dismay.

"What the fuck does that mean?" Mal asked, her attention bouncing back and forth from Zau to Voda.

Zau opened her eye and stared at her captain. "The undead, that's what it means."

Mal's reply took The Singa by surprise. "It's not like we haven't fucking dealt with undead before. Let's go!"

Matka sat on her garden bench and stared out into space. For the first time in her adult life, she was truly alone.

Her husband and children, all gone, as was her dream of a Sorbornef dynasty. This would reduce a lesser person to tears, wallowing in sorrow and self-pity. She, however, was not such a person.

Desperate times called for desperate measures, and she was not above using desperate measures.

An idea had formed upon waking, one that she had been pondering most of the day. It was time for the Sorbornef line to be reborn, different, stronger, with formidable allies. She would be the catalyst of such a line. Even if she wouldn't be around to witness it.

Suddenly standing, she smoothed the front of her dress and breathed deeply, taking in the fragrant bouquet of flowers blooming around her.

With a graceful yet determined stride, she passed the corral and barn, pausing at the door of the guest house.

Taking another deep breath, she peered around to make sure no one was watching, then knocked on the door.

A moment later she heard the latch turn and Bo-Lah's face appeared in the crack. His eyes shifted past the human to make sure she was alone, then he opened the door.

"Lady Sorbornef," the orange Tiikeri said, closing the door behind her. "What do I owe this pleasure?"

Matka surveyed the workshop turned into a makeshift Mawl bedroom with three bedding areas along the far wall. The two female Singas were preparing to depart.

Bo-Lah noted the human's questioning look.

"The Kan's almost here. They're going on a hunt," he explained.

"I've come to discuss recent events and future plans," Matka said.

"I see," Bo-Lah said, watching the Singas skulk out of the room. "Things may have taken a dramatic turn, but I hope you're not reconsidering our bargain."

"Quite the contrary. I'm proposing expanding our pact."

"Lady Sorbornef, I'm intrigued."

"You've paid in advance for the use of Staghorn for the next grand. How would you like to make the arrangement more... *permanent*?"

"And what might this permanent arrangement cost?"

Matka's eyes narrowed and the corners of her mouth turned upward in a sly smile. "Oh, I'm not talking about money, rather a strengthening of our alliance."

"What exactly did you have in mind?"

"A child."

This left the Tiikeri agent struck silent, staring at the brash human female. "I'm sorry, did you just say a child?"

"Not just *a* child, *our* child. They would be a new lord of Staghorn and a unique reemergence of the Sorbornef dynasty."

The Tiikeri anxiously rubbed the back of his neck. "I must say, Lady Sorbornef, you have me at a rare loss for words."

"You would come out of hiding," Matka said, reinforcing her proposal. "Have your own room in the manor house. Staghorn would forever be a haven for your kind."

"If the other River Lords despised the Dreeat, I can't imagine them accepting *my kind.*"

Matka gave an evil chuckle. "They would have to. Any child bore by me would be of noble blood. Besides, once word gets out about Lady Targoff's rather gruesome demise, they will fear the wrath of Staghorn."

"You realize there is a good chance you won't survive childbirth?"

"A chance I'm willing to take and a price I'm willing to pay to bring a superior, more powerful Sorbornef into the world. If I don't make it, you must promise to raise and protect our child until they are old enough to rule."

For the Tiikeri this was an offer so far beyond his mission and expectations, he simply could not let it pass.

"Lady Sorbornef, you make a compelling argument. I accept your generous offer."

"Call me Matka," she seductively said, taking a step back.

Reaching around behind her she unhooked the back of her dress and let it fall.

Initially, her thin, mature body did nothing for the Tiikeri. However, it had been a while and the thought of sex, even with a hairless human, was arousing him.

Stepping out of her dress she walked over to one of the straw beds.

Getting down on all fours, she lowered her head to the floor, arched her back, while thrusting her bare buttocks into the air in his direction.

Bo-Lah felt the tip of his penis sliding out of its sheath and poking out of his fur when he saw her engorged, exposed vulva.

"Let's get to it," she said, hearing him approach.

The entire skyline of square stone architecture, buried in sand to a greater or lesser degree, stretched for miles. Brilliant moonlight reflected off the fine white sand and building tops, creating long eerie shadows.

"Would ya look at this fucking place!" Mal said, taking in the partially interred architecture.

"And this is only part of it," Zau said, following Mal's gaze. "There's a vast network of tunnels and caverns below the city that extends far beneath the ground."

"What happened here?" Mal asked, her attention transfixed on the half buried, perfectly preserved buildings.

"There's a bunch of crazy legends floating around the oasis, but no one really knows," Zau replied. "It's been this way for thousands of grands."

"Quite the area to search," Alto said, looking over Mal's shoulder.

"Not as bad as you might think Mora," Zau said, keeping her attention on the ground. "Until recently there's only been one resident. Everyone gives this place a wide birth and It's well off any caravan route. Over the grands it's become a refuge for some very nasty critters, not to mention a crazy wizard. Any activity is going to stick out."

"You mean like those fucking guys," Mal said, directing their attention to dozens of humanoids shuffling in the sand between buildings.

"That would be them," Zau confirmed. "The Elders of Nof-Salom. They're slow but very strong. You don't want them to get ahold of you. They can even teleport short distances and can act as a conduit for the magic of the person who raised them."

Zaad had joined them, standing behind the command chairs. "Bet they taste like shit, just like the others."

"And just like back in Immor-Onn, if you encounter one, go for the head."

"There's the riding lizards and the wagon," Zau said, pointing down to where they tethered them. "And there's something else."

Without waiting for a reply, the Singa lifted her eye patch and the phantasmal globe projected in front of her. Tugging at the edges of the three-dimensional map, she zeroed in on their position. "I thought I felt something," she said, pointing to the blinking Flavian activity. "There's a trail that ends very close to that wagon. Someone or thing gated here very recently."

"Any idea who or what?" Mal asked.

The Singa lowered her patch and the map disappeared. "Nah," she replied, shaking her head. "It was relatively small and fast, more than likely a single entity. It came from over in Lumina."

"That's fucking great! Another player, just what we need."

"One thing's for sure captain," Zaad said, surveying the area below. "She's close."

"See that dome over there," Zau said, pointing a short distance away. "If you set us down close to it, I can guide us to just about anywhere in the area. And I might be able to get us a little help."

"Okay, Kumo take us in low. I don't want the moon casting our shadow and giving us away. Set us down there between those three buildings."

"Yes captain."

The *Haraka* swung around the outskirts of the city, ten feet off the ground. With Mal's direction, it landed just an easy walk from the domed building Zau referred to, as well as the wagon.

"All right," Mal said, coming to her feet once the craft settled. "You're sure you can lead us around here?"

"Absolutely positive captain," Zau replied.

The Spice Rat buckled her sword belt and slipped her pistol crossbow next to her blade.

"Let's go get Tally back!" Mal said. "Kumo drop the side hatch. Once we're off, set up a perimeter."

"You got a plan captain?" Zaad asked, after securing Bowbreaker.

"Yeah, kill as many of those little rat fucks as I can until they give up my kid!"

Thankfully, the entrance hallway was short enough that they didn't need to light up a gem. Mal could see moonlight streaming into the room just ahead. Drawing closer to the arched doorway, the group could hear the distinct sound of activity within.

The Spice Rat was grateful for the copious amounts of sand which covered the floors, muffling the sound of their approach. She paused at the entryway, raising her hand for those behind her to stop.

The octagon shaped room was immense, with a tall domed ceiling. A shaft of light streamed in from a small hole in the center of the dome's crest. The shaft of light widened into a cone which projected the night sky in a large circle on the smooth stone floor. To the right of the telescopic projection, a Bailian male moved small stone pieces about on a long worktable.

"Well don't just stand there staring," he casually said, not bothering to look up. "Come in, I've been expecting you."

Mal glanced back suspiciously at the others. Zau shook her head and rolled her eyes, irritated at the captain's unnecessary caution.

"He knows we're here," the Singa said, pushing past everyone.

The Bailian finally looked up when Zau led the astonished group into the room. He was of average height for a Bailian, with a bald head and thick puffy facial features. His eyes were large, like the others of his race, but his irises were a dull rusty red hue. A dried eyeball suspended from a thin gold necklace adorned his simple black robes.

"Zau Berin, so good to see you again," he greeted.

Mal noted this was the first time she had heard her navigator's full name.

"Master Garak," Zau said, returning the salutation with a touch of reverence in her voice.

"I knew you were not traveling alone," he said, walking over to them. "But I didn't expect you to be in the company of such wondrous creatures!" He stopped in front of Mal and Alto. "Humans, are you not?"

"Indeed we are, good sir," Alto said, bowing. "Alto de Gom, at your service."

The Bailian gave Zau a perplexed glance. "Do all of them speak in such a manor?"

"Nah," Mal broke in. "Some of us get right to the fucking point. Look we're here…"

"I know why you're here, my chart told me," he said in an amiable tone, pointing toward his worktable. "I've only heard of your race before."

He then stepped over to Zaad and stared up at his massive frame in amazement. "But I have never, never even *heard* of your kind!"

The EEtah chuckled. "Yeah, my people don't get over to this part of the Annigan very often."

Alto was staring at the large obsidian panels which hung on six of the eight walls. Each one had a Tanem Chart carved into its surface.

"I have seen those designs before," the swordmaster thoughtfully noted.

Garak's face brightened. "Oh, so you've been to Lor-Danta?"

"Yes, I saw them carved into the obsidian field by the oasis."

He indicated his panels with a sweep of his hand. "Zau Berin carved these and taught me how to read them. I, in turn, taught her the way of the runes."

"And her eye?" Mal asked. "She said you gave her that eye of hers."

Garak fingered the dried eyeball around his neck. "An eye for an eye."

There was a brief silence before Garak spun back to his worktable. Drawn onto its surface was a circle, divided into many slices, emanating from a central point. He'd sectioned dozens of small colored stones at various points.

"The ones you seek arrived not long before you," he said, pointing at the stones. "Amongst them was one brought against their will." He then pointed to stones in another section. "Soon after that, another joined them by use of a Flavian Portal. Then the Elders were raised."

"Master Garak can you help us with the Elders?" Zau asked, stepping over to the table.

"You do not need my help," he replied." Do you have your charts and runes?"

"They're always with me."

Garak waved his hand dismissively. "You possess all you need to deal with the Elders of Nof-Salom. You just need to be clever."

"Is there anything you can tell me?"

The Bailian mage gave a crafty smile. "The greatest answers sometimes come in the smallest vessels."

Beden didn't really enjoy hurting people. He was just good at it.

"Consider this a late payment penalty," Beden said, sending his knee upward into the man's groin. The unfortunate recipient of the disciplinary beat down doubled over and cried out in agony. An uppercut to his face immediately followed the assault, sending him sprawling onto the alley ground.

"Boka expects his payments on time!" preceded a kick to the ribs.

"This was a friendly warning," Beden said, kicking him again. "Next time, I'm gonna get rough."

Beden walked out onto the street hefting the pouch of gold coins and flapping his hand in pain from skinning his knuckles.

The Kan fog was rolling in, draping the end of the street in a steadily advancing cloudy white shroud. Through the ever-thickening mist, he spotted a hunched over figure just ahead. It was tottering along the side of the road, struggling with a bag.

"Mz. Prabina," he said, easily catching up with her. "Let me help you with that."

The old lady stopped and smiled sweetly, her wrinkled features crinkling with delight. "Oh Beden, you're such a good boy," she said, allowing the gangster to take the repulsive smelling bag of trash and waste.

"You're out late," Beden noted, offering her his other arm for support. "The Kan's setting in."

"Oh yes, I was talking with your mama a few streets over and time got away from us. Your mama is such a lovely woman. She loves you so much and always brags about her hard-working boy."

"That's nice," Beden said, knowing full well his mother died several grands ago.

Prabina and his mother had been the best of friends. She had even spoken at her funeral. Now Prabina, her mind slowly slipping, claimed to have frequent conversations with her.

"Let's get you back home," he said, dropping the bag of refuse into the cart bound for the Verr pyre at the lifting of the Kan. "The dampness isn't good for you."

He walked slowly beside the beloved old woman with her arm locked with his. When they reached their apartment building, she lovingly patted the side of his badly scarred cheek.

"Such a handsome boy. I'll make you something to eat tomorrow. How about a nice casserole?"

"Thank you Mz. Prabina. I always love your cooking."

"What's this?" she said, noticing his scraped knuckles. "You've hurt your hand."

"I got it at work. It's nothing."

"You shouldn't leave wounds open," she said, taking his hand and examining it. "It could fester. You come in; I fix you up."

Despite the precarious situation she found herself in, Taleeka wasn't afraid. She had been spending her time studying her captors and loosening her bonds.

The rat people were bigger than the Cul-Ta back home, but they were just as stupid and smelled just as bad. The unsavory imp like creatures with the sharp characteristics were devious and clever. Leading them all was the ruthless man-tiger.

The most recent arrivals were cause for concern. The lizard man in the long jacket brought quite a few odd-looking creatures with him. They also had sharp features and pointed ears, but he'd sown their mouths shut and they stared vacantly forward unless directed otherwise. All of them appeared to be preparing for something and virtually ignored her.

Taleeka had loosened the ropes around her wrists by the time the lizard-man moved her into the hallway for better observation. She propped herself against the wall and promptly started working on the bindings around her ankles, when she heard a loud commotion, followed by the squeals of rat creatures beyond the bend in the passageway. Several Ky-At left the room to investigate when the Tiikeri stopped them.

"Get ready," he ominously advised, and all but the undead pulled their weapons.

Taleeka drew an excited breath when she heard Zaad's roar reverberate through the building, followed by a high-pitched scream of pain. With a loud thump, the armless body of a dying Ky-Awat bounced off the hallway wall and crumpled to the floor, staining the surrounding sand red.

Mal rounded the corner first, followed by Alto and Zaad. Both Spice Rat and the child cried out when they saw each other. Mal sprinted toward Taleeka, sword in hand as Alto's warnings of a trap fell on her deaf ears.

Mal froze when she entered the room. A Kreetos standing near Taleeka put a dagger to her throat and hissed menacingly.

When Alto and Zaad followed her in, they stared around at the room full of adversaries and the EEtah gave a satisfied chuckle. With the surroundings finally spacious enough, Zaad drew Bowbreaker. Alto pulled Defari and the sword gave out a chilling howl.

Zau, still in the hall, flipped a shell on her belt and began rubbing the rune on the back when she felt a presence behind her. She quickly joined her companions inside when she saw the hall filling with zombies.

"Weapons are hardly necessary," Zo-Dah calmly said, extending a furry orange hand. "After all, this is a business transaction."

"Fuck you!" Mal spat. "I'm here to get my kid back."

All stood for a moment, staring apprehensively.

Da-Olman stepped forward breaking the tense standoff.

"Well I for one am glad to see us all here so nice and cozy," he said in a mocking tone before turning his attention to the Elders who accumulated out in the hall.

"Kill them all!" he sinisterly ordered.

Upon hearing the command, one zombie reached out and grabbed a nearby Ky-Awat by the head, then crushed it. The deceased man-rat dropped to the floor at the undead's feet.

Simultaneously, all the humanoid rats began squealing in panic, scrambling around the room.

Taleeka had survived living on the streets of the Narrows by capitalizing on a simple strategy that was now serving her well; Everyone underestimates a young girl.

With her hands now free, Taleeka reached up and grabbed the Kreetos' knife hand. She slid down the wall under the blade and guided the creature's wrists back toward its chest, plunging the blade into the startled sentient.

The Kreetos cried out at the knife jutting from his chest while Taleeka rolled away.

The room descended into chaos. Both Ky-Awat and Kreetos, realizing they had no allies, rushed about in a clamor, trying to evacuate the area. A growling Defari had just removed the heads of two Elders on her wielder's way over to Taleeka. The still bound young girl was shuffling along the floor on her back, attempting to untie the rope around her legs when the swordmaster gave out a whistle. She looked up in time to see Alto pull her knife from his sash and toss it to her.

Zo-Dah hung back watching the Malay when he spotted Da-Olman slipping out the door as the last of the undead shambled into the room. Snarling disdainfully, he began working himself around the edge of the room to follow.

The fight was mere moments old and all the Ky-Awat which hadn't escaped lay dead on the floor.

Alto bounded to Mal's back when he saw one elder teleport several feet and attack a Kreetos. On the ground, Taleeka crawled over to where Zau was crouching, defiantly holding her knife out in front of her.

"Stay low kid," the Singa advised, when she saw one elder attempt but fail to grab one of the Kreetos doubled over in pain.

Zaad was bellowing furiously and swinging Bowbreaker in a wide arc in front of him. The great sword's blade sliced cleanly through four zombies bounding toward him, arms extended. He sliced them in half, but the legs continued walking while the torsos pulled themselves across the floor.

"The head Zaad, aim for the head!" Alto yelled.

The EEtah, so close to a blood frenzy, didn't hear him.

Zau and Taleeka huddled against the wall in a defensive position. Even though they were out of the standing zombie's reach, two of the undead's torsos crawled toward them.

Pulling themselves ever closer, Zau retrieved one of the dead rat creature's short swords. Coming to her knees, she drove the blade down through the square of the nearest one's back. The tip punched through the chest and lodged between two stones, trapping the zombie to the floor. It mindlessly continued trying to pull itself along but remained pinned like an insect on display.

The other continued toward Taleeka. Zau peered back in horror when the young girl screamed. She was hacking away with inept abandon on the corpse that had grabbed both her legs and was attempting to rend her apart.

Flipping over another shell on her belt, she rubbed the rune with one hand and extended the other. Taleeka's screams and the din of combat drowned out Zau's soft chanting. Her palm began to glow orange.

Bending over, she touched her hand to the zombie's head. There was a slight flash and the Elder slumped, its head now a charred stump.

Mal was finding her thin bladed rapier ineffective on the undead attacking them. She had inflicted damage on several, keeping them at bay when she heard a snapping sound and Alto crying out in pain.

She spun to see one zombie wrenching Alto's main sword arm. It contorted in an unnatural angle and the bone jutted out. Defari toppled to the floor with a whimper and the swordmaster was frantically trying to draw his short sword through waves of intense pain.

Mal dropped her sword and dove for Defari. "Get 'em girl," she said, coming to her feet.

Defari growled when Mal sent the Etheria blade across the zombie's forearms that held Alto's limb. They severed cleanly but held on.

Mal's next swing was for the head which dropped the corpse and the arms loosened their grip and fell.

She continued her swing to the two she had been fighting. The sword howled when their heads flew from their bodies.

Zau was watching the badly outnumbered conflict with concern. With Alto badly injured, the odds were no longer in their favor. Something needed to be done.

Staring down at the zombie's burnt head, the voice of Master Garak echoed through her consciousness.

The greatest answers sometimes come in the smallest vessels.

"Tally, I've got an idea, but I need your help."

Taleeka peered up at her with a serious expression.

"We can't keep this up. I've got to try something. I need you to keep them off me while I do it. Can you do that?"

The nine-year-old nodded.

"This is going to take everything I've got, so I'm going to be defenseless afterwards even if it works. You're going to have to be my protector."

Taleeka held her knife up confidently. "I can do it!"

"Good kid!"

Zau turned yet another shell over on her belt. She closed her eyes and softly chanted while rubbing the rune.

Slowly, a swirling blue portal, a foot across, appeared in the floor beside her.

The small conduit shot out from the Corporal Reach, across the Middle Realms. It pierced the multi-verse opening a conduit to the Pasture Plain.

Kalaka, she called out under her breath. *Kalaka, your friends are in trouble. They need your help.*

Watching Da-Olman sneak up on the *Haraka*, Zo-Dah hadn't descended into a murderous rage, at least not yet. The Tiikeri agent always knew he couldn't trust the Gila and this was proof.

He had been easy to follow under the cloudless, moonlit sky. The arrogant lizard-man didn't even bother to conceal his movements, believing that his undead minions had done the messy work for him.

They nestled the airship in a narrow three-way intersection, hovering a few inches off the hard packed desert sand. It was far enough off the major streets so as not to attract attention—which made it a perfect target. Or so the Gila Etheriat thought.

Flexing his hands, the Tiikeri extended and retracted his claws while deciding what to do.

"Did you really think you could get away with this?" Zo-Dah said, stepping out from the building's shadow.

Da-Olman spun in surprise but immediately assumed a calm, confident demeanor. "If I didn't think I could get away with it, I wouldn't have tried."

"I suppose you know our little arrangement is no longer valid?"

"Oh, gods yes, that was never my intent—and that's close enough."

Undeterred by the warning, the Tiikeri kept walking. When he saw Da-Olman reach into his open coat, he lunged.

The Tiikeri tackled the Gila in his midsection, digging his claws into his back, just as he was pulling an Etheria grenade. The small glass orb flew from Da-Olman's hands and landed several feet away where it exploded, sending a plume of sand into the air.

Da-Olman screamed in pain and twisted his body to fling the Tiikeri off him. The throw succeeded but the man-tiger kept his claws dug in and both tumbled toward the parked craft.

It astonished each of the combatants when they didn't hit the ground, but an intricate sticky webbing suspended around the airship caught them instead.

Zo-Dah retracted his claws out of Da-Olman's back before beginning a futile effort to free himself. Testing the adhesive bonds, Da-Olman conserved his strength while the Tiikeri, already angry, thrashed wildly at his restraints. With each twist and thrash Zo-Dah became more irate and entangled.

He finally stopped when the back hatch dropped. Both captives saw the silhouette of the humanoid torso on the spider's body and Zo-Dah insolently growled.

Kumo quickly scampered across the web to examine her catch and both males felt the twinge of arousal as she came near, despite the danger.

She first hovered over Da-Olman, taking in the details of the man-lizard. Her face shriveled in disapproval and she shook her head before moving over to the Tiikeri.

Smiling, she reached down and caressed his orange fur.

"Pretty," she said in a soft, appreciative voice before pulling back her black sensuous lips and revealing two long, curved fangs.

Both captives cried out in surprise and horror just before she plunged them into the Tiikeri's neck.

The neurotoxin took effect almost immediately and the man-tiger's breath became shallow before stopping completely.

A second bite injected Zo-Dah with the digestive enzyme. While it took effect, Kumo started on his legs, rapidly encasing him. Da-Olman was quaking in terror while ropy white strands jetted from the Makari's thorax until it completely covered the Tiikeri.

The Gila could do nothing but lay immobile, looking up at the full moon and blanket of stars, listening in revulsion to Kumo's slurping away at the rapidly liquifying body of his former adversary.

Kumo stopped feeding when the sky went dark. She stared upward with Da-Olman to a massive undulating cloud that blocked out the sky. Swirling closer, both could hear a buzzing sound grow progressively louder.

Kumo had resumed feeding by the time the swarm was upon them. The air was thick with flying vermin and the roaring buzz of hundreds of thousands of rapidly beating wings was all but deafening.

Da-Olman knew the nature of the infestation and that he was in no danger.

These were funereal flies, and they had no use for the living. There was a reason there were no graves in the Dark Waste; these insects could completely devour a corpse in a luna, leaving nothing, not even bones.

The mass of thumb-sized flies briefly inundated the area, then swarmed as a single organism down the street and into the same building the conflict still raged in.

Someone had sounded the dinner bell, and the main course was going to be the Elders of Nof-Saloom.

Taleeka was becoming worried. Zau's eyes were growing heavy and the portal on the floor next to her was shrinking and fading.

Out in the center of the room, Mal, Alto and Zaad were holding their own, although still outnumbered by creatures that felt neither pain nor fear and wouldn't die until you removed their heads from their bodies.

Animated body parts littered the floor. The severed arms were the worst because they continued to crawl across the floor, reaching out for something to grab. Taleeka had already hacked up three of them which crawled too close to the incapacitated Singa.

Raucous, chaotic combat surrounded the child. The loudest of which was Zaad, who now was deep amid a blood frenzy. He roared at the top of his lungs with every swing of Bowbreaker. These brutal, unsophisticated attacks deposited more body parts on the ground which then continued to move on their own.

Mal was wielding Defari who growled and barked with each swing. Her attacks were more accurate, causing heads and bodies to fall. She marveled at the lightness and precision of the Etheria sword.

Alto, who was normally the epitome of grace in combat, struggled. He fought back-to-back with Mal using his short sword, grimacing in pain with every swing.

"I can't keep it open any longer," Zau said, slumping back against the wall with her eyes fluttering. When they finally closed, so did the portal.

Taleeka heard the buzzing coming down the hall just as a zombie struck Alto on his already badly broken arm.

The swordmaster went down on one knee and Taleeka screamed as a giant swarm of black, buzzing flies erupted through the doorway.

The swirling horde of insects quickly filled the room and went straight for the zombies and their various body parts strewn about the floor.

Once Taleeka realized these were not the same horse flies she had encountered in Otomoria, she ceased flailing her arms and squealing.

The air in the room grew thick with ravenous flies but they completely ignored the living. The undead found themselves completely covered and unable to continue their attack. They bumbled about blindly while the flies slowly devoured them.

Mal helped Alto to his feet, then rushed to Taleeka.

The two gave a brief relieved hug, then looked over at Zau who was slipping in and out of consciousness.

"What's wrong with Zau?" Taleeka asked, her childish face draped with worry.

"She used up all her energy keeping that portal open. She needs rest. I'll get her. You go to Alto. Stay away from Zaad, but we need to get the fuck out of here!"

Keeping well away from the berserking EEtah, Mal dragged the unconscious Zau across the limb scattered floor now covered with feasting flies. Taleeka, holding Alto's hand, led him out into the cool moonlight.

Once they made it to the *Haraka*, it surprised Mal to see the rear hatch open and Kumo and two captives in her web. She immediately recognized the cocoon wrapped, partially eaten Tiikeri body. Da-Olman hung right beside him, quaking in terror, his head turned away from the feasting spider-woman.

The terrified Gila looked over at the approaching Mal with a pleading expression.

"Oh, my pilot doesn't want to kill you," Mal's tone was merciless. "*I'm* the one that wants to kill you," she said, drawing her sword.

"Wait, wait, I didn't…"

"He wasn't one of the people who took me." Taleeka said, tugging at Mal's pant leg.

"See, see? Listen to the kid. I had nothing to do with taking her!"

"Get Alto inside and get one of those Dreeat candies in him."

Taleeka nodded and led the exhausted, pain wracked swordmaster away.

Once the duo was gone, Mal turned her attention to a still frightened Etheriat. Her look had not softened.

"You may not have been in on snatching my kid," she said, "but you told those creatures to kill us. Then you planned to heist my load. You sound like a real fucking pain in the ass. Why should I let you live?"

"Because I got skills you're gonna find real useful," the Gila replied, his staccato voice tense with desperation.

Mal lowered her blade. "Yeah, what kinda fucking skills are you talking about?"

"Crystals, Etheria Crystals. I'm an expert with them. I can make all kinds of things."

Mal raised her sword again and circled the tip at him. "Too bad you picked the wrong fucking friends, ass wipe."

"No, no, stop! Those weren't my friends, I swear!"

"Oh yeah?"

Da-Olman's face fell in defeat. "We were gonna split the Trinilic," he confessed.

Mal's mouth slowly pulled upward in a smile. A twinkle appeared in her eyes and she put her sword away. "And then try to beat us both out for the Etheria? By the goddess, I can respect that."

"Look, I've been a research whore my whole life," Da-Olman admitted, a sense of relief washing over him. "I plant my flag with anyone that can fund my work."

"I can respect that too." Mal said, sounding less enraged. "Do what ya love while all the while putting food on the table."

Da-Olman's face brightened. "So, you're gonna let me go?"

Mal gave an amused look and scoffed loudly. "Fuck no! You tried to kill us. There's no fucking way I trust you. But you're right, you just might be useful. I'll turn you over to the Valdurians. Let them decide what to do with you. In the meantime, my pilot here will make sure you're snug and secure for the trip back."

Beden didn't need to hear the Grand Turine ring out six bells to know the Kan was upon the high holy city of Zor. The fog was so thick he could barely make out Boka crossing the street.

At five-foot-six and one-hundred-twenty pounds, the mobster was hardly an imposing figure. It was his stare and cruel pouty mouth that made people think twice about crossing him.

To Beden, it was his distinct disheveled hair and beard which marked him, even at a distance.

"What ya got for me?" Beden asked, getting right down to business.

Boka instinctively looked around to see if anyone was within ear shot. Seeing no one, he stared back up at the much taller Beden.

"There's a guy named Flavio; he unloads cargo on dock sixteen. Last cycle he stiffed and roughed up one of the working girls over on High Street. When he's not on the docks, he's usually drinking at the Strange Brew Pub."

"That's over on High Street too isn't it?"

"Yeah."

"So, the idiot likes to shit in his own bed, huh?"

"He's into the girl for five silver. Then there's our recovery fee. I want you to make an example of this guy. Do it in public."

Beden snickered. "Before the Kan's over this dumbass fucker is going to realize how expensive pussy can get."

Both laughed and Boka started off. "Remember, make an example."

"Oh yeah, his friends are gonna see him cry like the little bitch he is. I'll head over there in a few. I've got something to take care of first."

Boka nodded, then disappeared into the fog.

Entering the front door of the apartment building he headed down the hall of the first floor instead of taking the stairs up to his.

He stopped in front of the third door down and gently knocked. At first there was no answer and he became a bit worried. He had seen Mz. Prabina return from his window just before the Kan, like normal. He always liked to check on her before going out on business, which he did under cover of the fog.

With the second knock he heard the latch turn. When the door opened, he stared in stunned surprise as a smiling, naked Prabina greeted him.

"Oh, hello," she said, oblivious to the situation. "Are you new around here? I always like to meet my new neighbors."

"Mz, Prabina, it's me, Beden. Shouldn't you get some clothes on?"

She ignored the question. "You're a friend of Beden? How nice to meet you. Well, any friend of Beden's... He is such a good boy."

"Mz. Prabina, *I'm* Beden!"

"Uh-huh," she said, turning and walking back into her room. "I've got something for him. He helped me last cycle and I promised I'd make him something nice. It's fresh and I've got it cooling by the window."

Beden watched the old woman's wrinkled, portly frame jiggle to a table by the room's solitary window.

She picked up a circular earthenware pan and brought it over to the saddened mobster, never losing her sweet smile.

"Here you go," she said, handing it to him. "If you would be so kind as to give this to Beden when you see him. And no picking at it! This is for your friend. He's such a nice boy. I just know he'll share."

Beden looked down at the pan filled with hardened mud, twigs and pebbles.

"Thanks, Mz. Prabina," he said with a sad smile. "I'll make sure he gets it."

They had been back in Zor for three cycles now and Taleeka barely left Mal's side. In fact, the entire trip back from the Dark Waste, the exhausted child had eaten and slept in her lap.

Now, making their way down the halls of the Zorian Forum, she held both Alto and Mal's hands tightly.

A broad grin adorned the Spice Rat's face. She was back at home, safe with the ones she loved and best of all, they were about to get paid.

Knocking on Joc' Valdur's office door got a resounding, "Come," from within.

The Valdurian Ambassador stood and came around from behind his desk when they entered.

"Back from the wild sands of the Dark Waste!" he heartily greeted.

"Yeah, and I don't mind saying, this one was a bitch," Mal said, letting go of Taleeka's hand.

"So I heard," Joc' said, placing a long, polished wooden box on his desk. "Well, you'll be happy to know that the Trinilic is already being put to good use by our Landagar friends and we are cautiously optimistic about the passenger you brought to us. I would say good job, but then you always do a good job." He then inspected Alto's frame. "How's the arm?"

"It feels fine," the swordmaster said, flexing it. "It is truly amazing what rune magic and Dreeat confections can accomplish."

"Well, we've got a little something here which will hopefully take the sting out of a 'bitch' of a job," Joc' said, opening the box.

"My favorite part of the gig," Mal said, watching him take a stack of six one-thousand-secor Air Notes.

"One for everyone in the crew, except your pilot. From what I understand she doesn't require compensation?"

"That's right," Mal replied. "All we have to do is keep her fed. Which can be a lot harder than it sounds."

He nodded and handed her the stack. "As usual, double share for the captain and even a share for Mz. Tally."

Joc' took a note off the top and handed it to the child who accepted it with a wide-eyed smile.

"What do you say?" Mal gently reminded.

"Thank you."

"You are welcome young lady. I hear you were a big help?"

Tally nodded enthusiastically. "I got to open locks and keep the icky undead things away from Zau. It was fun!"

The envoy smiled and returned his gaze to the adults. "And, I've got something special for you two," he said, reaching back into the box.

Taleeka was staring at the air note in wonder when Mal reached down and gently took it from her.

"This is an awful lot of money," she explained. "You don't want to lose it. I'll keep it safe for you."

Joc' removed two rolled-up pieces of paper. Stepping over to the pair, he ceremoniously handed one to both Mal and Alto.

"For your service to House Valdur and, quite frankly, mankind in general, by the power vested in me by the Zorian High Council I now bestow upon you the honor of Bespoke Names. These will forever mark you as heroes of the realm. Congratulations."

This left Mal too stunned to speak. She traded a delightedly surprised glance with Alto before opening the scroll.

"You may choose any name you wish," Joc' said, closing the box. "Any thoughts?"

Alto rolled the decree back up. "My father's name was Kameron. It would be a fitting tribute."

Mal paused for a moment, staring at the proclamation, then gazed lovingly at Alto and Taleeka. "Yeah, that sounds good."

This moved Alto beyond words. He could only stare in adoration at the woman who had shared his blade and his bed for the past four grands. Now she wished to share his name.

"Are you sure my love?" he could finally choke out.

"With all the shit we've been through, are you kidding?"

"What about me?" came a tiny voice from beside them.

All three looked down at the nine-year-old girl on the verge of tears.

Mal and Alto gave Joc' a questioning glance.

Joc' stepped over and knelt in front of Taleeka. "Are you certain young lady? This is a big decision."

Taleeka glanced up at Alto and Mal who stared tenderly at her. She then looked back at Joc' and excitedly nodded.

"Very well," Joc' said, standing. "I'll have the paperwork drawn up. From this day forward you shall be known as Alto, Maluria and Taleeka Kameron."

Across the many island chains and continents that comprised the Goyan Islands, the Kan represented different things to different people. For most, the thick fog and limited visibility represented a time of rest. Others used it to ply their trades in the service of the sleeping masses. A few, however, used the inescapable mist to shroud their nefarious activities.

Beden counted himself in the latter class and this Kan would prove no different. The fog was lighter due to a constant stiff breeze blowing in off the bay, punctuated by sustained gusts blowing open large swaths of mist.

From his third story perch, the mobster could see brief glimpses all the way to the docks. This would make his job more difficult, but not impossible. Soon, yet another person would learn the very painful lesson about crossing Boka.

Normally, Beden would already have been on the streets by now. He purposefully delayed his departure in hopes the breeze would die down allowing the fog to thicken; and because Mz. Prabina hadn't returned from her evening walk.

He was uneasy about the old woman's tardiness. Her mind seemed to be deteriorating at a faster pace as of late. This, combined with the agitated state of their Mawl neighbors, had the hardened mobster on edge.

For the last three cycles, Tiger Town had been especially restless. There were noticeable escalations of raucous altercations within its borders. The Mawls had become so territorial they constantly harassed humans if they dared enter or pass through. Even the city guards were hesitant of patrolling there.

This Kan, however, Tiger Town was eerily quiet.

When the current gust finally died and the fog grew thicker, Beden decided he'd wasted enough time and closed the window, when a strange feline cry went up from the Mawl encampment. This differed from the sounds of the cat-people's normal rowdy behavior, deeper and more prolonged.

Poking his head back out the window, another gust revealed the entire population of Mawls standing in a circle around the tent city's common area. The humanoid jaguar, dressed in robes, stood just outside the circle, arms raised to the sky, leading everyone in the unnerving chant.

Beden could feel the gust subsiding and knew he was about to lose his visibility when he saw something that caused his throat to tighten and stomach sink.

Thrust into the circle, was a naked Mz. Prabina. She was trembling and looking around in confused terror.

Beden heard her scream ring out above the discordant chant just as the fog closed in, leaving only the sounds of the atrocities below.

Moments later, another gust came along and he could see them shove her around the circle with the Mawls. They swatted at her when she passed, scratching small cuts across her body. She staggered about shrieking in agony and horror.

Another blinding wave of mist obscured his view and the mobster racked his brain for anything he could do. If he intervened, he would be all alone against larger and more powerful opponents whose senses allowed them to operate with impunity in the fog. If he cried out to draw attention to the slow slaughter, he would reveal himself.

Beden hadn't survived for as long as he had on the streets by being stupid. Beloved neighborhood matriarch or not, there was nothing Beden could do but helplessly observe her played to death by a pride of humanoid cat people.

When the fog cleared again, she was slumped in the middle of the circle, covered in blood and crying hysterically. The faces of the surrounding Mawls were one of diminishing excitement that their living toy could no longer amuse them.

Seeing her unable to continue, the man-jaguar entered the circle and stood dominantly over her. Reaching down, he grabbed her hair and yanked her head back. With a single slice of his claw, he severed her throat and the crying stopped with the chanting.

The Yagur priest dipped his finger in the open wound. The old woman's blood covered the digit when he pulled it out and he marked an X and I on her exposed forehead, before letting the body drop.

As fond as he was of Mz. Prabina, Beden felt relieved he didn't foolishly intervene. As soon as the woman's head hit the cobblestones, the ground trembled. All around the area, windows rattled and buildings shook. From under the woman's body, a fissure cracked open and the corpse tumbled into the jagged recess.

Moments later, a large black patch of primordial sludge oozed up from the crack in the street. It pooled just beside the opening. The entire surface of its amorphous body was flashing with small blue X's and I's. While the nebulous mass rose and took shape, the Mawls dropped to their knees chanting again.

The glob continued to shift and transform, the binary runes strobing across its slowly changing body. Its glyphs stopped lighting up when the blob finally formed into the basic shape of a humanoid feline. The newly formed body contained only the vaguest of discernible features, including two stubby cat ears on either side of its head.

Beden slumped to the floor below the window, his heart hammering and breath ragged. This exceeded anything his violent life had ever exposed him to on the streets of Zor.

He was frightened and enraged. He wanted to avenge her, but how?! He was so far out of his league; no plan would form in his mind.

This situation would require an action that was unthinkable before.

He was willing to risk something that would normally spell his death. Rafel, his dreaded nemesis, must be told.

He was going to violate the mobster's sacred oath of silence.

Tomorrow he would break the code of Tisina.

It had been a busy morning for the city of Zor. The earthquake during the Kan had been small and did negligible damage. The event was still enough to set tongues wagging and nerves on edge.

Patrol Captain Gasata was in Colonel Zekoff's office briefing him when Rafel poked his head in the door.

"Good, I'm glad I caught you both together," the spymaster said.

"More on the earthquake?" Zekoff wearily asked, watching Rafel take a seat next to Gasata.

"Of a sort," Rafel said with a grim nod. "I just had a conversation with a low-level leg breaker named Beden. He came to me."

With that revelation, Zekoff and Gasata traded curious glances.

"If he was willing to risk death breaking the criminal's code of silence, it must be serious," Gasata noted, stroking his mustache.

"He lives in an apartment in the Sisters, up on the third floor overlooking Tiger Town. He said he saw everything."

"What everything?" Zekoff asked, lighting his pipe. "It was a minor earthquake."

"Not quite so simple. According to our chatty friend, the Mawls caused it by performing some summoning ritual. They used a human sacrifice. An old lady that lived on the first floor of the building."

"My patrol sergeants reported Tiger Town as unusually quiet just before the quake." Gasata said, knowing his colonel liked any seemingly insignificant piece of information.

Zekoff sat puffing his pipe, silently taking in the news.

"Do we have a body?"

Rafel shook his head. "The quake supposedly opened up a small fissure that the body fell into and the thing came out of."

"What kind of thing?" Zekoff asked before blowing a column of evergreen scented smoke toward the ceiling.

Rafel gave a nervous sigh. "This is the truly disturbing part. According to Beden, it started out as a black ooze with glowing X's and I's all over it. The ooze then formed itself into a featureless Mawl that the Tiger Town population was worshiping on their knees."

The Zorian spymaster shifted anxiously in his chair. "And you know what? I believe him."

A moment of silence descended on the room with all three Zorian guards searching each other's faces.

"Stryder Aramos," Zekoff grimly said, breaking the silence.

"Sounds like it," Rafel confirmed. "Although just before he disappeared, he had dropped the Aramos name and was calling himself 'The Vicar of Pa-Waga.'"

Zekoff stared. "Well, they said the Mawls were religious refugees. At least now we know what religion."

"I suppose we should brace ourselves for more murders with blood runes on the wall." Gasata said with a touch of foreboding.

Zekoff shook his head. "Stryder was just getting started with those. I'm afraid if he's back there's bigger mischief afoot."

"What can we do?" Gasata asked.

Zekoff tapped out his pipe. "There's nothing we can do but be on guard. Have your patrols keep their eyes and ears open. Especially the ones in Tiger Town. Unfortunately, the first move if any, is Stryder's."

Gasata cleared his throat. "About those patrols Colonel. A lot of my men are nervous about patrolling there. The tension is pretty high and they're subject to constant harassment."

Zekoff nodded, contemplating his next action. "Is there anyone in charge over there?"

"Yes, a Yagur holy man by the name of Al-Zah."

Zekoff sighed and sat back in his chair. "I think it's time I go see firsthand what's going on and have a chat with this Al-Zah. Do we know anything about him?"

"Nothing," Rafel said flatly.

"Well then, this should be interesting," Zekoff said, opening the top drawer of his desk and pulling out a shard of Larimar. The milky white Etheria Crystal with blue striations had been a gift from Mal and Alto upon the return from their first mission to Nocturn. Its translating powers had proven useful repeatedly.

"Sir, surely you're not going alone?" Gasata said in surprise. "Let me send a few men with you."

Zekoff shook his head and pocketed the Diplomat Stone. "No, you said it yourself, tensions are high between the Mawls and your men. I'm going to try to lower the heat a bit and uniforms would probably be counterproductive."

The three exited the office, stepping into the busy hall.

"Just be careful sir," Rafel said, watching Zekoff walk off toward the front doors of the Zorian Guard's headquarters.

The colonel waved his hand in recognition but didn't look back.

"I'm going to go see Trenton," Rafel told Gasata, once Zekoff was out of ear shot. "He may not want uniforms around, but a couple of armed plainclothes Red Division in the crowd would make me a lot more comfortable about this meeting."

Zekoff could feel the eyes following him as he entered the boundaries of the tent city known as Tiger Town. Feline faces full of fear, resentment and rage scrutinized his every movement.

He could hear their disdainful murmurings too, even though they were unaware of his ability to understand them. Whispers of distrust and violence passed through the various groupings mostly situated just outside their open tents.

With his attention focused straight ahead, the old colonel's calm deliberate gait portrayed an air of unaggressive confidence.

By the time he reached the open common area he became aware he was being followed. Not letting on, he strolled up to the fissure in the cobblestone plaza.

The opening in the ground was three feet across and ten feet long with no discernible bottom. Peering into its recesses, Zekoff calmly retrieved his pipe, loaded and lit it.

Taking the pipe out of his mouth, he blew out the smoke while turning to address a group of seven young male Tiikeri and Singa. "Your leader is the priest named Al-Zah, is it not?"

The aggressive males, clearly perplexed that the human was speaking their language, glanced around, baffled.

"I would very much like to speak with him," Zekoff said before returning the pipe to his mouth and his attention to the pit, ignoring the intended intimidation.

Long moments passed. Zekoff circled the fissure, examining it from every angle while the crowd of curious Mawls gathered. Finally, an older Yagur pushed his way through the mass of bodies.

"I am Al-Zah," he said.

"Quite the hole you've got here," Zekoff said.

The humanoid jaguar's eyes narrowed suspiciously. "It opened last night during the Kan. My people had nothing to do with it."

Zekoff took another puff off his pipe. "Where are my manners? I'm Colonel Zekoff, commander of the Zorian City Guards." Zekoff examined the bowl of his pipe. "An old woman went missing around here last Kan." He looked up, staring Al-Zah directly in the eyes. "You wouldn't happen to know anything about that would you?"

"I'm a humble priest. I know nothing of missing humans."

"Funny, because witnesses placed her around here at the time of her disappearance."

"Colonel I find these questions insulting. Exactly what are you getting at?"

"Insulting you is not my intention. I am merely doing my job."

"I doubt if any humans were around here, especially during the Kan. We are a private people who dislike outsiders in our territory."

"This patch of ground where we stand is within the boundaries of the High Holy City of Zor. All citizens of this city are free to travel through here as they wish. It is not yours."

The Yagur scowled. "Your high council gave us sovereignty over this place!"

"I beg to differ. I am on the high council. You are mere guests in my city and by all reports, guests that are acting poorly."

Zekoff heard the term "blasphemer" yelled from behind just before someone struck him on the side of the head. Reeling to the side, another blow to the body followed which dropped the colonel to one knee.

"This is our land now," Al-Zah decreed, just before another blow sent Zekoff flat on his back.

Through the pain the commander of the city guards could hear the Mawls cursing at him while they delivered a series of punishing kicks to the body.

Just before losing consciousness Zekoff could hear Al-Zah give the order to "remove him from *our land*."

Sergeant Yemen de Uutu had been a member of Red Division for six grands and he truly enjoyed it. Coming from the Uutu Plat of the Seven Sisters, brutality had always been a way of life for him. Now he was getting paid for it. Unlike the regular Zorian Guards who kept the peace and investigated incidences, Red Division's policy of, "kill first, question later," really appealed to him.

Today's assignment didn't seem that perilous. He and three of his charges were to follow an unarmed Colonel Zekoff on his inspection of Tiger Town. Orders were to stay undercover; that meant they had to wait by the outskirts, close at hand, ready to intervene. Yemen didn't mind the assignment. It had been nine cycles since the Mawls arrived and he hadn't got a look at them yet.

Yemen's first glance at the cat people from Nocturn would be one he would never forget.

Heading straight for their position were two young male Singas dragging an unconscious Zekoff, one on each arm with a small crowd of Mawls following. Yemen would always recall the scraping sound the toes of the beloved commander's boots made when they yanked him across the cobblestones.

Snapping his fingers to catch his men's attention, he reached for his bow and forearm quiver beside the crate where he sat.

With looks of satisfied rage, the Singa's halted at the border of Tiger Town and tossed Zekoff to the ground just beyond the boundaries of the tent city.

They were dead before the old man's body hit the ground, each impaled with two arrows.

The crowd of Mawls gasped when the Singas joined the human on the street, then focused their attention on the four men aiming arrows at them. A Tiikeri roared in rage and charged, followed by a handful of Singas and mongrels.

With rapid precision they met the same fate. The men fired and reloaded so fast, the other Mawls could barely follow their movements. They froze in place, growling at the armed men in a tense standoff.

From the rear of the crowd there was a commotion and Al-Zah pushed his way forward.

"STOP. STOP!" he bellowed.

When he reached the front, he sadly looked around at the twelve dead Mawls and the humans with arrows nocked, ready to strike.

Raising his hands, he addressed the Mawls. "You must stop this violence. It does not reflect well on us and it is not our way!"

This took a bit of aggression off the crowd and the Yagur spun to face the humans who were more than ready to unleash another wave of death.

"Please, lower your weapons. We are a peace-loving people."

Yemen was unmoved by the priest's plea. "Turn over the ones responsible for attacking our commander! Do it now, or I'm going to assume you are all guilty and we'll kill you all!"

The Yagur sorrowfully gazed around at the dead Mawls. "You have already killed the ones responsible."

This seemed to satisfy the Red Division archers and they lowered their weapons but kept arrows nocked.

"Everyone stay put!" Yemen ordered the crowd. "You two," he addressed his men. "You get the colonel to Clerria House and you get Trenton and Gasata."

"Why are my people not free to go?" Al-Zah pleadingly asked.

"Because I need my superiors to decide what to do with you."

"What do you mean, 'do with us?'"

Yemen gave a malicious smirk. "Normally when they call me in, my job's simple. I'd just kill you all. Right now, I believe you. Some of your people might not have been involved, but that's not for me to decide. And if the colonel doesn't make it, you all may just end up dying anyway."

Bartol Aramos was quickly becoming accustomed to the trappings that being family patriarch provided. Mostly he was happy that his young wife Syleen, was busy setting up house in their Aris manor, leaving him the freedom of the royal life. After all, Zor was the real seat of power for all the human houses, not their ancestral homes up in the Goyodian Chain.

He looked over to the report on his desk from their new fixer in Makatooa. He knew that eventually he was going to have to address reopening the bank there, but that could wait. He'd finished work for the day and it was time to sample some of the pleasures his position provided.

Heaving a sigh of pleasure, he leaned back and peered down past his heaving rolls of belly fat to the face of his young runner and sex slave, Banavor. The young man with full lips, curly light brown hair and skin was enthusiastically sucking his tiny, rigid cock.

The portly Aramos felt the pressure building in his balls. He salaciously contemplated plastering the boy's face, when the smell of ammonia pulled his attention away from the oral devotion expertly given him.

"Do you smell that?" Bartol asked, feeling his member go soft.

"Hello brother, working hard I see." came a familiar voice from behind.

Bartol spun in his seat and the naked young boy stood and stepped back. Both stood face to face with a naked, very human looking Stryder.

"Stryder!" Bartol sputtered. "I thought you were dead!"

"Not dead brother, reborn."

"How did you get in? What are you doing here? What do you want?"

Stryder walked calmly to the center of the room and caressed Banavor's cheek with a nostalgic smile.

"So many questions," he said. "I'm simply here to assume my rightful role as spiritual leader of House Aramos."

"You're a little late for that brother," Bartol sneered.

Stryder's smile took on a confident note. "Am I?"

Banavor's eyes widened and he took a step back when Stryder's eyes and lips glowed blue. Bartol sat transfixed on his brother mouthing unintelligible words.

Benavor gasped in shock when his master's hand shakily opened the drawer in front of him and pulled out a tiny dagger used as a letter opener. He softly cried out when Bartol, his face filled with horrific disbelief, plunged the blade repeatedly into his neck.

Fountains of blood erupted all over his chest, lap and the top of the desk. With a final gurgle, he pitched forward onto the desk. His force striking the desktop drove the lodged dagger through his throat until the tip poked out the back.

Benavor was watching with a terrified expression, both hands over his mouth. His gaze slowly shifted from the dead body of his former master to Stryder's gloating naked frame.

"You belong to me now," Stryder proclaimed.

With a look of timid resignation, the naked young boy lowered his hands and walked over to Stryder. Without a word he dropped to his knees in front of Stryder's organless crotch and stared in bewilderment.

The Vicar of Pa-Waga reached down and gently rested his hand on the top of Benavor's head.

"I have evolved beyond such base needs," he whispered.

Benavor shuddered again at a fresh wave of ammonia, and the human before him changed. The boy cried out when the human facade faded away, leaving the black featureless form of a humanoid cat with strobing blue binary runes across its body.

When the transformation finished and the strobing stopped, it left Benavor quaking in dread. The Vicar of Pa-Waga looked down lovingly at the docile youngster, holding his barbed forefinger aloft.

"Don't be afraid," Stryder said in an assuring tone. "Your life is about to take an exciting new turn."

It had been raining nonstop for over fifteen cycles straight, flooding the streets of Makatooa, and the Cul-Ta could not continue with the city's repairs. For Gavin it meant fewer people on the streets which equated to fewer victims.

It had been a frustrating four cycles. He'd found no one suitable to help with his transformation. To make matters worse, the ghouls were growing hungrier each cycle and harder to deal with.

Now on cycle number five, a frustrated and empty-handed Gavin, soaked to the bone, stepped through the archway leading into the Old City. Water was still streaming down the stairs but at least it wasn't pouring down on him.

When he sloshed his way across the wet floors to his work room, it surprised him to see that he wasn't alone.

The Zoande clan were there of course, with their hungry, expectant looks.

Standing in front of the glass tank, Ve-Qua admired his collection of pinkie fingers which littered the bottom of the saline solution.

The petite Bailian was just as he remembered. The foreboding dark circles under her eyes set off her wild black hair. Just as before, he found the hardware which bolted her ample breasts together and held her vaginal lips open to be very disconcerting.

"Hello dearie, remember me?" she asked in a friendly tone.

"Yeah, you're that sadistic bitch from back in Tannimore!"

The Kinjuto giggled. "You're such a sweet talker."

"What the fuck do you want?"

"We had a deal."

"Yeah, well House Whitmar put an end to that."

"We didn't make a deal with House Whitmar. We made a deal with *you,* and you didn't live up to it."

"So, you're here to kill me?"

Ve-Qua gave a sensuous smile. "After a bit of fun."

"My friends down here won't let you do that."

"Oh, I'm afraid I've got a bit of bad news, you see, *your* friends are now *my* friends."

Almost on cue, a beautiful female Zoande with long black hair stepped over to Gavin, giving him a long, seductive look. Her pale white skin and large dark eyes entranced Gavin. She whispered something so soft he had to lean closer to hear it.

"I'm so hungry," she said, with a sudden vicious lunge.

Gavin screamed in pain when he felt sharpened teeth tear off part of his cheek. Ve-Qua reeled in ecstasy with the sudden flash of pain causing an electrical surge of power to course through her body.

Gavin's screams continued unabated. The ghouls descended on him, ripping off his clothes and biting off chunks of flesh.

Ve-Qua was now beside herself, energized by Gavin's torment from the ghouls eating him alive. Quickly, on wobbly legs, she found a place to sit. Thrusting her hand between her legs she began to masturbate.

"Chew slowly dearies," she cooed between his screams. "I want this to last."

Ambassador Za-Tarr gave out a startled cry when the door of his office flew open.

Standing in the doorway, a rolled piece of paper in hand, was a very determined looking Tate Whitmar. Towering behind the six-foot-two human was an EEtah twice his size, brandishing his Yudon harpoon.

"What's the meaning of this?!" the Tiikeri said with a snarl.

Marching into the office, Tate's nostrils flared at the ammonia smell. Stepping up to the desk the Whitmar envoy unrolled the piece of paper and slammed it down.

"I've just come from an emergency meeting of the Zorian Security Council. As Chairman of that council, it is my duty to inform you, that we are officially expelling your people from the High Holy City of Zor! Effective immediately. That includes *you*."

"You can't do that!" Za-Tarr sputtered.

Tate pointed to the paper in front of him. "That decree says I can!"

"For what reason?!"

"Piracy on the high seas against House Whitmar. Murderous rituals and assaulting a member of the Zorian High Council."

"This is outrageous! I demand the chance to defend myself and my people against these baseless charges!"

"I don't give a sow's udder what you demand. The council's decision is final. As we speak, we're rounding your people up and taking them down to the docks. The sergeant here is to escort you. There's a Calden transport ship due in port within the deci. You're leaving, so pack your things."

The Tiikeri trembled with anger, watching Tate turn and walk away. He lingered at the doorway and gazed back past the EEtah.

"You should thank whatever god you pray to that Colonel Zekoff is going to be okay. That old man is one of the most beloved figures in this city. If he would have died, we would have escorted your people to the executioner, not the docks."

After twenty straight cycles of rain, the clouds finally broke, allowing bright sunshine again to bathe the port city of Makatooa.

The return of pleasant weather also brought about the resumption of hammering and sawing across the city along with the chattering of Cul-Ta workers.

On a second-story balcony of the Hanara estate, Blyth Calden and Lord Hanara stood watching the city's reconstruction.

"Lord Hanara, using the Cul-Ta as labor is one thing but allowing them to live among us is quite another!"

The hammerhead EEtah laughed and patted Blyth on the shoulder. "Come now Mayor, to allow a race of sentients to labor above ground in your service, but live in the sewers, would quickly foster resentment. They deserve a place in society."

Blyth shook his head and scowled. "I'm already getting complaints from the city elders about this."

"Ah yes, grumbles from the old money anytime those of a class they deem inferior try to better themselves. Let me tell you about old money Your Honor. It's been my experience that old money is just dirty money that's had a few generations to wash it clean. They'll get used to it."

"Yeah, you don't have to listen to them. I do."

Hanara laughed again. "That's why you're in politics and I'm a captain of industry. As far as I'm concerned, they have nothing to say about the matter. I legally purchased this land and I can do anything I want with it so long as it doesn't violate our agreement. Besides, even with the weather delay, we're ahead of schedule. We'll finish the docks by the end of the quinte and we can get back to being a seaport again. The way those little bastards are working, the city will be back on a paying basis in no time. That spells the much-needed return of your tax base. All of these are good things. So, smile Mayor, things are looking up."

When captains Gasata and Trenton entered Zekoff's room at Clerria House, they were pleased to see their commander, sitting up in bed talking with Captain Rafel. Even with his head still in bandages, he appeared healthy.

"Sir, I'm glad to see you feeling better," Gasata said.

"It's been three cycles and I'm ready to get out of here," Zekoff said with a furrowed brow. "They won't let me have my pipe."

"You'll be up and about in no time," Gasata said in an optimistic tone.

Trenton stepped closer to the bed; his scarred, battle-hardened face sported a rare grin. "Sir, I'm happy to report that the Mawl issue has been resolved."

Zekoff appeared pleasantly surprised. "Oh?"

Trenton nodded. "Tate Whitmar called a Security Council meeting first thing at the lifting of the Kan this morning. They voted unanimously to expel. The ship sailed a couple of decis ago. We're dismantling Tiger Town now. We're going to have to burn those tents due to the smell."

Zekoff sighed deeply and shook his head. "If we expelled the Tiikeri Ambassador, you can expect some push back from Hai-Darr."

Trenton scoffed. "With Tate Whitmar as current chairman of the Security Council the Tiikeri can push all they want. He won't put up with their antics."

"I'm sure," Zekoff conceded. "But this probably signals trouble ahead."

"Nothing we can't handle sir."

"Speaking of the future," Zekoff said, sitting up straight. "As long as I've got you all here, I wanted to let you know first that I'm planning on retiring at the end of the quinti. This latest incident really showed me I'm too old to be traipsing around the streets putting myself in harm's way."

The three Zorian captains looked around at each other.

Gasata was the first able to speak. "Sir, I mean, if you're sure…"

"It's not like I'll be disappearing. A while ago I submitted a proposal to the University of Marassa's Board of Regents to teach a class on modern police techniques. They're willing to let me build the curriculum from the ground up."

"Congratulations sir," Rafel said. "Who's going to take your place?"

"No one," Zekoff replied firmly. "I'm promoting my protégé Lieutenant Vanir to captain of a new investigation

Division. You all don't need a commander; you know your jobs. All you need is to communicate with each other. All four of you should hold twice a cycle briefings. I'll be just over at the university in case you need a consultation."

The stunned captains nodded their acceptance begrudgingly.

"Come on," Zekoff cajoled. "Why the long faces? Like I said, I'm not going anywhere and I have a feeling we're still going to be working closely in the near future. I really don't think this Tiikeri incident is going to just blow over."

The Calden transport ship *Garraioa* sliced Westward through the waters of the deep ocean. Beside the crew, thirty-eight Mawls and six EEtah guards were on board.

Standing on the bow, his fur fluttering in the wind, Al-Zah stared mournfully out at the horizon. He had been successful at resurrecting the Vicar of Pa-Waga. But at what cost?

Amidst ship, former Ambassador Za-Tarr scowled at the Yagur then looked over at three mongrels and nodded.

Immediately, one hissed at the others and shoved them. A screaming cat fight ensued.

When the EEtah guards moved to quell the disturbance, Za-Tarr led two Tiikeri to the bow.

Without hesitation, the Tiikeri came up behind the meditating priest and pinned his arms to the railing. Looking around in a panic, he tried to move, with no success.

Za-Tarr quickly came up directly behind him and put his mouth by the Yagur's ear.

"Your zealotry cost the empire a great price!" he angrily growled. "Thanks to you we no longer have eyes in the human capital!"

Before Al-Zah could reply, the much larger man-tiger grabbed his head and twisted. When Za-Tarr heard the crunch of the neck snapping, he stepped back and the two Tiikeri threw the Yagur priest over the side. His body quickly disappeared beneath the ship's wake.

"Death to the enemies of the empire," he proclaimed.

"Death to the enemies of the empire," the Tiikeri repeated.

Tate Whitmar sat forward and leaned his arms on the conference table. "So, what ya got for us little lady?"

Marassa Hauts adjusted her glasses and glowered at the smiling man on the other side of the table.

"Chairman Whitmar, while I can appreciate that you meant no offense, I am not a little lady, nor am I anyone's darlin', sweetie, or any other patronizing pet names you contrive. I worked long and hard to rise to my current position."

The Whitmar envoy sat back, clapped his hands and laughed. "By golly I like you! You got spunk!"

Pierce Calden shifted nervously in his chair next to Tate, while Joc' Valdur closed his eyes and shook his head.

"Marassa Hauts, please continue."

Nodding her head, she placed a small bottle on the table.

"During the eclipse and the subsequent invasion," she recounted, "there was a Do-Tarr fighting on our side. Unfortunately, he died fighting and they lost his body in the waters by the turine in the harbor. We at the university had made prior arrangements with this Do-Tarr, that upon his demise we would receive his body for study."

Tate leaned in closer inspecting the bottle. His eyes squinted with confusion.

"The university employed a team of Piceans to find and retrieve his body from the bottom of the bay," Marassa Hauts continued. "After the usual departmental turf wars over who would lead the research, we got to work."

"And that's what you found?" Tate asked, pointing at the bottle.

Hauts shot the ambassador an irritated glance. "Having an actual body to examine produced a treasure trove of information on Do-Tarr physiology. A detailed report is being prepared."

Hauts picked up the bottle. "This was something we almost missed. Something I think the Security Council will want to know about immediately."

Pierce Calden leaned forward and squinted at the bottle. "What's so important that it couldn't wait for the report?"

"I'll spare you the technical jargon. It's an enzyme produced when you pulverize the Do-Tarr's glands. It acts as a highly effective pheromone blocker."

Tate and Pierce sat with puzzled looks while Joc' brightened in recognition. "Marassa Hauts, can you reproduce this?"

"Yes."

Joc' turned to Tate. "Si. Chairman, I would like to make a formal proposal to afford a grant for immediate production of this enzyme."

Tate quizzically cocked his head. "Funding for a grant is something usually taken up by the High Council. They control the purse strings."

Joc's expression turned serious and he shook his head. "I don't want this discovery to be made common knowledge. In fact, for security purposes, I'd like the entire production and any further research to be moved to Landagar."

With that statement the Valdurian Ambassador had captured the attention of everyone at the table.

"Joc', what's going on?" Pierce asked.

Joc' gave a devious smile. "The Marassa here has just handed us the biggest bargaining chip we could have ever hoped for in dealing with Nocturn."

Through a pain induced fog, Matka knew she was dying. The birth had been excruciating. She thought she was going to bite through the bit when she felt her child clawing its way out of her womb. She vaguely remembered seeing the tiny claws puncturing her belly from the inside. Over the baby's first cries she saw the attendant reach in, pull out the baby and cut the cord.

It was a boy. A beautiful combination of human and Tiikeri with very human features and pale tiger stripes across its body.

Matka managed a weak smile when they held the child up and presented it to her. Life slipped away with her blood, but she was happy she had succeeded in creating an heir and a legacy to the Sorbornef name.

When presented to Bo-Lah, the Tiikeri took the baby in his arms and stared down dispassionately at it.

Abomination! echoed through his head.

Every instinct told him to kill it, but he knew the child was the key to his people gaining a foothold in Lumina.

The world around Matka was growing dark, but she mouthed the words 'thank you' up at the Tiikeri.

"I am the new lord of Staghorn," she heard him defiantly declare, just before she slipped off into oblivion.

Wallack and Raydan really didn't like the weather in the Twilight Lands. They would much prefer the warm, brightly lit water of the Shallow Sea.

However, this was the Avatar's new home and the Bailians had opened their hearts to them.

The Do-Tarr workers had replicated the temple complex down to the last detail. The round, shallow pool was only a few inches deep. In the center, an open shell contained a lustrous pearl the size of a large melon.

Normally the ancient demi-god pulsed with a rhythmic song of life only the faithful could hear.

Now it throbbed and strobed to a more menacing beat, causing its fish head handlers to stop singing along and stare at each other in uncertainty.

The two Otick High Priests who were in the pool meditating suddenly tensed. Their eyes glowed the color of the pearl as they received their deity's message.

The entire episode was brief but left the Otick in an agitated state.

"It is like the warning from before," Raydan said.

Wallack nodded in agreement. "It is as the prophets teach: Only the most foolhardy ignores signs and wonders shown to them."

"Blessed be the fifth," they both chanted.

"We must get to the queen's spymaster," Raydan said, stepping from the pool. "Dark clouds loom on the horizon."

GLOSSARY

Spoiler warning: *The following is a master glossary for all the books in this series. Reading beyond specific word or phrase searches could result in spoilers.*

Term	Explanation
Adad Sunal	EEtah war collage belonging to House Bran. Its specialty is conducting internal security for House Bran.
Agress	Etheria Crystal, Green w/ red striations, which opens and closes doors, windows and hatches, negating any locks but not traps or wards.
Aiken	Semi-sentient clouds sent out across the Annigan by the Ghas-Tor. When placed against the backdrop of a blue sky they appear to be glowing blue clouds, all but indistinguishable from other clouds. They are remote viewing devices and record everything they experience, both on the ground and in the air across the Annigan. Aiken immediately send the visuals back to the mountain, which is the epicenter of air magic, however recent images remain in its limited memory. Avions and anyone possessing psychic abilities can access their recent memory by flying through them and communing.
Akina	Humanoid fox creatures native to the Barrens in the Twilight Lands. They're sly and excellent thieves.

Amarenian	Female human race formerly noted for their hatred and slavery of men and piracy.
Angona	Roasted eel on a stick. Sold from vendors' carts all over the City of Immor-Onn.
Annigan	The name of the world which is the setting for the various stories in the Tales of the Annigan Cycle.
Anointed Sister	The title for the Amarenian Queen.
Aquamarine	Pale blue Etheria crystal which reveals things true nature.
Ara-Fel Party	Political party of Amarenian farmers.
Arapa Fish	This large fish native to the back waters & tributaries of the Otoman River is torpedo shaped with large blackish-green scales and red markings. Streamlined and sleek, its dorsal and anal fin are set near its tail. Unlike other fish it has a fundamental dependence on surface air to breathe. In addition to gills, it has a modified and enlarged swim bladder composed of lung-like tissue, which enables it to extract oxygen from the air. The Dreeat especially covet its tough scaly skin to use as armor. The scales are so abrasive they sell them for nails.
Ash-Ta	Avion derogatory term (winged monster) for the humanoid bats which inhabit the rocky crags in widespread colonies stretching across of The Spine of the World.

	There have been six distinctive tribes noted by Avion scholars in the Ash' Ta Garia: the Molossi, Acero, Chiro, Ptero, Diaemus and Desmodus. Ash-Ta are allies with the Tiikeri and share an enemy in the Do-Tarr.
Astute	Amarenian title for high level politicians. Usually paired with the term "sister."
Aur-Quaz	Iridescent Etheria crystal stimulating energy.
Available Regions	Uninhabited areas of Immor-Onn waiting for the residence displaced by the recent Black Pearl Revolution to return and inhabit.
Avion	These proud sentients are the rulers of Lumina's sky. Incredibly beautiful and graceful to behold and unabashedly elitist, especially towards their distant cousins the humans. Avions refuse to wear any sort of armor and yet these fierce fighters have led the way in almost every major war fought. They are skilled Kel handlers, tending to huge herds of the flying lizards used as beasts of burden or harvested for food. Their scholars have contributed a great deal to the knowledge of everyone on Lumina. The four Great Houses occupy the air space and mountain tops of the Goyan Islands.
Avion Great Houses:	
House Azar	Avion House inhabiting the City of Mitar, on the Island of Dal, in the Tellasian chain, ruled by Queen Averin. Their territories include the

		skies over the Tellasian Chain, Otomoria, Zer-Tal Twins, and the Zerk Atoll. They are known for their healing Clerics of Neami and their beautiful music.
	House Eacher	Avion House inhabiting the Island of Wou, City of Picon & surrounding airspace. Ruled by King Sindil.
	House Pyre	Eldest, largest, and most powerful of all the Avion Houses. They inhabit the skies above the Island of Goya. Their magnificent city stronghold of Darmont Keep sits on the north face of Mt. Goya. Unlike the other Avion Houses who utilize air magic, they are the masters of Fire Magic drawing their power from the constantly erupting volcano.
	House Solas	Smallest and weakest of all the Avion houses. They inhabit the city of Adean on the island of Temil in the Outer Zerians and control the surrounding airspace.
Awal		First of the ten Quinte Grand Cycle, spring.
Azurite		Purple Etheria crystal which connects to the Middle realms.
Bailian		Predominate race of the western Twilight Lands. Descended from the Piceans they are a beautiful humanoid race with pale blue skin and large eyes.
Banja		Amarenian noble families. There are seventy-seven of them, eleven for each of the various seven provinces called Dors. There is a strict pecking order within each Dor and each

	Banja is always trying to elevate its status.
Banok Atoll	Island ring in the Southeastern Ocean of Lumina. It is the location of one of the largest permanent Flavian Portal. Its ripples extend out hundreds of miles and affects the entire southeastern Deep Ocean of Lumina.
Banok Run	Final test for admittance to the elite Brightstar Sailors of the Calden Navy. It comprises sailing a tight circle through the turbulent seas around the Banok Atoll, without the giant Flavian Portal located in those waters pulling you into it.
Bespoke Lords	Members of prominent families who have Bespoke Names and are advisors to the sovereign in a respective noble human house in the Goyan Islands.
Bespoke Names	In the Goyan Islands, these are personalized family names indicating wealth and status which can only be bestowed by a governor or higher, usually in reward for exemplary service to the crown.
Black Mural	Magical record of the Annigan in the Rod-Ema Trench in the Deep Oceans of Nocturn. It records each act of imbalance on the planet from great to small. When one side grows too powerful, it grows so large, it plunges into the planet's core killing all life, allowing it to start anew.
Black Talon	Special forces of the Aramos Army, the Fosvara Guard.
Boustian Mage	Bards who perform magic by singing, playing music and

	storytelling, located in the larger cities of the Goyodan Chain.
Brightstar	Elite sailors of House Calden qualified to sail the deep oceans and the storm-tossed waters of the twilight areas of the world. All captains in the Calden Navy are required to be Brightstar qualified. Brightstar only allows acceptance to their ranks upon completion of a sailing around one of the two massive Flavian portals, the Innaca Deep or the Banok Atoll. Once inducted they are qualified to wear the coveted star over swan pin.
Brom	Horse-size dragonflies which inhabit the steep southern foothills of the Amaren Mountains.
Brom Riders	Amarenians who catch, train, breed, and ride Broms.
Calcite	Clear Etheria crystal with aids in navigation.
Caldani	Privateers hired by human House Calden to patrol their waters.
Calden Intelligencer Service	Elite spy, protection, and secret police for House Calden. They draw almost all from the Calden Maritime Legion.
Calden Maritime Legion	House Calden's marines
Calisma	The main library in the University of Marassa, Zor.
Cali	Branch libraries and scriptoriums in the five human capital cities in the Goyodan Island Chain.
Carbana	Chewing tobacco rolled into a tight tube.
Cavernite	Etheria Crystal, pale green with pink striations. When placed on the

	interior side of all the structure's exterior walls it increases physical dimensions of the interiors size. The size of the increase will depend on the amount of Cavernite used and the amount of PSI it's powered with. This crystal must receive a constant supply of PSI power or the dimensions will revert back to their original size. For this reason, they are almost always attached to an Obsidian PSI battery.
Centi Elipse	Called a Centi for short. Unit of time in the Goyan Islands equaling a minute.
Celot	Amarenian term for a priestess.
Cevot	Large sentient spider creatures that inhabit the Os-Oni Mountains of the Twilight Lands, known for their silk.
Ched	Seventh of the ten Quinte Grand Cycle, autumn.
Cluster	Name for the grouping of ten cycles. The Annigan's version of a week. There are five clusters to a Quinte.
Cobalcite	Deep pink Etheria crystal used for healing.
Common	Short for the Common Tongue, a spoken only language used mostly by humans and those that do business with them.
Cocoonessa	Cocoon city of the Tinian Moth creatures on Mt. Natal in the Land of Mists, Nocturn. Also called the Silk City.
Corporal Reach, The	Otherwise known as the prime material plain of the middle realms. It is the Annigan resides.

Coxeter	Both the language and magic system of the Tinian race is a complex form of three-dimensional geometry. It is revealed in two different ways. The actual written language which is a cryptic mathematical notation using lines dots. The other more complex variation is in the three-dimensional mapping which is the way their mind perceives all math. It is displayed best in their silk weaving. Intricate geometric patterns are used to create everything from the simple walls created by the larva to the delicate patterns woven by the adult Tinians. Much like the rings of a tree a dissected pod wall revels when it was made and age of the maker. These patterns when combined with Etheria Crystals can be used to perform spells.
Croquis	Magitech mapping devise which projects a scalable three-dimensional holographic image of a desired location, including other planes and the multiverse.
Cub Prince	Heir to the throne of the Tiikeri Empire. All Tiikeri kings are a rare black tiger. Once a generation the king must breed an heir. All the prominent Tiikeri families offer their most eligible daughters to breed with the king. Only one will conceive a black tiger. All other cubs produced from this union are killed. The complete family that bore the Cub Prince are

	then moved into the palace and are also considered nobility. The Cub Prince is immediately groomed for the throne. When he comes of age, he must kill his father then take the throne.
Cul-Ta	Humanoid rat creatures found in almost every City in Lumina.
Cycle	Time period equivalent to a day.
Dag	Amarenian term for a common slave. A derogatory slang word for a male.
Darek Witch	Amarenian earth shamans acting as midwives and perform other shamanistic duties.
Darian Silk	High quality silk spun by the Cevot Spiders. They trade it to the On'Dara.
Darwan	This race is a cross between the Balians and the Fudomi. They are the most prolific humanoid native to the Barrens. Their villages are situated around Ghorn temples and must pay a tribute to the Onay horde of its region. Villages close to the borders of the hordes are always under threat. These creatures raise a herd animal called the Ng'Ombe which is the major food staple in the Barrens.
Dasam	Tenth of the ten Quinte Grand Cycle, winter.
Deci	Time unit in the Goyan Islands equivalent to one hour.
Derde	Third of the ten Quinte Grand Cycle, spring.
Diamond	Clear Etheria crystal which transfers power.

Diplomat Stone	Slang name for the Etheria Crystal, Larimar. It allows translation of all languages and to communicate from a distance. They are issued to diplomats serving in foreign lands.
Doggin	Derogatory term used for slave dock workers in the city of Aris.
Dolin	Etheria gem hunters mostly of the Gila race. They travel the Barrens in small caravans harvesting raw Etheria Crystals. They then take them back and sell them to the Zadim lapidaries of the Oasis in the Dark Waste Desert.
Dor	Title of the seven various provinces in Amarenia. Taia-Dor, Denat-Dor, Mivira-Dor, Amoso-Dor, Kinning-Dor, Rackam-Dor, Durik-Dor.
Do-Tarr	Sentient mantis hive mind creatures from the Land of Mists in Nocturn. They comprise two large hives in the north and south with precise tunnel networks beneath the ground. They are expert builders and are neutral in all forms of politics.
Dreamer in the Lake	Demi-God of the Os'Tor Forest and a Harbinger of Balance. She rests at the bottom of a large lake encased in mud and manifests herself on the lake's surface as a multicolored lotus. Her accolades are sentients from every race who sleep around the lake's shore. They send their ethereal bodies out into people's dreams and guide them.
Dreeat	Humanoid crocodile people who inhabit the area at the end of the western fork of the Otoman River in Otomoria. They grow sugar cane

	and make healing candies from it. They also harvest a meaty river fish as a major part of their diet. For thousands of grands, ever since their arrival humans have been attempting to eradicate them.
Dronning Mare	Female horse chosen to breed with the On'Dara chief.
EEtah	Large, powerful and aggressive humanoid sharks, professional warriors of Lumina trained in martial schools known as Sunals. After their egg birth in the hatcheries and their first year in the nursery they are sorted to one of the various Sunals of their House. Females enter House Nur and the males go through a highly competitive Sunal scouting, recruiting process with the nursery's called The Garess. Sunals then hire out bodyguards, sentries, mercenaries and virtually anything martial. This, and weapon manufacturing and sales, are the main revenue streams for the great houses.
EEtah Great Houses:	
House Nur	This Noble house is female only. Co-ruled secular Queen Mother and spiritual High Priestess. Temple of Drulain headquartered in the High Holy City of Zor. Specalties: Scribes, Clerics, Healers, Politics, Domestics.
House Crom	Three Sunals in the Tellasian Chain: Sedar Sunal on Roe Island. Specialty: Bodyguard.

	Boril Sunal on Uma Island. Specialty: Crom Internal Security. Zorod Sunal on Tel Island. Specialty: Castle and Town Defense.
House Bran	Four Sunals in the Goyodian Chain: Garf Sunal on Quell Island. Specialty: Long term inland duty. Tukk Sunal on Mobis Island. Specialty: Shipboard Security. Adad Sunal on Creos Island. Specialty: Bran Internal Security. Farak Sunal on Roust Island. Specialty: Bounty Hunter, Vengeance.
House Zed	Three Sunals in the Wouvian Islands: Dakor Sunal on Owling Island. Specialty: Shock Troops. Jut Sunal on Tor Island. Specialty: Zed Internal Security. Morrak Sunal on Billow Island. Specialty: Police, Executioners.
Elipse	A Unit of time in the Goyan Islands equaling a second.
Esteemed	Amarenian title for an ambassador, usually paired with the term 'sister'.
Etheria Crystal	Crystals that contain magical properties. Mostly found in the form of trees in the Barrens of the Twilight Lands. They harvest and process the crystals in the oases of the Dark Waste Desert. They are the primary form of magic in Nocturn.

Flavian Portals	Portals through space crossing to different points in the Annigan and seemingly instantaneously accessible. Each Flavian Portal is different. There are several large, fixed portals on both Lumina and Nocturn and hundreds of smaller dedicated Flavians.
	Certain animals, intoxicants and magical items can open smaller portals. Every Flavian Portal connects to its destination by passing through the inter-dimensional Middle Realms.
Frozen Sea	This vast expanse of open ice flows covers the vast majority of Nocturn and is the largest centrally occupied area in all of Annigan. The ice ranges from a slushy mixture with icebergs near the land masses to several hundred feet thick in the eastern areas.
Forsvara Guards	This is the rank-and-file foot soldier army of House Aramos.
Fudomi	Sentient humanoid ram creatures that inhabit the western Os-Oni Mountains of the Twilight Lands. They are constantly at odds with the Cevot Spider broods. They steal and sell the spiders silk and their eggs, which are considered a delicacy.
Galeb	Sea Gulls bred with a psychic connection to a handler. They are used to transporting messages across Lumina.
Garf Sunal	EEtah War college belonging to House Bran. Their specialty is long term inland duty.

Gar-Kal	Fish head humanoids living on the ocean floor of Nocturn. They are of low intelligence and aggressive.
Geta	Amarenian title for a master at a skill or craft, especially if they teach it.
Ghas-Tor	This is the tallest peak on the Annigan. It reaches upward 32,000 feet in the Os'Ani Mountain range, Twilight Lands. It is more than a mountain; it is a sentient being and the epicenter for Air Magic in the world.
Ghorn	Necromancers of the Barrens in Twilight Lands.
Ghost Suit	A grey, skintight jump suit used mostly by Valdurian forces to blend into the Kan fog.
Ghosts of the Kan	Mariners term for Rayth raiders. This is because of the ghost white chalk which covers their bodies and acts as camouflage when they attack during the Kan fog.
Gila	These are the main sentient race populating the Dark Waste. Their original stock comprised Bailian pilgrims and a now long-gone sentient lizard native to the region. They are an advanced race which occupies the three large oasis of the desert.
Golden One, The	Otick term for the Golden Avatar.
Goy-Ardia	Goyan fire mages trained at the University of Marassa.
Goyan Calander	Method of time keeping found only in the Goyan Islands. It consists of a Grand Cycle (year) which is comprised of 10 Quinte (months) named; Awal, Teine, Derde, Kvara, Peto, Sesto, Ched,

	Merve, Tisa and Dasam. Each Quinte is divided into 50 Cycles (days) with each cycle being divided into 50 Deci (hours) 25 being in sun and 25 in Kan. 10 cycles equal a Cluster (week) with 5 Clusters per Quinte.
Grand	Short for Grand Cycle. Time period equivalent to a year.
Grass Eater	Singa insult
Gustare'	Amarenian bath house and tavern.
Gyronite	Etheria Crystal which maintains balance.
Hackney	Etheria driven taxis of various sizes found in the major cities of Lumina.
Hand of the Wind	Assassin's guild of Annigan. All members worship Orad, goddess of death. Upper levels are clerics of Orad.
Hakim	A judge in the High Holy City of Zor.
Harbingers of Balance	Sentient creatures of all types who have given themselves to monitoring the balance of the Annigan and giving warning when something is about to upset the balance.
Hasteen	City of the Dreeat crocodile people.
Hill Sister	Hermaphroditic Amarenian warriors who inhabit the northern foothills of the Amaren Mountains. Even though they possess both male and female sex organs, they cannot procreate. Amarenian nobility use them as seneschal/bodyguards partly because they can have sex with them and not violate their 'no man' pledge.
Hoon	Word used in Zor to denote a pimp or the manager of a brothel.

Howlite	Grey Etheria Crystal used for glamour, disguise and polymorphing.
Humans	The human race is descended from the Avion race. In 5070 PA rebellious Avions which had joined Xandar the Mad doomed Great Kraken Incursion had their wings severed as punishment before they were banished and scattered to the Goyodan Chain. One hundred seventy-one years later the 7th Avatar Sang "The Song of Rebirth" and they evolved into a separate race. They formed their Great Houses and spread out across the Goyan Island Chain and eventually beyond The Shallow Sea.
Human Great Houses:	
House Aramos	This is the largest and wealthiest of the great human families directly descended from the First Men. The Capital city of Aris is on the Island of Vakai in The Goyodan Chain of Islands in the Northern Shallow Sea. They control the banking and finance in Lumina and are constantly hatching Machiavellian plots to expand their power over the other houses.
House Calden	This great house controls the seas with the largest military and commercial fleets. Their Capital City of Nader is on the Island of Tarla in the Goyodan Chain, but they command the island chain of the Zerk Atoll where their sailors are trained.

House Eldor	This great house control virtually all the agricultural islands of the eastern Goyan Islands. Their Capital City of Rophan is on the Island of Tolle in the Goyodan Chain of Islands in the Northern Shallow Sea.
House Valdur	This house is known for their incestuous practices to keep the family bloodline pure. Their capital city of Dryden is on the Island of Atar in The Goyodan Chain of Islands in the Northern Shallow Sea. They were all but destroyed in a surprise invasion by House Eldor called the Unification War. It was only through the discovery of lighter than air travel that their home island was spared by a fleet of war balloons. The rest of their agricultural lands were lost to Eldor. Their entire culture revolves around them now being a powerful Air guild, The Valdurian Air Service.
House Whitmar	This family runs the organized and sanctioned slave trade on Lumina from the city of Nier on the northern Goya coast. Their Capital City of Brinstan on the Island of Umin in the Goyodan Chain of Islands in the Northern Shallow Sea.
Immor-Onn	Large city on the western coast of the Twilight Lands. Home of the Bailian Empire.
Idonian Philosophy	Avion belief that humans are a scourge on the Annigan and should be wiped out. It is the driving belief of the Idonian Cabal of Avion House Pyre and Solas.

Innaca Deep	Giant whirlpool in the Northwestern Ocean of Lumina. It is the location of one of the largest Flavian Portal. Its ripples extend out hundreds of miles.
Innaca Run	Final test for admittance to the elite Brightstar Sailors. It comprises making a tight circle around the turbulent seas around the Banok Atoll without being pulled into the giant Flavian Portal there.
Ironmark	Brutal enforcers serving the Quartermasters in the Goyan Islands of Lumina. Each island chain has their own Ironmark, which specializes in a specific form of torture.
Itori	Shamans found throughout the agricultural western Goyan Islands to control mostly locust. They can control any insect and are immune to all insect poisons and stings.
Jangwa	These are elite desert commandos used by the two civilized oases in the Dark Waste Desert to defend the outer parameter of the oasis. They choose Jangwa from the ranks of the Oasis Guards, which show promise. Capable of traveling under the sand and rapidly over the surface of the desert, they make frequent scouting missions to the untamed Qua-Raman oasis and the Buried City of Nof-Saloom.
Kaefom	An Amarenian breeding ritual overseen by the Darek Witches.
Kan	Period of the day in the Goyan Islands when thick sea fogs rise. It is an effect caused by geothermal

	activities only found in the Goyan Islands and Shallow Sea. Citizens mostly use this time to sleep.
Kel	Flying lizards bred and tended by Avions for food and as beasts of burden.
Kharry Institute	Tiikeri medical facility in Hai-Darr specializing in the crossbreeding of Mawl races to produce Mongrels for specific duties. It is run by the brilliant and ruthless Dr. Met-Ge. The Institute is responsible for the Cheepas &. Ves-Lari.
Kinjuto Dominator	Sex mage specializing in BDSM techniques.
Konaleeta	Called the Island of the Lost. The entire island is caught in a permanent Flavian Loop. It bounces around from location to location across any of the planes of the Middle Realms, never staying in anyone place too long.
Kusars	Mawl bandits of the Dasos region in the Land of Mists.
Kvara	Fourth of the ten Quinte Grand Cycle, summer.
Ky-Awat	Sentient rat creatures of the Dark Waste Desert. They have bred them up from the Cul-Ta and are larger and more aggressive, but no smarter. Various factions use them as cannon fodder. They breed quickly and are plentiful, especially around the three main oases.
Land of Mists	This is the largest land mass in Nocturn. It is so named because the combination of cold temperatures in the air combined with the warmth of the ground results in a uniform

	constant low hanging fog over the entire continent.
	Three distinct landscapes cover the surface of the land, separated by the Kel-Raku Mountain range and dimly illuminated by bioluminescence, outcroppings of Etheria crystals and the moon and stars.
	The thick rainforest of Arboro lies to the north, and the vast savannah of Rovina runs to the south. They're connected by the Bor-Kaa Pass. The dense jungles and swamps of Dasos lie to the east.
Landagar Group	Research and development division of the Valdurian Air Service. It is in the balloon city of Landagar situated high in the mountains of the Valdurian home island of Atar.
Larimar	Etheria crystal used for communication. It is milky white with blue striations. When in proximity of the gem all parties hear what the other is saying in their head.
Learned Sister	The title given to Amarenian teachers, scribes & academics.
Lideri	Regional governess of Amarenia. There are eleven, one for each province or Dor. They act as a high council to the Amarenian queen.
Lor-Danta Oasis	The eastern most and sparsely populated major oasis in the Dark Waste Desert. The large obsidian field stretching from its shore contains six Tanum Charts of the skies used by the Arron-Nin Astrologers who dwell there.

Lumina	Half of the world in constant sunlight.
Luna	Term used for the lunar cycle by every culture in the Annigan except the humans in the Goyan Islands who cannot see the moon.
Luroh	Bolo/sash weapon used by the city guards of Mostas the Mahilia. The sash contains the person's rank and record. At either end are two metal balls which when twirled become an effective weapon.
Magitech	Fusion of magic and technology. This mostly refers to the use of Etheria Crystals and specific mechanical items (i.e., airship engines).
Mahilia	Amarenian Capital City of Mostar city guards.
Makari	Inter-dimensional race of sentient spiders from the Pasture Plain of the Middle Realms. They seeded the Cevot race in the Os'Tor Mountains in the Land of Mists.
	The males resemble hairy wolf spiders, the females resemble black widows.
	The females are always alluring to any male of any race. She will then feel the compulsion to kill them after sex.
Malachite	Light green Etheria crystal, which absorbs energy.
Marassa	Professor at the University of Marassa in Zor.
Masha	Amarenian for master.
Maudo Grass	Tall grass with a bright blue flowering tuft growing in the Land

	of Mists. The flowers are a favorite intoxicant for Mawls and especially coveted by the Tiikeri.
Mawl	Overall name for the humanoid cat races of the Land of Mists. It is also the term used for the common language they share.
Medikua	Medical officer aboard Calden naval vessels.
Merve	Eighth of the ten Quinte Grand Cycle, autumn.
Middle Realms	Constantly shifting inter-dimensional plane between worlds. Sometimes referred to as the Fairy or dream realms.
Mongrel	These are the product of cross breeding between the Mawl races. Pure breeds mostly shun them. The Tiikeri use them for slave labor. They can be found all over the Land of Mists.
Moonfall	Period of the cycle when Nocturn's main illuminating body the moon, dips below the horizon issuing in the Moonless
Moonless	Period of the cycle when Nocturn's main illuminating body the moon, orbits around to the Lumina side of the Annigan (night).
Mora	Term used for teacher or master in the Whovian Sword Schools of Rohina Takki.
Morasian Puff Boy	Male prostitute from the port City of Moras on Goya's west coast. Known for their distinctly feminine demeanor.
Mostas	Capital City of the Amarenian Empire on the western shore of Amarenia.

Najuka	Amarenian emasculation ritual performed on all males except those used for breeding purposes in the Kaefom Ritual.
Na-Kab	One of the three insectoid groups that live below the Land of Mists. They occupy the eastern most hive closest to Mount Natal and have a fire make-up under their exoskeleton. Their tail has a penis shaped stinger that can impregnate anything anyplace they sting.
Namesake	Term used for spouse when they share a bespoke last name.
Narrows, The	These are the slums of the Hidden City of Toriss in Otomoria. They are the remnants of an old iron mine.
Nocturn	Half the world in constant night
Nolton Boat	Ships made of Ukko wood in a secret shipyard on the island of Zer and mostly used by Brightstar sailors. They hover less than an inch above the water. Their rudder is also Ukko, so it guides and propels. The specific construction of the hull makes the boat unsinkable.
Noma	Poison from the Noma Viper.
Nurian Edicts	EEtah rules of conduct set down by House Nur which are the basis for all Sunal laws. The various Sunals can and do add their own individual laws to this baseline for all Sunals.
Nyanja	Large seahorses ridden as sea cavalry by the Calden Navy.
Obsidian	Black Etheria crystal which holds psychic energy.
Ol'daEE	Person able to cast spells while having sex under the influence of Oldust.

Oldust	Hallucinogenic powder derived from the spores of the rare Impia Mushroom. It increases magical abilities and can allow travel to the Middle Realms.
Onay	Humanoid wolf men of the Barrens. They band together their various packs in three distinct hordes.
On' Dara	Sentient horse creatures living on the Plains of Taka-Vir in the southeastern Twilight Lands. They raise and train horses, which they sell to the rest of the Annigan. They also trade for silk with the Cevot Spiders.
ooD	Shell worn on the back of the male Otick warriors as armor. They mark the warrior's rank and house on the outside of the shell and inscribe the inside with a record of their deeds. They place the ooD over the entrance to their home, which is a hole in the sand.
Oracle of the River	A demigod who dwells in the cypress swamp at the end of the western fork of the Otoman River. It appears as a giant catfish partially submerged. Its many whiskers are sunken into the water. Through them it perceives anything that happens in, on or around the waterway. It has been around for thousands of grands,
Orad	Air goddess of death and predominate deity of the assassin's guild, the Hand of the Wind.
Orad Dex	Initiates to the Orad priesthood. Street/entry level assassins.
Orad Con	(Taker of the divine wind) These are full priests of Orad. Their special

	skills are the kiss of death, the poison breath, and the Phantom Dagger.
Orad Sto	(Giver of the Divine Wind) High priests of Orad who can also restore life.
Otick	Humanoid crab people that inhabit the Shallow Sea. These are the first sentient creatures to rise from the ocean floor and are a proud, deeply spiritual and noble race.
	Goya's volcanic warmed waters provide home to the Otick's prolific oyster beds littering the floor of The Shallow Sea. From these beds arose the five great Pearl Avatars, creation gods whose songs brought life and sentience to Lumina. Otick society is organized into a highly structured caste system, Worker Class, Warrior Class and Mother Class. Otick society is organized in two main categories domestic and military. The three Otick Great Houses are known as the Shelled Triad. Each house tends their own oyster beds and competes for the birthplace of the next Avatar.
Otick Great Houses:	
House Awa	Home of the last two avatars. Located in the Tellasian Chain, in the capital city of Hidet on the Island of Zod. Mother Class specialization.
House Pewa	Located in the Goyodan Chain, in the capital city of Oniack, on the Island of Zak. Worker Class specialization.
House Sensu	Located in the Otoman Group, in the capital city of Sunico, on the Island

	of Lakia. Warrior Class specialization.
Otomoria	Large Island continent in the western Goyan Islands. One of the main agricultural islands producing grain.
Outer Clan EEtah	Shark creatures smaller in stature than regular EEtahs cast out from the three great EEtah Houses from the hatchery. The ones that survive banded together into loose clans. the contract themselves out as deck hands and lately have been volunteering in the Valdurian Marines.
Padi	Regional demi-god of water worshiped in and around the High Holy City of Zor, associated with the peace and calming effect of water and represented by a calm pond.
Palu EEtah	Rare hammerhead EEtahs. They are as big as outer clan EEtah but extremely intelligent. They tend to be reclusive loners.
Pappia	Members of the child street gangs of the Hidden City of Toriss. They live in the slum section of the city called The Narrows.
Pa-Waga	Lawful evil god of greed worshiped mostly by the Tiikeri. Its clerics practice binary blood rune magic comprising "X" and "I."
Peace Babies	Children born of a union between any of the five major human houses.
Peto	Fifth of the ten Quinte Grand Cycle, summer.
Piceans	Humanoid fish people of Lumina. They have the capability of breathing above and below the water

	and are impervious to the ocean's depths. Their gill flaps are large enough to fold over their ears. When the sound waves of the voice pass through the membrane, it translates it. This makes them valuable translators in all seaports of the Goyan Islands.
Piety Watch	Militant, religious police faction of the Pa-Waga church. They roam the city arresting anyone who is caught begging, idle, or not being productive. Minor offences are punished by beating with thin cane rods. They wear black capes with high pointed collars that resemble cat ears and red shirts.
Pisar	Bailian title for a scholar.
Pomaku	Humanoid leopard people (Mawl) native to the Arboro region in the Land of Mists, Nocturn.
Protocol 13	Code phrase used by EEtah House Nur requesting a meeting between an intelligence asset and their Handler.
PSI	Short for psychic energy. It is the underlying force which powers all magic in the Annigan.
Qua-Raman Oasis	Oasis in the central Dark Waste Desert. Because its location is just south of the Tur-Qua Pass, it is a major trading post with the gems harvested in the Barrens to the north.
Quartermaster	Collector of taxes and tariffs in the Goyan Islands. They use the Ironmark for enforcing their rule.
Quinte	Time period equivalent to a month.

Ramu	This gambling dismemberment game has been banned throughout the entire Goyan Islands. The Free City of Tannimore is the only place that permits it.
Rayth	Pirate faction of the Amarenian people in open revolt and attempting to form their own nation.
Rod-Ema Trench	Massive abysmal fissure running the equator in the western ocean floor in Nocturn. At its head is the Agar Goyot. On its north wall dipping into the depths is the Black Mural.
Rohina Takii	Sword school originating on the island of Wou. Its distinctive characteristic is the strike while drawing technique.
Salar Winds	The turbulent winds surrounding the peak of Mount Goya which must be navigated to enter the Avion City of Darmont on the mountain's northwestern face. Avion term of exasperation, "By the mighty winds of Salar!"
Secor	Street name for the Imperial Gold Ingot equivalent to ten struck gold coins.
Sesto	Sixth of the ten Quinte Grand Cycle, autumn.
Si	The term for Mr. in the Common Tongue spoken in the Goyan Islands.
Shrouding Stone	A hybrid Etheria crystals (Magitech) consisting of Howlite for glamour, and Planchite, which connects to air magic. When powered with PSI it bends the light around the being or object attached to, rendering it invisible. The invisible object still

	has substance and can be collided with or struck. It is ineffective on creatures that have sonic or infrared capabilities.
Sikari	Female Singa hunter/killer squads. They travel in groups of two or more. They have crossed bandoleros on their chests filled with sickle shaped throwing blades.
Silent Partner	Organized crime families in the Goyan islands. There are seven cabals, each organized by local.
Simikort	Round engraved coin which acts as an Amarenian noble's calling card.
Singa	Humanoid lion people (Mawl) that inhabit the southern Rovina area of the land of Mists.
Skirting the Upwinds	Dangerous maneuver practiced by only a few airship pilots. It involves taking the airship up to the edge of the atmosphere, then down to your destination. Allowing long distance travel in a short period.
Society of Whispers	Term used for the general intelligence communities of the five human Noble Houses.
Spice Rat	Smugglers that operate mostly in the Spice Islands chains (Zerian Reef Chain and Outer Zerians) and occasionally in the entire western side of the Goyan Islands.
Spooks	Street term for spies and operatives in the Society of Whispers.
Strasta	Ancient prophet in the folklore of the Cevot spider people of the Os-Ani Mountains.
Sunal	EEtah war college specializing in a martial skill.

Szoldos mercenaries	One of several small private armies for hire on the Goyan continent.
Taking it Upstairs	Airship pilot slang for Skirting the Upwinds
Tanum Charts	Six maps of Nocturn's night sky. The Arron-Nin Astrologers use them for divination and sometimes the opening of Flavian Portals.
Teine	Second of the ten Quinte Grand Cycle, spring.
Ten - Fifty	Cliche phrase in the Goyan Islands referring to the ten cycles in the cluster (week) and fifty decis of the cycle. The equivalent of 24/7.
Tenable Sister	Title given to Amarenian lawyers
Tiikeri	Sentient Tiger creatures of the Dasos region in the eastern Land of Mists.
Tisa	Ninth of the ten Quinte Grand Cycle, winter.
Tisina, Code of,	Mobster code of silence in the city of Zor. Because no organized crime is allowed, the various independent criminals adopted a complete "no cooperation" rule with the city guards. The smallest violation is punishable by death.
Trinilic	Orange Etheria crystal, which connects with fire magic.
Turine	Tidal clocks used in the Goyan Islands.
Ukkonite	Bronze Etheria crystal with natural repellant properties. It is the crystal equivalent to Ukko wood found only in Nocturn.
Ukko wood	Magical wood from the world tree harvested only on the island of Zer in the eastern Goyan Islands. It has natural repellant properties. This makes it perfect for shields. They

	also use it as currency and to make Brightstar Nolton Boats.
Ulana	Chaotic Evil goddess of the sea worshiped by a small sect of Amarenian Rayth in the province of Durik-Dor.
Unification War	Conflict started by House Eldor in 2 P.A. against the eastern agricultural islands of House Valdur. It ended as quickly as it began when House Aramos forced them to the negotiating table by threatening to freeze both houses' accounts in the Imperial Bank.
Valorous Sister	Amarenian title for heroic acts which affected the realm.
Vedette	Small fast Nolton Boats crewed by a single ex-Brightstar sailor. They use them for fast, anonymous travel around the oceans of Lumina.
Velocomite	Etheria Crystal, Pale blue w/ red bands, which increases or decreases an objects speed in which it's travelling.
Veros Pearls	Highest quality pearl cultivated in the sacred Otick oyster beds. They can hold a magical charge.
Ves-Lari	Mawl mongrels bred by the Tiikeri for rowing and poling. They are a combination of Pomaku (leopard) and Duma (Cheetah). Crews can pole or row for hundreds of miles at a time without stopping. They keep crews together to promote unity but switch them out after long trips for rest.
Virago	Amarenian title for a female warlord.

Wraith	Deep cover agents for House Aramos. They are drawn from the elite Black Talons unit.
Yagur	Humanoid jaguars (Mawl) from the Arboro region of the Land of Mists. They are seers, healers and shamans, and serve all the various Mawl races.
Yudon	Harpoon and standard weapon of every Sunal EEtah. They rifle the shaft for accuracy in throwing.
Yupik	Also called Ice Clans, these are one hundred and sixty-five humanoid clans of Eskimo like people. They divide into 3 major groups. The nomadic wanderers of the western flows always in competition for food and resources. They are constantly being harassed from the Ash-Ta as prey. The largest group inhabits the vast eastern flows and has semi-permanent settlements all surrounding the Ice City of Mos-Agar'.
Zadim	Lapidaries which operate in the three large oasis of the Dark Waste Desert.
Zerian Rangers	Woodsmen fighters who belong to any of nine different clans which occupy the forests of the Island continent of Zer in the Goyan Islands.
Zorian Monetary Council	A ruling body controlling all banking located in the High Holy City of Zor. They regulate all exchanges of money, goods and services, including the collecting of taxes and tariffs through the Quartermasters Guild.

R.W. Marcus

MAPS

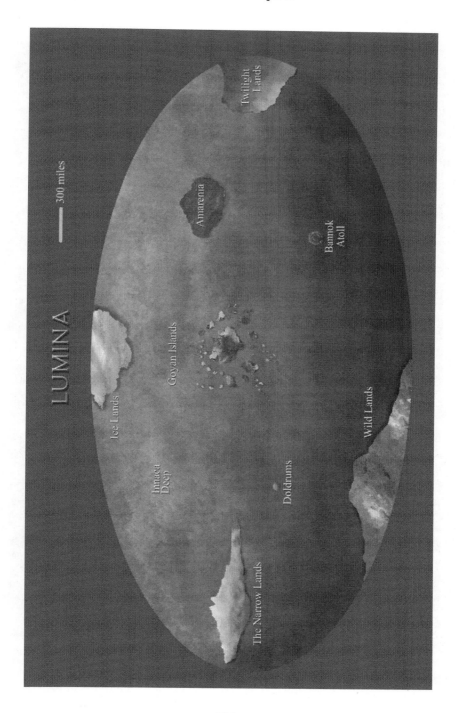

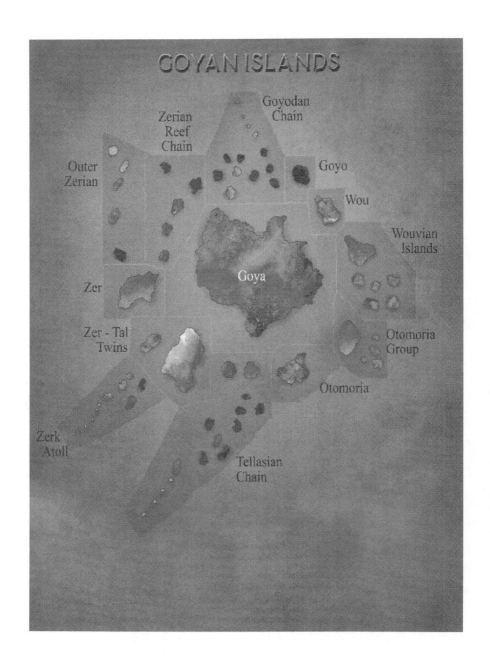

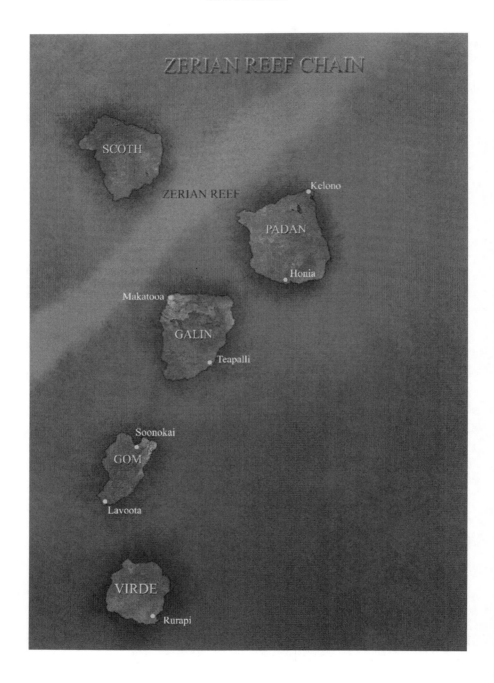

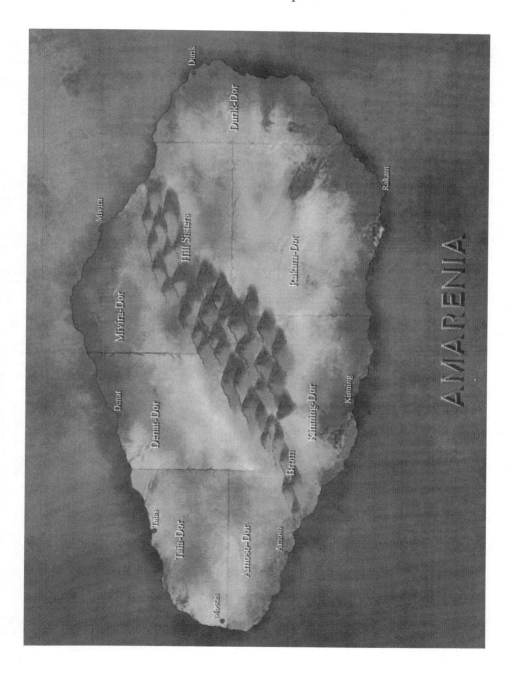

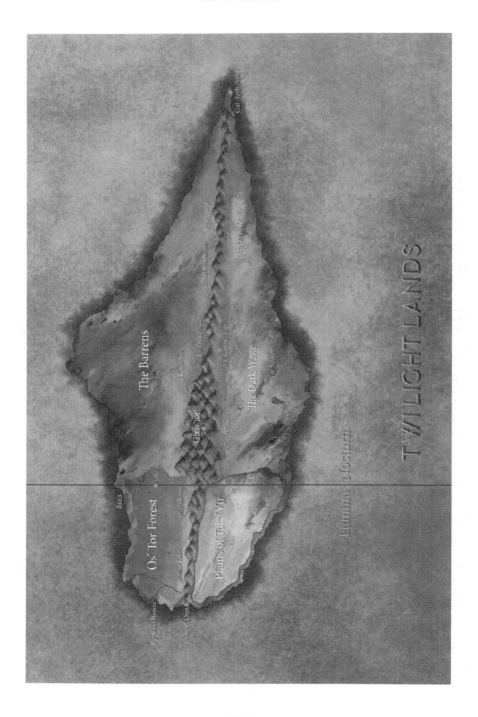

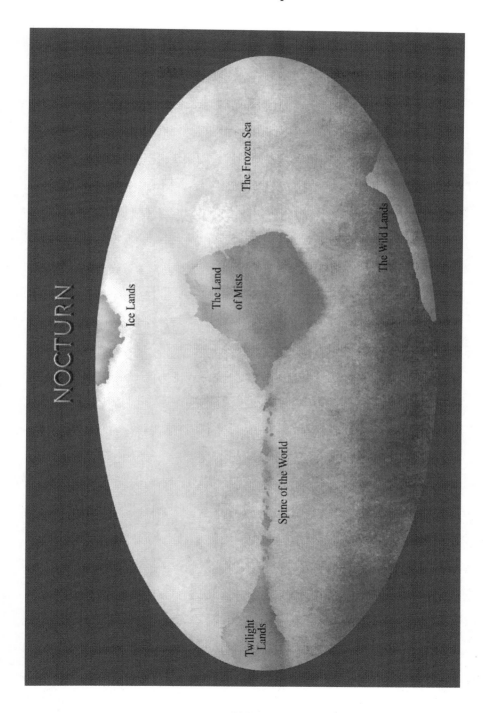

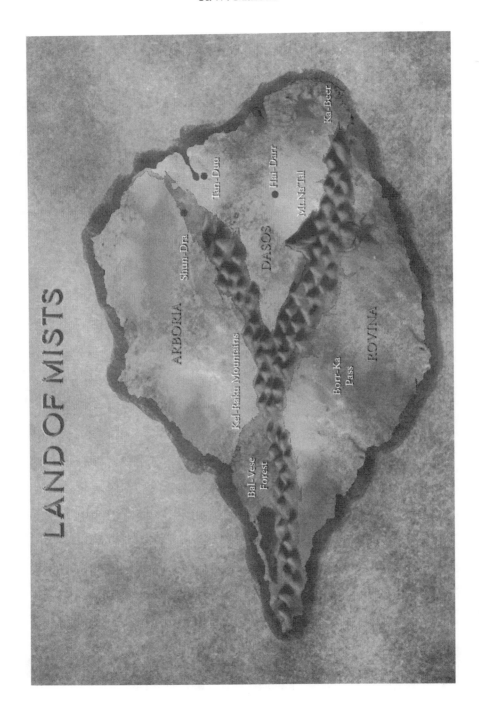

LAND OF MISTS

ABOUT THE AUTHOR

R.W. Marcus spent most of his life selling books. Along the way he managed to become a Falconer, 3rd Dan Black Belt in Yoshukai Karate, Freemason, Freelance Photographer, Ad Copywriter and WMNF Radio Disc Jockey. Marcus' radio commercials and freelance photography won numerous awards, including Best of Shows and Best of the Bay Addy Awards for work with Creative Keys and Laughing Bird Productions. R.W. Marcus was also Founder and Creative Director of United Game Masters, where he cowrote the UGM Universal Gaming System which he used to create and playtest a role-playing game based in the world of the Annigan Cycle. He formally held the title of Director of Incunabula at Griffon's Medieval Manuscripts, where he

penned his first nonfiction title, *The Ship of Fools to 1500*, which Amazon called "an authoritative guide to one of the most popular works of secular writing." Now retired, he created a new genre of fiction—Pulp Fantasy Noir—to exorcise the darker side of his good nature. He currently resides in Tallahassee, Florida.

CONNECT
WEBSITE: https://AnniganCycle.com
FACEBOOK: https://www.facebook.com/noirrwmarcus/
TWITTER: @NoirRWMarcus
EMAIL: RWMarcus@yahoo.com

R.W. Marcus

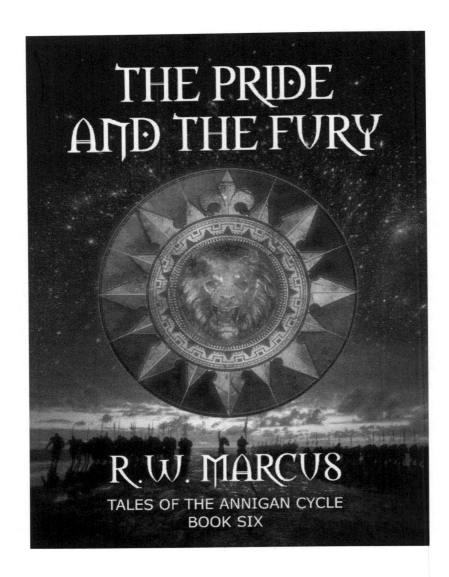

The PRIDE and the FURY
TALES OF THE ANNIGAN CYCLE
BOOK SIX
COMING SOON FROM LAUGHING BIRD PUBLISHING